# THE BEST SCIENCE FICTION OF THE YEAR

## #7

Terry Carr,
Editor

A Del Rey Book

BALLANTINE BOOKS • NEW YORK

A Del Rey Book
Published by Ballantine Books



Library of Congress Catalog Card Number: 72-195467

ISBN 0-345-27338-9

Manufactured in the United States of America

First Edition: July 1978

## ACKNOWLEDGMENTS

"Lollipop and the Tar Baby" by John Varley: Copyright © 1977 by Damon Knight. From *Orbit 19,* by permission of the author and his agents, Kirby McCauley, Ltd.

"Stardance" by Spider and Jeanne Robinson: Copyright © 1977 by The Conde-Nast Publications, Inc. From *Analog,* March 1977, by permission of the authors and their agents, Kirby McCauley, Ltd.

"The House of Compassionate Sharers" by Michael Bishop: Copyright © 1977 by Baronet Publishing Co. From *Cosmos,* May 1977, by permission of the author and his agent, Virginia Kidd.

"The Screwfly Solution" by Raccona Sheldon: Copyright © 1977 by The Conde-Nast Publications, Inc. From *Analog,* June 1977, by permission of the author and her agents, Robert P. Mills Ltd.

"Aztecs" by Vonda N. McIntyre: Copyright © 1977 by Vonda N. McIntyre. From *2076: The American Tricentennial,* by permission of the author and her agents, Rodell-Collin Literary Agency.

"Tropic of Eden" by Lee Killough: Copyright © 1977 by Mercury Press, Inc. From *Fantasy and Science Fiction,* August 1977, by permission of the author.

"Victor" by Bruce McAllister: Copyright © 1977 by Mercury Press, Inc. From *Fantasy and Science Fiction,* July 1977, by permission of the author.

"The Family Monkey" by Lisa Tuttle: Copyright © 1977 by Lisa Tuttle. From *New Voices in Science Fiction,* by permission of the author.

"A Rite of Spring" by Fritz Leiber: Copyright © 1977 by Terry Carr. From *Universe 7,* by permission of the author and his agents, Robert P. Mills Ltd.

## Contents

# Introduction

Every time I meet a science fiction reader, it seems, I get asked the same questions: "How do you choose the stories for *The Best Science Fiction of the Year*? Do you *really* read every sf story published? And what about the other 'best science fiction' anthologies?—your selections seldom coincide with the ones in Donald Wollheim's anthology or Gardner Dozois's. Who's right about what the best stories are?"

I'm not surprised that people ask; the appearance each year of three different editors' anthologies, each claiming to present the best stories, must inevitably provoke some wonder and even a bit of skepticism. The fact that the Science Fiction Writers of America issue an annual volume of *their* choice of the best stories adds to the confusion. —Plus, of course, the announcements each year of the Hugo Awards, Apollo Awards, *Locus* Awards, etc.

To be honest, I don't really believe there's any such thing as "the best science fiction of the year." It's a matter of individual taste: *you* may like to read only stories with detailed explications of the scientific extrapolation behind them; another person may prefer fast-action adventure stories set on other worlds; someone else may be interested in stylistic experimentation, or predictions of near-future problems, or allegories of The Human Condition revealed in radically different future societies . . . and so on. Any given reader's choice of the "best" science fiction stories is likely to differ greatly from the preferences of most other readers.

All this is not to say that there's no difference in quality between stories; obviously there is, else you'd enjoy equally every story that happens to fit your ideas of what science fiction should be. But these other considerations are important, so you're likely to respond more favorably to a "pretty good" story of the type you prefer than you will to even an exceptionally well done story of some other type.

This is why it's commercially feasible for several "best sf" anthologies to be published each year: the different editors have variant tastes, and once we've made our choices of the stories we consider outstanding, you're free to buy the book or books offered by editors whose tastes most closely coincide with your own.

As to how these stories are chosen . . . well, I can't speak for the other editors, but in my own case, Yes, I *do* read every sf story published—or at least I *start* to read every one. Some of them just don't interest me, so I don't finish them. Most are interesting enough to keep me reading to the end even if I don't consider them Excellent, Superb, or Mind-bending.

When I finish a story, I write a "grade" next to its title on the contents page. (If I don't finish it, I put a check-mark there to let me know later that I've at least tried it.) When I read a story that especially pleases me, I type a file-card noting the title, author, wordage, where it appeared, and as much of the plot as I can synopsize in one paragraph.

Perhaps an example would be appropriate. Here's the card I wrote for a story that eventually appeared in last year's anthology:

Science fiction
15,000 words

Varley, John
THE PHANTOM OF KANSAS (B)

Fox, who banks her memories in a bank recently robbed, wakes to find she's been murdered—three times, each time being reborn in clone with implanted memories. While police & Central Computer try to catch killer, she composes new environment show, storm over "Kansas disneyland," artificial cave under Moon. Meets killer amid storm, finds it's *her,* as a man—illegally cloned by accident, then abandoned. He only wants to die now, but she saves him & takes him to outpost world where his lack of registration with population-control won't matter. One fascinating idea after another.

*Galaxy,* Feb 76

I listed the story as science fiction to differentiate it from fantasy stories, which I try not to use in this anthology because I know that only a comparatively small percentage of science-fiction readers also enjoy tales of vampires, sorcerers, and ghosts. (I write cards for fantasy stories I like, too, and keep them in a separate box, because I also edit anthologies of fantasy—including, beginning this year, an annual called *Year's Finest Fantasy.*)

And if you think a "B" is a low rating for a story I deemed one of the best of the year, you should know that I'm a very tough grader. Indeed, in the many years I've edited anthologies I've rated only one story an "A," and just one an "A-minus."

I file these cards throughout the year, and when deadline-time comes I check through the cards and pick 125,000 words of stories for inclusion in the book; the stories that don't get chosen are listed in the Recommended Reading section. (You can get a good idea of how much I agree with the other anthologists' choices by comparing their contents pages not only with mine but also with the Recommended Reading list.)

All in all, it sounds like a simple method—but it's somewhat more complicated than that. My estimation of the quality of the stories is by far the most important criterion, of course, but there are other things I feel I must consider too. For instance, I shy away from choosing more than one story a year by a particular author.

(Though this isn't a hard-and-fast rule: writers such as Roger Zelazny, R. A. Lafferty, Robert Silverberg, and John Varley have all had two stories reprinted in the same volume when I absolutely couldn't resist.) I also limit myself to reprinting no more than one story a year from my own original-stories anthology series *Universe,* since my personal involvement with them might unduly influence my judgment. (You'll find no stories here that I wrote myself, either.)

There is, furthermore, the matter of "editorial balance," which leads me to try not to fill any book with stories about first-landings-on-alien-planets, or warnings of ecological doom, or a plethora of robot stories, time travel stories, tales of mutants or the problems of clones. I do my best to avoid preponderances of "downbeat" stories, tales of romantic love or the ennui of immortals, stories based on biology, psychology, physics, or Zen Buddhism.

Variety is a virtue, I believe; and since science fiction offers more opportunity for variety than does any other fiction form, I feel a science-fiction anthology should reflect this.

So it boils down to this: *The Best Science Fiction of the Year* is a title that doesn't mean its contents consist of a computer-rated determination of the most sensitive and trail-blazing scientific extrapolations recently published; instead, it describes the very best book of science-fiction short stories, novelettes, and novellas that I-as-an-individual-human-being can shape from the offerings of sf's finest writers, famous or otherwise, during the past year.

This means about the same thing, frankly. There's *always* a great deal of variety in themes, styles, and ideas among the top science-fiction stories of the year, so I really have little "balancing" to do; and there are so many good stories appearing that when I do bypass a story for these reasons, there's another one just as good that I can choose. Every story that appears in these books is one that I consider among the best . . . and the stories that I think are the *very* best are always included, of course.

This year's selection includes stories of adventure, humor, romance, skulduggery, compassion, battles of wits, and strange catastrophes. Who could ask for more?

—TERRY CARR
January 1978

# Lollipop and the Tar Baby

**John Varley**

# *Lollipop and the Tar Baby*

## John Varley

John Varley's stories have been appearing in print for fewer than half a dozen years, but he's already established himself as one of the most popular authors in science fiction. He's a teller of stories and wonders who keeps up with the latest scientific discoveries and extrapolates them fascinatingly as he imagines a future history of Earth and the solar system that's consistent from story to story. His first novel, *The Ophiuchi Hotline,* was published in 1977 and was widely praised; he recently completed his second novel.

"Lollipop and the Tar Baby" is part of his future history, but as usual, you needn't have read any of the other stories in order to enjoy this one. It's an imaginative, playful and ultimately moving novelette about a young woman who searches for black holes in space—and finds one that talks to her. It has important things to tell her, too . . . .

---

"Zzzzello. *Zzz.* Hello. Hello." Someone was speaking to Xanthia from the end of a ten-kilometer metal pipe, shouting to be heard across a roomful of gongs and cymbals being knocked over by angry giant bees. She had never heard such interference.

"Hello?" she repeated. "What are you doing on my wavelength?"

"Hello." The interference was still there, but the voice was slightly more distinct. "Wavelength. Searching, searching wavelength . . . get best reception with . . . Hello? Listening?"

"Yes, I'm listening. You're talking over . . . my radio isn't even . . ." She banged the radio panel with her palm in the ancient ritual humans employ when their creations are being balky. "My goddamn *radio* isn't even on. Did you know that?" It was a relief to feel anger boiling up inside her. Anything was preferable to feeling lost and silly.

"Not necessary."

"What do you mean, not—who *are* you?"

"Who. Having . . . *I'm,* pronoun, yes, I'm having difficulty. Bear with. Me? Yes, pronoun. Bear with me. I'm not who. What. *What* am I?"

"All right. *What* are you?"

"Space-time phenomenon. I'm gravity and causality-sink. Black hole."

Xanthia did not need black holes explained to her. She had spent her entire eighteen years hunting them, along with her clone-sister, Zoetrope. But she was not used to having them talk to her.

"Assuming for the moment that you really are a black hole," she said, beginning to wonder if this might be some elaborate trick played on her by Zoe, "just taking that as a tentative hypothesis—how are you able to talk to me?"

There was a sound like an attitude thruster going off, a rumbling pop. It was repeated.

"I manipulate space-time framework . . . no, please hold line . . . *the* line. I manipulate the space-time framework with controlled gravity waves projected in narrow . . . a narrow cone. I direct at the speaker in your radio. You hear. Me."

"What was that again?" It sounded like a lot of crap to her.

"I elaborate. I will elaborate. I cut through space itself, through—hold the line, hold the line, reference." There was a sound like a tape reeling rapidly through playback heads. "This is the BBC," said a voice that was recognizably human, but blurred by static. The tape whirred again. "gust the third, in the year of our Lord nineteen fifty-seven. Today in—" Once again the tape hunted.

"chelson-Morley experiment disproved the existence of the ether, by ingeniously arranging a rotating prism—" Then the metallic voice was back.

"Ether. I cut through space itself, through a—hold the line." This time the process was shorter. She heard a fragment of what sounded like a video adventure serial. "Through a space warp made through the ductile etheric continuum—"

"Hold on there. That's not what you said before."

"I was elaborating."

"Go on. Wait, what were you doing? With that tape business?"

The voice paused, and when the answer came the line had cleared up quite a bit. But the voice still didn't sound human. Computer?

"I am not used to speech. No need for it. But I have learned your language by listening to radio transmissions. I speak to you through use of indeterminate statistical concatenations. Gravity waves and probability, which is not the same thing in a causality singularity, enables a nonrational event to take place."

"Zoe, this is really you, isn't it?"

Xanthia was only eighteen Earth-years old, on her first long orbit into the space beyond Pluto, the huge cometary zone where space is truly flat. Her whole life had been devoted to learning how to find and capture black holes, but one didn't come across them very often. Xanthia had been born a year after the beginning of the voyage and had another year to go before the end of it. In her whole life she had seen and talked to only one other human being, and that was Zoe, who was one hundred and thirty-five years old and her identical twin.

Their home was the *Shirley Temple,* a fifteen-thousand-tonne fusion-drive ship registered out of Lowell, Pluto. Zoe owned *Shirley* free and clear; on her first trip, many years ago, she had found a scale-five hole and had become instantly rich. Most hole hunters were not so lucky.

Zoe was also unusual in that she seemed to thrive on solitude. Most hunters who made a strike settled down to live in comfort, buy a large company or put the money into safe investments and live off the interest. They were unwilling or unable to face another twenty years alone. Zoe had gone out again, and a third time after the second trip had proved fruitless. She had found a hole on her third trip, and was now almost through her fifth.

But for some reason she had never adequately explained to Xanthia, she had wanted a companion this time. And what better company than herself? With the medical facilities aboard *Shirley* she had grown a copy of herself and raised the little girl as her daughter.

Xanthia squirmed around in the control cabin of *The Good Ship Lollipop,* stuck her head through the hatch leading to the aft exercise room, and found nothing. What she had expected, she didn't know. Now she crouched in midair with a screwdriver, attacking the service panels that protected the radio assembly.

"What are you doing by yourself?" the voice asked.

"Why don't *you* tell *me,* Zoe?" she said, lifting the panel off and tossing it angrily to one side. She peered into the gloomy interior, wrinkling her nose at the smell of oil and paraffin. She shone her pencil-beam into the space, flicking it from one component to the next, all as familiar to her as neighborhood corridors would be to a planet-born child. There was nothing out of place, nothing that shouldn't be there. Most of it was sealed into plastic blocks to prevent moisture or dust from getting to critical circuits. There were no signs of tampering.

"I am failing to communicate. I am not your mother, I am a gravity and causality—"

"She's not my mother," Xanthia snapped.

"My records show that she would dispute you."

Xanthia didn't like the way the voice said that. But she was admitting to herself that there was no way Zoe could have set this up. That left her with the alternative: She really was talking to a black hole.

"She's not my mother," Xanthia repeated. "And if you've been listening in, you *know* why I'm out here in a lifeboat. So why do you ask?"

"I wish to help you. I have heard tension building between the two of you these last years. You are growing up."

Xanthia settled back in the control chair. Her head did not feel so good.

Hole hunting was a delicate economic balance, a tightrope walked between the needs of survival and the limitations of mass. The initial investment was tremendous and the return was undependable, so the potential hole hunter had to have a line to a source of speculative credit or be independently wealthy.

No consortium or corporation had been able to turn a profit at the business by going at it in a big way. The government of Pluto maintained a monopoly on the use of one-way robot probes, but they had found over the years that when a probe succeeded in finding a hole, a race usually developed to see who would reach it and claim it first. Ships sent after such holes had a way of disappearing in the resulting fights, far from law and order.

The demand for holes was so great that an economic niche remained which was filled by the solitary prospector, backed by people with tax write-offs to gain. Prospectors had a ninety percent bankruptcy rate. But as with gold and oil in earlier days, the potential profits were huge, so there was never a lack of speculators.

Hole hunters would depart Pluto and accelerate to the limits of engine power, then coast for ten to fifteen years, keeping an eye on the mass detector. Sometimes they would be half a light-year from Sol before they had to decelerate and turn around. Less mass equaled more range, so the solitary hunter was the rule.

Teaming of ships had been tried, but teams that discovered a hole seldom came back together. One of them tended to have an accident. Hole hunters were a greedy lot, self-centered and self-sufficient.

Equipment had to be reliable. Replacement parts were costly in terms of mass, so the hole hunter had to make an agonizing choice with each item. Would it be better to leave it behind and chance a possibly fatal failure, or take it along, decreasing the range, and maybe miss the glory hole that is sure to be lurking just one more AU away? Hole hunters learned to be handy at repairing, jury-rigging, and bashing, because in twenty years even fail-safe triplicates can be on their last legs.

Zoe had sweated over her faulty mass detector before she admitted it was beyond her skills. Her primary detector had failed ten years into the voyage, and the second one had begun to act up six years later. She tried to put together one functioning detector with parts cannibalized from both. She nursed it along for a year with the equivalents of bobby pins and bubblegum. It was hopeless.

But *Shirley Temple* was a palace among prospecting ships. Having found two holes in her career, Zoe had her own money. She had stocked spare parts, beefed up the drive, even included that incredible luxury, a lifeboat.

The lifeboat was sheer extravagance, except for one thing. It had a mass detector as part of its astrogational equipment. She had bought it mainly for that reason, since it had only an eighteen-month range and would be useless except at the beginning and end of the trip, when they were close to Pluto. It made extensive use of plug-in components, sealed in plastic to prevent tampering or accidents caused by inexperienced passengers. The mass detector on board did not have the range or accuracy of the one on *Shirley*. It could be removed or replaced, but not recalibrated.

They had begun a series of three-month loops out from the mother ship. Xanthia had flown most of them earlier, when Zoe did not trust her to run *Shirley*. Later they had alternated.

"And that's what I'm doing out here by myself," Xanthia said. "I have to get out beyond ten million kilometers from *Shirley* so its mass doesn't affect the detector. My instrument is calibrated to ignore only the mass of this ship, not *Shirley*. I stay out here for three months, which is a reasonably safe time for the life systems on *Lollipop,* and time to get pretty lonely. Then back for refueling and supplying."

"The *Lollipop*?"

Xanthia blushed. "Well, I named this lifeboat that, after I started spending so much time on it. We have a tape of Shirley Temple in the library, and she sang this song, see—"

"Yes, I've heard it. I've been listening to radio for a very long time. So you no longer believe this is a trick by your mother?"

"She's *not* . . ." Then she realized she had referred to Zoe in the third person again.

"I don't know what to think," she said miserably. "Why are you doing this?"

"I sense that you are still confused. You'd like some proof that I am what I say I am. Since you'll think of it in a minute, I might as well ask you this question. Why do you suppose I haven't yet registered on your mass detector?"

Xanthia jerked in her seat, then was brought up short by the straps. It was true, there was not the slightest wiggle on the dials of the detector.

"All right, why haven't you?" She felt a sinking sensation. She was sure the punch line came now, after she'd shot off her mouth about *Lollipop*—her secret from Zoe—and made such a point of the fact that Zoe was not her mother. It was her own private rebellion, one that she had not had the nerve to face Zoe with.

Now she's going to reveal herself and tell me how she did it, and I'll feel like a fool, she thought.

"It's simple," the voice said. "You weren't in range of me yet. But now you are. Take a look."

The needles were dancing, giving the reading of a scale-seven hole. A scale-seven would mass about a tenth as much as the asteroid Ceres.

"Mommy, what *is* a black hole?"

The little girl was seven years old. One day she would call herself Xanthia, but she had not yet felt the need for a name and her mother had not seen fit to give her one. Zoe reasoned that you needed two of something before you needed names. There was only one other person on *Shirley*. There was no possible confusion. When the girl thought about it at all, she assumed her name must be Hey, or Darling.

She was a small child, as Zoe had been. She was recapitulating the growth Zoe had already been through a hundred years ago. Though she didn't know it, she was pretty: dark eyes with an Oriental fold, dark skin, and kinky blond hair. She was a genetic mix of Chinese and Negro, with dabs of other races thrown in for seasoning.

"I've tried to explain that before," Zoe said. "You don't have the math for it yet. I'll get you started on space-time equations, then in about a year you'll be able to understand."

"But I want to know now." Black holes were a problem for the child. From her earliest memories the two of them had done nothing but hunt them, yet they never found one. She'd been doing a lot of reading—there was little else to do—and was wondering if they might inhabit the same category where she had tentatively placed Santa Claus and leprechauns.

"If I try again, will you go to sleep?"

"I promise."

So Zoe launched into her story about the Big Bang, the time in the long-ago when little black holes could be formed.

"As far as we can tell, all the little black holes like

the ones we hunt were made in that time. Nowadays other holes can be formed by the collapse of very large stars. When the fires burn low and the pressures that are trying to blow the star apart begin to fade, gravity takes over and starts to pull the star in on itself." Zoe waved her hands in the air, forming cups to show bending space, flailing out to indicate pressures of fusion. These explanations were almost as difficult for her as stories of sex had been for earlier generations. The truth was that she was no relativist and didn't really grasp the slightly incredible premises behind black-hole theory. She suspected that no one could really visualize one, and if you can't do that, where are you? But she was practical enough not to worry about it.

"And what's gravity? I forgot." The child was rubbing her eyes to stay awake. She struggled to understand but already knew she would miss the point yet another time.

"Gravity is the thing that holds the universe together. The glue, or the rivets. It pulls everything toward everything else, and it takes energy to fight it and overcome it. It feels like when we boost the ship, remember I pointed that out to you?"

"Like when everything wants to move in the same direction?"

"That's right. So we have to be careful, because we don't think about it much. We have to worry about where things are because when we boost, everything will head for the stern. People on planets have to worry about that all the time. They have to put something strong between themselves and the center of the planet, or they'll go down."

"Down." The girl mused over that word, one that had been giving her trouble as long as she could remember, and thought she might finally have understood it. She had seen pictures of places where down was always the same direction, and they were strange to the eye. They were full of tables to put things on, chairs to sit in, and funny containers with no tops. Five of the six walls of rooms on planets could hardly be used at all. One, the "floor," was called on to take all the use.

"So they use their legs to fight gravity with?" She was yawning now.

"Yes. You've seen pictures of the people with the funny legs. They're not so funny when you're in gravity. Those flat things on the ends are called feet. If they had peds like us, they wouldn't be able to walk so good. They always have to have one foot touching the floor, or they'd fall toward the surface of the planet."

Zoe tightened the strap that held the child to her bunk, and fastened the velcro patch on the blanket to the side of the sheet, tucking her in. Kids needed a warm snug place to sleep. Zoe preferred to float free in her own bedroom, tucked into a fetal position and drifting.

"G'night, Mommy."

"Good night. You get some sleep, and don't worry about black holes."

But the child dreamed of them, as she often did. They kept tugging at her, and she would wake breathing hard and convinced that she was going to fall into the wall in front of her.

"You don't mean it? I'm rich!"

Xanthia looked away from the screen. It was no good pointing out that Zoe had always spoken of the trip as a partnership. She owned *Shirley* and *Lollipop*.

"Well, you too, of course. Don't think you won't be getting a real big share of the money. I'm going to set you up so well that you'll be able to buy a ship of your own, and raise little copies of yourself if you want to."

Xanthia was not sure that was her idea of heaven, but said nothing.

"Zoe, there's a problem, and I . . . well, I was—" But she was interrupted again by Zoe, who would not hear Xanthia's comment for another thirty seconds.

"The first data is coming over the telemetry channel right now, and I'm feeding it into the computer. Hold on a second while I turn the ship. I'm going to start decelerating in about one minute, based on these figures. You get the refined data to me as soon as you have it."

There was a brief silence.

"What problem?"

"It's talking to me, Zoe. The hole is talking to me."

This time the silence was longer than the minute it took the radio signal to make the round trip between ships. Xanthia furtively thumbed the contrast knob, turning her sister-mother down until the screen was blank. She could look at the camera and Zoe wouldn't know the difference.

Damn, damn, she thinks I've flipped. But I *had* to tell her.

"I'm not sure what you mean."

"Just what I *said*. I don't understand it, either. But it's been talking to me for the last hour, and it says the *damnedest* things."

There was another silence.

"All right. When you get there, don't do anything, repeat, *anything*, until I arrive. Do you understand?"

"Zoe, I'm not crazy. I'm *not*."

Then why am I crying?

"Of course you're not, baby, there's an explanation for this and I'll find out what it is as soon as I get there. You just hang on. My first rough estimate puts me alongside you about three hours after you're stationary relative to the hole."

*Shirley* and *Lollipop*, traveling parallel courses, would both be veering from their straight-line trajectories to reach the hole. But Xanthia was closer to it; Zoe would have to move at a more oblique angle and would be using more fuel. Xanthia thought four hours was more like it.

"I'm signing off," Zoe said. "I'll call you back as soon as I'm in the groove."

Xanthia hit the off button on the radio and furiously unbuckled her seat belt. Damn Zoe, damn her, damn her, *damn her*. Just sit tight, she says. I'll be there to explain the unexplainable. It'll be all right.

She knew she should start her deceleration, but there was something she must do first.

She twisted easily in the air, grabbing at braces with all four hands, and dived through the hatch to the only other living space in *Lollipop*: the exercise area. It was cluttered with equipment that she had neglected to fold into the walls, but she didn't mind; she liked close places. She squirmed through the maze like a fish gliding through coral, until she reached the wall she was looking for. It had been taped over with discarded manual pages, the only paper she could find on *Lollipop*. She started ripping at the paper, wiping tears from her cheeks with one ped as she worked. Beneath the paper was a mirror.

How to test for sanity? Xanthia had not considered the question; the thing to do had simply presented itself and she had done it. Now she confronted the mirror and searched for . . . what? Wild eyes? Froth on the lips?

What she saw was her mother.

Xanthia's life had been a process of growing slowly into the mold Zoe represented. She had known her pug nose would eventually turn down. She had known what baby fat would melt away. Her breasts had grown just into the small cones she knew from her mother's body and no further.

She hated looking in mirrors.

Xanthia and Zoe were small women. Their most striking feature was the frizzy dandelion of yellow hair, lighter than their bodies. When the time had come for naming, the young clone had almost opted for Dandelion, until she came upon the word *xanthic* in a dictionary. The radio call-letters for *Lollipop* happened to be X-A-N, and the word was too good to resist. She knew, too, that Orientals were thought of as having yellow skin, though she could not see why.

Why had she come here, of all places? She strained toward the mirror, fighting her repulsion, searching her face for signs of insanity. The narrow eyes were a little puffy, and as deep and expressionless as ever. She put her hands to the glass, startled in the silence to hear the multiple clicks as the long nails just missed touching the ones on the other side. She was always forgetting to trim them.

Sometimes, in mirrors, she knew she was not seeing herself. She could twitch her mouth, and the image would not move. She could smile, and the image would frown. It had been happening for two years, as her body put the finishing touches on its eighteen-year process of duplicating Zoe. She had not spoken of it, because it scared her.

"And this is where I come to see if I'm sane," she said aloud, noting that the lips in the mirror did not move. "Is she going to start talking to me now?" She waved her arms wildly, and so did Zoe in the mirror. At least it wasn't that bad yet; it was only the details that failed to match: the small movements, and especially the facial expressions. Zoe was inspecting her dispassionately and did not seem to like what she saw. That small curl at the edge of the mouth, the almost brutal narrowing of the eyes . . .

Xanthia clapped her hands over her face, then peeked out through the fingers. Zoe was peeking out, too. Xanthia began rounding up the drifting scraps of paper and walling her twin in again with new bits of tape.

The beast with two backs and legs at each end writhed, came apart, and resolved into Xanthia and Zoe, drifting, breathing hard. They caromed off the walls like monkeys, giving up their energy, gradually getting breath back under control. Golden, wet hair and sweaty skin brushed against each other again and again as they came to rest.

Now the twins floated in the middle of the darkened bedroom. Zoe was already asleep, tumbling slowly with that total looseness possible only in free fall. Her leg rubbed against Xanthia's belly and her relative motion stopped. The leg was moist. The room was close, thick with the smell of passion. The recirculators whined quietly as they labored to clear the air.

Pushing one finger gently against Zoe's ankle, Xanthia turned her until they were face to face. Frizzy blond hair tickled her nose, and she felt warm breath on her mouth.

Why can't it always be like this?

"You're not my mother," she whispered. Zoe had no reaction to this heresy. "You're *not.*"

Only in the last year had Zoe admitted the relationship was much closer. Xanthia was now fifteen.

And what was different? Something, there had to be something beyond the mere knowledge that they were not mother and child. There was a new quality in their relationship, growing as they came to the end of the voyage. Xanthia would look into those eyes where she had seen love and now see only blankness, coldness.

"Oriental inscrutability?" she asked herself, half seriously. She knew she was hopelessly unsophisticated. She had spent her life in a society of two. The only other person she knew had her own face. But she had thought she knew Zoe. Now she felt less confident with every glance into Zoe's face and every kilometer passed on the way to Pluto.

Pluto.

Her thoughts turned gratefully away from immediate problems and toward that unimaginable place. She would be there in only four more years. The cultural adjustments she would have to make were staggering. Thinking about that, she felt a sensation in her chest that she guessed was her heart leaping in anticipation. That's what happened to characters in tapes when they got excited, anyway. Their hearts were forever leaping, thudding, aching, or skipping beats.

She pushed away from Zoe and drifted slowly to the viewport. Her old friends were all out there, the only friends she had ever known, the stars. She greeted them all one by one, reciting childhood mnemonic riddles and rhymes like bedtime prayers.

It was a funny thought that the view from her window would terrify many of those strangers she was going to meet on Pluto. She'd read that many tunnel-raised people could not stand open spaces. What it was that scared them, she could not understand. The things that scared her were crowds, gravity, males, and mirrors.

"Oh, damn. Damn! I'm going to be just *hopeless*. Poor little idiot girl from the sticks, visiting the big city." She brooded for a time on all the thousands of things she had never done, from swimming in the gigantic underground disneylands to seducing a boy.

"To *being* a boy." It had been the source of their first big argument. When Xanthia had reached adolescence, the time when children want to begin experimenting, she had learned from Zoe that *Shirley Temple* did not carry the medical equipment for sex changes. She was doomed to spend her critical formative years as a sexual deviate, a unisex.

"It'll stunt me forever," she had protested. She had been reading a lot of pop psychology at the time.

"Nonsense," Zoe had responded, hard pressed to explain why she had not stocked a viro-genetic imprinter and the companion Y-alyzer. Which, as Xanthia pointed out, *any* self-respecting home surgery kit should have.

"The human race got along for millions of years without sex changing," Zoe had said. "Even after the Invasion. We were a highly technological race for hundreds of years before changing. Billions of people lived and died in the same sex."

"Yeah, and look what they were like."

Now, for another of what seemed like an endless series of nights, sleep was eluding her. There was the worry of Pluto, and the worry of Zoe and her strange behavior, and no way to explain anything in her small universe which had become unbearably complicated in the last years.

*I wonder what it would be like with a man.*

Three hours ago Xanthia had brought *Lollipop* to a careful rendezvous with the point in space her instruments indicated contained a black hole. She had long since understood that even if she ever found one she would never see it, but she could not restrain herself from squinting into the starfield for some evidence. It was silly; though the hole massed ten to the fifteenth tonnes (the original estimate had been off one order of magnitude) it was still only a fraction of a millimeter in diameter. She was staying a good safe hundred kilometers from it. Still, you ought to be able to sense something like that, you ought to be able to *feel* it.

It was no use. This hunk of space looked exactly like any other.

"There is a point I would like explained," the hole said. "What will be done with me after you have captured me?"

The question surprised her. She still had not got around to thinking of the voice as anything but some annoying aberration like her face in the mirror. How was she supposed to deal with it? Could she admit to herself that it existed, that it might even have feelings?

"I guess we'll just mark you, in the computer, that is. You're too big for us to haul back to Pluto. So we'll hang around you for a week or so, refining your trajectory until we know precisely where you're going to be, then we'll leave you. We'll make some maneuvers on the way in so no one could retrace our path and find out where you are, because they'll know we found a big one when we get back."

"How will they know that?"

"Because we'll be renting . . . well, *Zoe* will be chartering one of those big monster tugs, and she'll come out here and put a charge on you and tow you . . . say, how do you feel about this?"

"Are you concerned with the answer?"

The more Xanthia thought about it, the less she liked it. If she really was not hallucinating this experience, then she was contemplating the capture and imprisonment of a sentient being. An innocent sentient being who had been wandering around the edge of the system, suddenly to find him- or herself . . .

"Do you have a sex?"

"No."

"All right, I guess I've been kind of short with you. It's just because you *did* startle me, and I *didn't* expect it, and it was all a little alarming."

The hole said nothing.

"You're a strange sort of person, or whatever," she said.

Again there was a silence.

"Why don't you tell me more about yourself? What's it like being a black hole, and all that?" She still couldn't fight down the ridiculous feeling those words gave her.

"I live much as you do, from day to day. I travel from star to star, taking about ten million years for the trip. Upon arrival, I plunge through the core of the star. I do this as often as is necessary, then I depart by a slingshot maneuver through the heart of a massive planet. The Tunguska Meteorite, which hit Siberia in 1908, was a black hole gaining momentum on its way to Jupiter, where it could get the added push needed for solar escape velocity."

One thing was bothering Xanthia. "What do you mean, 'as often as is necessary'?"

"Usually five or six thousand passes is sufficient."

"No, no. What I mean is *why* is it necessary? What do you get out of it?"

"Mass," the hole said. "I need to replenish my mass. The Relativity Laws state that nothing can escape from a black hole, but the Quantum Laws, specifically the Heisenberg Uncertainty Principle, state that below a certain radius the position of a particle cannot be determined. I lose mass constantly through tunneling. It is not all wasted, as I am able to control the direction and form of the escaping mass, and to use the energy that results to perform functions that your present-day physics says are impossible."

"Such as?" Xanthia didn't know why, but she was getting nervous.

"I can exchange inertia for gravity, and create energy in a variety of ways."

"So you can move yourself."

"Slowly."

"And you eat . . ."

"Anything."

Xanthia felt a sudden panic, but she didn't know what was wrong. She glanced down at her instruments and felt her hair prickle from her wrists and ankles to the nape of her neck.

The hole was ten kilometers closer than it had been.

"How could you *do* that to me?" Xanthia raged. "I trusted you, and that's how you repaid me, by trying to sneak up on me and . . . and—"

"It was not intentional. I speak to you by means of controlled gravity waves. To speak to you at all, it is necessary to generate an attractive force between us. You were never in any danger."

"I don't believe that," Xanthia said angrily. "I think you're doubletalking me. I don't think gravity works like that, and I don't think you really tried very hard to tell me how you talk to me, back when we first started." It occurred to her now, also, that the hole was speaking much more fluently than in the beginning. Either it was a very fast learner, or that had been intentional.

The hole paused. "This is true," it said.

She pressed her advantage. "Then why did you do it?"

"It was a reflex, like blinking in a bright light, or drawing one's hand back from a fire. When I sense matter, I am attracted to it."

"The proper cliché would be 'like a moth to a flame.' But you're not a moth, and I'm not a flame. I don't believe you. I think you could have stopped yourself if you wanted to."

Again the hole hesitated. "You are correct."

"So you were trying to . . . ?"

"I was trying to eat you."

"Just like *that?* Eat someone you've been having a conversation with?"

"Matter is matter," the hole said, and Xanthia thought she detected a defensive note in its voice.

"What do you think of what I said we're going to do with you? You were going to tell me, but we got off on that story about where you came from."

"As I understand it, you propose to return for me. I will be towed to near Pluto's orbit, sold, and eventually come to rest in the heart of an orbital power station, where your species will feed matter into my gravity well, extracting power cheaply from the gravitational collapse."

"Yeah, that's pretty much it."

"It sounds ideal. My life is struggle. Failing to find matter to consume would mean loss of mass until I am smaller than an atomic nucleus. The loss rate would increase exponentially, and my universe would disappear. I do not know what would happen beyond that point. I have never wished to find out."

How much could she trust this thing? Could it move very rapidly? She toyed with the idea of backing off still farther. The two of them were now motionless relative to each other, but they were both moving slowly away from the location she had given Zoe.

It didn't make sense to think it could move in on her fast. If it could, why hadn't it? Then it could eat her and wait for Zoe to arrive—Zoe, who was helpless to detect the hole with her broken mass detector.

She should relay the new vectors to Zoe. She tried to calculate where her twin would arrive, but was distracted by the hole speaking.

"I would like to speak to you now of what I initially contacted you for. Listening to Pluto radio, I have become aware of certain facts that you should know, if, as I suspect, you are not already aware of them. Do you know of Clone Control Regulations?"

"No, what are they?" Again, she was afraid without knowing why.

The genetic statutes, according to the hole, were the soul of simplicity. For three hundred years, people had been living just about forever. It had become necessary to limit the population. Even if everyone had only one child—the Birthright—population would still grow. For a while, clones had been a loophole. No more. Now, only one person had the right to any one set of genes. If two possessed them, one was excess, and was summarily executed.

"Zoe has prior property rights to her genetic code," the hole concluded. "This is backed up by a long series

"So I'm—"

of court decisions."

"Excess."

Zoe met her at the air lock as Xanthia completed the docking maneuver. She was smiling, and Xanthia felt the way she always did when Zoe smiled these days: like a puppy being scratched behind the ears. They kissed, then Zoe held her at arm's length.

"Let me look at you. Can it only be three months? You've *grown*, my baby."

Xanthia blushed. "I'm not a baby anymore, Mother." But she was happy. Very happy.

"No, I should say not." She touched one of Xanthia's breasts, then turned her around slowly. "I should say not. Putting on a little weight in the hips, aren't we?"

"And the bosom. One inch while I was gone. I'm almost there." And it was true. At sixteen, the young clone was almost a woman.

"Almost there," Zoe repeated, and glanced away from her twin. But she hugged her again, and they kissed, and began to laugh as the tension was released.

They made love, not once and then to bed, but many times, feasting on each other. One of them remarked—Xanthia could not remember who because it seemed so accurate that either of them might have said it—that the only good thing about these three-month separations was the homecoming.

"You did very well," Zoe said, floating in the darkness and sweet exhausted atmosphere of their bedroom many hours later. "You handled the lifeboat like it was part of your body. I watched the docking. I *wanted* to see you make a mistake, I think, so I'd know I still have something on you." Her teeth showed in the starlight, rows of lights below the sparkles of her eyes and the great dim blossom of her hair.

"Ah, it wasn't that hard," Xanthia said, delighted, knowing full well that it *was* that hard.

"Well, I'm going to let you handle it again the next swing. From now on, you can think of the lifeboat as *your* ship. You're the skipper."

It didn't seem like the time to tell her that she already thought of it that way. Nor that she had christened the ship.

Zoe laughed quietly. Xanthia looked at her.

"I remember the day I first boarded my own ship," she said. "It was a big day for me. My own ship."

"This is the way to live," Xanthia agreed. "Who needs all those people? Just the two of us. And they say hole hunters are crazy. I . . . wanted to . . ." The words stuck in her throat, but Xanthia knew this was the time to get them out, if there ever would be a time. "I don't want to stay too long at Pluto, Mother. I'd like to get right back out here with you." There, she'd said it.

Zoe said nothing for a long time.

"We can talk about that later."

"I love you, Mother," Xanthia said, a little too loudly.

"I love you, too, baby," Zoe mumbled. "Let's get some sleep, okay?"

She tried to sleep, but it wouldn't happen. What was *wrong?*

Leaving the darkened room behind her, she drifted through the ship, looking for something she had lost, or was losing, she wasn't sure which. What had happened, after all? Certainly nothing she could put her finger on. She loved her mother, but all she knew was that she was choking on tears.

In the water closet, wrapped in the shower bag with warm water misting around her, she glanced in the mirror.

"Why? Why would she do a thing like that?"

"Loneliness. And insanity. They appear to go together. This is her solution. You are not the first clone she has made."

She had thought herself beyond shock, but the clarity that simple declarative sentence brought to her mind was explosive. Zoe had always needed the companionship Xanthia provided. She needed a child for diversion in the long, dragging years of a voyage; she needed someone to talk to. *Why couldn't she have brought a dog?* She saw herself now as a shipboard pet, and felt sick. The local leash laws would necessitate the destruction of the animal before landing. Regrettable, but there it was. Zoe had spent the last year working up the courage to do it.

How many little Xanthias? They might even have chosen that very name; they would have been that much like her. Three, four? She wept for her forgotten sisters. Unless . . .

"How do I know you're telling me the truth about this? How could she have kept it from me? I've seen tapes of Pluto. I never saw any mention of this."

"She edited those before you were born. She has been careful. Consider her position: there can be only one of you, but the law does not say which it has to be. With her death, you become legal. If you had known that, what would life have been like in *Shirley Temple?*"

"I don't believe you. You've got something in mind, I'm sure of it."

"Ask her when she gets here. But be careful. Think it out, all the way through."

She had thought it out. She had ignored the last three calls from Zoe while she thought. All the options must be considered, all the possibilities planned for. It was an impossible task; she knew she was far too emotional to think clearly, and there wasn't time to get herself under control.

But she had done what she could. Now *The Good Ship Lollipop,* outwardly unchanged, was a ship of war.

Zoe came backing in, riding the fusion torch and headed for a point dead in space relative to Xanthia. The fusion drive was too dangerous for *Shirley* to complete the rendezvous; the rest of the maneuver would be up to *Lollipop.*

Xanthia watched through the telescope as the drive went off. She could see *Shirley* clearly on her screen, though the ship was fifty kilometers away.

Her screen lit up again, and there was Zoe. Xanthia turned her own camera on.

"There you are," Zoe said. "Why wouldn't you talk to me?"

"I didn't think the time was ripe."

"Would you like to tell me how come this nonsense about talking black holes? What's gotten into you?"

"Never mind about that. There never was a hole, anyway. I just needed to talk to you about something you forgot to erase from the tape library in the *Lol* . . . in the lifeboat. You were pretty thorough with the tapes in *Shirley,* but you forgot to take the same care here. I guess you didn't think I'd ever be using it. Tell me, what are Clone Control Regulations?"

The face on the screen was immobile. Or was it a mirror, and was she smiling? Was it herself or Zoe she watched? Frantically, Xanthia thumbed a switch to put her telescope image on the screen, wiping out the face. Would Zoe try to talk her way out of it? If she did, Xanthia was determined to do nothing at all. There was no way she could check out any lie Zoe might tell her, nothing she could confront Zoe with except a fantastic story from a talking black hole.

*Please say something. Take the responsibility out of my hands.* She was willing to die, tricked by Zoe's fast talk, rather than accept the hole's word against Zoe's.

But Zoe was acting, not talking, and the response was exactly what the hole had predicted. The attitude-control jets were firing, *Shirley Temple* was pitching and yawing slowly, the nozzles at the stern hunting for a speck in the telescope screen. When the engines were aimed, they would surely be fired, and Xanthia and the whole ship would be vaporized.

But she was ready. Her hands had been poised over the thrust controls. *Lollipop* had a respectable acceleration, and every g of it slammed her into the couch as she scooted away from the danger spot.

*Shirley*'s fusion engines fired, and began a deadly hunt. Xanthia could see the thin, incredibly hot stream playing around her as Zoe made finer adjustments in her orientation. She could evade it for only a short time, but that was all she needed.

Then the light went out. She saw her screen flare up as the telescope circuit became overloaded with an intense burst of energy. And it was over. Her radar screen showed nothing at all.

"As I predicted," the hole said.

"Why don't you shut up?" Xanthia sat very still, and trembled.

"I shall, very soon. I did not expect to be thanked. But what you did, you did for yourself."

"And you too, you . . . you *ghoul!* Damn you, damn you to hell." She was shouting through her tears. "Don't think you've fooled me, not completely, anyway. I know what you did, and I know how you did it."

"Do you?" The voice was unutterably cool and distant. She could see that now that the hole was out of danger, it was rapidly losing interest in her.

"Yes, I do. Don't tell me it was coincidence that when you changed direction it was just enough to be near Zoe when she got here. You had this planned from the start."

"From much further back than you know," the hole said. "I tried to get you both, but it was impossible. The best I could do was take advantage of the situation as it was."

"Shut up, shut up."

The hole's voice was changing from the hollow, neutral tones to something that might have issued from a tank of liquid helium. She would never have mistaken it for human.

"What I did, I did for my own benefit. But I saved your life. She was going to try to kill you. I maneuvered her into such a position that when she tried to turn her fusion drive on you, she was heading into a black hole she was powerless to detect."

"You *used* me."

"You used me. You were going to imprison me in a power station."

"But you said you wouldn't *mind!* You said it would be the perfect place."

"Do you believe that eating is all there is to life? There is more to do in the wide universe than you can even suspect. I am slow. It is easy to catch a hole if your mass detector is functioning; Zoe did it three times. But I am beyond your reach now."

"What do you mean? What are you going to do? What am *I* going to do?" That question hurt so much that Xanthia almost didn't hear the hole's reply.

"I am on my way out. I converted *Shirley* into energy; I absorbed very little mass from her. I beamed the energy very tightly, and am now on my way out of your system. You will not see me again. You have two options. You can go back to Pluto and tell everyone what happened out here. It would be necessary for scientists to rewrite natural laws if they believed you. It has been done before, but usually with more persuasive evidence. There will be questions asked concerning the fact that no black hole has ever evaded capture, spoken, or changed velocity in the past. You can explain that when a hole has a chance to defend itself, the hole hunter does not survive to tell the story."

"I will. I *will* tell them what happened! Xanthia was eaten by a horrible doubt. Was it possible there had been a solution to her problem that did not involve Zoe's death? Just how badly had the hole tricked her?

"There is a second possibility," the hole went on, relentlessly. "Just what *are* you doing out here in a lifeboat?"

"What am I . . . I told you, we had . . ." Xanthia stopped. She felt herself choking.

"It would be easy to see you as crazy. You discovered something in *Lollipop*'s library that led you to know you must kill Zoe. This knowledge was too much for you. In defense, you invented me to trick you into doing what you had to do. Look in the mirror and tell me if you think your story will be believed. Look closely, and be honest with yourself."

She heard the voice laugh for the first time, from down in the bottom of its hole, like a voice from a well. It was an extremely unpleasant sound.

Maybe Zoe had died a month ago, strangled or poisoned or slashed with a knife. Xanthia had been sitting in her lifeboat, catatonic, all that time, and had constructed this episode to justify the murder. It *had* been self-defense, which was certainly a good excuse, and a very convenient one.

But she knew. She was sure, as sure as she had ever been of anything, that the hole was out there, that everything had happened as she had seen it happen. She saw the flash again in her mind, the awful flash that had turned Zoe into radiation. But she also knew that the other explanation would haunt her for the rest of her life.

"I advise you to forget it. Go to Pluto, tell everyone that your ship blew up and you escaped and you are Zoe. Take her place in the world, and never, *never* speak of talking black holes."

The voice faded from her radio. It did not speak again.

After days of numb despair and more tears and recriminations than she cared to remember, Xanthia did as the hole had predicted. But life on Pluto did not agree with her. There were too many people, and none of them looked very much like her. She stayed long enough to withdraw Zoe's money from the bank and buy a ship, which she named *Shirley Temple*. It was massive, with power to blast to the stars if necessary. She had left something out there, and she meant to search for it until she found it again.

## *Stardance*

### Spider and Jeanne Robinson

Spider Robinson was born in New York but currently lives in Nova Scotia, Canada, in a 150-year-old house that was, according to him, "unquestionably built by a dwarf who leaned to the left at a 45-degree angle." In 1974 he tied with Lisa Tuttle for the John W. Campbell Memorial Award for new writers in science fiction; in 1977 his novella "By Any Other Name" won a Hugo Award, tied with a story by James Tiptree, Jr. (He remarks that he "seems fit to be tied.")

Jeanne Robinson, originally from Boston, lives in Nova Scotia with Spider and their daughter, Luanna Mountainborne. She's a dancer, choreographer, and dance teacher who had no intention of ever becoming a writer of science fiction, but . . . when Spider started writing "Stardance," Jeanne "began reading each day's output and frowning. Ever so diplomatically, she began correcting minor points of terminology or dance lore, then suggesting small bits, then tactfully criticizing a phrase here, a paragraph there. I took the story off down a horrid blind alley, and she told me so . . . 'I'm sorry,' she said, 'but Shara just wouldn't *do* that,' and then she proceeded to explain my character to me." Spider rewrote the scene her way and asked her what she figured would happen next. "Although she never set finger to typewriter, the resulting novella was at least as much hers as mine," Spider says. (Most of the choreography is hers, for instance.)

Presently they're collaborating on a sequel, "Starseed," which together with "Stardance" will form a complete novel. While you're waiting for it you can enjoy the first half, which is complete in itself: a story of dancing in free-fall, of love and courage in the face of an alien invasion.

---

I can't really say that I knew her, certainly not the way Seroff knew Isadora. All I know of her childhood and adolescence are the anecdotes she chanced to relate in my hearing—just enough to make me certain that all three of the contradictory biographies on the current best-seller list are fictional. All I know of her adult life are the hours she spent in my presence and on my monitors—more than enough to tell me that every newspaper account I've seen is fictional. Carrington probably believed he knew her better than I, and in a limited sense he was correct—but he would never have written of it, and now he is dead.

But I was her video man, since the days when you touched the camera with your hands, and I knew her backstage: a type of relationship like no other on Earth or off it. I don't believe it can be described to anyone not of the profession—you might think of it as somewhere between co-workers and combat buddies. I was with her the day she came to Skyfac, terrified and determined, to stake her life upon a dream. I watched her work and worked with her for that whole two months, through endless rehearsals, and I have saved every tape and they are not for sale.

And, of course, I saw the Stardance. I was there; I taped it.

I guess I can tell you some things about her.

To begin with, it was not, as Cahill's *Shara* and Von Derski's *Dance Unbound: The Creation of New Modern* suggest, a lifelong fascination with space and space travel that led her to become the race's first zero-gravity dancer. Space was a means to her, not an end, and its vast empty immensity scared her at first. Nor was it, as Melberg's hardcover tabloid *The Real Shara Drummond* claims, because she lacked the talent to make it as a dancer on Earth. If you think free-fall dancing is easier than conventional dance, you try it. Don't forget your dropsickness bag.

But there is a grain of truth in Melberg's slander, as there is in all the best slanders. She could *not* make it on Earth—but not through lack of talent.

I first saw her in Toronto in July of 1984. I headed Toronto Dance Theater's video department at that time, and I hated every minute of it. I hated everything in those days. The schedule that day called for spending the entire afternoon taping students, a waste of time and tape which I hated more than anything except the phone company. I hadn't seen the year's new crop yet, and was not eager to. I love to watch dance done well—the efforts of a tyro are usually as pleasing to me as a first-year violin student in the next apartment is to you.

My leg was bothering me even more than usual as I walked into the studio. Norrey saw my face and left a group of young hopefuls to come over. "Charlie . . . ?"

"I know, I know. They're tender fledglings, Charlie, with egos as fragile as an Easter egg in December. Don't bite them, Charlie. Don't even bark at them if you can help it, Charlie."

She smiled. "Something like that. Leg?"

"Leg."

Norrey Drummond is a dancer who gets away with looking like a woman because she's small. There's about a hundred and fifteen pounds of her, and most of it is heart. She stands about five four, and is perfectly capable of seeming to tower over the tallest student. She has more energy than the North American Grid, and uses it as efficiently as a vane pump (have you ever studied the principle of a standard piston-type pump? Go look up the principle of a vane pump. I wonder what the original conception of *that* notion must have been like, as an emotional experience). There's a signaturelike uniqueness to her dance, the only reason I can see why she got so few of the really juicy parts in company productions until Modern gave way to New Modern. I liked her because she didn't pity me.

"It's not only the leg," I admitted. "I hate to see the tender fledglings butcher your choreography."

"Then you needn't worry. The piece you're taping today is by . . . one of the students."

"Oh, fine. I knew I should have called in sick." She made a face. "What's the catch?"

"Eh?"

"Why did the funny thing happen to your voice just as you got to 'one of my students'?"

She blushed. "Dammit, she's my sister."

Norrey and I are the very oldest and closest of friends, but I'd never chanced to meet a sister—not unusual these days, I suppose.

My eyebrows rose. "She must be good then."

"Why thank you, Charlie."

"Bullshit. I give compliments right-handed or not at all—I'm not talking about heredity. I mean that you're so hopelessly ethical you'd bend over backward to avoid nepotism. For you to give your own sister a feature like that, she must be *terrific*."

"Charlie, she is," Norrey said simply.

"We'll see. What's her name?"

"Shara." Norrey pointed her out, and I understood the rest of the catch. Shara Drummond was ten years younger than her sister—and seven inches taller, with thirty or forty more pounds. I noted absently that she was stunningly beautiful, but it didn't deter my dismay—in her best years, Sophia Loren could never have become a modern dancer. Where Norrey was small, Shara was big, and where Norrey was big, Shara was bigger. If I'd seen her on the street I might have whistled appreciatively—but in the studio I frowned.

"My God, Norrey, she's enormous."

"Mother's second husband was a football player," she said mournfully. "She's awfully good."

"If she *is* good, that *is* awful. Poor girl. Well, what do you want me to do?"

"What makes you think I want you to do anything?"

"You're still standing here."

"Oh. I guess I am. Well . . . have lunch with us, Charlie?"

"Why?" I knew perfectly well why, but I expected a polite lie.

Not from Norrey Drummond. "Because you two have something in common, I think."

I paid her honesty the compliment of not wincing. "I suppose we do."

"Then you will?"

"Right after the session."

She twinkled and was gone. In a remarkably short time she had organized the studioful of wandering, chattering young people into something that resembled a dance ensemble if you squinted. They warmed up during the twenty minutes it took me to set up and check out my equipment. I positioned one camera in front of them, one behind, and kept one in my hands for walk-around close-up work. I never triggered it.

There's a game you play in your mind. Every time someone catches or is brought to your attention, you begin making guesses about them. You try to extrapolate their character and habits from their appearance. Him? Surly, disorganized—leaves the cap off the toothpaste and drinks boilermakers. Her? Art-student type, probably uses a diaphragm and writes letters in a stylized calligraphy of her own invention. Them? They look like schoolteachers from Miami, probably here to see what snow looks like, attend a convention. Sometimes I come pretty close. I don't know how I typecast Shara

Drummond, in those first twenty minutes. The moment she began to dance, all preconceptions left my mind. She became something elemental, something unknowable, a living bridge between our world and the one the Muses live in.

I know, on an intellectual and academic level, all there is to know about dance, and I could not categorize or classify or even really comprehend the dance she danced that afternoon. I saw it, I even appreciated it, but I was not equipped to understand it. My camera dangled from the end of my arm, next to my jaw. Dancers speak of their "center," the place their motion centers around, often quite near the physical center of gravity. You strive to "dance from your center," and the "contraction-and-release" idea which underlies much of Modern dance depends on the center for its focus of energy. Shara's center seemed to move about the room under its own power, trailing limbs that attached to it by choice rather than necessity. What's the word for the outermost part of the sun, the part that still shows in an eclipse? Corona? That's what her limbs were: four lengthy tongues of flame that followed the center in its eccentric, whirling orbit, writhing fluidly around its surface. That the lower two frequently contacted the floor seemed coincidental—indeed, the other two touched the floor nearly as regularly.

There were other students dancing. I know this because the two automatic videocameras, unlike me, did their job and recorded the piece as a whole. It was called *Birthing,* and depicted the formation of a galaxy that ended up resembling Andromeda. It was only vaguely accurate, literally, but it wasn't intended to be. Symbolically, it felt like the birth of a galaxy.

In retrospect. At the time I was aware only of the galaxy's heart: Shara. Students occluded her from time to time, and I simply never noticed. It hurt to watch her.

If you know anything about dance, this must all sound horrid to you. A dance about a *nebula?* I know, I know. It's a ridiculous notion. And it worked. In the most gut-level, cellular way it worked—save only that Shara was too good for those around her. She did not belong in that eager crew of awkward, half-trained apprentices. It was like listening to the late Stephen Wonder trying to work with a pickup band in a Montreal bar.

But that wasn't what hurt.

Le Maintenant was shabby, but the food was good and the house brand of grass was excellent. Show a Diner's Club card in there and they'd show you a galley full of dirty dishes. It's gone now. Norrey and Shara declined a toke, but in my line of work it helps. Besides, I needed a few hits. How to tell a lovely lady her dearest dream is hopeless?

I didn't need to ask Shara to know that her dearest dream was to dance. More: to dance professionally. I have often speculated on the motives of the professional artist. Some seek the narcissistic assurance that others will actually pay cash to watch or hear them. Some are so incompetent or disorganized that they can support themselves in no other way. Some have a message which they feel needs expressing. I suppose most artists combine elements of all three. This is no complaint—what they do for us is necessary. We should be grateful that there *are* motives.

But Shara was one of the rare ones. She danced because she needed to. She needed to say things which could be said in no other way, and she needed to take her meaning and her living from the saying of them. Anything else would have demeaned and devalued the essential statement of her dance. I know this, from watching that one dance.

Between toking up and keeping my mouth full and then toking again (a mild amount to offset the slight down that eating brings), it was over half an hour before I was required to say anything, beyond an occasional grunted response to the luncheon chatter of the ladies. As the coffee arrived, Shara looked me square in the eye and said, "Do you talk, Charlie?"

She was Norrey's sister, all right.

"Only inanities."

"No such thing. Inane people, maybe."

"Do you enjoy dancing, Miss Drummond?"

She answered seriously. "Define 'enjoy.' "

I opened my mouth and closed it, perhaps three times. You try it.

"And for God's sake tell me why you're so intent on not talking to me. You've got me worried."

"Shara!" Norrey looked dismayed.

"Hush. I want to know."

I took a crack at it. "Shara, before he died I had the privilege of meeting Bertram Ross. I had just seen him dance. A producer who knew and liked me took me backstage, the way you take a kid to see Santa Claus. I had expected him to look even older off stage, at rest. He looked younger, as if that incredible motion of his was barely in check. He talked to me. After a while I stopped opening my mouth, because nothing ever came out."

She waited, expecting more. Only gradually did she comprehend the compliment and its dimension. I had assumed it would be obvious. Most artists *expect* to be complimented. When she did twig, she did not blush or simper. She did not cock her head and say "Oh, come on." She did not say "You flatter me." She did not look away.

She nodded slowly and said, "Thank you, Charlie. That's worth a lot more than idle chatter." There was a suggestion of sadness in her smile, as if we shared a bitter joke.

"You're welcome."

"For heaven's sake, Norrey, what are you looking so upset about?"

The cat now had Norrey's tongue.

"She's disappointed in me," I said. "I said the wrong thing."

"That was the wrong thing?"

"It should have been 'Miss Drummond, I think you ought to give up dancing.' "

"It should have been '*Shara,* I think you ought' . . . *what?*"

"Charlie," Norrey began.

"I was supposed to tell you that we can't all be professional dancers, that they also surf who only sand and wade. Shara, I was supposed to tell you to dump the dance—before it dumps you."

In my need to be honest with her, I had been more brutal than was necessary, I thought. I was to learn that bluntness never dismayed Shara. She demanded it.

"Why you?" was all she said.

"We're inhabiting the same vessel, you and I. We've both got an itch that our bodies just won't let us scratch."

Her eyes softened. "What's your itch?"

"The same as yours."

"Eh?"

"The man was supposed to come and fix the phone on Thursday. My roommate, Karen, and I had an all-day rehearsal. We left a note. Mister telephone man, we had to go out, and we sure couldn't call you, heh heh. Please get the key from the concierge and come on in; the phone's in the bedroom. The phone man never showed up. They never do." My hands seemed to be shaking. "We came home up the back stairs from the alley. The phone was still dead, but I never thought to take down the note on the front door. I got sick the next morning. Cramps. Vomiting. Karen and I were just friends, but she stayed home to take care of me. I suppose on a Friday night the note seemed even more plausible. He slipped the lock with a piece of plastic, and Karen came out of the kitchen as he was unplugging the stereo. He was so indignant he shot her. Twice. The noise scared him; by the time I got there he was halfway out the door. He just had time to put a slug through my hip joint, and then he was gone. They never got him. They never even came to fix the phone." My hands were under control now. "Karen was a damned good dancer, but I was better. In my head, I still am."

Her eyes were round. "You're not Charlie . . . Charles *Armstead.*"

I nodded.

"Oh my God. So *that's* where you went."

I was shocked by how she looked. It brought me back from the cold and windy border of self-pity. I began a little to pity her. I should have guessed the depth of her empathy. And in the way that really mattered, we were too damned alike—we *did* share the same bitter joke. I wondered why I had wanted to shock her.

"They couldn't repair the joint?" she asked softly.

"I can walk splendidly. Given a strong enough motivation, I can even run short distances. I can't dance worth a damn."

"So you became a video man."

"Three years ago. People who know both video and dance are about as common as garter belts these days. Oh, they've been taping dance since the seventies—with the imagination of a network news cameraman. If you film a stage play with two cameras in the orchestra pit, is it a movie?"

"You do for dance what the movie camera did for drama?"

"Pretty fair analogy. Where it breaks down is that dance is more analogous to music than to drama. You can't stop and start it, or go back and retake a scene that didn't go in the can right, or reverse the chronology to get a tidy shooting schedule. The event happens and you record it. What I am is what the record industry pays top dollar for—a mix-man with savvy enough to know which ax is wailing at the moment and mike it high—and the sense to have given the heaviest dudes the best mikes. There are a few others like me. I'm the best."

She took it the way she had the compliment to herself—at face value. Usually when I say things like that I don't give a damn what reaction I get, or I'm being salty and hoping for outrage. But I was pleased at her acceptance, pleased enough for it to bother me. A faint irritation made me go brutal again, *knowing* it wouldn't work.

"So what all this leads to is that Norrey was hoping I'd suggest some similar form of sublimation for you. Because I'll make it in dance before you will."

She stubborned up. "I don't buy that, Charlie. I know what you're talking about, I'm not a fool, but I think I can beat it."

"Sure you will. *You're too damned big, lady.* You've got tits like both halves of a prize honeydew melon and an ass that any actress in Hollywood would sell her parents for, and in Modern dance that makes you d-e-d dead, you haven't got a chance. Beat it? You'll beat your head in first, how'm I doing, Norrey?"

"For Christ's sake, Charlie!"

I softened. I can't work Norrey into a tantrum—I like her too much. "I'm sorry, hon. My leg's giving me the mischief, and I'm stinkin' mad. She *ought* to make it—and she won't. She's your sister, and so it saddens you. Well I'm a total stranger, and it enrages me."

"How do you think it makes me feel?" Shara blazed, startling us both. I hadn't known she had so much voice. "So you want me to pack it in and rent me a camera, huh, Charlie? Or maybe sell apples outside the studio?" A ripple ran up her jaw. "Well I will be damned by all the gods in Southern California before I'll pack it in. God gave me the large economy size, but there is not a surplus pound on it and it fits me like a glove and I can by Jesus *dance* it and I will. You may be right—I may beat my head in first. But I will get it done." She took a deep breath. "Now I thank you for your kind intentions, Char—Mr. Armst— Oh shit." The tears came and she left hastily, spilling a quarter cup of cold coffee on Norrey's lap.

"Charlie," Norrey said through clenched teeth, "why do I like you so much?"

"Dancers are dumb." I gave her my handkerchief.

"Oh." She patted at her lap awhile. "How come you like me?"

"Video men are smart."

"Oh."

I spent the afternoon in my apartment, reviewing the footage I'd shot that morning, and the more I watched, the madder I got.

Dance requires intense motivation at an extraordinarily early age—a blind devotion, a gamble on the as-yet-unrealized potentials of heredity and nutrition. You can begin, say, classical ballet training at age six—and at fourteen find yourself broad-shouldered, the years of total effort utterly wasted. Shara had set her sights on Modern dance—and found out too late that God had dealt her the body of a woman.

She was not fat—you have seen her. She was tall, big-boned tall, and on that great frame was built a rich, ripely female body. As I ran and reran the tapes of *Birthing,* the pain grew in me until I even forgot the ever-present aching of my own leg. It was like watching a supremely gifted basketball player who stood four feet tall.

To make it in Modern dance, it is essential to get into a company. You cannot be seen unless you are visible. Norrey had told me, on the walk back to the studio, of Shara's efforts to get into a company—and I could have predicted nearly every word.

"Merce *Cunningham* saw her dance, Charlie. Martha Graham saw her dance, just before she died. Both of them praised her warmly, for her choreography as much as for her technique. Neither offered her a position. I'm not even sure I blame them—I can sort of understand."

Norrey could understand all right. It was her own defect magnified a hundredfold: uniqueness. A company member must be capable of excellent solo work—but she must also be able to blend into group effort, in ensemble work. Shara's very uniqueness made her virtually useless as a company member. She could not help but draw the eye.

And, once drawn, the male eye at least would never leave. Modern dancers must sometimes work nude these days, and it is therefore meet that they have the body of a fourteen-year-old boy. We may have ladies dancing with few or no clothes on up here, but by God it is Art. An actress or a musician or a singer or a painter may be lushly endowed, deliciously rounded—but a dancer must be nearly as sexless as a high-fashion model. Perhaps God knows why. Shara could not have purged her dance of her sexuality even if she had been interested in trying, and as I watched her dance on my monitor and in my mind's eye, I knew she was not.

Why did her genius have to lie in the only occupation besides model and nun in which sexiness is a liability? It broke my heart, by empathic analogy.

"It's no good at all, is it?"

I whirled and barked. "Dammit, you made me bite my tongue."

"I'm sorry." She came from the doorway into my living room. "Norrey told me how to find the place. The door was ajar."

"I forgot to shut it when I came home."

"You leave it open?"

"I've learned the lesson of history. No junkie, no matter how strung out he is, will enter an apartment with the door ajar and the radio on. Obviously there's someone home. And you're right, it's no damn good at all. Sit down."

She sat on the couch. Her hair was down now, and I liked it better that way. I shut off the monitor and popped the tape, tossing it on a shelf.

"I came to apologize. I shouldn't have blown up at you at lunch. You were trying to help me."

"You had it coming. I imagine by now you've built up quite a head of steam."

"Five years' worth. I figured I'd start in the States instead of Canada. Go farther faster. Now I'm back in Toronto and I don't think I'm going to make it here either. You're right, Mr. Armstead—I'm too damned big. Amazons don't dance."

"It's still Charlie. Listen, something I want to ask you. That last gesture, at the end of *Birthing*—what was that? I thought it was a beckoning, Norrey says it was a farewell, and now that I've run the tape it looks like a yearning, a reaching out."

"Then it worked."

"Pardon?"

"It seemed to me that the birth of a galaxy called for all three. They're so close together in spirit it seemed silly to give each a separate movement."

"Mmm." Worse and worse. Suppose Einstein had had aphasia. "Why couldn't you have been a rotten dancer? That'd just be irony. This,"—I pointed to the tape—"is high tragedy."

"Aren't you going to tell me I can still dance for myself?"

"No. For you that'd be worse than not dancing at all."

"My God, you're perceptive. Or am I that easy to read?"

I shrugged.

"Oh, Charlie," she burst out, "what am I going to do?"

"You'd better not ask me that." My voice sounded funny.

"Why not?"

"Because I'm already two thirds in love with you. And because you're not in love with me and never will be. And so that is the sort of question you shouldn't ask me."

It jolted her a little, but she recovered quickly. Her eyes softened, and she shook her head slowly. "You even know why I'm not, don't you?"

"And why you won't be."

I was terribly afraid she was going to say "Charlie, I'm sorry." But she surprised me again. What she said was "I can count on the fingers of one foot the number of grown-up men I've ever met. I'm grateful for you. I guess ironic tragedies come in pairs?"

"Sometimes."

"Well, now all I have to do is figure out what to do with my life. That should kill the weekend."

"Will you continue your classes?"

"Might as well. It's never a waste of time to study. Norrey's teaching me things."

All of a sudden my mind started to percolate. Man is a rational animal, right? Right? "What if I had a better idea?"

"If you've got another idea, it's better. Speak."

"Do you have to have an audience? I mean, does it have to be *live?*"

"What do you mean?"

"Maybe there's a back way in. Look, they're building tape facilities into all the TVs nowadays, right? And by now everybody has collected all the old movies and Ernie Kovacs programs and such that they always wanted, and now they're looking for new stuff. Exotic stuff, too esoteric for network or local broadcast, stuff that—"

"The independent video companies, you're talking about."

"Right. TDT is thinking of entering the market, and the Graham company already has."

"So?"

"So suppose we go freelance? You and me? You dance it and I'll tape it: a straight business deal. I've got a few connections, and maybe I can get more. I could name you ten acts in the music business right now that never go on tour—just record and record. Why don't you bypass the structure of the dance companies and take a chance on the public? Maybe word-of-mouth could . . ."

Her face was beginning to light up like a jack-o'-lantern. "Charlie, do you think it could work? Do you really think so?"

"I don't think it has a snowball's chance." I crossed the room, opened up the beer fridge, took out the snowball I keep there in the summer, and tossed it at her. She caught it, but just barely, and when she realized what it was, she burst out laughing. "I've got just enough faith in the idea to quit working for TDT and put my time into it. I'll invest my time, my tape, my equipment, and my savings. Ante up."

She tried to get sober, but the snowball froze her fingers and she broke up again. "A snowball in July. You madman. Count me in. I've got a little money saved.

And . . . and I guess I don't have much choice, do I?"

"I guess not."

The next three years were some of the most exciting years of my life, of both our lives. While I watched and taped, Shara transformed herself from a potentially great dancer into something truly awesome. She did something I'm not sure I can explain.

She became dance's analogy of the jazzman.

Dance was, for Shara, self-expression, pure and simple, first, last and always. Once she freed herself of the attempt to fit into the world of company dance, she came to regard choreography per se as an *obstacle* to her self-expression, as a preprogrammed rut, inexorable as a script and as limiting. And so she devalued it.

A jazzman may blow *Night in Tunisia* for a dozen consecutive nights, and each evening will be a different experience, as he interprets and reinterprets the melody according to his mood of the moment. Total unity of artist and his art: spontaneous creation. The melodic starting point distinguishes the result from pure anarchy.

In just this way Shara devalued preperformance choreography to a starting point, a framework on which to build whatever the moment demanded, and then jammed around it. She learned in those three busy years to dismantle the interface between herself and her dance. Dancers have always tended to sneer at improv dancing, even while they practiced it, in the studio, for the looseness it gave. They failed to see that *planned* improv, improv around a theme fully thought out in advance, was the natural next step in dance. Shara took the step. You must be very, very good to get away with that much freedom. She was good enough.

There's no point in detailing the professional fortunes of Drumstead Enterprises over those three years. We worked hard, we made some magnificent tapes, and we couldn't sell them for paperweights. A home video cassette industry indeed existed—and they knew as much about Modern dance as the record industry knew about the blues when *they* started. The big outfits wanted credentials, and the little outfits wanted cheap talent. Finally we even got desperate enough to try the schlock houses—and learned what we already knew. They didn't have the distribution, the prestige, or the technical specs for the critics to pay any attention to them. Word-of-mouth advertising is like a gene pool—if it isn't a certain minimum size to start with, it doesn't get anywhere. "Spider" John Koerner is an incredibly talented musician and songwriter who has been making and selling his own records since 1972. How many of you have ever heard of him?

In May of 1987 I opened my mailbox in the lobby and found the letter from VisuEnt Inc., terminating our option with deepest sorrow and no severance. I went straight over to Shara's apartment, and my leg felt as if the bone marrow had been replaced with thermite and ignited. It was a very long walk.

She was working on *Weight Is a Verb* when I got there. Converting her big living room into a studio had cost time, energy, skullsweat, and a fat bribe to the landlord, but it was cheaper than renting time in a studio, considering the sets we wanted. It looked like high mountain country that day, and I hung my hat on a fake alder when I entered.

She flashed me a smile and kept moving, building up to greater and greater leaps. She looked like the most beautiful mountain goat I ever saw. I was in a foul mood and I wanted to kill the music (McLaughlin and Miles together, leaping some themselves), but I never could interrupt Shara when she was dancing. She built it gradually, with directional counterpoint, until she seemed to hurl herself into the air, stay there until she was damned good and ready, and then hurl herself down again. Sometimes she rolled when she hit and sometimes she landed on her hands, and always the energy of falling was transmuted into something instead of being absorbed. It was total energy output, and by the time she was done I had calmed down enough to be almost philosophical about our mutual professional ruin.

She ended up collapsed in upon herself, head bowed, exquisitely humbled in her attempt to defy gravity. I couldn't help applauding. It felt corny, but I couldn't help it.

"Thank you, Charlie."

"I'll be damned. Weight *is* a verb. I thought you were crazy when you told me the title."

"It's one of the strongest verbs in dance—and you can make it do *anything.*"

"Almost anything."

"Eh?"

"VisuEnt gave us our contract back."

"Oh." Nothing showed in her eyes, but I knew what was behind them. "Well, who's next on the list?"

"There is no one left on the list."

*"Oh."* This time it showed. "Oh."

"We should have remembered. Great artists are never honored in their own lifetime. What we ought to do is drop dead—then we'd be all set."

In my way I was trying to be strong for her, and she knew it and tried to be strong for me.

"Maybe what we should do is go into death insurance, for artists," she said. "We pay the client premiums against a controlling interest in his estate, and we insure that he'll die."

"We can't lose. And if he becomes famous in his lifetime he can buy out."

"Terrific. Let's stop this before I laugh myself to death."

"Yeah."

She was silent for a long time. My own mind was racing efficiently, but the transmission seemed to be blown—it wouldn't *go* anywhere. Finally she got up and turned off the music machine, which had been whining softly ever since the tape ended. It made a loud *click.*

"Norrey's got some land in Prince Edward Island," she said, not meeting my eyes. "There's a house."

I tried to head her off with the punch line from the

old joke about the kid shoveling out the elephant cage in the circus whose father offers to take him back and set him up with a decent job. "What? And leave show business?"

"Screw show business," she said softly. "If I went out to PEI now, maybe I could get the land cleared and plowed in time to get a garden in." Her expression changed. "How about you?"

"Me? I'll be okay. TDT asked me to come back."

"That was six months ago."

"They asked again. Last week."

"And you said no. Moron."

"Maybe so, maybe so."

"The whole damn thing was a waste of time. All that time. All that energy. All that work. I might as well have been farming in PEI—by now the soil'd be starting to bear well. What a waste, Charlie, what a stinking waste."

"No, I don't think so, Shara. It sounds glib to say that 'nothing is wasted,' but—well, it's like that dance you just did. Maybe you can't beat gravity—but it surely is a beautiful thing to *try*."

"Yeah, I know. Remember the Light Brigade. Remember the Alamo. They tried." She laughed, a bitter laugh.

"Yes, and so did Jesus of Nazareth. Did you do it for material reward, or because it needed doing? If nothing else, we now have several hundred thousand feet of the most magnificent dance recordings on tape, commercial value zero, real value incalculable, and by me that is no waste. It's over now, and we'll both go do the next thing, but it was *not a waste*." I discovered that I was shouting, and stopped.

She closed her mouth. After a while she tried a smile. "You're right, Charlie. It wasn't waste. I'm a better dancer than I ever was."

"Damn right. You've transcended choreography."

She smiled ruefully. "Yeah. Even Norrey thinks it's a dead end."

"It is *not* a dead end. There's more to poetry than

haiku and sonnets. Dancers don't *have* to be robots, delivering memorized lines with their bodies."

"They do if they want to make a living."

"We'll try again in a few years. Maybe they'll be ready then."

"Sure. Let me get us some drinks."

I slept with her that night, for the first and last time. In the morning I broke down the set in the living room while she packed. I promised to write. I promised to come and visit when I could. I carried her bags down to the car, and stowed them inside. I kissed her and waved good-bye. I went looking for a drink, and at four o'clock the next morning a mugger decided I looked drunk enough and I broke his jaw, his nose, and two ribs, and then sat down on him and cried. On Monday morning I showed up at the studio with my hat in my hand and a mouth like a bus-station ashtray and crawled back into my old job. Norrey didn't ask any questions. What with rising food prices, I gave up eating anything but bourbon, and in six months I was fired. It went like that for a long time.

I never did write to her. I kept getting bogged down after "Dear Shara . . ."

When I got to the point of selling my video equipment for booze, a relay clicked somewhere and I took stock of myself. The stuff was all the life I had left, and so I went to the local Al-Anon instead of the pawn shop and got sober. After a while my soul got numb, and I stopped flinching when I woke up. A hundred times I began to wipe the tapes I still had of Shara—she had copies of her own—but in the end I could not. From time to time I wondered how *she* was doing, and I could not bear to find out. If Norrey heard anything, she didn't tell me about it. She even tried to get me my job back a third time, but it was hopeless. Reputation can be a terrible thing once you've blown it. I was lucky to land a job with an educational TV station in New Brunswick.

It was a long couple of years.

Vidphones were coming out by 1990, and I had

breadboarded one of my own without the knowledge or consent of the phone company, which I still hated more than anything. When the peanut bulb I had replaced the damned bell with started glowing softly on and off one evening in June, I put the receiver on the audio pickup and energized the tube, in case the caller was also equipped. "Hello?"

She was. When Shara's face appeared, I got a cold cube of fear in the pit of my stomach, because I had quit seeing her face everywhere when I quit drinking, and I had been thinking lately of hitting the sauce again. When I blinked and she was still there, I felt a little better and tried to speak. It didn't work.

"Hello, Charlie. It's been a long time."

The second time it worked. "Seems like yesterday. Somebody else's yesterday."

"Yes, it does. It took me *days* to find you. Norrey's in Paris, and no one else knew where you'd gone."

"Yeah. How's farming?"

"I . . . I've put that away, Charlie. It's even more creative than dancing, but it's not the same."

"Then what *are* you doing?"

"Working."

*"Dancing?"*

"Yes. Charlie, I need you. I mean, I have a job for you. I need your cameras and your eye."

"Never mind the qualifications. Any kind of need will do. *Where are you?* When's the next plane there? Which cameras do I pack?"

"New York, an hour from now, and none of them. I didn't mean 'your cameras' literally—unless you're using GLX-5000s and a Hamilton Board lately."

I whistled. It hurt my mouth. "Not on my budget. Besides, I'm old-fashioned—I like to hold 'em with my hands."

"For this job you'll use a Hamilton, and it'll be a twenty-input Masterchrome, brand new."

"You grew poppies on that farm? Or just struck diamonds with the rototiller?"

"You'll be getting paid by Bryce Carrington."

I blinked.

"Now will you catch that plane so I can tell you about it? The New Age, ask for the Presidential Suite."

"The hell with the plane, I'll walk. Quicker." I hung up.

According to the *Time* magazine in my dentist's waiting room, Bryce Carrington was the genius who had become a multimillionaire by convincing a number of giants of industry to underwrite Skyfac, the great orbiting complex that kicked the bottom out of the crystals market. As I recalled the story, some rare poliolike disease had wasted both his legs and put him in a wheelchair. But the legs had lost strength, not function—in lessened gravity, they worked well enough. So he created Skyfac, establishing mining crews on Luna to supply it with cheap raw materials, and lived in orbit under reduced gravity. His picture made him look like a reasonably successful author (as opposed to writer). Other than that I knew nothing about him. I paid little attention to news and none at all to space news.

The New Age was *the* hotel in New York in those days, built on the ruins of the Sheraton. Ultraefficient security, bulletproof windows, carpet thicker than the outside air, and a lobby of an architectural persuasion that John D. MacDonald once called "Early Dental Plate." It stank of money. I was glad I'd made the effort to locate a necktie, and I wished I'd shined my shoes. An incredible man blocked my way as I came in through the air lock. He moved and was built like the toughest, fastest bouncer I ever saw, and he dressed and acted like God's butler. He said his name was Perry. He asked if he could help me, as though he didn't think so.

"Yes, Perry. Would you mind lifting up one of your feet?"

"Why?"

"I'll bet twenty dollars you've shined your soles."

Half his mouth smiled, and he didn't move an inch. "Whom did you wish to see?"

"Shara Drummond."

"Not registered."

"The Presidential Suite."

"Oh." Light dawned. "Mr. Carrington's lady. You should have said so. Wait here, please." While he phoned to verify that I was expected, keeping his eye on me and his hand near his pocket, I swallowed my heart and rearranged my face. It took some time. So that was how it was. All right then. That was how it was.

Perry came back and gave me the little button-transmitter that would let me walk the corridors of the New Age without being cut down by automatic laser fire, and explained carefully that it would blow a largish hole in me if I attempted to leave the building without returning it. From his manner I gathered that I had just skipped four grades in social standing. I thanked him, though I'm damned if I knew why.

I followed the green fluorescent arrows that appeared on the bulbless ceiling, and came after a long and scenic walk to the Presidential Suite. Shara was waiting at the door, in something like an angel's pajamas. It made all that big body look delicate. "Hello, Charlie."

I was jovial and hearty. "Hi, babe. Swell joint. How've you been keeping yourself?"

"I haven't been."

"Well, how's Carrington been keeping you, then?" Steady, boy.

"Come in, Charlie."

I went in. It looked like where the Queen stayed when she was in town, and I'm sure she enjoyed it. You could have landed an airplane in the living room without waking anyone in the bedroom. It had two pianos. Only one fireplace, barely big enough to barbecue a buffalo—you have to scrimp somewhere, I guess. Roger Kellaway was on the quadio, and for a wild moment I thought he was actually in the suite, playing some unseen third piano. So this was how it was.

"Can I get you something, Charlie?"

"Oh, sure. Hash oil, Tangier Supreme. Dom Perignon for the pipe."

Without cracking a smile she went to a cabinet, which looked like a midget cathedral, and produced precisely what I had ordered. I kept my own features impassive and lit up. The bubbles tickled my throat, and the rush was exquisite. I felt myself relaxing, and when we had passed the narghile's mouthpiece a few times I felt her relax. We looked at each other then—really looked at each other—then at the room around us and then at each other again. Simultaneously we roared with laughter, a laughter that blew all the wealth out of the room and let in richness. Her laugh was the same whooping, braying belly laugh I remembered so well, an unselfconscious and lusty laugh, and it reassured me tremendously. I was so relieved I couldn't stop laughing myself, and that kept *her* going, and just as we might have stopped she pursed her lips and blew a stuttered arpeggio. There's an old recording called the *Spike Jones Laughing Record,* where the tuba player tries to play "The Flight of the Bumblebee" and falls down laughing, and the whole band breaks up and horse-laughs for a full two minutes, and every time they run out of air the tuba player tries another flutter and roars and they all break up again, and once when Shara was blue I bet her ten dollars that she couldn't listen to that record without at least giggling and I won. When I understood now that she was quoting it, I shuddered and dissolved into great whoops of new laughter, and a minute later we had reached the stage where we literally laughed ourselves out of our chairs and lay on the floor in agonies of mirth, weakly pounding the floor and howling. I take that laugh out of my memory now and then and rerun it—but not often, for such records deteriorate drastically with play.

At last we Dopplered back down to panting grins, and I helped her to her feet.

"What a perfectly dreadful place," I said, still chuckling.

She glanced around and shuddered. "Oh God, it *is*, Charlie. It must be awful to need this much front."

"For a horrid while I thought *you* did."

She sobered, and met my eyes. "Charlie, I wish I could resent that. In a way I do need it."

My eyes narrowed. "Just what do you mean?"

"I need Bryce Carrington."

"This time you can trot out the qualifiers. *How* do you need him?"

"I need his money," she cried.

How can you relax and tense up at the same time? "Oh, *damn* it, Shara! Is *that* how you're going to get to dance? Buy your way in? What does a critic go for, these days?"

"Charlie, stop it. I need Carrington to get seen. He's going to rent me a hall, that's all."

"If that's all, let's get out of the dump right now. I can bor . . . get enough cash to rent you any hall in the world, and I'm just as willing to risk my money."

"Can you get me Skyfac?"

*"Uh?"*

I couldn't for the life of me imagine why she proposed to go to Skyfac to dance. Why not Antarctica?

"Shara, you know even less about space than I do, but you must know that a satellite broadcast doesn't have to be made from a satellite?"

"Idiot. It's the setting I want."

I thought about it. "Moon'd be better, visually. Mountains. Light. Contrast."

"The visual aspect is secondary. I don't want one-sixth g, Charlie. I want zero gravity."

My mouth hung open.

"And I want you to be my video man."

God, she was a rare one. What I needed then was to sit there with my mouth open and think for several minutes. She let me do just that, waiting patiently for me to work it all out.

"Weight isn't a verb anymore, Charlie," she said finally. "That dance ended on the assertion that you can't beat gravity—you said so yourself. Well, that statement is incorrect—obsolete. The dance of the twenty-first century will have to acknowledge that."

"And it's just what you need to make it. A new kind of dance for a new kind of dancer. Unique. It'll catch the public eye, and you should have the field entirely to yourself for years. I like it, Shara. I like it. But can you pull it off?"

"I thought about what you said: that you can't beat gravity but it's beautiful to try. It stayed in my head for months, and then one day I was visiting a neighbor with a TV and I saw newsreels of the crew working on Skyfac Two. I was up all night thinking, and the next morning I came up to the States and got a job in Skyfac One. I've been up there for nearly a year, getting next to Carrington. I can do it, Charlie, I can make it work." There was a ripple in her jaw that I had seen before—when she told me off in Le Maintenant. It was a ripple of determination.

Still I frowned. "With Carrington's backing."

Her eyes left mine. "There's no such thing as a free lunch."

"What does he charge?"

She failed to answer, for long enough to answer me. In that instant, I began believing in God again, for the first time in years, just to be able to hate Him.

But I kept my mouth shut. She was old enough to manage her own finances. The price of a dream gets higher every year. Hell, I'd half expected it from the moment she'd called me.

But only half.

"Charlie, don't just sit there with your face all knotted up. Say something. Cuss me out, call me a whore, *something.*"

"Nuts. You be your own conscience, I have trouble enough being my own. You want to dance, you've got a patron. So now you've got a video man."

I hadn't intended to say that last sentence at all.

Strangely, it almost seemed to disappoint her at first. But then she relaxed and smiled. "Thank you, Charlie. Can you get out of whatever you're doing right away?"

"I'm working for an educational station in Shediac. I even got to shoot some dance footage. A dancing bear from the London Zoo. The amazing thing was how well he danced." She grinned. "I can get free."

"I'm glad. I don't think I could pull this off without you."

"I'm working for you. Not for Carrington."

"All right."

"Where is the great man, anyway? Scuba diving in the bathtub?"

"No," came a quiet voice from the doorway. "I've been sky diving in the lobby."

His wheelchair was a mobile throne. He wore a four-hundred-dollar suit the color of strawberry ice cream, a powder-blue turtleneck and one gold earring. The shoes were genuine leather. The watch was that newfangled bandless kind that literally tells you the time. He wasn't tall enough for her, and his shoulders were absurdly broad, although the suit tried hard to deny both. His eyes were like twin blueberries. His smile was that of a shark wondering which part will taste best. I wanted to crush his head between two boulders.

Shara was on her feet. "Bryce, this is Charles Armstead. I told you . . ."

"Oh yes. The video chap." He rolled forward and extended an impeccably manicured hand. "I'm Bryce Carrington, Armstead."

I remained seated, hands in my lap. "Oh yes. The rich chap."

One eyebrow rose an urbane quarter inch. "Oh, my. Another rude one. Well, if you're as good as Shara says you are, you're entitled."

"I'm rotten."

The smile faded. "Let's stop fencing, Armstead. I don't expect manners from creative people, but I have far more significant contempt than yours available if I need any. Now I'm tired of this damned gravity and I've had a rotten day testifying for a friend and it looks like they're going to recall me tomorrow. Do you want the job or don't you?"

He had me there. I did. "Yeah."

"All right, then. Your room is 2772. We'll be going up to Skyfac in two days. Be here at eight A.M."

"I'll want to talk with you about what you'll be needing, Charlie," Shara said. "Give me a call tomorrow."

I whirled to face her, and she flinched from my eyes.

Carrington failed to notice. "Yes, make a list of your requirements by tomorrow, so it can go up with us. Don't scrimp—if you don't fetch it, you'll do without. Good night, Armstead."

I faced him. "Good night, Mr. Carrington." Suh.

He turned toward the narghile, and Shara hurried to refill the chamber and bowl. I turned away hastily and made for the door. My leg hurt so much I nearly fell on the way, but I set my jaw and made it. When I reached the door I said to myself, You will now open the door and go through it, and then I spun on my heel. "Carrington!"

He blinked, surprised to discover I still existed. "Yes?"

"Are you *aware* that she doesn't love you in the slightest? Does that matter to you in any way?" My voice was high, and my fists were surely clenched.

"Oh," he said, and then again, "Oh. So that's what it is. I didn't *think* success alone merited that much contempt." He put down the mouthpiece and folded his fingers together. "Let me tell you something, Armstead. No one has ever loved me, to my knowledge. This suite does not love me." His voice took on human feeling for the first time. "But it is *mine*. Now get out."

I opened my mouth to tell him where to put his job, and then I saw Shara's face, and the pain in it suddenly made me deeply ashamed. I left at once, and when the door closed behind me I vomited on a rug that was worth slightly less than a Hamilton Masterchrome board. I was sorry then that I'd worn a necktie.

The trip to Pike's Peak Spaceport, at least, was aesthetically pleasurable. I enjoy air travel, gliding among stately clouds, watching the rolling procession of mountains and plains, vast jigsaws of farmland and intricate mosaics of suburbia unfolding below.

But the jump to Skyfac in Carrington's personal shuttle, *That First Step,* might as well have been an old

*Space Commando* rerun. I *know* they can't put portholes in space ships—but dammit, a shipboard video relay conveys no better resolution, color values, or presence than you get on your living-room tube. The only differences are that the stars don't "move" to give the illusion of travel, and there's no director editing the POV to give you dramatically interesting shots.

Aesthetically speaking. The *experiential* difference is that they do not, while you are watching the Space Commando sell hemorrhoid remedies, strap you into a couch, batter you with thunders, make you weigh better than half a ton for an unreasonably long time, and then drop you off the edge of the world into weightlessness. I had been half expecting nausea, but what I got was even more shocking: the sudden, unprecedented, total absence of pain in my leg. At that, Shara was hit worse than I was, barely managing to deploy her dropsickness bag in time. Carrington unstrapped and administered an antinausea injection with sure movements. It seemed to take forever to hit her, but when it did there was an enormous change—color and strength returned rapidly, and she was apparently fully recovered by the time the pilot announced that we were commencing docking and would everyone please strap in and shut up. I half expected Carrington to bark manners into him, but apparently the industrial magnate was not that sort of fool. He shut up and strapped himself down.

My leg didn't hurt in the slightest. Not at all.

The Skyfac complex looked like a disorderly heap of bicycle tires and beach balls of various sizes. The one our pilot made for was more like a tractor tire. We matched course, became its axle, and matched spin, and the damned thing grew a spoke that caught us square in the air lock. The air lock was "overhead" of our couches, but we entered and left it feet first. A few yards into the spoke, the direction we traveled became "down," and handholds became a ladder. Weight increased with every step, but even when we had emerged in a rather large cubical compartment it was far less than Earth normal. Nonetheless, my leg resumed biting me.

The room tried to be a classic reception room, high-level ("Please be seated. His Majesty will see you shortly."), but the low g and the p-suits racked along two walls spoiled the effect. Unlike the Space Commando's armor, a real pressure suit looks like nothing so much as a people-shaped baggie, and they look particularly silly in repose. A young dark-haired man in tweed rose from behind a splendidly gadgeted desk and smiled. "Good to see you, Mr. Carrington, I hope you had a pleasant jump."

"Fine thanks, Tom. You remember Shara, of course. This is Charles Armstead. Tom McGillicuddy." We both displayed our teeth and said we were delighted to meet each other. I could see that beneath the pleasantries McGillicuddy was upset about something.

"Nils and Mr. Longmire are waiting in your office, sir. There's . . . there's been another sighting."

"God *damn* it," Carrington began, and cut himself off. I stared at him. The full force of my best sarcasm had failed to anger this man. "All right. Take care of my guests while I go hear what Longmire has to say." He started for the door, moving like a beach ball in slow motion but under his own power. "Oh yes—the *Step* is loaded to the gun'ls with bulky equipment, Tom. Have her brought around to the cargo bays. Store the equipment in Six." He left, looking worried. McGillicuddy activated his desk and gave the necessary orders.

"What's going on, Tom?" Shara asked when he was through.

He looked at me before replying. "Pardon my asking, Mr. Armstead, but—are you a newsman?"

"Charlie. No, I'm not. I am a video man, but I work for Shara."

"Mmmm. Well, you'll hear about it sooner or later. About two weeks ago, an object appeared within the orbit of Neptune, just appeared out of nowhere. There were . . . certain other anomalies. It stayed put for half a day and then vanished again. The Space Command slapped a hush on it, but it's common knowledge on board Skyfac."

"And the thing has been sighted again?" Shara asked.

"Just beyond the orbit of Jupiter."

I was only mildly interested. No doubt there was an explanation for the phenomenon, and since Isaac Asimov wasn't around I would doubtless never understand a word of it. Most of us gave up on intelligent nonhuman life when the last intersystem probe came back empty. "Little green men, I suppose. Can you show us the lounge, Tom? I understand it's just like the one we'll be working in."

He seemed to welcome the change of subject. "Sure thing."

McGillicuddy led us through a p-door opposite the one Carrington had used, through long halls whose floors curved up ahead of and behind us. Each was outfitted differently, each was full of busy, purposeful people, and each reminded me somehow of the lobby of the New Age, or perhaps of the old movie *2001*. Futuristic Opulence, so understated as to fairly shriek. Wall Street lifted bodily into orbit—the *clocks* were on Wall Street time. I tried to make myself believe that cold, empty space lay a short distance away in any direction, but it was impossible. I decided it was a good thing spacecraft didn't have portholes—once he got used to the low gravity, a man might forget and open one to throw out a cigar.

I studied McGillicuddy as we walked. He was immaculate in every respect, from necktie down to nail polish, and he wore no jewelry at all. His hair was short and black, his beard inhibited, and his eyes surprisingly warm in a professionally sterile face. I wondered what he had sold his soul for. I hoped he had gotten his price.

We had to descend two levels to get to the lounge. The gravity on the upper level was kept at one-sixth normal, partly for the convenience of the lunar personnel who were Skyfac's only regular commuters, and mostly (of course) for the convenience of Carrington. But descending brought a subtle increase in weight, to perhaps a fifth or a quarter normal. My leg complained bitterly, but I found to my surprise that I preferred the pain to its absence. It's a little scary when an old friend goes away like that.

The lounge was a larger room than I had expected, quite big enough for our purposes. It encompassed all three levels, and one whole wall was an immense video screen, across which stars wheeled dizzily, joined with occasional regularity by a slice of mother Terra. The floor was crowded with chairs and tables in various groupings, but I could see that, stripped, it would provide Shara with entirely adequate room to dance; equally important, my feet told me that it would make a splendid dancing surface. Then I remembered how little use the floor was liable to get.

"Well," Shara said to me with a smile, "this is what home will look like for the next six months. The Ring Two lounge is identical to this one."

"Six?" McGillicuddy said. "Not a chance."

*"What do you mean?"* Shara and I said together.

He blinked at our combined volume. "Well, *you'll* probably be good for that long, Charlie. But Shara's already had over a year of low g, while she was in the typing pool."

"So what?"

"Look, you expect to be in free fall for long periods of time, if I understand this correctly?"

"Twelve hours a day," Shara agreed.

He grimaced. "Shara, I hate to say this . . . but I'll be surprised if you last a month. A body designed for a one-g environment doesn't work properly in zero g."

"But it will adapt, won't it?"

He laughed mirthlessly. "Sure. That's why we rotate all personnel Earthside every fourteen months. Your body will adapt. One way. No return. Once you've fully adapted, returning to Earth will stop your heart—if some other major systemic failure doesn't occur first. Look, you were just Earthside for three days—did you have any chest pains? Dizziness? Bowel trouble? Dropsickness on the way up?"

"All of the above," she admitted.

"There you go. You were close to the nominal fourteen-month limit when you left. And your body will adapt even faster under no gravity at all. The successful free-fall endurance record of about eight months was set by a Skyfac construction gang with bad deadline problems—and they hadn't spent a year in one-sixth g first, *and* they weren't straining their hearts the way you will be. Hell, there are four men on Luna now, from the original dozen in the first mining team, who will never see Earth again. Eight of their teammates tried. Don't you two know *any*thing about space?"

"But I've got to have at least four months. Four months of solid work, every day. I *must*." She was dismayed, but fighting hard for control.

McGillicuddy started to shake his head, and then thought better of it. His warm eyes were studying Shara's face. I knew exactly what he was thinking, and I liked him for it.

He was thinking, *How to tell a lovely lady her dearest dream is hopeless?*

He didn't know the half of it. I *knew* how much Shara had already—irrevocably—invested in this dream, and something in me screamed.

And then I saw her jaw ripple and I dared to hope.

Dr. Panzarella was a wiry old man with eyebrows like two fuzzy caterpillars. He wore a tight-fitting jumpsuit which would not foul a p-suit's seals should he have to get into one in a hurry. His shoulder-length hair, which should have been a mane on that great skull, was clipped securely back against a sudden absence of gravity. A cautious man. To employ an obsolete metaphor, he was a suspenders-*and*-belt type. He looked Shara over, ran tests, and gave her just under a month and a half. Shara said some things. I said some things. McGillicuddy said some things. Panzarella shrugged, made further, very careful tests, and reluctantly cut loose of the suspenders. Two months. Not a day over. Possibly less, depending on subsequent monitoring of her body's reactions to extended weightlessness. Then a year Earth-side before risking it again. Shara seemed satisfied.

I didn't see how we could do it.

McGillicuddy had assured us that it would take Shara at least a month simply to learn to handle herself competently in zero g, much less dance. Her familiarity with one-sixth g would, he predicted, be a liability rather than an asset. Then figure three weeks of choreography and rehearsal, a week of taping, and just maybe we could broadcast one dance before Shara had to return to Earth. Not good enough. She and I had calculated that we would need three successive shows, each well received, to make a big enough dent in the dance world for Shara to squeeze into it. A year was far too big a spacing—*and who knew how soon Carrington would tire of her?* So I hollered at Panzarella.

"Mr. Armstead," he said hotly, "I am specifically contractually forbidden to allow this young lady to commit suicide." He grimaced sourly. "I'm told it's terrible public relations."

"Charlie, it's okay," Shara insisted. "I can fit in three dances. We may lose some sleep, but we can do it."

"I once told a man nothing was impossible. He asked me if I could ski through a revolving door. You haven't got . . ."

My brain slammed into hyperdrive, thought about things, kicked itself in the ass a few times, and returned to real time in time to hear my mouth finish without a break: ". . . much choice, though. Okay, Tom, have that damned Ring Two lounge cleaned out, I want it naked and spotless, and have somebody paint over that damned video wall, the same shade as the other three, and I mean *the same*. Shara, get out of those clothes and into your leotard. Doctor, we'll be seeing you in twelve hours. Quit gaping and *go,* Tom—we'll be going over there at once; *where the hell are my cameras?"*

McGillicuddy sputtered.

"Get me a torch crew—I'll want holes cut through the walls, cameras behind them, one-way glass, six locations, a room adjacent to the lounge for a mixer console the size of a jetliner cockpit, and bolt a Norelco coffee machine next to the chair. I'll need another room for editing, complete privacy and total darkness, size of an efficiency kitchen, another Norelco."

McGullicuddy finally drowned me out. "Mr. *Armstead,* this is the Main Ring of the Skyfac One complex, the administrative offices of one of the wealthiest corporations in existence. If you think this whole Ring is going to stand on its head for you . . ."

So we brought the problem to Carrington. He told McGillicuddy that henceforth Ring Two was *ours,* as well as any assistance whatsoever that we requested. He looked rather distracted. McGillicuddy started to tell him by how many weeks all this would put off the opening of the Skyfac Two complex. Carrington replied very quietly that he could add and subtract quite well, thank you, and McGillicuddy got white and quiet.

I'll give Carrington that much. He gave us a free hand.

Panzarella ferried over to Skyfac Two with us. We were chauffeured by lean-jawed astronaut types, on vehicles looking, for all the world, like pregnant broomsticks. It was as well that we had the doctor with us—Shara fainted on the way over. I nearly did myself, and I'm sure that broomstick has my thigh-prints on it yet—falling through space is a scary experience the first time. Shara responded splendidly once we had her inboard again, and fortunately her dropsickness did not return—nausea can be a nuisance in free fall, a disaster in a p-suit. By the time my cameras and mixer had arrived, she was on her feet and sheepish. And while I browbeat a sweating crew of borrowed techs into installing them faster than was humanly possible, Shara began learning how to move in zero g.

We were ready for the first taping in three weeks.

Living quarters and minimal life support were rigged for us in Ring Two so that we could work around the clock if we chose, but we spent nearly half of our nominal "off-hours" in Skyfac One. Shara was required to spend half of three days a week there with Carrington, and spent a sizable portion of her remaining putative sack time out in space, in a p-suit. At first it was a conscious attempt to overcome her gut-level fear of all that emptiness. Soon it became her meditation, her retreat, her artistic reverie, an attempt to gain from contemplation of the cold black depths enough insight into the meaning of extraterrestrial existence to dance of it.

I spent my own time arguing with engineers and electricians and technicians and a damn fool union legate who insisted that the second lounge, finished or not, belonged to the hypothetical future crew and administrative personnel. Securing his permission to work there wore the lining off my throat and the insulation off my nerves. Far too many nights I spent slugging instead of sleeping. Minor example: Every interior wall in the whole damned second Ring was painted the identical shade of turquoise—and they couldn't duplicate it to cover that godforsaken video wall in the lounge. It was McGillicuddy who saved me from gibbering apoplexy—at his suggestion, I washed off the third latex job, unshipped the outboard camera that fed the wall screen, brought it inboard, and fixed it to scan an interior wall in an adjoining room. That made us friends again.

It was all like that: jury-rig, improvise, file to fit and paint to cover. If a camera broke down, I spent sleep time talking with off-shift engineers, finding out what parts in stock could be adapted. It was simply too expensive to have anything shipped up from Earth's immense gravity well, and Luna didn't have what I needed.

At that, Shara worked harder than I did. A body must totally recoordinate itself to function in the absence of weight—she had to forget literally everything she had ever known or learned about dancing and acquire a whole new set of skills. This turned out to be even harder than we had expected. McGillicuddy had been right: What Shara had learned in her year of one-sixth g was an exaggerated attempt to *retain* terrestrial patterns of coordination—rejecting them altogether was actually easier for *me*.

But I couldn't keep up with her—I had to abandon any thought of handheld camera work and base my plans solely on the six fixed cameras. Fortunately GLX-5000s have a ball-and-socket mount; even behind that damned one-way glass I had about forty degrees of traverse on each one. Learning to coordinate all six simultaneously on the Hamilton Board did a truly extraordinary thing to me—it lifted me that one last step to unity with my art. I found that I could learn to be aware of all six monitors with my mind's eye, to perceive almost spherically, to—not share my attention among the six—to *encompass* them all, seeing like a six-eyed creature from many angles at once. My mind's eye became holographic, my awareness multilayered. I began to really understand, for the first time, three-dimensionality.

It was that fourth dimension that was the kicker. It took Shara two days to decide that she could not possibly become proficient enough in free-fall maneuvering to sustain a half-hour piece in the time required. So she rethought her work plan too, adapting her choreography to the demands of exigency. She put in six hard days under normal Earth weight.

And for her, too, the effort brought her that one last step toward apotheosis.

On Monday of the fourth week we began taping *Liberation.*

Establishing shot:

A great turquoise box, seen from within. Dimensions unknown, but the color somehow lends an impression of immensity, of vast distances. Against the far wall, a swinging pendulum attests that this is a standard-gravity environment; but the pendulum swings so slowly and is so featureless in construction that it is impossible to estimate its size and so extrapolate that of the room.

Because of this *trompe l'oeil* effect, the room seems rather smaller than it really is when the camera pulls back and we are wrenched into proper perspective by the appearance of Shara, prone, inert, face down on the floor, facing us.

She wears beige leotard and tights. Hair the color of fine mahogany is pulled back into a loose ponytail which fans across one shoulder blade. She does not appear to breathe. She does not appear to be alive.

Music begins. The aging Mahavishnu, on obsolete nylon acoustic, establishes a Minor E in no hurry at all. A pair of small candles in simple brass holders appear inset on either side of the room. They are larger than life, though small beside Shara. Both are unlit.

Her body . . . there is no word. It does not move, in the sense of motor activity. One might say that a ripple passes through it, save that the motion is clearly all outward from her center. She *swells,* as if the first breath of life were being taken by her whole body at once. She lives.

The twin wicks begin to glow, oh, softly. The music takes on quiet urgency.

Shara raises her head to us. Her eyes focus somewhere beyond the camera yet short of infinity. Her body writhes, undulates, and the glowing wicks are coals (that this brightening takes place in slow motion is not apparent).

A violent contraction raises her to a crouch, spilling the ponytail across her shoulder. Mahavishnu begins a cyclical cascade of runs, in increasing tempo. Long, questing tongues of yellow-orange flame begin to blossom *downward* from the twin wicks, whose coals are turning to blue.

The contraction's release flings her to her feet. The twin skirts of flame about the wicks curl up over themselves, writhing furiously, to become conventional candle flames, flickering now in normal time. Tablas, tambouras, and a bowed string bass join the guitar, and they segue into an energetic interplay around a minor seventh that keeps trying, fruitlessly, to find resolution in the sixth. The candles stay in perspective, but dwindle in size until they vanish.

Shara begins to explore the possibilities of motion. First she moves only perpendicular to the camera's line of sight, exploring that dimension. Every motion of arms or legs or head is clearly seen to be a defiance of gravity, of a force as inexorable as radioactive decay, as entropy itself. The most violent surges of energy succeed only for a time—the outflung leg falls, the outthrust arm drops. She must struggle or fall. She pauses in thought.

Her hands and arms reach out toward the camera, and at the instant they do we cut to a view from the left-hand wall. Seen from the right side, she reaches out into this new dimension, and soon begins to move in it. (As she moves backward out of the camera's field, its entire image shifts right on our screen, butted out of the way by the incoming image of a second camera, which picks her up as the first loses her without a visible seam.)

The new dimension too fails to fulfill Shara's desire for freedom from gravity. Combining the two, however, presents so many permutations of movement that for a while, intoxicated, she flings herself into experimentation. In the next fifteen minutes, Shara's entire background and history in dance are recapitulated, in a blinding tour de force that incorporates elements of jazz, Modern, and the more graceful aspects of Olympic-level mat gymnastics. Five cameras come into play, singly and in pairs on splitscreen, as the "bag of tricks" amassed in a lifetime of study and improvisation are rediscovered and performed by a superbly trained and versatile body, in a pyrotechnic display that would shout of joy if her expression did not remain aloof, almost arrogant. *This is the offering,* she seems to say, *which you would not accept. This, by itself, was not good enough.*

And it is not. Even in its raging energy and total control, her body returns again and again to the final compromise of mere erectness, that last simple refusal to fall.

Clamping her jaw, she works into a series of leaps,

ever longer, ever higher. She seems at last to hang suspended for full seconds, straining to fly. When, inevitably, she falls, she falls reluctantly, only at the last possible instant tucking and rolling back onto her feet. The musicians are in a crescendoing frenzy. We see her now only with the single original camera, and the twin candles have returned, small but burning fiercely.

The leaps begin to diminish in intensity and height, and she takes longer to build to each one. She has been dancing flat out for nearly twenty minutes; as the candle flames begin to wane, so does her strength. At last she retreats to a place beneath the indifferent pendulum, gathers herself with a final desperation, and races forward toward us. She reaches incredible speed in a short space, hurls herself into a double roll, and bounds up into the air off one foot, seeming a full second later to push off against empty air for a few more inches of height. Her body goes rigid, her eyes and mouth gape wide, the flames reach maximum brilliance, the music peaks with the tortured wail of an electric guitar, and—she falls, barely snapping into a roll in time, rising only as far as a crouch. She holds there for a long moment, and gradually her head and shoulders slump, defeated, toward the floor. The candle flames draw in upon themselves in a curious way and appear to go out. The string bass saws on, modulating down to D.

Muscle by muscle, Shara's body gives up the struggle. The air seems to tremble around the wicks of the candles, which have now grown nearly as tall as her crouching form.

Shara lifts her face to the camera with evident effort. Her face is anguished, her eyes nearly shut. A long beat.

All at once she opens her eyes wide, squares her shoulders, and contracts. It is the most exquisite and total contraction ever dreamed of, filmed in real time but seeming almost to be in slow motion. She holds it. Mahavishnu comes back in on guitar, building in increasing tempo from a down-tuned bass string to a D with a flatted fourth. Shara holds.

We shift for the first time to an overhead camera, looking down on her from a great height. As Mahavishnu's picking increases to the point where the chord seems a sustained drone, Shara slowly lifts her head, still holding the contraction, until she is staring directly up at us. She poises there for an eternity, like a spring wound to the bursting point . . .

. . . and explodes upward toward us, rising higher and faster than she possibly can in a soaring flight that *is* slow motion now, coming closer and closer until her hands disappear off either side and her face fills the screen, flanked by two candles which have bloomed into gouts of yellow flame in an instant. The guitar and bass are submerged in an orchestra.

Almost at once she whirls away from us, and the POV switches to the original camera, on which we see her fling herself down ten meters to the floor, reversing her attitude in mid-flight and twisting. She comes out of her roll in an absolutely flat trajectory that takes her the length of the room. She hits the far wall with a crash audible even over the music, shattering the still pendulum. Her thighs soak up the kinetic energy and then release it, and once again she is racing toward us, hair streaming straight out behind her, a broad smile of triumph growing larger in the screen.

In the next five minutes all six cameras vainly try to track her as she caroms around the immense room like a hummingbird trying to batter its way out of a cage, using the walls, floor and ceiling the way a jai alai master does, *existing in three dimensions.* Gravity is defeated. The basic assumption of all dance is transcended.

Shara is transformed.

She comes to rest at last at vertical center in the forefront of the turquoise cube, arms-legs-fingers-toes-face straining *outward,* turning gently end over end. All four cameras that bear on her join in a four-way splitscreen, the orchestra resolves into its final E Major, and—fade out.

I had neither the time nor the equipment to create the special effects that Shara wanted. So I found ways to warp reality to my need. The first candle segment was a twinned shot of a candle being blown out from above—in ultra-slow-motion, and in reverse. The second segment was a simple recording of reality. I had lit the candle, started taping—and had the Ring's spin killed. A candle behaves oddly in zero g. The low-density combustion gases do not rise up from the flame, allowing air to reach it from beneath. The flame does not go out: It becomes dormant. Restore gravity within a minute or so, and it blooms back to life again. All I did was monkey with speeds a bit to match in with the music and Shara's dance. I got the idea from Harry Stein, Skyfac's construction foreman, who was helping me design the next dance.

I set up a screen in the Ring One lounge, and everyone in Skyfac who could cut work crowded in for the broadcast. They saw exactly what was being sent out over worldwide satellite hookup (Carrington had sufficient pull to arrange twenty-five minutes without commercial interruption) almost a full half-second before the world did.

I spent the broadcast in the Communications Room, chewing my fingernails. But it went without a hitch, and I slapped my board dead and made it to the lounge in time to see the last half of the standing ovation. Shara stood before the screen, Carrington sitting beside her, and I found the difference in their expressions instructive. Her face showed no surprise or modesty. She had had faith in herself throughout, had approved this tape for broadcast—she was aware, with that incredible detachment of which so few artists are capable, that the wild applause was only what she deserved. But her face showed that she was deeply surprised—and deeply grateful—to be given what she deserved.

Carrington, on the other hand, registered a triumph strangely mingled with relief. He too had had faith in Shara, backing it with a large investment—but his faith was that of a businessman in a gamble he believes will pay off, and as I watched his eyes and the glisten of sweat on his forehead, I realized that no businessman ever takes an expensive gamble without worrying that it may be the fiasco that will begin the loss of his only essential commodity: face.

Seeing his kind of triumph next to hers spoiled the moment for me, and instead of thrilling for Shara I found myself almost hating her. She spotted me, and waved me to join her before the cheering crowd, but I turned and literally flung myself from the room. I borrowed a bottle from Harry Stein and got stinking.

The next morning my head felt like a fifteen-amp fuse on a forty-amp circuit, and I seemed to be held together only by surface tension. Sudden movements frightened me. It's a long fall off that wagon, even at one-sixth g.

The phone chimed—I hadn't had time to rewire it—and a young man I didn't know politely announced that Mr. Carrington wished to see me in his office. At once, I spoke of a barbed-wire suppository and what Mr. Carrington might do with it, at once. Without changing expression, he repeated his message and disconnected.

So I crawled into my clothes, decided to grow a beard, and left. Along the way I wondered what I had traded my independence for, and why.

Carrington's office was oppressively tasteful, but at least the lighting was subdued. Best of all, its filter system would handle smoke—the sweet musk of pot lay on the air. I accepted a macrojoint of "Maoi-Zowie" from Carrington with something approaching gratitude, and began melting my hangover.

Shara sat next to his desk, wearing a leotard and a layer of sweat. She had obviously spent the morning rehearsing for the next dance. I felt ashamed, and consequently snappish, avoiding her eyes and her hello. Panzarella and McGillicuddy came in on my heels, chattering about the latest sighting of the mysterious object from deep space, which had appeared this time in the neighborhood of Mercury. They were arguing over whether it displayed signs of sentience or not, and I wished they'd shut up.

Carrington waited until we had all seated ourselves and lit up, then rested a hip on his desk and smiled. "Well, Tom?"

McGillicuddy beamed. "Better than we expected, sir. All the ratings agree we had about seventy-four percent of the world audience—"

"The hell with the Nielsons," I snapped. *"What did the critics say?"*

McGillicuddy blinked. "Well, the general reaction so far is that Shara was a smash. The *Times*—"

I cut him off again. "What was the less-than-general reaction?"

"Well, nothing is ever unanimous."

"Specifics. The dance press? Liz Zimmer? Migdalski?"

"Uh. Not as good. Praise, yes—only a blind man could've panned that show. But guarded praise. Uh, Zimmer called it a magnificent dance spoiled by a gimmicky ending."

"And Migdalski?" I insisted.

"He headed his review, 'But What Do You Do For An Encore?' " McGillicuddy admitted. "His basic thesis was that it was a charming one-shot. But the *Times*—"

"Thank you, Tom," Carrington said quietly. "About what we expected, isn't it, my dear? A big splash, but no one's willing to call it a tidal wave yet."

She nodded. "But they will, Bryce. The next two dances will sew it up."

Panzarella spoke up. "Ms. Drummond, may I ask why you played it the way you did? Using the null-g interlude only as a brief adjunct to conventional dance—surely you must have expected the critics to call it gimmickry."

Shara smiled and answered. "To be honest, Doctor, I had no choice. I'm learning to use my body in free fall, but it's still a conscious effort, almost a pantomine. I need another few weeks to make it second nature, and it *has* to be if I'm to sustain a whole piece in it. So I dug a conventional dance out of the trunk, tacked on a five-minute ending that used every zero-g move I knew, and found to my extreme relief that they made thematic sense together. I told Charlie my notion, and he made it work visually and dramatically—that whole business of the candles was his, and it underlined what I was trying to say better than any set we could have built."

"So you have not yet completed what you came here to do?" Panzarella asked Shara.

"Oh, no. Not by any means. The next dance will show the world that dance is more than controlled falling. And the third . . . the third will be what this has all been for." Her face lit, became animated. "The third dance will be the one I have wanted to dance all my life. I can't entirely picture it yet—but I know that when I become capable of dancing it, I will create it, and it will be my greatest dance."

Panzarella cleared his throat. "How long will it take you?"

"Not long," she said. "I'll be ready to tape the next dance in two weeks, and I can start on the last one almost at once. With luck, I'll have it in the can before my month is up."

"Ms. Drummond," Panzarella said gravely, "I'm afraid you don't have another month."

Shara went white as snow, and I half rose from my seat. Carrington looked intrigued.

"How much time?" Shara asked.

"Your latest tests have not been encouraging. I had assumed that the sustained exercise of rehearsal and practice would tend to slow your system's adaptation. But most of your work has been in total weightlessness, and I failed to realize the extent to which your body is accustomed to sustained exertion—in a terrestrial environment."

*"How much time?"*

"Two weeks. Possibly three, if you spend three separate hours a day at hard exercise in two gravities."

"That's ridiculous," I burst out. "Don't you understand about dancers' spines? She could ruin herself in two gees."

"I've got to have four weeks," Shara said.

"Ms. Drummond, I am sorry."

"I've got to have four weeks."

Panzarella had that same look of helpless sorrow that McGillicuddy and I had had in our turn, and I was suddenly sick to death of a universe in which people had to keep looking at Shara that way. "Dammit," I roared, "she needs four weeks."

Panzarella shook his shaggy head. "If she stays in zero g for four working weeks, she may die."

Shara sprang from her chair. "Then I'll die," she cried. "I'll take that chance. I *have* to."

Carrington coughed. "I'm afraid I can't permit you to, darling."

She whirled on him furiously.

"This dance of yours is excellent PR for Skyfac," he said calmly, "but if it were to kill you it might boomerang, don't you think?"

Her mouth worked, and she fought desperately for control. My own head whirled. Die? Shara?

"Besides," he added, "I've grown quite fond of you."

"Then I'll stay up here in space," she burst out.

"Where? The only areas of sustained weightlessness are factories, and you're not qualified to work in one."

"Then for God's sake give me one of the new pods, the small spheres. Bryce, I'll give you a higher return on your investment than a factory pod, and I'll . . . " Her voice changed. "I'll be available to you always."

He smiled lazily. "Yes, but I might not *want* you always, darling. My mother warned me strongly against making irrevocable decisions about women. Especially informal ones. Besides, I find zero-g sex rather too exhausting as a steady diet."

I had almost found my voice, and now I lost it again. I was glad Carrington was turning her down—but the way he did it made me yearn to drink his blood.

Shara too was speechless for a time. When she spoke,

her voice was low, intense, almost pleading. "Bryce, it's a matter of timing. If I broadcast two more dances in the next four weeks, I'll have a world to return to. If I have to go Earthside and wait a year or two, that third dance will sink without a trace—no one'll be looking, and they won't have the memory of the first two. This is my only option, Bryce—*let me take the chance*. Panzarella can't guarantee four weeks will kill me."

"I can't guarantee your survival," the doctor said.

"You can't guarantee that any one of us will live out the day," she snapped. She whirled back to Carrington, held him with her eyes. "Bryce, *let me risk it*." Her face underwent a massive effort, produced a smile that put a knife through my heart. "I'll make it worth your while."

Carrington savored that smile and the utter surrender in her voice like a man enjoying a fine claret. I wanted to slay him with my hands and teeth, and I prayed that he would add the final cruelty of turning her down. But I had underestimated his true capacity for cruelty.

"Go ahead with your rehearsal, my dear," he said at last. "We'll make a final decision when the time comes. I shall have to think about it."

I don't think I've ever felt so hopeless, so . . . impotent in my life. Knowing it was futile, I said, "Shara, I can't let you risk your life—"

"I'm going to do this, Charlie," she cut me off, "with or without you. No one else knows my work well enough to tape it properly, but if you want out I can't stop you." Carrington watched me with detached interest. "Well?"

I said a filthy word. "You know the answer."

"Then let's get to work."

Tyros are transported on the pregnant broomsticks. Old hands hang outside the air lock, dangling from handholds on the outer surface of the spinning Ring. They face in the direction of the spin, and when their destination comes under the horizon, they just drop off. Thruster units built into gloves and boots supply the necessary course corrections. The distances involved are small. Shara and I, having spent more weightless hours than some technicians who'd been in Skyfac for years, were old hands. We made scant and efficient use of our thrusters, chiefly in canceling the energy imparted to us by the spin of the Ring we left. We had throat mikes and hearing-aid-sized receivers, but there was no conversation on the way across the void. I spent the journey appreciating the starry emptiness through which I fell—I had come, perforce, to understand the attraction of sky diving—and wondering whether I would ever get used to the cessation of pain in my leg. It even seemed to hurt less under spin those days.

We grounded, with much less force than a sky diver does, on the surface of the new studio. It was an enormous steel globe, studded with sunpower screens and heat-losers, tethered to three more spheres in various stages of construction, on which p-suited figures were even now working. McGillicuddy had told me that the complex when completed would be used for "controlled density processing," and when I said, "How nice," he added, "Dispersion foaming and variable density casting," as if that explained everything. Perhaps it did. Right at the moment, it was Shara's studio.

The air lock led to a rather small working space around a smaller interior sphere some fifty meters in diameter. It too was pressurized, intended to contain a vacuum, but its locks stood open. We removed our p-suits, and Shara unstrapped her thruster bracelets from a bracing strut and put them on, hanging by her ankles from the strut while she did so. The anklets went on next. As jewelry they were a shade bulky—but they had twenty minutes' continuous use each, and their operation was not visible in normal atmosphere and lighting. Indoor zero-gee dance without them would have been enormously more difficult.

As she was fastening the last strap I drifted over in front of her and grabbed the strut. "Shara . . ."

"Charlie, I can beat it. I'll exercise in *three* gravities, and I'll sleep in two, and I'll make this body last. I know I can."

"You could skip *Mass Is a Verb* and go right to the *Stardance*."

She shook her head. "I'm not ready yet—and neither is the audience. I've got to lead myself and them through dance in a sphere first—in a contained space—before I'll be ready to dance in empty space, or for them to appreciate it. I have to free my mind, and theirs, from just about every preconception of dance, change the postulates. Even two stages is too few—but it's the irreducible minimum." Her eyes softened. "Charlie—I must."

"I know," I said gruffly and turned away. Tears are a nuisance in free fall—they don't *go* anywhere. I began hauling myself around the surface of the inner sphere toward the camera emplacement I was working on, and Shara entered the inner sphere to begin rehearsal.

I prayed as I worked on my equipment, snaking cables among the bracing struts and connecting them to drifting terminals. For the first time in years I prayed, prayed that Shara would make it. That we both would.

The next twelve days were the toughest of my life. Shara worked twice as hard as I did. She spent half of every day working in the studio, half of the rest in exercise under two and a quarter gravities (the most Dr. Panzarella would permit), and half of the rest in Carrington's bed, trying to make him contented enough to let her stretch her time limit. Perhaps she slept in the few hours left over. I only know that she never looked tired, never lost her composure or her dogged determination. Stubbornly, reluctantly, her body lost its awkwardness, took on grace even in an environment where grace required enormous concentration. Like a child learning to walk, Shara learned how to fly.

I even began to get used to the absence of pain in my leg.

What can I tell you of *Mass*, if you have not seen it? It cannot be described, even badly, in mechanistic terms, the way a symphony could be written out in words. Conventional dance terminology is, by its built-in assumptions, worse than useless, and if you are at all familiar with the new nomenclature you *must* be familiar with *Mass Is a Verb,* from which it draws *its* built-in assumptions.

Nor is there much I can say about the technical aspects of *Mass.* There were no special effects; not even music. Brindle's superb score was composed *from the dance,* and added to the tape with my permission two years later, but it was for the original, silent version that I was given the Emmy. My entire contribution, aside from editing and installing the two trampolines, was to camouflage batteries of wide-dispersion light sources in clusters around each camera eye, and wire them so that they energized only when they were out-of-frame with respect to whichever camera was on at the time—insuring that Shara was always lit from the front, presenting two (not always congruent) shadows. I made no attempt to employ flashy camera work; I simply recorded what Shara danced, changing POV only as she did.

No. *Mass Is a Verb* can be described only in symbolic terms, and then poorly. I can say that Shara demonstrated that mass and inertia are as able as gravity to supply the dynamic conflict essential to dance. I can tell you that from them she distilled a kind of dance that could have been imagined only by a group-head consisting of an acrobat, a stunt diver, a skywriter, and an underwater ballerina. I can tell you that she dismantled the last interface between herself and utter freedom of motion, subduing her body to her will and space itself to her need.

And still I will have told you next to nothing. For Shara sought more than freedom—she sought meaning. *Mass* was, above all, a spiritual event—its title pun paralleling its thematic ambiguity between the technological and the theological. Shara made the human confrontation with existence a transitive act, literally meeting God halfway. I do not mean to imply that her dance at any time addressed an exterior God, a discrete entity with or without white beard. Her dance addressed reality, gave successive expression to the Three Eternal Questions asked by every human being who ever lived.

Her dance observed her *self,* and asked, *How have I come to be here?*

Her dance observed the universe in which self existed, and asked, *How did all this come to be here with me?*

And at last, observing her self in relation to its universe, *Why am I so alone?*

And, having asked these questions, having earnestly asked them with every muscle and sinew she possessed, she paused, hung suspended in the center of the sphere, her body and soul open to the universe, and when no answer came, she contracted. Not in a dramatic, ceiling-spring sense as she had in *Liberation,* a compressing of energy and tension. This was physically similar, but an utterly different phenomenon. It was a focusing inward, an act of introspection, a turning of the mind's (soul's?) eye in upon itself, to seek answers that lay nowhere else. Her body too, therefore, seemed to fold in upon itself, compacting her mass, so evenly that her position in space was not disturbed.

And reaching within herself, she closed on emptiness. The camera faded out, leaving her alone, rigid, encapsulated, yearning. The dance ended, leaving her three questions unanswered, the tension of their asking unresolved. Only the expression of patient waiting on her face blunted the shocking edge of the non-ending, made it bearable, a small, blessed sign whispering, "To be continued."

By the eighteenth day we had it in the can, in rough form. Shara put it immediately out of her mind and began choreographing *Stardance,* but I spent two hard days of editing before I was ready to release the tape for broadcast. I had four days until the half-hour of prime time Carrington had purchased—but that wasn't the deadline I felt breathing down the back of my neck.

McGillicuddy came into my workroom while I was editing, and although he saw the tears running down my face he said no word. I let the tape run, and he watched in silence, and soon his face was wet, too. When the tape had been over for a long time he said, very softly, "One of these days I'm going to have to quit this stinking job."

I said nothing.

"I used to be a karate instructor. I was pretty good. I could teach again, maybe do exhibition work, make ten percent of what I do now."

I said nothing.

"The whole damned Ring's bugged, Charlie. The desk in my office can activate and tap any vidphone in Skyfac. Four at a time, actually."

I said nothing.

"I saw you both in the air lock, when you came back the last time. I saw her collapse. I saw you bringing her around. I heard her make you promise not to tell Dr. Panzarella."

I waited. Hope stirred.

He dried his face. "I came in here to tell you I was going to Panzarella, to tell him what I saw. He'd bully Carrington into sending her home right away."

"And now?" I said.

"I've seen that tape."

"And you know the *Stardance* will probably kill her?"

"Yes."

"And you know we have to let her do it?"

"Yes."

Hope died. I nodded. "Then get out of here and let me work."

He left.

On Wall Street and aboard Skyfac it was late afternoon when I finally had the tape edited to my satisfaction. I called Carrington, told him to expect me in half an hour, showered, shaved, dressed, and left.

A major of the Space Command was there with him when I arrived, but he was not introduced and so I ignored him. Shara was there too, wearing a thing made of orange smoke that left her breasts bare. Carrington had obviously made her wear it, as an urchin writes filthy words on an altar, but she wore it with a perverse and curious dignity that I sensed annoyed him. I looked her in the eye and smiled. "Hi, kid. It's a good tape."

"Let's see," Carrington said. He and the major took seats behind the desk, and Shara sat beside it.

I fed the tape into the video rig built into the office wall, dimmed the lights, and sat across from Shara. It ran twenty minutes, uninterrupted, no soundtrack, stark naked.

It was terrific.

"Aghast" is a funny word. To make you aghast, a thing must hit you in a place you haven't armored over with cynicism yet. I seem to have been born cynical; I have been aghast three times that I can remember. The first was when I learned, at the age of three, that there were people who could deliberately hurt kittens. The second was when I learned, at age seventeen, that there were people who could actually take LSD and then hurt other people for fun. The third was when *Mass Is a Verb* ended and Carrington said in perfectly conversational tones, "Very pleasant; very graceful. I like it," when I learned, at age forty-five, that there were men, not fools or cretins but intelligent men, who could watch Shara Drummond dance and fail to *see*. We all, even the most cynical of us, always have some illusion which we cherish.

Shara simply let it bounce off her somehow, but I could see that the major was as aghast as I, controlling his features with a visible effort.

Suddenly welcoming a distraction from my horror and dismay, I studied him more closely, wondering for the first time what he was doing here. He was my age, lean and more hardbitten than I am, with silver fuzz on top of his skull and an extremely tidy mustache on the front. I'd taken him for a crony of Carrington's, but three things changed my mind. Something indefinable about his eyes told me that he was a military man of long combat experience. Something equally indefinable about his carriage told me that he was on duty at the moment. And something quite definable about the line his mouth made told me that he was disgusted with the duty he had drawn.

When Carrington went on, "What do you think, Major?" in polite tones, the man paused for a moment, gathering his thoughts and choosing his words. When he did speak, it was not to Carrington.

"Ms. Drummond," he said quietly, "I am Major William Cox, commander of S.C. *Champion,* and I am honored to meet you. That was the most profoundly moving thing I have ever seen."

Shara thanked him most gravely. "This is Charles Armstead, Major Cox. He made the tape."

Cox regarded me with new respect. "A magnificent job, Mr. Armstead." He stuck out his hand, and I shook it.

Carrington was beginning to understand that we three shared a thing which excluded him. "I'm glad you enjoyed it, Major," he said with no visible trace of sincerity. "You can see it again on your television tomorrow night, if you chance to be off duty. And eventually, of course, cassettes will be made available. Now perhaps we can get to the matter at hand."

Cox's face closed as if it had been zippered up, became stiffly formal. "As you wish, sir."

Puzzled, I began what I thought was the matter at hand. "I'd like your own Comm Chief to supervise the actual transmission this time, Mr. Carrington. Shara and I will be too busy to—"

"My Comm Chief will supervise the broadcast, Armstead," Carrington interrupted, "but I don't think you'll be particularly busy."

I was groggy from lack of sleep; my uptake was rather slow.

He touched his desk delicately. "McGillicuddy, report at once," he said, and released it. "You see, Armstead, you and Shara are both returning to Earth. At once."

*"What?"*

"Bryce, you *can't,*" Shara cried. "You *promised.*"

"I promised I would think about it, my dear," he corrected.

"The hell you say. That was weeks ago. Last night you *promised.*"

"Did I? My dear, there were no witnesses present last night. Altogether for the best, don't you agree?"

I was speechless with rage.

McGillicuddy entered. "Hello, Tom," Carrington said pleasantly. "You're fired. You'll be returning to Earth at once, with Ms. Drummond and Mr. Armstead, aboard Major Cox's vessel. Departure in one hour, and don't leave anything you're fond of." He glanced from McGillicuddy to me. "From Tom's desk you can tap any vidphone in Skyfac. From my desk you can tap Tom's desk."

Shara's voice was low. "Bryce, two days. God damn you, name your price."

He smiled slightly. "I'm sorry, darling. When informed of your collapse, Dr. Panzarella became most specific. Not even one more day. Alive you are a distinct plus for Skyfac's image—you are my gift to the world. Dead you are an albatross around my neck. I cannot allow you to die on my property. I anticipated that you might resist leaving, and so I spoke to a friend in the"—he glanced at Cox—"*higher* echelons of the Space Command, who was good enough to send the Major here to escort you home. You are not under arrest in the legal sense—but I assure you that you have no choice. Something like protective custody applies. Goodbye, Shara." He reached for a stack of reports on his desk, and I surprised myself considerably.

I cleared the desk entirely, tucked head catching him squarely in the sternum. His chair was belted to the deck and so it snapped clean. I recovered so well that I had time for one glorious right. Do you know how, if you punch a basketball squarely, it will bounce up from the floor? That's what his head did, in low-g slow motion.

Then Cox had hauled me to my feet and shoved me into the far corner of the room. "Don't," he said to me, and his voice must have held a lot of that "habit of command" they talk about, because it stopped me cold. I stood breathing in great gasps while Cox helped Carrington to his feet.

The millionaire felt his smashed nose, examined the blood on his fingers, and looked at me with raw hatred. "You'll never work in video again, Armstead. You're through. Finished. Un-em-ployed, you get that?"

Cox tapped him on the shoulder, and Carrington spun on him. "What the hell do you want?" he barked.

Cox smiled. "Carrington, my late father once said, 'Bill, make your enemies by choice, not by accident.' Over the years I have found that to be excellent advice. You suck."

"And not particularly well," Shara agreed.

Carrington blinked. Then his absurdly broad shoulders swelled and he roared, "Out, all of you! *Off my property at once!*"

By unspoken consent, we waited for McGillicuddy, who knew his cue. "Mr. Carrington, it is a rare privilege and a great honor to have been fired by you. I shall think of it always as a Pyrrhic defeat." And he half bowed and we left, each buoyed by a juvenile feeling of triumph that must have lasted ten seconds.

The sensation of falling that comes with zero g is literal truth, but your body quickly learns to treat it as an illusion. Now, in zero g for the last time, for the half-hour before I would be back in Earth's own gravitational field, I felt I was falling. Plummeting into some bottomless gravity well, dragged down by the anvil that was my heart, the scraps of a dream that should have held me aloft fluttering overhead.

The *Champion* was three times the size of Carrington's yacht, which childishly pleased me until I recalled that he had summoned it here without paying for either fuel or crew. A guard at the air lock saluted as we entered. Cox led us to a compartment aft of the air lock where we were to strap in. He noticed along the way that I used only my left hand to pull myself along, and when we stopped he said, "Mr. Armstead, my late father also told me, 'Hit the soft parts with your hand. Hit the hard parts with a utensil.' Otherwise I can find no fault with your technique. I wish I could shake your hand."

I tried to smile, but I didn't have it in me. "I admire your taste in enemies, Major."

"A man can't ask for more. I'm afraid I can't spare time to have your hand looked at until we've grounded. We begin reentry immediately."

"Forget it."

He bowed to Shara, did *not* tell her how deeply sorry he was to et cetera, wished us all a comfortable journey, and left. We strapped into our acceleration couches to await ignition. There ensued a long and heavy silence, compounded of a mutual sadness that bravado could only have underlined. We did not look at each other, as though our combined sorrow might achieve some kind of critical mass. Grief struck us dumb, and I believe that remarkably little of it was self-pity.

But then a whole lot of time seemed to have gone by. Quite a bit of intercom chatter came faintly from the next compartment, but ours was not in circuit. At last we began to talk, desultorily, discussing the probable critical reaction to *Mass Is a Verb,* whether analysis was worthwhile or the theater really dead, anything at all except future plans. Eventually there was nothing else to talk about, so we shut up again. I guess I'd say we were in shock.

For some reason I came out of it first. "What in hell is taking them so long?" I barked irritably.

McGillicuddy started to say something soothing, then glanced at his watch and yelped. "You're right. It's been nearly an hour."

I looked at the wall clock, got hopelessly confused until I realized it was on Greenwich time rather than Wall Street, and realized he was correct. "Chrissakes," I shouted, "the whole bloody *point* of this exercise is to protect Shara from overexposure to free fall! I'm going forward."

"Charlie, hold it." McGillicuddy, with two good hands, unstrapped faster than I. "Dammit, stay right there and cool off. I'll go find out what the holdup is."

He was back in a few minutes, and his face was slack. "We're not going anywhere. Cox has orders to sit tight."

"What? Tom, what the *hell* are you talking about?"

His voice was all funny. "Red fireflies. More like bees, actually. In a balloon."

He simply *could not* be joking with me, which meant he flat out *had* to have gone completely round the bend, which meant that somehow I had blundered into my favorite nightmare where everyone but me goes crazy, and begins gibbering at me. So I lowered my head like an enraged bull, and charged out of the room so fast the door barely had time to get out of my way.

It just got worse. When I reached the door to the bridge I was going much too fast to be stopped by anything short of a body block, and the crewmen present were caught flatfooted. There was a brief flurry at the door, and then I was on the bridge, and then I decided that I had gone crazy too, which somehow made everything all right.

The forward wall of the bridge was one enormous video tank—and just enough off center to faintly irritate me, standing out against the black deep as clearly as cigarettes in a darkroom, there truly did swarm a multitude of red fireflies.

The conviction of unreality made it okay. But then Cox snapped me back to reality with a bellowed *"Off this bridge, mister."* If I'd been in a normal frame of mind it would have blown me out the door and into the farthest corner of the ship; in my current state it managed to jolt me into acceptance of the impossible situation. I shivered like a wet dog and turned to him.

"Major," I said desperately, "What is going on?"

As a king may be amused by an insolent varlet who refuses to kneel, he was bemused by the phenomenon of someone failing to obey him. It bought me an answer.

"We are confronting intelligent alien life," he said concisely. "I believe them to be sentient plasmoids."

I had never for a moment believed that the mysterious object which had been leapfrogging around the solar system since I came to Skyfac was *alive*. I tried to take it in, then abandoned the task and went back to my main priority. "I don't care if they're eight tiny reindeer; you've got to get this can back to Earth *now*."

"Sir, this vessel is on Emergency Red Alert and on Combat Standby. At this moment the suppers of everyone in North America are getting cold. I will consider myself fortunate if I ever see Earth again. Now get off my bridge."

"But you don't *understand*. Sustained free fall might kill Shara. That's what you came up here to prevent, dammit—"

"*MR. ARMSTEAD!* This is a military vessel. We are facing nearly a dozen intelligent beings who appeared out of hyperspace near here twenty minutes ago, beings who therefore use a drive beyond my conception with no visible parts. If it makes you feel any better, I am aware that I have a passenger aboard of greater intrinsic value to my species than this ship and everyone else on her, and if it is any comfort to you this knowledge already provides a distraction I need like an auxiliary anus, and I can no more leave this orbit than I can grow horns. Now will you get off this bridge or will you be dragged?"

I didn't get a chance to decide: They dragged me.

On the other hand, by the time I got back to our compartment Cox had put our vidphone screen in circuit with the tank on the bridge. Shara and McGillicuddy were studying it with rapt attention. Having nothing better to do, I did too.

McGillicuddy had been right. They *did* act more like bees, in the swarming rapidity of their movement. It was a while before I could get an accurate count: ten of them. And they *were* in a balloon—a faint, barely tangible thing on the fine line between transparency and translucency. Though they darted like furious red gnats, it was only within the confines of the spheroid balloon—they never left it or seemed to touch its inner surface.

As I watched, the last of the adrenalin rinsed out of my kidneys, but it left a sense of frustrated urgency. I tried to grapple with the fact that these *Space Commando* special effects represented something that was—more important than Shara. It was a primevally disturbing notion, but I could not reject it.

In my mind were two voices, each hollering questions at the top of their lungs, each ignoring the other's questions. One yelled: *Are those things friendly? Or hostile? Or do they even use those concepts? How big are they? How far away? From where?* The other voice was less ambitious but just as loud: all it said, over and over again, was: *How much longer can Shara remain in free fall without dooming herself?*

Shara's voice was full of wonder. "They're . . . they're *dancing.*"

I looked closer. If there was a pattern to the flies-on-garbage swarm they made. I couldn't detect it. "Looks random to me."

"Charlie, look. All that furious activity, and they never bump into each other or the walls of that envelope they're in. They must be in orbits as carefully choreographed as those of electrons."

"Do atoms dance?"

She gave me an odd look. "Don't they, Charlie?"

"Laser beam," McGillicuddy said.

We looked at him.

"Those things have to be plasmoids—the man I talked to said they were first spotted on radar. That means they're ionized gases of some kind—the kind of thing that used to cause UFO reports." He giggled, then caught himself. "If you could slice through that envelope with a laser, I'll bet you could deionize them pretty good—besides, that envelope has to hold their life support, whatever it is they metabolize."

I was dizzy. "Then we're not defenseless?"

"You're both talking like soldiers," Shara burst out. "I tell you they're dancing. Dancers aren't fighters."

"Come on, Shara," I barked. "Even if those things happen to be remotely like us, that's not true. Samurai, karate, kung fu—they're dance." I nodded to the screen. "All we know about these animated embers is that they travel interstellar space. That's enough to scare me."

"Charlie, look at them," she commanded.

I did.

By God, they didn't look threatening. They did, the more I watched, seem to move in a dancelike way, whirling in mad adagios just too fast for the eye to follow. Not like conventional dance—more analogous to what Shara had begun with *Mass Is a Verb*. I found myself wanting to switch to another camera for contrast of perspective, and that made my mind start to wake up at last. Two ideas surfaced, the second one necessary in order to sell Cox the first.

"How far do you suppose we are from Skyfac?" I asked McGillicuddy.

He pursed his lips. "Not far. There hasn't been much more than maneuvering acceleration. The damn things were probably attracted to Skyfac in the first place—it must be the most easily visible sign of intelligent life in this system." He grimaced. "Maybe they don't *use* planets."

I reached forward and punched the audio circuit. "Major Cox."

*"Get off this circuit."*

"How would you like a closer view of those things?"

"We're staying put. Now stop jiggling my elbow and get off this circuit or I'll—"

"Will you listen to me? I have four mobile cameras in space, remote-control, self-contained power source and light, and better resolution than you've got. They were set up to tape Shara's next dance."

He shifted gears at once. "Can you patch them into my ship?"

"I think so. But I'll have to get back to the master board in Ring One."

"No good, then. I can't tie myself to a top—what if I have to fight or run?"

"Major—how far a walk is it?"

It startled him a bit. "A mile or two, as the crow flies. But you're a groundlubber."

"I've been in free fall for most of two months. Give me a portable radar and I can ground on Phobos."

"Mmmm. You're a civilian—but dammit, I need better video. Permission granted."

Now for the first idea. "Wait—one thing more. Shara and Tom must come with me."

"Nuts. This isn't a field trip."

"Major Cox—Shara *must* return to a gravity field as quickly as possible. Ring One'll do—in fact, it'd be ideal, if we can enter through the 'spoke' in the center. She can descend very slowly and acclimatize gradually, the way a diver decompresses in stages, but in reverse. McGillicuddy will have to come along to stay with her—if she passes out and falls down the tube, she could break a leg even in one-sixth g. Besides, he's better at EVA than either of us."

He thought it over. "Go."

We went.

The trip back to Ring One was far longer than any Shara or I had ever made, but under McGillicuddy's guidance we made it with minimal maneuvering. Ring, *Champion,* and aliens formed an equiangular triangle about a mile and a half on a side. Seen in perspective, the aliens took up about as much volume as Shea Stadium. They did not pause or slacken in their mad gyration, but somehow they seemed to watch us cross the gap to Skyfac. I got an impression of a biologist studying the strange antics of a new species. We kept our suit radios off to avoid distraction, and it made me just a little bit more susceptible to suggestion.

I left McGillicuddy with Shara and dropped down the tube six rings at a time. Carrington was waiting for me in the reception room, with two flunkies. It was plain to see that he was scared silly, and trying to cover it with anger. "Goddammit, Armstead, those are my bloody cameras."

"Shut up, Carrington. If you put those cameras in the hands of the best technician available—me—and if I put their data in the hands of the best strategic mind in space—Cox—we *might* be able to save your damned factory for you. And the human race for the rest of us." I moved forward, and he got out of my way. It figured. Putting all humanity in danger might just be bad PR.

After all the practicing I'd done, it wasn't hard to direct four mobile cameras through space simultaneously by eye. The aliens ignored their approach. The Skyfac comm crew fed my signals to the *Champion* and patched me in to Cox on audio. At his direction I bracketed the balloon with the cameras, shifting POV at his command. Space Command Headquarters must have recorded the video, but I couldn't hear their conversation with Cox, for which I was grateful. I gave him slow-motion replay, close-ups, splitscreens—everything at my disposal. The movements of individual fireflies did not appear particularly symmetrical, but patterns began to repeat. In slow motion they looked more than ever as though they were dancing, and although I couldn't be sure, it seemed to me that they were increasing their tempo. Somehow the dramatic tension of their dance seemed to build.

And then I shifted POV to the camera which included Skyfac in the background, and my heart turned to hard vacuum and I screamed in pure primal terror—halfway between Ring One and the swarm of aliens, coming up on them slowly but inexorably, was a p-suited figure that had to be Shara.

With theatrical timing, McGillicuddy appeared in the doorway, leaning heavily on the chief engineer, his face drawn with pain. He stood on one foot, the other leg plainly broken.

"Guess I can't . . . go back to exhibition work . . . after all," he gasped. "Said . . . 'I'm sorry, Tom' . . . knew she was going to swing on me . . . wiped me out anyhow. Oh, dammit, Charlie, I'm sorry." He sank into an empty chair.

Cox's voice came urgently. "What the hell is going on? Who is that?"

She *had* to be on our frequency. "Shara!" I screamed. "Get your ass back in here!"

"I can't, Charlie." Her voice was startlingly loud, and very calm. "Halfway down the tube my chest started to hurt like hell."

"Ms. Drummond," Cox rapped, "if you approach any closer to the aliens I will destroy you."

She laughed, a merry sound that froze my blood. "Bullshit, Major. You aren't about to get gay with laser beams near those things. Besides, you need me as much as you do Charlie."

"What do you mean?"

"These creatures communicate by dance. It's their equivalent of speech, it has to be a sophisticated kind of sign language, like hula."

"You can't know that."

"I *feel* it. I know it. Hell, how else do you communicate in airless space? Major Cox, I am the only qualified interpreter the human race has at the moment. Now will you kindly shut up so I can try to learn their 'language'?"

"I have no authority to—"

I said an extraordinary thing. I should have been gibbering, pleading with Shara to come back, even racing for a p-suit to *bring* her back. Instead I said, "She's right. Shut up, Cox."

"What are you trying to do?"

"Damn you, *don't waste her last effort.*"

He shut up.

Panzarella came in, shot McGillicuddy full of painkiller, and set his leg right there in the room, but I was oblivious. For over an hour I watched Shara watch the aliens. I watched them myself, in the silence of utter despair, and for the life of me I could not follow their dance. I strained my mind, trying to suck meaning from their crazy whirling, and failed. The best I could do to aid Shara was to record everything that happened, for a hypothetical posterity. Several times she cried out softly, small muffled exclamations, and I ached to call out to her in reply, but did not. With the last exclamation, she used her thrusters to bring her closer to the alien swarm, and hung there for a long time.

At last her voice came over the speaker, thick and slurred at first, as though she were talking in her sleep. "God, Charlie. Strange. So strange. I'm beginning to read them."

"How?"

"Every time I begin to understand a part of the dance, it . . . it brings us closer. Not telepathy, exactly. I just . . . know them better. Maybe it is telepathy, I don't know. By dancing what they feel, they give it enough intensity to make me understand. I'm getting about one concept in three. It's stronger up close."

Cox's voice was gentle but firm. "What have you learned, Shara?"

"That Tom and Charlie were right. They are warlike. At least there's a flavor of arrogance to them—conviction of superiority. Their dance is a challenging, a dare. Tell Tom they *do* use planets."

"What?"

"I think at one stage of their development they're corporeal, planetbound. Then when they have matured sufficiently, they . . . become these fireflies, like caterpillars becoming butterflies, and head out into space."

"Why?" from Cox.

"To find spawning grounds. They want Earth."

There was a silence lasting perhaps ten seconds. Then Cox spoke up quietly. "Back away, Shara. I'm going to see what lasers will do to them."

"No!" she cried, loud enough to make a really first-rate speaker distort.

"Shara, as Charlie pointed out to me, you are not only expendable, you are for all practical purposes expended."

"No!" This time it was me shouting.

"Major," Shara said urgently, "that's not the way.

Believe me, they can dodge or withstand anything you or Earth can throw at them. I *know.*"

"Hell and damnation, woman," Cox said, "what do you want me to do? Let them have the first shot? There are vessels from four countries on their way right now."

"Major, wait. Give me time."

He began to swear, then cut off. "How much time?"

She made no direct reply. "If only this telepathy thing works in reverse . . . it must. I'm no more strange to them than they are to me. Probably less so; I get the idea they've been around. Charlie?"

"Yeah."

"This is a take."

I knew. I had known since I first saw her in open space on my monitor. And I knew what she needed now, from the faint trembling of her voice. It took everything I had, and I was only glad I had it to give. With extremely realistic good cheer, I said, "Break a leg, kid," and killed my mike before she could hear the sob that followed.

And she danced.

It began slowly, the equivalent of one-finger exercises, as she sought to establish a vocabulary of motion that the creatures could comprehend. *Can you see,* she seemed to say, *that* this *movement is a reaching, a yearning? Do you see that* this *is a spurning,* this *an unfolding,* that *a graduated elision of energy? Do you feel the ambiguity in the way I distort this arabesque, or that the tension can be resolved* so?

And it seemed that Shara was right, that they had infinitely more experience with disparate cultures than we, for they were superb linguists of motion. It occurred to me later that perhaps they had selected motion for communication because of its very universality. At any rate, as Shara's dance began to build, their own began to slow down perceptibly in speed and intensity, until at last they hung motionless in space, watching her.

Soon after that Shara must have decided that she had sufficiently defined her terms, at least well enough for pidgin communication—for now she began to dance in earnest. Before she had used only her own muscles and the shifting masses of her limbs. Now she added thrusters, singly and in combination, moving within as well as in space. Her dance became a true dance: more than a collection of motions, a thing of substance and meaning. It was unquestionably the *Stardance,* just as she had choreographed it, as she had always intended to dance it. That it had something to say to utterly alien creatures, of man and his nature, was not at all a coincidence: It was the essential and ultimate statement of the greatest artist of her age, and it had something to say to God himself.

The camera lights struck silver from her p-suit, gold from the twin air tanks on her shoulders. To and fro against the black backdrop of space, she wove the intricacies of her dance, a leisurely movement that seemed somehow to leave echoes behind it. And the meaning of these great loops and whirls slowly became clear, drying my throat and clamping my teeth.

For her dance spoke of nothing more and nothing less than the tragedy of being alive, and being human. It spoke, most eloquently, of pain. It spoke, most knowingly, of despair. It spoke of the cruel humor of limitless ambition yoked to limited ability, of eternal hope invested in an ephemeral lifetime, of the driving need to try and create an inexorably predetermined future. It spoke of fear, and of hunger, and, most clearly, of the basic loneliness and alienation of the human animal. It described the universe through the eyes of man: a hostile environment, the embodiment of entropy, into which we are all thrown alone, forbidden by our nature to touch another mind save secondhand, by proxy. It spoke of the blind perversity which forces man to strive hugely for a peace which, once attained, becomes boredom. And it spoke of folly, of the terrible paradox by which man is simultaneously capable of reason and unreason, forever unable to cooperate even with himself.

It spoke of Shara and her life.

Again and again, cyclical statements of hope began, only to collapse into confusion and ruin. Again and again, cascades of energy strove for resolution, and found only frustration. All at once she launched into a pattern that seemed familiar, and in moments I recognized it: the closing movement of *Mass Is a Verb* recapitulated—not repeated but reprised, echoed, the Three Questions given a more terrible urgency by this new altar on which they were piled. And as before, it segued into that final relentless contraction, that ultimate drawing-inward of all energies. Her body became derelict, abandoned, drifting in space, the essence of her being withdrawn to her center and invisible.

The quiescent aliens stirred for the first time.

And suddenly she exploded, blossoming from her contraction not as a spring uncoils, but as a flower bursts from a seed. The force of her release flung her through the void as though she were tossed like a gull in a hurricane by galactic winds. Her center appeared to hurl itself through space and time, yanking her body into a new dance.

And the new dance said, *This is what it is to be human: to see the essential existential futility of all action, all striving—and to act, to strive. This is what it is to be human: to reach forever beyond your grasp. This is what it is to be human: to live forever or die trying. This is what it is to be human: to perpetually ask the unanswerable questions, in the hope that the asking of them will somehow hasten the day when they will be answered. This is what it is to be human: to strive in the face of the certainty of failure.*

*This is what it is to be human: to persist.*

It said all this with a soaring series of cyclical movements that held all the rolling majesty of grand symphony, as uniquely different from each other as snowflakes, and as similar. And the new dance *laughed,* and it laughed as much at tomorrow as it did at yesterday, and it laughed most of all at today.

*For this is what it means to be human: to laugh at what another would call tragedy.*

The aliens seemed to recoil from the ferocious energy, startled, awed, and faintly terrified by Shara's indomitable spirit. They seemed to wait for her dance to wane, for her to exhaust herself, and her laughter sounded on my speaker as she redoubled her efforts, became a pinwheel, a Catherine wheel. She changed the focus of her dance, began to dance *around* them, in pyrotechnic spatters of motion that came ever closer to the intangible spheroid which contained them. They cringed inward from her, huddling together in the center of the envelope, not so much physically threatened as cowed.

*This,* said her body, *is what it means to be human: to commit hara-kiri, with a smile, if it becomes needful.*

And before that terrible assurance, the aliens broke. Without warning fireflies and balloon vanished, gone, *elsewhere.*

I know that Cox and McGillicuddy were still alive, because I saw them afterward, and that means they were probably saying and doing things in my hearing and presence, but I neither heard nor saw them then; they were as dead to me as everything except Shara. I called out her name, and she approached the camera that was lit, until I could make out her face behind the plastic hood of her p-suit.

"We may be puny, Charlie," she puffed, gasping for breath. "But by Jesus we're tough."

"Shara—come on in now."

"You know I can't."

"Carrington'll *have* to give you a free-fall place to live now."

"A life of exile? For what? To dance? Charlie, *I haven't got anything more to say.*"

"Then I'll come out there."

"Don't be silly. Why? So you can hug a p-suit? Tenderly bump hoods one last time? Balls. It's a good exit so far—let's not blow it."

*"Shara!"* I broke completely, just caved in on myself and collapsed in great racking sobs.

"Charlie, listen now," she said softly, but with an urgency that reached me even in my despair. "Listen now, for I haven't much time. I have something to give you. I hoped you'd find it for yourself, but . . . will you listen?"

"Y—yes."

"Charlie, zero-g dance is going to get awful popular all of a sudden. I've opened the door. But you know how fads are, they'll bitch it all up unless you move fast. I'm leaving it in your hands."

"What . . . what are you talking about?"

"About you, Charlie. You're going to dance again."

Oxygen starvation, I thought. But she can't be that low on air already. "Okay. Sure thing."

"For God's sake stop humoring me—I'm straight, I tell you. You'd have seen it yourself if you weren't so damned stupid. Don't you understand? *There's nothing wrong with your leg in free fall!*"

My jaw dropped.

"Do you hear me, Charlie? You can dance again!"

"No," I said, and searched for a reason why not. "I . . . you can't . . . it's . . . dammit, the leg's not strong enough for inside work."

"Forget for the moment that inside work'll be less than half of what you do. Forget it and remember that smack in the nose you gave Carrington. Charlie, when you leaped over the desk, *you pushed off with your right leg.*"

I sputtered for a while and shut up.

"There you go, Charlie. My farewell gift. You know I've never been in love with you . . . but you must know that I've always loved you. Still do."

"I love you, Shara."

"So long, Charlie. Do it right."

And all four thrusters went off at once. I watched her go down. A while after she was too far to see, there was a long golden flame that arced above the face of the globe, waned, and then flared again as the air tanks went up.

There's a tired old hack plot about the threat of alien invasion unifying mankind overnight. It's about as realistic as Love Will Find a Way—if those damned fireflies ever come back, they'll find us just as disorganized as we were the last time. There you go.

Carrington, of course, tried to grab all the tapes and all the money—but neither Shara nor I had ever signed a contract, and her will was most explicit. So he tried to buy the judge, and he picked the wrong judge, and when it hit the papers and he saw how public and private opinion were going, he left Skyfac in a p-suit with no thrusters. I think he wanted to go the same way she had, but he was unused to EVA and let go too late. He was last seen heading in the general direction of Betelgeuse. The Skyfac board of directors picked a new man who was most anxious to wash off the stains, and he offered me continued use of all facilities.

And so I talked it over with Norrey, and she was free, and that's how the Shara Drummond Company of New Modern Dance was formed. We specialize in good dancers who couldn't cut it on Earth for one reason or another, and there are a surprising hell of a lot of them.

I enjoy dancing with Norrey. Together we're not as good as Shara was alone—but we mesh well. In spite of the obvious contraindications, I think our marriage is going to work.

That's the thing about us humans: We persist.

# *The House of Compassionate Sharers*

## Michael Bishop

Science fiction has given us countless examples of alien beings who seem, and often are, incomprehensible to humans; this is, after all, a literature of strangeness, and the exploration of variant modes of thinking can be much more fascinating than any description of the appearance or physiology of weird monsters. But what about the human beings who live among us but are unable to feel a sense of communion with their/our own people? Michael Bishop realizes that "alienation" is an increasingly important problem in human life, and in this thoughtful novelette he tells of one future man who has lost his psychological birthright because he's been forced to adopt a nonhuman form himself. Can he regain his humanity? Should he *want* to?

Michael Bishop lives with his wife and two children in Georgia; he holds an M.A. degree and has written a thesis on Dylan Thomas. He's published three remarkable novels and an impressive number of shorter science-fiction stories. "The House of Compassionate Sharers" strikes me as the most moving novelette he's written.

*And he was there, and it was not far enough, not yet, for the earth hung overhead like a rotten fruit, blue with mold, crawling, wrinkling, purulent and alive.*

—DAMON KNIGHT, "Masks"

In the Port Iranani Galenshall I awoke in the room Diderits liked to call the "Black Pavilion." I was an engine, a system, a series of myoelectric and neuromechanical components, and The Accident responsible for this clean and enamel-hard enfleshing lay two full D-years in the past. This morning was an anniversary of sorts. I ought by now to have adjusted. And I had. I had reached an absolute accommodation with myself. Narcissistic, one could say. And that was the trouble.

"Dorian? Dorian Lorca?"

The voice belonged to KommGalen Diderits, wet and breathy even though it came from a small metal speaker to which the sable curtains of the dome were attached. I stared up into the ring of curtains.

"Dorian, it's Target Day. Will you answer me, please?"

"I'm here, my galen. Where else would I be?" I stood up, listening to the almost-musical ratcheting that I make when I move, a sound like the concatenation of tiny bells or the purring of a stope-car. The sound is conveyed through the tempered porcelain plates, metal vertebrae, and osteoid polymers holding me together, and no one else can hear it.

"Rumer's here, Dorian. Are you ready for her to come in?"

"If I agreed, I suppose I'm ready."

"Dammit, Dorian, don't feel you're bound by *honor* to see her! We've spent the last several brace-weeks preparing you for a resumption of normal human contact." Diderits began to enumerate: "Chameleodrene treatments . . . hologramic substitution . . . stimulus-response therapy . . . You ought to want Rumer to come in to you, Dorian."

*Ought*. My brain was—is—my own, but the body Diderits and the other kommgalens had given me had "instincts" and "tropisms" peculiar to itself, ones whose templates had a mechanical rather than a biological origin. What I ought to feel, in human terms, and what I in fact felt, as the inhabitant of a total prosthesis, were as dissimilar as blood and oil.

"Do you *want* her to come in, Dorian?"

"All right. I do." And I did. After all the biochemical and psychiatric preparation, I wanted to see what my reaction would be. Still sluggish from some drug, I had no exact idea how Rumer's presence would affect me.

At a parting of the pavilion's draperies, only two or three meters from my couch, appeared Rumer Montieth, my wife. Her garment of overlapping latex scales, glossy black in color, was a hauberk designed to reveal only her hands, face, and hair. The way Rumer was dressed was one of Diderits's deceits, or "preparations": I was supposed to see my wife as little different from myself, a creature as intricately assembled and synapsed as the engine I had become. But the hands, the face, the hair—nothing could disguise their unaugmented humanity, and revulsion swept over me like a tide.

"Dorian?" And her voice—wet, breath-driven, expelled between parted lips . . .

I turned away from her. "No," I told the speaker overhead. "It hasn't worked, my galen. Every part of me cries out against this."

Diderits said nothing. Was he still out there? Or was he trying to give Rumer and me a privacy I didn't want?

"Disassemble me," I urged him. "Link me to the control systems of a delta-state vessel and let me go out from Diroste for good. You don't want a zombot among you, Diderits—an unhappy anproz. Damn you all, you're torturing me!"

"And you, us," Rumer said quietly. I faced her. "As you're very aware, Dorian, as you're very aware . . . Take my hand."

"No." I didn't shrink away; I merely refused.

"Here. Take it."

Fighting my own disgust, I seized her hand, twisted it over, showed her its back. "Look."

"I *see* it, Dor." I was hurting her.

"Surfaces, that's all you see. Look at this growth, this wen." I pinched the growth. "Do you see that, Rumer? That's sebum, fatty matter. And the smell, if only you could—"

She drew back, and I tried to quell a mental nausea almost as profound as my regret . . . To go out from Diroste seemed to be the only answer. Around me I wanted machinery—thrumming, inorganic machinery—and the sterile, actinic emptiness of outer space. I wanted to be the probeship *Dorian Lorca.* It hardly seemed a step down from my position as "prince consort" to the Governor of Diroste.

"Let me out," Rumer commanded the head of the Port Iranani Galenshall, and Diderits released her from the "Black Pavilion."

Then I was alone again in one of the few private chambers of a surgical complex given over to adapting Civi Korps personnel to our leprotic little planet's fume-filled mine shafts. The Galenshall was also devoted to patching up these civkis after their implanted respirators had atrophied, almost beyond saving, the muscles of their chests and lungs.

Including administrative personnel, Kommfleet officials, and the Civi Korps laborers in the mines, in the year I'm writing of there were over a half million people on Diroste. Diderits was responsible for the health of all of them not assigned to the outlying territories. Had I not been the husband of Diroste's first governor, he might well have let me die along with the seventeen "expendables" on tour with me in the Fetneh District when the roof of the Haft Paykar diggings fell in on us. Rumer, however, made Diderits's duty clear to him, and I am as I am because the resources were at hand in Port Iranani and Diderits saw fit to obey his Governor.

Alone in my pavilion, I lifted a hand to my face and heard a caroling of minute copper bells . . .

Nearly a month later I observed Rumer, Diderits, and a stranger by closed-circuit television as they sat in one of the Galenshall's wide conference rooms. The stranger was a woman, bald but for a scalplock, who wore gold silk pantaloons that gave her the appearance of a clown, and a corrugated green jacket that somehow reversed this impression. Even on my monitor I could see the thick sunlight pouring into their room.

"This is Wardress Kefa," Rumer informed me.

I greeted her through a microphone and tested the cosmetic work of Diderits's associates by trying to smile for her.

"She's from Earth, Dor, and she's here because KommGalen Diderits and I asked her to come."

"Forty-six lights," I murmured, probably inaudibly. I was touched and angry at the same time. To be constantly the focus of your friends' attentions, especially when they have more urgent matters to see to, can lead to either a corrosive cynicism or a humility just as crippling.

"We want you to go back with her on *Nizami*," Diderits said, "when it leaves Port Iranani tomorrow night."

"Why?"

"Wardress Kefa came all this way," Rumer responded, "because we wanted to talk to her. As a final stage in your therapy she's convinced us that you ought to visit her . . . her establishment there. And if this fails, Dorian, I give you up; if that's what you want, I relinquish you." Today Rumer was wearing a yellow sarong, a tasseled gold shawl, and a nun's hood of yellow and orange stripes. When she spoke she averted her eyes from the conference room's monitor and looked out its high windows instead. At a distance, I could appreciate the spare aesthetics of her profile.

"Establishment? What sort of establishment?" I studied the tiny Wardress, but her appearance volunteered nothing.

"The House of Compassionate Sharers," Diderits began. "It's located in Earth's western hemisphere, on the North American continent, nearly two hundred kilometers southwest of the gutted Urban Nucleus of Denver. It can be reached from Manitou Port by 'rail."

"Good. I shouldn't have any trouble finding it. But what is it, this mysterious house?"

Wardress Kefa spoke for the first time: "I would prefer that you learn its nature and its purposes from me, Mr. Lorca, when we have arrived safely under its several roofs."

"Is it a brothel?" This question fell among my three interlocutors like a heavy stone.

"No," Rumer said after a careful five-count. "It's a unique sort of clinic for the treatment of unique emotional disorders." She glanced at the Wardress, concerned that she had revealed too much.

"Some would call it a brothel," Wardress Kefa admitted huskily. "Earth has become a haven of misfits and opportunists, a crossroads of Glatik Komm influence and trade. The House, I must confess, wouldn't prosper if it catered only to those who suffer from rare dissociations of feeling. Therefore a few—a very few—of those who come to us are kommthors rich in power and exacting in their tastes. But these people are exceptions, Governor Montieth, KommGalen Diderits; they represent an uneasy compromise we must make in order to carry out the work for which the House was originally envisioned and built."

A moment later Rumer announced, "You're going, Dor. You're going tomorrow night. Diderits and I, well, we'll see you in three E-months." That said, she gathered in her cloak with both hands and rearranged it on her shoulders. Then she left the room.

"Good-bye, Dorian," Diderits said, standing.

Wardress Kefa fixed upon the camera conveying her picture to me a keen glance made more disconcerting by her small, naked face. "Tomorrow, then."

"Tomorrow," I agreed. I watched my monitor as the galen and the curious-looking Wardress exited the conference room together. In the room's high windows Diroste's sun sang a capella in the lemon sky.

They gave me a private berth on *Nizami*. I used my "nights," since sleep no longer meant anything to me, to prowl through those nacelles of shipboard machinery not forbidden to passengers. Although I wasn't permitted in the forward command module, I did have access to the computer-ringed observation turret and two or three corridors of auxiliary equipment necessary to the maintenance of a continuous probe-field. In these places I secreted myself and thought seriously about the likelihood of an encephalic/neural linkage with one of Kommfleet's interstellar frigates.

My body was a trial. Diderits had long ago informed me that it—that *I*—was still "sexually viable," but this was something I hadn't yet put to the test, nor did I wish to. Tyrannized by morbidly vivid images of human viscera, human excreta, human decay, I had been rebuilt of metal, porcelain, and plastic *as if* from the very substances—skin, bone, hair, cartilage—that these inorganic materials derided. I was a contradiction, a quasi-immortal masquerading as one of the ephemera who had saved me from their own short-lived lot. Still another paradox was the fact that my aversion to the organic was itself a human (i.e., an organic) emotion. That was why I so fervently wanted out. For over a year and a half on Diroste I had hoped that Rumer and the others would see their mistake and exile me not only from themselves, but from the body that was a deadly daily reminder of my total estrangement.

But Rumer was adamant in her love, and I had been a prisoner in the Port Iranani Galenshall—with but one chilling respite—ever since the Haft Paykar explosion and cave-in. Now I was being given into the hands of a new wardress, and as I sat amid the enamel-encased engines of *Nizami* I couldn't help wondering what sort of prison the House of Compassionate Sharers must be . . .

Among the passengers of a monorail car bound outward from Manitou Port, Wardress Kefa in the window seat beside me, I sat tense and stiff. Anthrophobia.

Lorca, I told myself repeatedly, you must exercise self-control. Amazingly, I did. From Manitou Port we rode the sleek underslung bullet of our car through rugged, sparsely populated terrain toward Wolf Run Summit, and I controlled myself.

"You've never been 'home' before?" Wardress Kefa asked me.

"No. Earth isn't home. I was born on GK-world Dai-Han, Wardress. And as a young man I was sent as an administrative colonist to Diroste, where—"

"Where you were born again," Wardress Kefa interrupted. "Nevertheless, this is where we began."

The shadows of the mountains slid across the wrap-around glass of our car, and the imposing white pylons of the monorail system flashed past us like the legs of giants. Yes. Like huge, naked cyborgs hiding among the mountains' aspens and pines.

"Where I met Rumer Montieth, I was going to say; where I eventually got married and settled down to the life of a bureaucrat who happens to be married to power. You anticipate me, Wardress." I didn't add that now Earth and Diroste were equally alien to me, that the probeship *Nizami* had bid fair to assume first place among my loyalties.

A 'rail from Wolf Run came sweeping past us toward Manitou Port. The sight pleased me; the vibratory hum of the passing 'rail lingered sympathetically in my hearing, and I refused to talk, even though the Wardress clearly wanted to draw me out about my former life. I was surrounded and beset. Surely this woman had all she needed to know of my past from Diderits and my wife. My annoyance grew.

"You're very silent, Mr. Lorca."

"I have no innate hatred of silences."

"Nor do I, Mr. Lorca—unless they're empty ones."

Hands in lap, humming bioelectrically, inaudibly, I looked at my tiny guardian with disdain. "There are some," I told her, "who are unable to engage in a silence without stripping it of its unspoken cargo of significance."

To my surprise the woman laughed heartily. "That certainly isn't true of you, is it?" Then, a wry expression playing on her lips, she shifted her gaze to the hurtling countryside and said nothing else until it came time to disembark at Wolf Run Summit.

Wolf Run was a resort frequented principally by Kommfleet officers and members of the administrative hierarchy stationed in Port Manitou. Civi Korps personnel had built quaint, gingerbread chateaus among the trees and engineered two of the slopes above the hamlet for year-round skiing. "Many of these people," Wardress Kefa explained, indicating a crowd of men and women beneath the deck of Wolf Run's main lodge, "work inside Shays Mountain, near the light-probe port, in facilities built originally for satellite tracking and missile-launch detection. Now they monitor the display boards for Kommfleet orbiters and shuttles; they program the cruising and descent lanes of these vehicles. Others are demographic and wildlife managers, bent on resettling Earth as efficiently as it may be done. Tedious work, Mr. Lorca. They come here to play." We passed below the lodge on a path of unglazed vitrifoam. Two or three of Wolf Run's bundled visitors stared at me, presumably because I was in my tunic sleeves and conspicuously undaunted by the spring cold. Or maybe their stares were for my guardian . . .

"How many of these people are customers of yours, Wardress?"

"That isn't something I can divulge." But she glanced back over her shoulder as if she had recognized someone.

"What do they find at your establishment they can't find in Manitou Port?"

"I don't know, Mr. Lorca; I'm not a mind reader."

To reach the House of Compassionate Sharers from Wolf Run, we had to go on foot down a narrow path worked reverently into the flank of the mountain. It was very nearly a two-hour hike. I couldn't believe the distance or Wardress Kefa's stamina. Swinging her arms, jolting herself on stiff legs, she went down the mountain with a will. And in all the way we walked we met no other hikers.

At last we reached a clearing giving us an open view of a steep, pine-peopled glen: a grotto that fell away beneath us and led our eyes to an expanse of smooth white sky. But the Wardress pointed directly down into the foliage.

"There," she said. "The House of Compassionate Sharers."

I saw nothing but afternoon sunlight on the aspens, boulders huddled in the mulch cover, and swaying tunnels among the trees. Squinting, I finally made out a geodesic structure built from the very materials of the woods. Like an upland sleight, a wavering mirage, the House slipped in and out of my vision, blending, emerging, melting again. It was a series of irregular domes as hard to hold as water vapor—but after several red-winged blackbirds flew noisily across the plane of its highest turret, the House remained for me in stark relief; it had shed its invisibility.

"It's more noticeable," Wardress Kefa said, "when its external shutters have been cranked aside. Then the House sparkles like a dragon's eye. The windows are stained glass."

"I'd like to see that. Now it appears camouflaged."

"That's deliberate, Mr. Lorca. Come."

When we were all the way down, I could see of what colossal size the House really was: It reared up through the pine needles and displayed its interlocking polygons to the sky. Strange to think that no one in a passing helicraft was ever likely to catch sight of it . . .

Wardress Kefa led me up a series of plank stairs, spoke once at the door, and introduced me into an antechamber so clean and military that I thought "barracks" rather than "bawdyhouse." The ceiling and walls were honeycombed, and the natural flooring was redolent of the outdoors. My guardian disappeared, returned without her coat, and escorted me into a much smaller room shaped like a tapered well. By means of a wooden hand-crank she opened the shutters, and varicolored light filtered in upon us through the room's slant-set windows. On elevated cushions that snapped and rustled each time we moved, we sat facing each other.

"What now?" I asked the Wardress.

"Just listen: The Sharers have come to the House of their own volition, Mr. Lorca; most lived and worked on extrakomm worlds toward Glaktik Center before being approached for duty here. The ones who are here accepted the invitation. They came to offer their presences to people very like yourself."

"Me? Are they misconceived machines?"

"I'm not going to answer that. Let me just say that the variety of services the Sharers offer is surprisingly wide. As I've told you, for some visitants the Sharers are simply a convenient means of satisfying exotically aberrant tastes. For others they're a way back to the larger community. We take whoever comes to us for help, Mr. Lorca, in order that the Sharers not remain idle nor the House vacant."

"So long as whoever comes is wealthy and influential?"

She paused before speaking. "That's true enough. But the matter's out of my hands, Mr. Lorca. I'm an employee of Glaktik Komm, chosen for my empathetic abilities. I don't make policy. I don't own title to the House."

"But you *are* its madam. Its 'wardress,' rather."

"True. For the last twenty-two years. I'm the first and only wardress to have served here, Mr. Lorca, and I love the Sharers. I love their devotion to the fragile mentalities who visit them. Even so, despite the time I've lived among them, I still don't pretend to understand the source of their transcendent concern. That's what I wanted to tell you."

"You think me a 'fragile mentality'?"

"I'm sorry—but you're here, Mr. Lorca, and you certainly aren't fragile of *limb*, are you?" The Wardress laughed. "I also wanted to ask you to . . . well, to restrain your crueler impulses when the treatment itself begins."

I stood up and moved away from the little woman. How had I borne her presence for as long as I had?

"Please don't take my request amiss. It isn't *specifically* personal, Mr. Lorca. I make it of everyone who comes to the House of Compassionate Sharers. Restraint is an unwritten corollary of the only three rules we have here. Will you hear them?"

I made a noise of compliance.

"First, that you do not leave the session chamber once you've entered it. Second, that you come forth immediately upon my summoning you . . ."

"And third?"

"That you do not kill the Sharer."

All the myriad disgusts I had been suppressing for seven or eight hours were now perched atop the ladder of my patience, and rung by painful rung, I had to step them back down. Must a rule be made to prevent a visitant from murdering the partner he had bought? Incredible. The Wardress herself was just perceptibly sweating, and I noticed too how grotesquely distended her earlobes were.

"Is there a room in this establishment for a wealthy and influential patron? A private room?"

"Of course," she said. "I'll show you."

It had a full-length mirror. I undressed and stood in front of it. Only during my first "period of adjustment" on Diroste had I spent much time looking at what I had became. Later, back in the Port Iranani Galenshall, Diderits had denied me any sort of reflective surface at all—looking glasses, darkened windows, even metal spoons. The waxen perfection of my features ridiculed the ones another Dorian Lorca had possessed before the Haft Paykar Incident. Cosmetic mockery. Faintly corpselike, speciously paradigmatic, I was both more than I was supposed to be and less.

In Wardress Kefa's House the less seemed preeminent. I ran a finger down the inside of my right arm, scrutinizing the track of one of the intubated veins through which circulated a serum that Dederits called hematocybin: an efficient, "low-maintenance" blood substitute, combative of both fatigue and infection, which requires changing only once every six D-months. With a proper supply of hematocybin and a plastic recirculator I can do the job myself, standing up. That night, however, the ridge of my vein, mirrored only an arm's length away, was more horror than miracle. I stepped away from the looking glass and closed my eyes.

Later that evening Wardress Kefa came to me with a candle and a brocade dressing gown. She made me put on the gown in front of her, and I complied. Then, the robe's rich and symbolic embroidery on my back, I followed her out of my first-floor chamber to a rustic stairwell seemingly connective to all the rooms in the House.

The dome contained countless smaller domes and five or six primitive staircases, at least. Not a single other person was about. Lit flickeringly by Wardress Kefa's taper as we climbed one of these sets of stairs, the House's mid-interior put me in mind of an Escheresque drawing in which verticals and horizontals become hopelessly confused and a figure who from one perspective seems to be going up a series of steps seems from another to be coming down them. Presently the Wardress and I stood on a landing above this topsy-turvy well of stairs (though there were still more stairs above us), and, looking down, I experienced an unsettling reversal of perspectives. Vertigo. Why hadn't Diderits, against so human a susceptibility, implanted tiny gyrostabilizers in my head? I clutched a railing and held on.

"You can't fall," Wardress Kefa told me. "It's an illusion. A whim of the architects."

"Is it an illusion behind this door?"

"Oh, the Sharer's real enough, Mr. Lorca. Please. Go on in." She touched my face and left me, taking her candle with her.

After hesitating a moment I went through the door to my assignation, and the door locked of itself. I stood with my hand on the butterfly shape of the knob and felt the night working in me and the room. The only light came from the stove-bed on the opposite wall, for the fitted polygons overhead were still blanked out by their shutters and no candles shone here. Instead, reddish embers glowed behind an isinglass window beneath the stove-bed, strewn with quilts, on which my Sharer awaited me.

Outside, the wind played harp music in the trees.

I was trembling rhythmically, as when Rumer had come to me in the "Black Pavilion." Even though my eyes adjusted rapidly, automatically, to the dark, it was still difficult to see. Temporizing, I surveyed the dome. In its high central vault hung a cage in which, disturbed by my entrance, a bird hopped skittishly about. The cage swayed on its tether.

*Go on,* I told myself.

I advanced toward the dais and leaned over the unmoving Sharer who lay there. With a hand on either side of the creature's head, I braced myself. The figure beneath me moved, moved weakly, and I drew back. But because the Sharer didn't stir again, I reassumed my previous stance: the posture of either a lover or a man called upon to identify a disfigured corpse. But identification was impossible; the embers under the bed gave too feeble a sheen. In the chamber's darkness even a lover's kiss would have fallen clumsily . . .

"I'm going to touch you," I said. "Will you let me do that?"

The Sharer lay still.

Then, willing all of my senses into the cushion of synthetic flesh at my forefinger's tip, I touched the Sharer's face.

Hard, and smooth, and cool.

I moved my finger from side to side; and the hardness, smoothness, coolness continued to flow into my pressuring fingertip. It was like touching the pate of a death's-head, the cranial cap of a human being: bone rather than metal. My finger distinguished between these two possibilities, deciding on bone; and, half panicked, I concluded that I had traced an arc on the skull of an intelligent being who wore his every bone on the outside, like an armor of calcium. Could that be? If so, how could this organism—this entity, this *thing*—express compassion?

I lifted my finger away from the Sharer. Its tip hummed with a pressure now relieved and emanated a faint warmth.

A death's-head come to life . . .

Maybe I laughed. In any case, I pulled myself onto the platform and straddled the Sharer. I kept my eyes closed, though not tightly. It didn't seem that I was straddling a skeleton.

"Sharer," I whispered. "Sharer, I don't know you yet."

Gently, I let my thumbs find the creature's eyes, the sockets in the smooth exoskeleton, and both thumbs returned to me a hardness and a coldness that were unquestionably metallic in origin. Moreover, the Sharer didn't flinch—even though I'd anticipated that probing his eyes, no matter how gently, would provoke at least an involuntary pulling away. Instead, the Sharer lay still and tractable under my hands.

*And why not?* I thought. *Your eyes are nothing but two pieces of sophisticated optical machinery* . . .

It was true. Two artificial, light-sensing, image-integrating units gazed up at me from the sockets near which my thumbs probed, and I realized that even in this darkness my Sharer, its vision mechanically augmented beyond my own, could *see* my blind face staring down in a futile attempt to create an image out of the information my hands had supplied me. I opened my eyes and held them open. I could see only shadows, but my thumbs could *feel* the cold metal rings that held the Sharer's photosensitive units so firmly in its skull.

"An animatronic construct," I said, rocking back on my heels. "A soulless robot. Move your head if I'm right."

The Sharer continued motionless.

"All right. You're a sentient creature whose eyes

have been replaced with an artificial system. What about that? Lord, are we brothers then?"

I had a sudden hunch that the Sharer was very old, a senescent being owing its life to prosthetics, transplants, and imitative organs of laminated silicone. Its life, I was certain, had been *extended* by these contrivances, not saved. I asked the Sharer about my feeling, and very, very slowly it moved the helmetlike skull housing its artificial eyes and its aged, compassionate mind. Uncharitably I then believed myself the victim of a deception, whether the Sharer's or Wardress Kefa's I couldn't say. Here, after all, was a creature who had chosen to prolong its organic condition rather than to escape it, and it had willingly made use of the same materials and methods Diderits had brought into play to save me.

"You might have died," I told it. "Go too far, Sharer—go too far with these contrivances and you may forfeit suicide as an option."

Then, leaning forward again, saying, "I'm still not through, I still don't know you," I let my hands come down the Sharer's bony face to its throat. Here a shield of cartilage graded upward into its jaw and downward into the plastically silken skin covering the remainder of its body, internalizing all but the defiantly naked skull of the Sharer's skeletal structure. A death's-head with the body of a man . . .

That was all I could take. I rose from the stove-bed and, cinching my dressing gown tightly about my waist, crossed to the other side of the chamber. There was no furniture in the room but the stove-bed (if that qualified), and I had to content myself with sitting in a lotus position on the floor. I sat that way all night, staving off dreams.

Diderits had said that I needed to dream. If I didn't dream, he warned, I'd be risking hallucinations and eventual madness; in the Port Iranani Galenshall he'd seen to it that drugs were administered to me every two days and my sleep period monitored by an ARC machine and a team of electroencephalographers. But my dreams were almost always nightmares, descents into klieg-lit charnel houses, and I infinitely preferred the risk of going psychotic. There was always the chance someone would take pity and disassemble me, piece by loving piece. Besides, I had lasted two E-weeks now on nothing but grudging catnaps, and so far I still had gray matter upstairs instead of scrambled eggs . . .

I crossed my fingers.

A long time after I'd sat down, Wardress Kefa threw open the door. It was morning. I could tell because the newly canted shutters outside our room admitted a singular roaring of light. The entire chamber was illumined, and I saw crimson wall hangings, a mosaic of red and purple stones on the section of the floor, and a tumble of scarlet quilts. The bird in the suspended cage was a red-winged blackbird.

"Where is it from?"

"You could use a more appropriate pronoun."

*"He? She?* Which is the more appropriate, Wardress Kefa?"

"Assume the Sharer masculine, Mr. Lorca."

"My sexual proclivities have never run that way, I'm afraid."

"Your sexual proclivities," the Wardress told me stingingly, "enter into this only if you persist in thinking of the House as a brothel rather than a clinic and the Sharers as whores rather than therapists!"

"Last night I heard two or three people clomping up the stairs in their boots, that and a woman's raucous laughter."

"A visitant, Mr. Lorca, *not* a Sharer."

"I didn't think she was a Sharer. But it's difficult to believe I'm in a 'clinic' when that sort of noise disrupts my midnight meditations, Wardress."

"I've explained that. It can't be helped."

"All right, all right. Where is *he* from, this 'therapist' of mine?"

"An interior star. But where he's from is of no consequence in your treatment. I matched him to your needs, as I see them, and soon you'll be going back to him."

"Why? To spend another night sitting on the floor?"

"You won't do that again, Mr. Lorca. And you needn't worry. Your reaction wasn't an uncommon one for a newcomer to the House."

"Revulsion?" I cried. "Revulsion's therapeutic?"

"I don't think you were as put off as you believe."

"Oh? Why not?"

"Because you talked to the Sharer. You addressed him directly, not once but several times. Many visitants never get that far during their first session, Mr. Lorca."

"Talked to him?" I said dubiously. "Maybe. Before I found out what he was."

"Ah. Before you found out what he was." In her heavy green jacket and swishy pantaloons the tiny woman turned about and departed the well of the sitting room.

I stared bemusedly after her for a long time.

Three nights after my first "session," the night of my conversation with Wardress Kefa, I entered the Sharer's chamber again. Everything was as it had been, except that the dome's shutters were open and moonlight coated the mosaic work on the floor. The Sharer awaited me in the same recumbent, unmoving posture, and inside its cage the red-winged blackbird set one of its perches to rocking back and forth.

Perversely, I had decided not to talk to the Sharer this time—but I did approach the stove-bed and lean over him. *Hello,* I thought, and the word very nearly came out. I straddled the Sharer and studied him in the stained moonlight. He looked just as my sense of touch had led me to conclude previously . . . like a skull, oddly flattened and beveled, with the body of a man. But despite the chemical embers glowing beneath his dais the Sharer's body had no warmth, and to know him more fully I resumed tracing a finger over his alien parts.

I discovered that at every conceivable pressure point a tiny scar existed, or the tip of an implanted electrode, and that miniature canals into which wires had been sunk veined his inner arms and legs. Just beneath his sternum a concave disc about eight centimeters across, containing neither instruments nor any other surface features, had been set into the Sharer's chest like a stainless-steel brooch. It seemed to hum under the pressure of my finger as I drew my nail silently around the disc's circumference. What was it for? What did it mean? Again, I almost spoke.

I rolled toward the wall and lay stretched out beside the unmoving Sharer. Maybe he *couldn't* move. On my last visit he had moved his dimly phosphorescent head for me, of course, but that only feebly, and maybe his immobility was the result of some cybergamic dysfunction. I had to find out. My resolve not to speak deserted me, and I propped myself up on my elbow.

"Sharer . . . Sharer, can you move?"

The head turned toward me slightly, signaling . . . well, what?

"Can you get off this platform? Try. Get off this dais under your own power."

To my surprise, the Sharer nudged a quilt to the floor and in a moment stood facing me. Moonlight glinted from the photosensitive units serving the creature as eyes and gave his bent, elongated body the appearance of a piece of Inhodlef Era statuary, primitive work from the extrakomm world of Glaparcus.

"Good," I praised the Sharer, "very good. Can you tell me what you're supposed to share with me? I'm not sure we have as much in common as our Wardress seems to think."

The Sharer extended both arms toward me and opened his tightly closed fists. In the cups of his palms he held two items I hadn't discovered during my tactile examination of him. I accepted these from the Sharer. One was a small metal disc, the other a thin metal cylinder. Looking them over, I found that the disc reminded me of the larger, mirrorlike bowl set in the alien's chest, while the cylinder seemed to be a kind of penlight.

Absently, I pulled my thumb over the head of the penlight; a ridged metal sheath followed the motion of my thumb, uncovering a point of ghostly red light stretching away into the cylinder seemingly deeper than the penlight itself. I pointed this instrument at the wall, at our bedding, at the Sharer himself—but it emitted no beam. When I turned the penlight on my wrist, the results were predictably similar: Not even a faint red shadow appeared along the edge of my arm. Nothing. The cylinder's light existed internally, a beam continuously transmitted and retransmitted between the penlight's two poles. Pulling back the sheath on the instrument's head had in no way interrupted the operation of its self-regenerating circuit.

I stared wonderingly into the hollow of redness, then looked up. "Sharer, what's this thing for?"

The Sharer reached out and took from my other hand the disc I had so far ignored. Then he placed this small circle of metal in the smooth declivity of the larger disc in his chest, where it apparently adhered—for I could no longer see it. That done, the Sharer stood distressingly immobile, even more like a statue than he had seemed a moment before, one arm frozen across his body and his hand stilled at the edge of the sunken plate in which the smaller disc had just adhered. He looked dead and self-commemorating.

"Lord!" I exclaimed. "What've you done, Sharer? Turned yourself off? That's right, isn't it?"

The Sharer neither answered nor moved.

Suddenly I felt sickeningly weary, opiate-weary, and I knew that I wouldn't be able to stay on the dais with this puzzle-piece being from an anonymous sun standing over me like a dark angel from my racial subconscious. I thought briefly of manhandling the Sharer across the room, but didn't have the will to touch this catatonically rigid being, this sculpture of metal and bone, and so dismissed the idea. Nor was it likely that Wardress Kefa would help me, even if I tried to summon her with murderous poundings and cries—a bitterly amusing prospect. Wellaway, another night propped against the chamber's far wall, keeping sleep at bay . . .

Is this what you wanted me to experience, Rumer? The frustration of trying to piece together my own "therapy"? I looked up through one of the dome's unstained polygons in lethargic search of the constellation Auriga. Then I realized that I wouldn't recognize it even if it happened to lie within my line of sight. Ah, Rumer, Rumer . . .

"You're certainly a pretty one," I told the Sharer. Then I pointed the penlight at his chest, drew back the sheath on its head, and spoke a single onomatopoeic word: *"Bang."*

Instantly a beam of light sang between the instrument in my hand and the plate in the Sharer's chest. The beam died at once (I had registered only its shattering brightness, not its color), but the disc continued to glow with a residual illumination.

The Sharer dropped his frozen arm and assumed a posture more limber, more suggestive of life. He looked . . . expectant.

I could only stare. Then I turned the penlight over in my hands, pointed it again at the Sharer, and waited for another coursing of light. To no purpose. The instrument still burned internally, but it wouldn't relume the alien's inset disc, which, in any case, continued to glow dimly. Things were all at once interesting again. I gestured with the penlight.

"You've rejoined the living, haven't you?"

The Sharer acknowledged this with a slight turn of the head.

"Forgive me, Sharer, but I don't want to spend another night sitting on the floor. If you can move again, how about over there?" I pointed at the opposite wall. "I don't want you hovering over me."

Oddly, he obeyed. But he did so oddly, without turning around. He cruised backward as if on invisible casters—his legs moving a little, yes, but not enough to propel him so smoothly, so quickly, across the chamber. Once against the far wall, the Sharer settled into the motionless but expectant posture he had assumed after his "activation" by the penlight. I could see that he still had some degree of control over his own movements, for his long fingers curled and uncurled and his skull nodded eerily in the halo of moonlight pocketing him. Even so, I realized that he had truly moved only at my voice command and my simultaneous gesturing with the penlight. And what did *that* mean?

. . . Well, that the Sharer had relinquished control of his body to the man-machine Dorian Lorca, retaining for himself just those meaningless reflexes and stirrings that convince the manipulated of their own autonomy. It was an awesome prostitution, even if Wardress Kefa would have frowned to hear me say so. Momentarily I rejoiced in it, for it seemed to free me from the demands of an artificial eroticism, from the need to figure through what was expected of me. The Sharer would obey my simplest wrist-turning, my briefest word; all I had to do was *use* the control he had literally handed to me.

This virtually unlimited power, I thought then, was a therapy whose value Rumer would understand only too well. This was a harsh assessment, but, penlight in hand, I felt that I too was a kind of marionette . . .

Insofar as I could, I tried to come to grips with the physics of the Sharer's operation. First, the disc-within-a-disc on his chest apparently broke the connections ordinarily allowing him to exercise the senile powers that were still his. And, second, the penlight's beam restored and amplified these powers but delivered them into the hands of the speaker of imperatives who wielded the penlight. I recalled that in Earth's lunar probeship yards were crews of animatronic laborers programmed for fitting and welding. A single trained supervisor could direct from fifteen to twenty receiver-equipped laborers with one penlight and a microphone—

"Sharer," I commanded, blanking out this reverie, pointing the penlight, "go there . . . No, no, not like that. Lift your feet. March for me . . . That's right, a *goosestep*."

While Wardress Kefa's third rule rattled in the back of my mind like a challenge, for the next several hours I toyed with the Sharer. After the marching I set him to calisthenics and interpretative dance, and he obeyed, moving more gracefully than I would have imagined possible. Here—then there—then back again. All he lacked was Beethoven's piano sonatas for an accompaniment.

At intervals I rested, but always the fascination of the penlight drew me back, almost against my will, and I once again played puppetmaster.

"Enough, Sharer, enough." The sky had a curdled quality suggestive of dawn. Catching sight of the cage overhead, I was taken by an irresistible impulse. I pointed the penlight at the cage and commanded, "Up, Sharer. Up, up, up."

The Sharer floated up from the floor and glided effortlessly toward the vault of the dome: a beautiful, aerial walk. Without benefit of hawsers or scaffolds or wings the Sharer levitated. Hovering over the stove-bed he had been made to surrender, hovering over everything in the room, he reached the cage and swung before it with his hands touching the scrolled ironwork on its little door. I dropped my own hands and watched him. So tightly was I gripping the penlight, however, that my knuckles must have resembled the caps of four tiny bleached skulls.

A great deal of time went by, the Sharer poised in the gelid air awaiting some word from me.

Morning began coming in the room's polygonal windows.

"Take the bird out," I ordered the Sharer, moving my penlight. "Take the bird out of the cage and kill it." This command, sadistically heartfelt, seemed to me a foolproof, indirect way of striking back at Rumer, Diderits, the Wardress, and the Third Rule of the House of Compassionate Sharers. More than anything, against all reason, I wanted the red-winged blackbird dead. And I wanted the Sharer to kill it.

Dawn made clear the cancerous encroachment of age in the Sharer's legs and hands, as well as the full horror of his cybergamically rigged death's-head. He looked as if he had been unjustly hanged. And when his hands went up to the cage, instead of opening its door the Sharer lifted the entire contraption off the hook fastening it to its tether, and then accidentally lost his grip on the cage.

I watched the cage fall—land on its side—bounce—bounce again. The Sharer stared down with his bulging, silver-ringed eyes, his hands still spread wide to accommodate the fallen cage.

"Mr. Lorca." Wardress Kefa was knocking at the door. "Mr. Lorca, what's going on, please?"

I arose from the stove-bed, tossed my quilt aside, straightened my heavy robes. The Wardress knocked again. I looked at the Sharer swaying in the half-light like a sword or a pendulum, an instrument of severance. The night had gone faster than I liked.

Again, the purposeful knocking.

"Coming," I barked.

In the dented cage there was a flutter of crimson, a stillness, and then another bit of melancholy flapping. I hurled my penlight across the room. When it struck the wall, the Sharer rocked back and forth for a moment without descending so much as a centimeter. The knocking continued.

"You have the key, Wardress. Open the door."

She did, and stood on its threshold taking stock of the games we had played. Her eyes were bright but devoid of censure, and I swept past her wordlessly, burning with shame and bravado.

I slept that day—all that day—for the first time since leaving my own world. And I dreamed. I dreamed that I was connected to a mechanism pistoning away on the edge of the Haft Paykar diggings, siphoning deadly gases out of the shafts and perversely recirculating them through the pump with which I shared a symbiomechanic linkage. Amid a series of surreal turquoise sunsets and intermittent gusts of sand, this pistoning went on, and on, and on. When I awoke I lifted my hands to my face, intending to scar it with my nails. But a moment later, as I had known it would, the mirror in my chamber returned me a perfect, unperturbed Dorian Lorca . . .

"May I come in?"

"I'm the guest here, Wardress. So I suppose you may."

She entered and, quickly intuiting my mood, walked to the other side of the chamber. "You slept, didn't you? And you dreamed?"

I said nothing.

"You dreamed, didn't you?"

"A nightmare, Wardress. A long and repetitious nightmare, notable only for being different from the ones I had on Diroste."

"A start, though. You weren't monitored during your sleep, after all, and even if your dream *was* a nightmare, Mr. Lorca, I believe you've managed to survive it. Good. All to the good."

I went to the only window in the room, a hexagonal pane of dark blue through which it was impossible to see anything. "Did you get him down?"

"Yes. And restored the birdcage to its place." Her tiny feet made pacing sounds on the hardwood. "The bird was unharmed."

"Wardress, what's all this about? Why have you paired me with . . . with this particular Sharer?" I turned around. "What's the point?"

"You're not estranged from your wife only, Mr. Lorca. You're—"

"I know that. I've *known* that."

"And I know that you know it. Give me a degree of credit . . . You also know," she resumed, "that you're estranged from yourself, body and soul at variance—"

"Of course, dammit! And the argument between them's been stamped into every pseudo-organ and circuit I can lay claim to!"

"Please, Mr. Lorca, I'm trying to explain. This interior 'argument' you're so aware of . . . it's really a metaphor for an attitude you involuntarily adopted after

Diderits performed his operations. And a metaphor can be taken apart and explained."

"Like a machine."

"If you like." She began pacing again. "To take inventory you have to surmount that which is to be inventoried. You go outside, Mr. Lorca, in order to come back in." She halted and fixed me with a colorless, lopsided smile.

"All of that," I began cautiously, "is clear to me. 'Know thyself,' saith Diderits and the ancient Greeks . . . Well, if anything, my knowledge has *increased* my uneasiness about not only myself, but others—and not only others, but the very phenomena permitting us to spawn." I had an image of crimson-gilled fish firing upcurrent in a roiling, untidy barrage. "What I know hasn't cured anything, Wardress."

"No. That's why we've had you come here. To extend the limits of your knowledge and to involve you in relationships demanding a recognition of others as well as self."

"As with the Sharer I left hanging up in the air?"

"Yes. Distance is advisable at first, perhaps inevitable. You needn't feel guilty. In a night or two you'll be going back to him, and then we'll just have to see."

"Is this the only Sharer I'm going to be . . . working with?"

"I don't know. It depends on the sort of progress you make."

But for the Wardress Kefa, the Sharer in the crimson dome, and the noisy, midnight visitants I had never seen, there were times when I believed myself the only occupant of the House. The thought of such isolation, although not unwelcome, was an anchoritic fantasy: I knew that breathing in the chambers next to mine, going about the arcane business of the lives they had bartered away, were humanoid creatures difficult to imagine; harder still, once lodged in the mind, to put out of it. To what number and variety of beings had Wardress Kefa indentured her love . . . ?

I had no chance to ask this question. We heard an

insistent clomping on the steps outside the House and then muffled voices in the antechamber.

"Who's that?"

The Wardress put up her hand to silence me and opened the door to my room. "A moment," she called. "I'll be with you in a moment." But her husky voice didn't carry very well, and whoever had entered the House set about methodically knocking on doors and clomping from apartment to apartment, all the while bellowing the Wardress's name. "I'd better go talk with them," she told me apologetically.

"But who is it?"

"Someone voice-coded for entrance, Mr. Lorca. Nothing to worry about." And she went into the corridor, giving me a scent of spruce needles and a vision of solidly hewn rafters before the door swung to.

But I got up and followed the Wardress. Outside I found her face to face with two imposing persons who looked exactly alike in spite of their being one a man and the other a woman. Their faces had the same lantern-jawed mournfulness, their eyes a hooded look under prominent brows. They wore filigreed pea jackets, ski leggings, and fur-lined caps bearing the interpenetrating-galaxies insignia of Glaktik Komm. I judged them to be in their late thirties, E-standard, but they both had the domineering, glad-handing air of high-ranking veterans in the bureaucratic establishment, people who appreciate their positions just to the extent that their positions can be exploited. I knew. I had once been an official of the same stamp.

The man, having been caught in mid-bellow, was now trying to laugh. "Ah, Wardress, Wardress."

"I didn't expect you this evening," she told the two of them.

"We were granted a proficiency leave for completing the Salous blueprint in advance of schedule," the woman explained, "and so caught a late 'rail from Manitou Port to take advantage of the leave. We hiked down in the dark." Along with her eyebrows she lifted a hand lantern for our inspection.

"We *took* a proficiency leave," the man said, "even if we *were* here last week. And we deserved it too." He went on to tell us that "Salous" dealt with reclaiming the remnants of aboriginal populations and pooling them for something called integrative therapy. "The Great Plains will soon be our bordello, Wardress. There, you see: You and the Orhas are in the same business . . . at least until we're assigned to stage-manage something more prosasic." He clapped his gloved hands together and looked at me. "You're new, aren't you? Who are you going to?"

"Pardon me," the Wardress interjected wearily. "Who do *you* want tonight?"

The man looked at his partner with a mixture of curiosity and concern. "Cleva?"

"The mouthless one," Cleva responded at once. "Drugged, preferably."

"Come with me, Orhas," the Wardress directed. She led them first to her own apartment and then into the House's mid-interior, where the three of them disappeared from my sight. I could hear them climbing one of the sets of stairs.

Shortly thereafter the Wardress returned to my room.

"They're twins?"

"In a manner of speaking, Mr. Lorca. Actually they're clonemates: Cleva and Cleirach Orha, specialists in Holosyncretic Management. They do abstract computer planning involving indigenous and alien populations, which is why they know of the House at all and have an authorization to come here."

"Do they always appear here together? Go upstairs together?"

The Wardress's silence clearly meant yes.

"That's a bit kinky, isn't it?"

She gave me an angry look whose implications immediately silenced me. I started to apologize, but she said: "The Orhas are the only visitants to the House who arrive together, Mr. Lorca. Since they share a common upbringing, the same genetic material, and identical biochemistries, it isn't surprising that their sexual preferences should coincide. In Manitou Port, I'm told, is a third clonemate who was permitted to marry, and her I've never seen either here or in Wolf Run Summit. It seems there's a *degree* of variety even among clonal siblings."

"Do these two come often?"

"You heard them in the House several days ago."

"They have frequent leaves then?"

"Last time was an overnighter. They returned to Manitou Port in the morning, Mr. Lorca. Just now they were trying to tell me that they intend to be here for a few days."

"For treatment," I said.

"You know better. You're baiting me, Mr. Lorca." She had taken her graying scalplock into her fingers, and was holding its fan of hair against her right cheek. In this posture, despite her preoccupation with the arrival of the Orhas, she looked very old and very innocent.

"Who is the 'mouthless one,' Wardress?"

"Good night, Mr. Lorca. I only returned to tell you good night." And with no other word she left.

It was the longest I had permitted myself to talk with her since our first afternoon in the House, the longest I had been in her presence since our claustrophobic 'rail ride from Manitou Port. Even the Orhas, bundled to the gills, as vulgar as sleek bullfrogs, hadn't struck me as altogether insufferable.

Wearing neither coat nor cap, I took a walk through the glens below the House, touching each wind-shaken tree as I came to it and trying to conjure out of the darkness a viable memory of Rumer's smile . . .

"Sex as weapon," I told my Sharer, who sat propped on the stove-bed amid ten or twelve quilts of scarlet and off-scarlet. "As prince consort to the Governor of Diroste, that was the only weapon I had access to . . . Rumer employed me as an emissary, Sharer, an espionage agent, a protocol officer, whatever state business required. I received visiting representatives of Glaktik

Komm, mediated disputes in the Port Iranani business community, and went on biannual inspection tours of the Fetneh and Furak District mines. I did a little of everything, Sharer."

As I paced, the Sharer observed me with a macabre, but somehow not unsettling, penetration. The hollow of his chest was exposed, and, as I passed him, an occasional metallic wink caught the corner of my eye.

I told him the story of my involvement with a minor official in Port Iranani's department of immigration, a young woman whom I had never called by anything but her maternal surname, Humay. There had been others besides this woman, but Humay's story was the one I chose to tell. Why? Because alone among my ostensible "lovers," Humay I had never lain with. I had never chosen to.

Instead, to her intense bewilderment, I gave Humay ceremonial pendants, bracelets, ear-pieces, brooches, necklaces, and die-cut cameos of gold on silver, all from the collection of Rumer Montieth, Governor of Diroste—anything, in short, distinctive enough to be recognizable to my wife at a glance. Then, at those state functions requiring Rumer's attendance upon a visiting dignitary, I arranged for Humay to be present; sometimes I accompanied her myself, sometimes I found her an escort among the unbonded young men assigned to me as aides. Always I insured that Rumer should see Humay, if not in a reception line then in the promenade of the formal recessional. Afterwards I asked Humay, who never seemed to have even a naïve insight into the purposes of my game, to hand back whatever piece of jewelry I had given her for ornament, and she did so. Then I returned the jewelry to Rumer's sandalwood box before my wife could verify what her eyes had earlier that evening tried to tell her. Everything I did was designed to create a false impression of my relationship with Humay, and I wanted my dishonesty in the matter to be conspicuous.

Finally, dismissing Humay for good, I gave her a cameo of Rumer's that had been crafted in the Furak

District. I learned later that she had flung this cameo at an aide of mine who entered the offices of her department on a matter having nothing to do with her. She created a disturbance, several times raising my name. Ultimately (in two days' time), she was disciplined by a transfer to the frontier outpost of Yagme, the administrative center of the Furak District, and I never saw her again.

"Later, Sharer, when I dreamed of Humay, I saw her as a woman with mother-of-pearl flesh and ruby eyes. In my dreams she *became* the pieces of jewelry with which I'd tried to incite my wife's sexual jealousy—blunting it even as I incited it."

The Sharer regarded me with hard but sympathetic eyes.

Why? I asked him. Why had I dreamed of Humay as if she were an expensive clockwork mechanism, gilded, beset with gemstones, invulnerably enameled? And why had I so fiercely desired Rumer's jealousy?

The Sharer's silence invited confession.

After the Haft Paykar Incident (I went on, pacing), after Diderits had fitted me with a total prosthesis, my nightmares often centered on the young woman who'd been exiled to Yagme. Although in Port Iranani I hadn't once touched Humay in an erotic way, in my monitored nightmares I regularly descended into either a charnel catacomb or a half-fallen quarry—it was impossible to know which—and there forced myself, without success, on the bejeweled automaton she had become. In every instance Humay waited for me underground; in every instance she turned me back with coruscating laughter. Its echoes always drove me upward to the light, and in the midst of nightmare I realized that I wanted Humay far less than I did residency in the secret, subterranean places she had made her own. The klieg lights that invariably directed my descent always followed me back out, too, so that Humay was always left kilometers below exulting in the dark . . .

My Sharer got up and took a turn around the room,

a single quilt draped over his shoulders and clutched loosely together at his chest. This was the first time since I had been coming to him that he had moved so far of his own volition, and I sat down to watch. Did he understand me at all? I had spoken to him as if his understanding were presupposed, a certainty—but beyond a hopeful *feeling* that my words meant something to him I'd had no evidence at all, not even a testimonial from Wardress Kefa. All of the Sharer's "reactions" were really nothing but projections of my own ambiguous hopes.

When he at last returned to me, he extended both hideously canaled arms and opened his fists. In them, the disc and the penlight. It was an offering, a compassionate, selfless offering, and for a moment I stared at his open hands in perplexity. What did they want of me, this Sharer, Wardress Kefa, the people who had sent me here? How was I supposed to buy either their forbearance or my freedom? By choosing power over impotency? By manipulation? . . . But these were altogether different questions, and I hesitated.

The Sharer then placed the small disc in the larger one beneath his sternum. Then, as before, a thousand esoteric connections severed, he froze. In the hand still extended toward me, the penlight glittered faintly and threatened to slip from his insensible grasp. I took it carefully from the Sharer's fingers, pulled back the sheath on its head, and gazed into its red-lit hollow. I released the sheath and pointed the penlight at the disc in his chest.

If I pulled the sheath back again, he would become little more than a fully integrated, *external* prosthesis—as much at my disposal as the hands holding the penlight.

"No," I said. "Not this time." And I flipped the penlight across the chamber, out of the way of temptation. Then, using my fingernails, I pried the small disc out of its electromagnetic moorings above the Sharer's heart.

He was restored to himself.

As was I to myself. As was I.

A day later, early in the afternoon, I ran into the Orhas in the House's mid-interior. They were coming unaccompanied out of a lofty, seemingly sideways-canted door as I stood peering upward from the access corridor. Man and woman together, mirror images ratcheting down a Möbius strip of stairs, the Orhas held my attention until it was too late for me to slip away unseen.

"The new visitant," Cleirach Orha informed his sister when he reached the bottom step. "We've seen you before."

"Briefly," I agreed. "The night you arrived from Manitou Port for your proficiency leave."

"What a good memory you have," Cleva Orha said. "We also saw you the day *you* arrived from Manitou Port. You and the Wardress were just setting out from Wolf Run Summit together. Cleirach and I were beneath the ski lodge, watching."

"You wore no coat," her clonemate said in explanátion of their interest.

They both stared at me curiously. Neither was I wearing a coat in the well of the House of Compassionate Sharers—even though the temperature inside hovered only a few degrees above freezing and we could see our breaths before us like the ghosts of ghosts . . . I was a queer one, wasn't I? My silence made them nervous and brazen.

"No coat," Cleva Orha repeated, "and the day cold enough to fur your spittle. 'Look at that one,' Cleirach told me, 'thinks he's a polar bear.' We laughed about that, studling. We laughed heartily."

I nodded, nothing more. A coppery taste of bile, such as I hadn't experienced for several days, flooded my mouth, and I wanted to escape the Orhas' warty good humor. They were intelligent people, otherwise they would never have been cloned, but, face to face with their flawed skins and their loud, insinuative sexuality, I began to feel my new-found stores of tolerance overbalancing like a tower of blocks. It was a bitter test, this meeting below the stairs, and one I was on the edge of failing.

"We seem to be the only ones in the House this month," the woman volunteered. "Last month the Wardress was gone, the Sharers had a holiday, and Cleirach and I had to content ourselves with incestuous buggery in Manitou Port."

"Cleva!" the man protested, laughing.

"It's true." She turned to me. "It's true, studling. And that little she-goat—Kefa, I mean—won't even tell us why the 'Closed' sign was out for so long. Delights in mystery, that one."

"That's right," Cleirach went on. "She's an exasperating woman. She begrudges you your privileges. You have to tread lightly on her patience. Sometimes you'd like to take *her* into a chamber and find out what makes her tick. A bit of exploratory surgery, hey-la!" Saying this, he showed me his trilling tongue.

"She's a maso-ascetic, Brother."

"I don't know. There are many mansions in this House, Cleva, several of which she's refused to let us enter. Why?" He raised his eyebrows suggestively, as Cleva had done the night she lifted her hand-lantern for our notice. The expressions were the same.

Cleva Orha appealed to me as a disinterested third party: "What do you think, studling? Is Wardress Scalplock at bed and at bone with one of her Sharers? Or does she lie by herself, maso-ascetically, under a hide of untanned elk hair? What do you think?"

"I haven't really thought about it." Containing my anger, I tried to leave. "Excuse me, Orha clones."

"Wait, wait, wait," the woman said mincingly, half humorously. "You know our names and a telling bit of our background. That puts you up, studling. We won't have that. You can't go without giving us a name."

Resenting the necessity, I told them my name.

"From where?" Cleirach Orha asked.

"Colony World GK-11. We call it Diroste."

Brother and sister exchanged a glance of sudden enlightment, after which Cleva raised her thin eyebrows and spoke in a mocking rhythm: "Ah ha, the mystery solved. Out and back our Wardress went and therefore closed her House."

"Welcome, Mr. Lorca. Welcome."

"We're going up to Wolf Run for an after-bout of toddies and P-nol. What about you? Would you like to go? The climb wouldn't be anything to a warmblooded studling like you. Look, Cleirach. Biceps unbundled and his sinuses still clear."

In spite of the compliment I declined.

"Who have *you* been with?" Cleirach Orha wanted to know. He bent forward conspiratorially. "We've been with a native of an extrakomm world called Trope. That's the local name. Anyhow, there's not another such being inside of a hundred light-years, Mr. Lorca."

"It's the face that intrigues us," Cleva Orha explained, saving me from an immediate reply to her brother's question. And then she reached out, touched my arm, and ran a finger down my arm to my hand. "Look. Not even a goose bump. Cleirach, you and I are suffering the shems and trivs, and our earnest Mr. Lorca's standing here bare-boned."

Brother was annoyed by this analysis. There was something he wanted to know, and Cleva's non sequiturs weren't advancing his case. Seeing that he was going to ask me again, I rummaged about for an answer that was neither informative nor tactless.

Cleva Orha, meanwhile, was peering intently at her fingertips. Then she looked at my arm, again at her fingers, and a second time at my arm. Finally she locked eyes with me and studied my face as if for some clue to the source of my reticence.

Ah, I thought numbly, she's recognized me for what I am . . .

"Mr. Lorca can't tell you who he's been with, Cleirach," Cleva Orha told her clonemate, "because he's not a visitant to the House at all and he doesn't choose to violate the confidences of those who are."

Dumbfounded, I said nothing.

Cleva put her hand on her brother's back and guided

him past me into the House's antechamber. Over her shoulder she bid me good afternoon in a toneless voice. Then the Orha clones very deliberately let themselves out the front door and began the long climb to Wolf Run Summit.

What had happened? It took me a moment to figure it out. Cleva Orha had recognized me as a human-machine and from this recognition drawn a logical but mistaken inference: She believed me, like the "mouthless one" from Trope, a slave of the House . . .

During my next tryst with my Sharer I spoke for an hour, two hours, maybe more, of Rumer's infuriating patience, her dignity, her serene ardor. I had moved her—maneuvered her—to the expression of these qualities by my own hollow commitment to Humay and the others before Humay who had engaged me only physically. Under my wife's attentions, however, I preened sullenly, demanding more than Rumer—than any woman in Rumer's position—had it in her power to give. My needs, I wanted her to know, my needs were as urgent and as real as Diroste's.

And at the end of one of these vague encounters Rumer seemed both to concede the legitimacy of my demands and to decry their intemperance by removing a warm pendant from her throat and placing it like an accusation in my palm.

"A week later," I told the Sharer, "was the inspection tour of the diggings at Haft Paykar."

These things spoken, I did something I had never done before in the Wardress's House: I went to sleep under the hand of my Sharer. My dreams were dreams rather than nightmares, and clarified ones at that, shot through with light and accompanied from afar by a peaceful funneling of sand. The images that came to me were haloed arms and legs orchestrated within a series of shifting yellow, yellow-orange, and subtly-red discs. The purr of running sand behind these movements conferred upon them the benediction of mortality, and that, I felt, was good.

I awoke in a blast of icy air and found myself alone. The door to the Sharer's apartment was standing open on the shaft of the stairwell, and I heard faint, angry voices coming across the emptiness between. Disoriented, I lay on my stove-bed staring toward the door, a square of shadow feeding its chill into the room.

*"Dorian!"* a husky voice called. *"Dorian!"*

Wardress Kefa's voice, diluted by distance and fear. A door opened, and her voice hailed me again, this time with more clarity. Then the door slammed shut, and every sound in the House took on a smothered quality, as if mumbled through cold, semiporous wood.

I got up, dragging my bedding with me, and reached the narrow porch on the stairwell with a clear head. Thin starlight filtered through the unshuttered windows in the ceiling. Nevertheless, looking from stairway to stairway to stairway inside the House, I had no idea behind which door the Wardress now must be.

Because there existed no connecting stairs among the staggered landings of the House, my only option was to go down. I took the steps two at a time, very nearly plunging.

At the bottom I found my Sharer with both hands clenched about the outer stair rail. He was trembling. In fact, his chest and arms were quivering so violently that he seemed about to shake himself apart. I put my hands on his shoulders and tightened my grip until the tremors wracking him threatened to wrack my systems, too. Who would come apart first?

"Go upstairs," I told the Sharer. "Get the hell upstairs."

I heard the Wardress call my name again. Although by now she had squeezed some of the fear out of her voice, her summons was still distance-muffled and impossible to pinpoint.

The Sharer either couldn't or wouldn't obey me. I coaxed him, cursed him, goaded him, tried to turn him around so that he was heading back up the steps. Nothing availed. The Wardress, summoning me, had inadvertently called the Sharer out as my proxy, and he now had no intention of giving back to me the role he'd just usurped. The beautifully faired planes of his skull turned toward me, bringing with them the stainless-steel rings of his eyes. These were the only parts of his body that didn't tremble, but they were helpless to countermand the agues shaking him. As inhuman and unmoving as they were, the Sharer's features still managed to convey stark, unpitiable entreaty . . .

I sank to my knees, felt about the insides of the Sharer's legs, and took the penlight and the disc from the two pocketlike incisions tailored to these instruments. Then I stood and used them.

"Find Wardress Kefa for me, Sharer," I commanded, gesturing with the penlight at the windows overhead. "Find her."

And the Sharer floated up from the steps through the mid-interior of the House. In the crepuscular starlight, rocking a bit, he seemed to pass through a knot of curving stairs into an open space where he was all at once brightly visible.

"Point to the door," I said, jabbing the penlight uncertainly at several different landings around the well. "Show me the one."

My words echoed, and the Sharer, legs dangling, inscribed a slow half-circle in the air. Then he pointed toward one of the nearly hidden doorways.

I stalked across the well, found a likely-seeming set of stairs, and climbed them with no notion at all of what was expected of me.

Wardress Kefa didn't call out again, but I heard the same faint, somewhat slurred voices that I'd heard upon waking and knew that they belonged to the Orhas. A burst of muted female laughter, twice repeated, convinced me of this, and I hesitated on the landing.

"All right," I told my Sharer quietly, turning him around with a turn of the wrist, "go on home."

Dropping through the torus of a lower set of stairs, he found the porch in front of our chamber and settled upon it like a clumsily handled puppet. And why not? I was a clumsy puppetmaster. Because there seemed to be nothing else I could do, I slid the penlight into a pocket of my dressing gown and knocked on the Orhas' door.

"Come in," Cleva Orha said. "By all means, Sharer Lorca, come in."

I entered and found myself in a room whose surfaces were all burnished as if with beeswax. The timbers shone. Whereas in the other chambers I had seen nearly all the joists and rafters were rough-hewn, here they were smooth and splinterless. The scent of sandalwood pervaded the air, and opposite the door was a carved screen blocking my view of the chamber's stove-bed. A tall wooden lamp illuminated the furnishings and the three people arrayed around the lamp's border of light like iconic statues.

"Welcome," Cleirach Orha said. "Your invitation was from the Wardress, however, not us." He wore only a pair of silk pantaloons drawn together at the waist with a cord, and his right forearm was under Wardress Kefa's chin, restraining her movement without quite cutting off her wind.

His disheveled clonemate, in a dressing gown very much like mine, sat cross-legged on a cushion and toyed with a wooden stiletto waxed as the beams of the chamber were waxed. Her eyes were too wide, too lustrous, as were her brother's, and I knew this was the result of too much placenol in combination with too much Wolf Run small-malt in combination with the Orhas' innate meanness. The woman was drugged, and drunk, and, in consequence of these things, malicious to a turn. Cleirach didn't appear quite so far gone as his sister, but all he had to do to strangle the Wardress, I understood, was raise the edge of his forearm into her trachea. I felt again the familiar sensation of being out of my element, gill-less in a sluice of stinging salt water . . .

"Wardress Kefa—" I began.

"She's all right," Cleva Orha assured me. "Perfectly all right." She tilted her head so that she was gazing at me out of her right eye alone, and then barked a hoarse, deranged-sounding laugh.

"Let the Wardress go," I told her clonemate.

Amazingly, Cleirach Orha looked intimidated. "Mr. Lorca's an anproz," he reminded Cleva. "That little letter opener you're cleaning your nails with, it's not going to mean anything to him."

"Then let her go, Cleirach. Let her go."

Cleirach released the Wardress, who, massaging her throat with both hands, ran to the stove-bed. She halted beside the carved screen and beckoned me with a doll-like hand. "Mr. Lorca . . . Mr. Lorca, please . . . will you see to him first? I beg you."

"I'm going back to Wolf Run Summit," Cleirach informed his sister, and he slipped on a night jacket, gathered up his clothes, and left the room. Cleva Orha remained seated on her cushion, her head tilted back as if she were tasting a bitter potion from a heavy metal goblet.

Glancing doubtfully at her, I went to the Wardress. Then I stepped around the wooden divider to see her Sharer.

The Tropeman lying there was a slender creature, almost slight. There was a ridge of flesh where his mouth ought to be, and his eyes were an organic variety of crystal, uncanny and depthful stones. One of these brandy-colored stones had been dislodged in its socket by Cleva's "letter opener"; and although the Orhas had failed to pry the eye completely loose, the Tropeman's face was streaked with blood from their efforts. The streaks ran down into the bedding under his narrow, fragile head and gave him the look of an aborigine in war paint. Lacking external genitalia, his sexless body was spread-eagled atop the quilts so that the burn marks on his legs and lower abdomen cried out for notice as plangently as did his face.

"Sweet light, sweet light," the Wardress chanted softly, over and over again, and I found her locked in my arms, hugging me tightly above her beloved, butchered ward, this Sharer from another star.

"He's not dead," Cleva Orha said from her cushion. "The rules . . . the rules say not to kill 'em, and we go by the rules, brother and I."

"What can I do, Wardress Kefa?" I whispered, holding her. "What do you want me to do?"

Slumped against me, the Wardress repeated her consoling chant and held me about the waist. So, fearful that this being with eyes like precious gems would bleed to death as we delayed, each of us undoubtedly ashamed of our delay, we delayed—and I held the Wardress, pressed her head to my chest, gave her a warmth I hadn't before believed in me. And she returned this warmth in undiluted measure.

Wardress Kefa, I realized, was herself a Compassionate Sharer; she was as much a Sharer as the bleeding Tropeman on the stove-bed or that obedient creature whose electrode-studded body and luminous death's-head had seemed to mock the efficient, mechanical deadness in myself—a deadness that, in turning away from Rumer, I had made a god of. In the face of this realization my disgust with the Orhas was transfigured into something very unlike disgust: a mode of perception, maybe; a means of adapting. An answer had been revealed to me, and, without its being either easy or uncomplicated, it was still, somehow, very simple: I, too, was a Compassionate Sharer. Monster, machine, anproz, the designation didn't matter any longer. Wherever I might go, I was forevermore a ward of this tiny woman's House—my fate, inescapable and sure.

The Wardress broke free of my embrace and kneeled beside the Tropeman. She tore a piece of cloth from the bottom of her tunic. Wiping the blood from the Sharer's face, she said, "I heard him calling me while I was downstairs, Mr. Lorca. Encephalogoi. 'Brain words,' you know. And I came up here as quickly as I could. Cleirach took me aside. All I could do was shout for you. Then, not even that."

Her hands touched the Sharer's burns, hovered over the wounded eye, moved about with a knowledge the Wardress herself seemed unaware of.

"We couldn't get it all the way out," Cleva Orha laughed. "Wouldn't come. Cleirach tried and tried."

I found the cloned woman's pea jacket, leggings, and

tunic. Then I took her by the elbow and led her down the stairs to her brother. She reviled me tenderly as we descended, but otherwise didn't protest.

"You," she predicted once we were down, ". . . you we'll never get."

She was right. It was a long time before I returned to the House of Compassionate Sharers, and, in any case, upon learning of their sadistic abuse of one of the wards of the House, the authorities in Manitou Port denied the Orhas any future access to it. A Sharer, after all, was an expensive commodity.

But I did return. After going back to Diroste and living with Rumer the remaining forty-two years of her life, I applied to the House as a novitiate. I am here now. In fact as well as in metaphor, I am today one of the Sharers.

My brain cells die, of course, and there's nothing anyone can do to stop utterly the depredations of time—but my body seems to be that of a middle-aged man and I still move inside it with ease. Visitants seek comfort from me, as once, against my will, I sought comfort here; and I try to give it to them . . . even to the ones who have only a muddled understanding of what a Sharer really is. My battles aren't really with these unhappy people; they're with the advance columns of my senility (I don't like to admit this) and the shock troops of my memory, which is still excessively good . . .

Wardress Kefa has been dead seventeen years, Diderits twenty-three, and Rumer two. That's how I keep score now. Death has also carried off the gem-eyed Tropeman and the Sharer who drew the essential Dorian Lorca out of the prosthetic rind he had mistaken for himself.

I intend to be here a while longer yet. I have recently been given a chamber into which the light sifts with a painful white brilliance reminiscent of the sands of Diroste or the snows of Wolf Run Summit. This is all to the good. Either way, you see, I die at home . . .

# *The Screwfly Solution*

## Raccoona Sheldon

You're probably more familiar with "Raccoona Sheldon" under her more famous pen-name "James Tiptree, Jr." Actually, as I explained in last year's book, her real name is Alice B. Sheldon, and most everyone in the science-fiction field was stunned (and many delighted) to learn that the author who had written so many excellent stories in a crisp, supposedly "masculine" style is a woman. Under the "Tiptree" name she's published three collections of short stories and most recently a novel, *Up the Walls of the World*—on which she's identified only as "Tiptree," though the dust jacket includes a photo of her, thus no doubt confusing some readers while delighting others who enjoy the shaking-up of preconceptions about masculine and feminine characteristics.

The fact is, of course, that personal data about an author is seldom if ever relevant to our enjoyment of stories; what matters is simply the quality of the stories. "The Screwfly Solution," a tale of a mysterious psychological plague that steadily increases in suspense and delivers a startling explanation at the end, was originally published under the "Raccoona Sheldon" byline and is therefore reprinted here under that name.

The young man sitting at 2° N, 75° W sent a casually venomous glance up at the nonfunctional shoofly *ventilador* and went on reading his letter. He was sweating heavily, stripped to his shorts in the hotbox of what passed for a hotel room in Cuyapán.

How do other wives *do* it? I stay busy-busy with the Ann Arbor grant review programs and the seminar, saying brightly "Oh yes, Alan is in Colombia setting up a biological pest control program, isn't it wonderful?" But inside I imagine you surrounded by nineteen-year-old raven-haired cooing beauties, every one panting with social dedication and filthy rich. And forty inches of bosom busting out of her delicate lingerie. I even figured it in centimeters, that's 101.6 centimeters of busting. Oh, darling, darling, do what you want only *come home safe*.

Alan grinned fondly, briefly imagining the only body he longed for. His girl, his magic Anne. Then he got up to open the window another cautious notch. A long pale mournful face looked in—a goat. The room opened on the goatpen, the stench was vile. Air, anyway. He picked up the letter.

Everything is just about as you left it, except that the Peedsville horror seems to be getting worse. They're calling it the Sons of Adam cult now. Why can't they *do* something, even if it is a religion? The Red Cross has set up a refugee camp in Ashton, Georgia. Imagine, refugees in the U.S.A. I heard two little girls were carried out all slashed up. Oh, Alan.

Which reminds me, Barney came over with a wad of clippings he wants me to send you. I'm putting them in a separate envelope; I know what happens to very fat letters in foreign POs. He says, in case you don't get them, what do the following have in common? Peedsville, Sao Paulo, Phoenix, San Diego, Shanghai, New Delhi, Tripoli, Brisbane, Johannesburg, and Lubbock, Texas. He says the hint is, remember where the Intertropical Convergence Zone is now. That makes no sense to me, maybe it will to your superior ecological brain. All I could see about the clippings was that they were fairly horrible accounts of murders or massacres of women. The worst was the New Delhi one, about "rafts of female corpses" in the river. The funniest (!) was the Texas Army officer who shot his wife, three daughters, and his aunt, because God told him to clean the place up.

Barney's such an old dear, he's coming over Sunday to help me take off the downspout and see what's blocking it. He's dancing on air right now, since you left his spruce bud-worm-moth antipheromone program finally paid off. You know he tested over 2,000 compounds? Well, it seems that good old 2,097 *really* works. When I asked him what it does he just giggles, you know how shy he is with women. Anyway, it seems that a one-shot spray program will save the forests, without harming a single other thing. Birds and people can eat it all day, he says.

Well sweetheart, that's all the news except Amy goes back to Chicago to school Sunday. The place will be a tomb, I'll miss her frightfully in spite of her being at the stage where I'm her worst enemy. The sullen sexy subteens, Angie says. Amy sends love to her Daddy. I send you my whole heart, all that words can't say.

Your Anne

Alan put the letter safely in his notefile and glanced over the rest of the thin packet of mail, refusing to let himself dream of home and Anne. Barney's "fat envelope" wasn't there. He threw himself on the rumpled bed, yanking off the lightcord a minute before the town generator went off for the night. In the darkness the list of places Barney had mentioned spread themselves around a misty globe that turned, troublingly, briefly in his mind. Something . . .

But then the memory of the hideously parasitized children he had worked with at the clinic that day took possession of his thoughts. He set himself to considering the data he must collect. *Look for the vulnerable link in the behavioral chain*—how often Barney—Dr. Barnhard Braithwaite—had pounded it into his skull. Where was it, where? In the morning he would start work on bigger canefly cages . . .

At that moment, five thousand miles North, Anne was writing:

Oh, darling, darling, your first three letters are here, they all came together. I *knew* you were writing. Forget what I said about swarthy heiresses, that was all a joke. My darling, I know, I know . . . us. Those dreadful canefly larvae, those poor little kids. If you weren't my husband I'd think you were a saint or something. (I do anyway.)

I have your letters pinned up all over the house, makes it a lot less lonely. No real news here except things feel kind of quiet and spooky. Barney and I got the downspout out, it was full of a big rotted hoard of squirrel-nuts. They must have been dropping them down the top, I'll put a wire over it. (Don't worry, I'll use a ladder this time.)

Barney's in an odd, grim mood. He's taking this Sons of Adam thing very seriously, it seems he's going to be on the investigation committee if that ever gets off the ground. The weird part is that nobody seems to be doing anything, as if it's just too big. Selina Peters has been printing some acid comments, like When one man kills his wife you call it murder, but when enough do it we call it a lifestyle. I think it's spreading, but nobody knows because the media have been asked to downplay it. Barney says it's being viewed as a form of contagious hysteria. He insisted I send you this ghastly interview. It's *not* going to be published, of course. The quietness is worse, though, it's like something terrible was going on just out of sight. After reading Barney's thing I called up Pauline in San Diego to make sure she was all right. She sounded funny, as if she wasn't saying everything . . . my own sister. Just after she said things were great she suddenly asked if she could come and stay here awhile next month. I said come right away, but she wants to sell her house first. I wish she'd hurry.

Oh, the diesel car is okay now, it just needed its filter changed. I had to go out to Springfield to get one but Eddie installed it for only $2.50. He's going to bankrupt his garage.

In case you didn't guess, those places of Barney's are all about latitude 30° N or S—the horse latitudes. When I said not exactly, he said remember the equatorial convergence zone shifts in winter, and to add in Libya, Osaka, and a place I forget—wait, Alice Springs, Australia. What has this to do with anything, I asked. He said, "Nothing—I hope." I leave it to you, great brains like Barney can be weird.

Oh my dearest, here's all of me to all of you. Your letters make life possible. But don't feel you *have* to, I can tell how tired you must be. Just know we're together, always everywhere.

Your Anne

PS I had to open this to put Barney's thing in, it wasn't the secret police. Here it is. All love again. A.

In the goat-infested room where Alan read this, rain was drumming on the roof. He put the letter to his nose to catch the faint perfume once more, and folded it away. Then he pulled out the yellow flimsy Barney had sent and began to read, frowning.

PEEDSVILLE CULT/SONS OF ADAM SPECIAL. Statement by driver Sgt. Willard Mews, Globe Fork, Ark. We hit the roadblock about 80 miles west of Jacksonville. Major John Heinz of Ashton was expecting us, he gave us an escort of two riot vehicles headed by Capt. T. Parr. Major Heinz appeared shocked to see that the NIH medical team included two women doctors. He warned us in the strongest terms of the danger. So Dr. Patsy Putnam (Urbana, Ill.), the psychologist, decided to stay behind at the Army cordon. But Dr. Elaine Fay (Clinton, N.J.) insisted on going with us, saying she was the episomething (epidemiologist).

We drove behind one of the riot cars at 30 mph for about an hour without seeing anything unusual. There were two big signs saying SONS OF ADAM—LIBERATED ZONE. We passed some small pecan packing plants and a citrus processing plant. The men there looked at us but did not do anything unusual. I didn't see any children or women of course. Just outside Peedsville we stopped at a big barrier made of oil drums in front of a large citrus warehouse. This area is old, sort of a shantytown and trailer park. The new part of town with the shopping center and developments is about a mile further on. A warehouse worker with a shotgun came out and told us to wait for the Mayor. I don't think he saw Dr. Elaine Fay then, she was sitting sort of bent down in back.

Mayor Blount drove up in a police cruiser and our chief, Dr. Premack, explained our mission from the Surgeon General. Dr. Premack was very careful not to make any remarks insulting to the Mayor's religion. Mayor Blount agreed to let the party go on into Peedsville to take samples of the soil and water and so on and talk to the doctor who lives there. The mayor was about 6'2", weight maybe 230 or 240, tanned, with grayish hair. He was smiling and chuckling in a friendly manner.

Then he looked inside the car and saw Dr. Elaine Fay and he blew up. He started yelling we had to all get the hell back. But Dr. Premack talked to him and cooled him down and finally the Mayor said Dr. Fay should go into the warehouse office and stay there with the door closed. I had to stay there too and see she didn't come out, and one of the Mayor's men would drive the party.

So the medical people and the Mayor and one of the riot vehicles went on into Peedsville and I took Dr. Fay back into the warehouse office and sat down. It was real hot and stuffy. Dr. Fay opened a window, but when I heard her trying to talk to an old man outside I told her she couldn't do that and closed the window. The old man went away. Then she wanted to talk to me but I told her I did not feel like conversing. I felt it was real wrong, her being there.

So then she started looking through the office files and reading papers there. I told her that was a bad idea, she shouldn't do that. She said the government expected her to investigate. She showed me a booklet or magazine they had there, it was called *Man Listens to God* by Reverend McIllhenny. They had a cartonful in the office. I started reading it and Dr. Fay said she wanted to wash her hands. So I took her back along a kind of enclosed hallway beside the conveyor to where the toilet was. There were no doors or windows so I went back. After a while she called out that there was a cot back there, she was going to lie down. I figured that was all right because of the no windows, also I was glad to be rid of her company.

When I got to reading the book it was very intriguing. It was very deep thinking about how man is now on trial with

God and if we fulfill our duty God will bless us with a real new life on Earth. The signs and portents show it. It wasn't like, you know, Sunday-school stuff. It was deep.

After a while I heard some music and saw the soldiers from the other riot car were across the street by the gas tanks, sitting in the shade of some trees and kidding with the workers from the plant. One of them was playing a guitar, not electric, just plain. It looked so peaceful.

Then Mayor Blount drove up alone in the cruiser and came in. When he saw I was reading the book he smiled at me sort of fatherly, but he looked tense. He asked me where Dr. Fay was and I told him she was lying down in back. He said that was okay. Then he kind of sighed and went back down the hall, closing the door behind him. I sat and listened to the guitar man, trying to hear what he was singing. I felt really hungry, my lunch was in Dr. Premack's car.

After a while the door opened and Mayor Blount came back in. He looked terrible, his clothes were messed up and he had bloody scrape marks on his face. He didn't say anything, he just looked at me hard and fierce, like he might have been disoriented. I saw his zipper was open and there was blood on his clothing and also on his (private parts).

I didn't feel frightened, I felt something important had happened. I tried to get him to sit down. But he motioned me to follow him back down the hall, to where Dr. Fay was. "You must see," he said. He went into the toilet and I went into a kind of little room there, where the cot was. The light was fairly good, reflected off the tin roof from where the walls stopped. I saw Dr. Fay lying on the cot in a peaceful appearance. She was lying straight, her clothing was to some extent different but her legs were together. I was glad to see that. Her blouse was pulled up and I saw there was a cut or incision on her abdomen. The blood was coming out there, or it had been coming out there, like a mouth. It wasn't moving at this time. Also her throat was cut open.

I returned to the office. Mayor Blount was sitting down, looking very tired. He had cleaned himself off. He said, "I did it for you. Do you understand?"

He seemed like my father, I can't say it better than that. I realized he was under a terrible strain, he had taken a lot on himself for me. He went on to explain how Dr. Fay was very dangerous, she was what they call a cripto-female (crypto?), the most dangerous kind. He had exposed her and purified the situation. He was very straightforward, I didn't feel confused at all, I knew he had done what was right.

We discussed the book, how man must purify himself and show God a clean world. He said some people raise the question of how can man reproduce without women but such people miss the point. The point is that as long as man depends on the old filthy animal way God won't help him. When man gets rid of his animal part which is woman, this is the signal God is awaiting. Then God will reveal the new true clean way, maybe angels will come bringing new souls, or maybe we will live forever, but it is not our place to speculate, only to obey. He said some men here had seen an Angel of the Lord. This was very deep, it seemed like it echoed inside me, I felt it was an inspiration.

Then the medical party drove up and I told Dr. Premack that Dr. Fay had been taken care of and sent away, and I got in the car to drive them out of the Liberated Zone. However four of the six soldiers from the roadblock refused to leave. Capt. Parr tried to argue them out of it but finally agreed they could stay to guard the oil-drum barrier.

I would have liked to stay too the place was so peaceful but they needed me to drive the car. If I had known there would be all this hassle I never would have done them the favor. I am not crazy and I have not done anything wrong and my lawyer will get me out. That is all I have to say.

In Cuyapán the hot afternoon rain had temporarily ceased. As Alan's fingers let go of Sergeant Williard Mews's wretched document he caught sight of pencil-scrawled words in the margin. Barney's spider hand. He squinted.

*"Man's religion and metaphysics are the voices of his glands. Schönweiser, 1878."*

Who the devil Schönweiser was Alan didn't know, but he knew what Barney was conveying. This murderous crackpot religion of McWhosis was a symptom, not a cause. Barney believed something was physically affecting the Peedsville men, generating psychosis, and a local religious demagog had sprung up to "explain" it.

Well, maybe. But, cause or effect, Alan thought only of one thing: eight hundred miles from Peedsville to Ann Arbor. Anne should be safe. She *had* to be.

He threw himself on the lumpy cot, his mind going back exultantly to his work. At the cost of a million bites and cane-cuts he was pretty sure he'd found the weak link in the canefly cycle. The male mass-mating behavior, the comparative scarcity of ovulant females. It would be the screwfly solution all over again with the sexes reversed. Concentrate the pheromone, release sterilized females. Luckily the breeding populations were comparatively isolated. In a couple of seasons they ought to have it. Have to let them go on spraying poison meanwhile, of course; damn pity, it was slaughtering everything and getting in the water, and the caneflies had evolved to immunity anyway. But in a couple of seasons, maybe three, they could drop the canefly populations below reproductive viability. No more tormented human bodies with those stinking larvae in the nasal passages and brain . . . He drifted off for a nap, grinning.

Up north, Anne was biting her lip in shame and pain.

Sweetheart, I shouldn't admit it but your wife is ~~scared~~ a bit jittery. Just female nerves or something, nothing to worry about. Everything is normal up here. It's so eerily normal, nothing in the papers, nothing anywhere except what I hear through Barney and Lillian. But Pauline's phone won't answer out in San Diego; the fifth day some strange man yelled at me and banged the phone down. Maybe she's sold her house—but why wouldn't she call?

Lillian's on some kind of Save-the-Women committee, like we were an endangered species, ha-ha—you know Lillian. It seems the Red Cross has started setting up camps. But she says, after the first rush, only a trickle are coming out of what they call "the affected areas." Not many children, either, even little boys. And they have some air-photos around Lubbock showing what look like mass graves. Oh, Alan . . . so far it seems to be mostly spreading west, but something's happening in St. Louis, they're cut off. So many places seem to have just vanished from the news, I had a nightmare that there isn't a woman left alive down there. And nobody's *doing* anything. They talked about spraying with tranquilizers for a while and then that died out. What could it do? Somebody at the U.N. has proposed a convention on—you won't believe this—*femicide.* It sounds like a deodorant spray.

Excuse me, honey, I seem to be a little hysterical. George Searles came back from Georgia talking about God's Will—Searles the lifelong atheist. Alan, something crazy is happening.

But there aren't any facts. Nothing. The Surgeon General issued a report on the bodies of the Rahway Rip-Breast Team—I guess I didn't tell you about that. Anyway, they could find no pathology. Milton Baines wrote a letter saying in the present state of the art we can't distinguish the brain of a saint from a psychopathic killer, so how could they expect to find what they don't know how to look for?

Well, enough of these jitters. It'll be all over by the time you get back, just history. Everything's fine here, I fixed the car's muffler again. And Amy's coming home for the vacations, *that'll* get my mind off faraway problems.

Oh, something amusing to end with—Angie told me what Barney's enzyme does to the spruce budworm. It seems it blocks the male from turning around after he connects with the female, so he mates with her *head* instead. Like clockwork with a cog missing. There're going to be some pretty puzzled female spruceworms. Now why couldn't Barney tell me that? He really is such a sweet shy old dear. He's given me some stuff to put in, as usual. I didn't read it.

Now don't worry, my darling, everything's fine.

I love you, I love you so.

Always, all ways your Anne

Two weeks later in Cuyapán, when Barney's enclosures slid out of the envelope, Alan didn't read them either. He stuffed them into the pocket of his bush jacket with a shaking hand and started bundling his notes together on the rickety table, with a scrawled note to Sister Dominique on top. The hell with the canefly, the hell with everything except that tremor in his Anne's firm handwriting. The hell with being five thousand miles away from his woman, his child, while some deadly madness raged. He crammed his meager belongings into his duffel. If he hurried he could catch the bus through to Bogotá and maybe make the Miami flight.

He made it, but in Miami he found the planes north jammed. He failed a quick standby; six hours to wait. Time to call Anne. When the call got through some difficulty he was unprepared for the rush of joy and relief that burst along the wires.

"Thank God—I can't believe it—Oh, Alan, my darling, are you really—I can't believe—"

He found he was repeating too, and all mixed up with the canefly data. They were both laughing hysterically when he finally hung up.

Six hours. He settled in a frayed plastic chair opposite Aerolineas Argentinas, his mind half back at the clinic, half on the throngs moving by him. Something was oddly different here, he perceived presently. Where was the decorative fauna he usually enjoyed in Miami, the parade of young girls in crotch-tight pastel jeans? The flounces, boots, wild hats and hairdos, and startling expanses of newly tanned skin, the brilliant fabrics barely confining the bob of breasts and buttocks? Not here—but wait; looking closely, he glimpsed two young faces hidden under unbecoming parkas, their bodies draped in bulky nondescript skirts. In fact, all down the long vista he could see the same thing: hooded ponchos, heaped-on clothes and baggy pants, dull colors. A new style? No, he thought not. It seemed to him their movements suggested furtiveness, timidity. And they moved in groups. He watched a lone girl struggle to catch up with others ahead of her, apparently strangers. They accepted her wordlessly.

They're frightened, he thought. Afraid of attracting notice. Even that gray-haired matron in a pantsuit resolutely leading a flock of kids was glancing around nervously.

And at the Argentine desk opposite he saw another odd thing: two lines had a big sign over them, MUJERES. Women. They were crowded with the shapeless forms, and very quiet.

The men seemed to be behaving normally: hurrying, lounging, griping and joking in the lines as they kicked their luggage along. But Alan felt an undercurrent of tension, like an irritant in the air. Outside the line of storefronts behind him a few isolated men seemed to be handing out tracts. An airport attendant spoke to the nearest man; he merely shrugged and moved a few doors down.

To distract himself Alan picked up a *Miami Herald* from the next seat. It was surprisingly thin. The international news occupied him for a while; he had seen none for weeks. It too had a strange empty quality; even the bad news seemed to have dried up. The African war which had been going on seemed to be over, or went unreported. A trade summit-meeting was haggling over grain and steel prices. He found himself at the obituary pages, columns of close-set type dominated by the photo of a defunct ex-senator. Then his eye fell on two announcements at the bottom of the page. One was too flowery for quick comprehension, but the other stated in bold plain type:

THE FORSETTE FUNERAL HOME REGRETFULLY
ANNOUNCES IT WILL NO LONGER ACCEPT
FEMALE CADAVERS

Slowly he folded the paper, staring at it numbly. On the back was an item headed "Navigational Hazard Warning," in the shipping news. Without really taking it in, he read:

AP/NASSAU. The excursion liner *Carib Swallow* reached port under tow today after striking an obstruction in the

Gulf Stream off Cape Hatteras. The obstruction was identified as part of a commercial trawler's seine floated by female corpses. This confirms reports from Florida and the Gulf of the use of such seines, some of them over a mile in length. Similar reports coming from the Pacific coast and as far away as Japan indicate a growing hazard to coastwise shipping.

Alan flung the thing into the trash receptacle and sat rubbing his forehead and eyes. Thank God he had followed his impulse to come home. He felt totally disoriented, as though he had landed by error on another planet. Four and a half hours more to wait . . . At length he recalled the stuff from Barney he had thrust in his pocket, and pulled it out and smoothed it.

The top item seemed to be from the *Ann Arbor News*. Dr. Lillian Dash, together with several hundred other members of her organization, had been arrested for demonstrating without a permit in front of the White House. They had started a fire in a garbage can, which was considered particularly heinous. A number of women's groups had participated; the total struck Alan as more like thousands than hundreds. Extraordinary security precautions were being taken, despite the fact that the President was out of town at the time.

The next item had to be Barney's acerbic humor.

UP/VATICAN CITY 19 JUNE. Pope John IV today intimated that he does not plan to comment officially on the so-called Pauline Purification cults advocating the elimination of women as a means of justifying man to God. A spokesman emphasized that the Church takes no position on these cults but repudiates any doctrine involving a "challenge" to or from God to reveal His further plans for man.

Cardinal Fazzoli, spokesman for the European Pauline movement, reaffirmed his view that the Scriptures define woman as merely a temporary companion and instrument of Man. Women, he states, are nowhere defined as human, but merely as a transitional expedient or state. "The time of transition to full humanity is at hand," he concluded.

The next item appeared to be a thin-paper Xerox from a recent issue of *Science:*

SUMMARY REPORT OF THE AD HOC
EMERGENCY COMMITTEE ON FEMICIDE

The recent worldwide though localized outbreaks of femicide appear to represent a recurrence of similar outbreaks by groups or sects which are not uncommon in world history in times of psychic stress. In this case the root cause is undoubtedly the speed of social and technological change, augmented by population pressure, and the spread and scope are aggravated by instantaneous world communications, thus exposing more susceptible persons. It is not viewed as a medical or epidemiological problem; no physical pathology has been found. Rather it is more akin to the various manias which swept Europe in the 17th century, e.g., the Dancing Manias, and like them, should run its course and disappear. The chiliastic cults which have sprung up around the affected areas appear to be unrelated, having in common only the idea that a new means of human reproduction will be revealed as a result of the "purifying" elimination of women.

We recommend that (1) inflammatory and sensational reporting be suspended; (2) refugee centers be set up and maintained for women escapees from the focal areas: (3) containment of affected areas by military cordon be continued and enforced; and (4) after a cooling-down period and the subsidence of the mania, qualified mental health teams and appropriate professional personnel go in to undertake rehabilitation.

SUMMARY OF THE MINORITY
REPORT OF THE AD HOC COMMITTEE

The nine members signing this report agree that there is no evidence for epidemiological contagion of femicide in the strict sense. *However*, the geographical relation of the focal areas of outbreak strongly suggest that they cannot be dismissed as purely psychosocial phenomena. The initial outbreaks have occurred around the globe near the 30th parallel, the area of principal atmospheric downflow of upper winds coming from the Intertropical Convergence Zone. An agent or condition in the upper equatorial atmosphere would thus be expected to reach ground level along the 30th parallel, with certain seasonal variations. One principal variation is that the downflow moves north over the East Asian continent during the late winter months, and those areas south of it (Arabia, Western India, parts of North Africa) have in fact been free of outbreaks until recently, when the downflow zone moved south. A similar downflow occurs in the Southern Hemisphere, and outbreaks have been reported along the 30th parallel running through Pretoria and Alice Springs, Australia. (Information from Argentina is currently unavailable.)

This geographical correlation cannot be dismissed, and it is therefore urged that an intensified search for a physical cause be instituted. It is also urgently recommended that the rate of spread from known focal points be correlated with wind conditions. A watch for similar outbreaks along the secondary down-welling zones at 60° north and south should be kept.

(signed for the minority)
Barnhard Braithwaite

Alan grinned reminiscently at his old friend's name, which seemed to restore normalcy and stability to the world. It looked as if Barney was on to something, too, despite the prevalence of horses' asses. He frowned, puzzling it out.

Then his face slowly changed as he thought how it would be, going home to Anne. In a few short hours his arms would be around her, the tall, secretly beautiful body that had come to obsess him. Theirs had been a late-blooming love. They'd married, he supposed now, out of friendship, even out of friends' pressure. Everyone said they were made for each other, he big and chunky and blond, she willowy brunette; both shy, highly controlled, cerebral types. For the first few years the friendship had held, but sex hadn't been all that much. Conventional necessity. Politely reassuring each other, privately—he could say it now—disappointing.

But then, when Amy was a toddler, something had happened. A miraculous inner portal of sensuality had slowly opened to them, a liberation into their own secret unsuspected heaven of fully physical bliss . . . Jesus, but it had been a wrench when the Colombia thing had come up. Only their absolute sureness of each other had made him take it. And now, to be about to have her again, trebly desirable from the spice of separation —feeling-seeing-hearing-smelling-grasping. He shifted in his seat to conceal his body's excitement, half mesmerized by fantasy.

And Amy would be there, too; he grinned at the memory of that prepubescent little body plastered against him. She was going to be a handful, all right. His manhood understood Amy a lot better than her mother did; no cerebral phase for Amy . . . But Anne, his exquisite shy one, with whom he'd found the way into the almost unendurable transports of the flesh . . . First the conventional greeting, he thought: the news, the unspoken, savored, mounting excitement behind their eyes; the light touches; then the seeking of their own room, the falling clothes, the caresses, gentle at first—the flesh, the *nakedness*—the delicate teasing, the grasp, the first thrust—

—A terrible alarm-bell went off in his head. Exploded from his dream, he stared around, then finally down at his hands. *What was he doing with his open clasp-knife in his fist?*

Stunned, he felt for the last shreds of his fantasy, and realized that the tactile images had not been of caresses, but of a frail neck strangling in his fist, the thrust had been the plunge of a blade seeking vitals. In his arms, legs, phantasms of striking and trampling bones cracking. And Amy—

Oh God. Oh God—

Not sex, bloodlust.

That was what he had been dreaming. The sex was there, but it was driving some engine of death.

Numbly he put the knife away, thinking only over

and over, It's got me. It's got me. Whatever it is, it's got me. *I can't go home.*

After an unknown time he got up and made his way to the United counter to turn in his ticket. The line was long. As he waited, his mind cleared a little. What could he do, here in Miami? Wouldn't it be better to get back to Ann Arbor and turn himself in to Barney? Barney could help him, if anyone could. Yes, that was best. But first he had to warn Anne.

The connection took even longer this time. When Anne finally answered he found himself blurting unintelligibly; it took awhile to make her understand he wasn't talking about a plane delay.

"I tell you, I've caught it. Listen, Anne, for God's sake. If I should come to the house don't let me come near you. I mean it. I mean it. I'm going to the lab, but I might lose control and try to get to you. Is Barney there?"

"Yes, but, darling—"

"Listen. Maybe he can fix me, maybe this'll wear off. But I'm not safe, Anne, Anne, I'd kill you, can you understand? Get a—get a weapon. I'll try not to come to the house. But if I do, don't let me get near you. Or Amy. It's a sickness, it's real. Treat me—treat me like a fucking wild animal. Anne, say you understand, say you'll do it."

They were both crying when he hung up.

He went shaking back to sit and wait. After a time his head seemed to clear a little more. *Doctor, try to think.* The first thing he thought of was to take the loathsome knife and throw it down a trash slot. As he did so he realized there was one more piece of Barney's material in his pocket. He uncrumpled it; it seemed to be a clipping from *Nature.*

At the top was Barney's scrawl: "Only guy making sense. U.K. infected now. Oslo, Copenhagen out of communication. Damfools still won't listen. Stay put."

COMMUNICATION FROM PROFESSOR MACINTYRE, GLASGOW UNIV.

A potential difficulty for our species has always been implicit in the close linkage between the behavioural expression of aggression/predation and sexual reproduction in the male. This close linkage involves (a) many neuromuscular pathways which are utilized both in predatory and sexual pursuit: grasping, mounting, etc., and (b) similar states of adrenergic arousal which are activated in both. The same linkage is seen in the males of many other species; in some, the expression of aggression and copulation alternate or even coexist, an all-too-familiar example being the common house cat. Males of many species bite, claw, bruise, tread, or otherwise assault receptive females during the act of intercourse; indeed, in some species the male attack is necessary for female ovulation to occur.

In many if not all species it is the aggressive behaviour which appears first, and then changes to copulatory behaviour when the appropriate signal is presented (*e.g.*, the three-tined stickleback and the European robin). Lacking the inhibiting signal, the male's fighting response continues and the female is attacked or driven off.

It seems therefore appropriate to speculate that the present crisis might be caused by some substance, perhaps at the viral or enzymatic level, which effects a failure of the switching or triggering function in the higher primates. (Note: Zoo gorillas and chimpanzees have recently been observed to attack or destroy their mates; rhesus not.) Such a dysfunction could be expressed by the failure of mating behaviour to modify or supervene over the aggressive/predatory response; *i.e.*, sexual stimulation would produce attack only, the stimulation discharging itself through the destruction of the stimulating object.

In this connection it might be noted that exactly this condition is a commonplace of male functional pathology, in those cases where murder occurs as a response to and apparent completion of sexual desire.

It should be emphasized that the aggression/copulation linkage discussed here is specific to the male; the female response (*e.g.*, lordotic reflex) being of a different nature.

Alan sat holding the crumpled sheet a long time; the dry, stilted Scottish phrases seemed to help clear his head, despite the sense of brooding tension all around him. Well, if pollution or whatever had produced some substance, it could presumably be countered, filtered, neutralized. Very very carefully, he let himself consider his life with Anne, his sexuality. Yes: Much of their loveplay could be viewed as genitalized, sexually gentled savagery. Play-predation . . . He turned his mind quickly away. Some writer's phrase occurred to him: "The panic element in all sex." Who? Fritz Leiber? The violation of social distance, maybe; another threatening element. Whatever, it's our weak link, he thought. Our vulnerability . . . The dreadful feeling of *rightness* he had experienced when he found himself knife in hand, fantasizing violence, came back to him. As though it was the right, the only way. Was that what Barney's budworms felt when they mated with their females wrong-end-to?

At long length, he became aware of body need and sought a toilet. The place was empty, except for what he took to be a heap of clothes blocking the door of the far stall. Then he saw the red-brown pool in which it lay, and the bluish mounds of bare, thin buttocks. He backed out, not breathing, and fled into the nearest crowd, knowing he was not the first to have done so.

Of course. Any sexual drive. Boys, men, too.

At the next washroom he watched to see men enter and leave normally before he ventured in.

Afterward he returned to sit, waiting, repeating over and over to himself: *Go to the lab. Don't go home. Go straight to the lab.* Three more hours; he sat numbly at 26°N, 81°W, breathing, breathing . . .

* * *

Dear diary. Big scene tonite. Daddy came home!!! Only he acted so funny, he had the taxi wait and just held on to the doorway, he wouldn't touch me or let us come near him. (I mean funny weird, not funny Ha-ha.) He said, I have something to tell you, this is getting worse not better. I'm going to sleep in the lab but I want you to get out. Anne, Anne, I can't trust myself anymore. First thing in the morning you both get on the plane for Martha's and stay there. So I thought he had to be joking, I mean with the dance next week and Aunt Martha lives in Whitehorse where there's nothing nothing nothing. So I was yelling and Mother was yelling and Daddy was groaning, Go now! And then he started crying. Crying!!! So I realized, wow, this is serious, and I started to go over to him but Mother yanked me back and then I saw she had this big KNIFE!!! And she shoved me in back of her and started crying too Oh Alan, Oh Alan, like she was insane. So I said, Daddy, I'll never leave you, it felt like the perfect thing to say. And it was thrilling, he looked at me real sad and deep like I was a grown-up while Mother was treating me like I was a mere infant as usual. But Mother ruined it raving Alan the child is mad, darling go. So he ran out the door yelling Be gone, Take the car, Get out before I come back.

Oh I forgot to say I was wearing what but my gooby green with my curltites still on, wouldn't you know of all the shitty luck, how could I have known such a beautiful scene was ahead we never know life's cruel whimsy. And mother is dragging out suitcases yelling Pack your things hurry! So she's going I guess but I am not repeat not going to spend the fall sitting in Aunt Martha's grain silo and lose the dance and all my summer credits. And Daddy was trying to *communicate* with us, right? I think their relationship is obsolete. So when she goes upstairs I am splitting, I am going to go over to the lab and see Daddy.

Oh PS Diane tore my yellow jeans she promised me I could use her pink ones Ha-ha that'll be the day.

* * *

. . . I ripped that page out of Amy's diary when I heard the squad car coming. I never opened her diary before but when I found she'd gone I looked . . . Oh, my darling girl. She went to him, my little girl, my poor little fool child. Maybe if I'd taken time to explain, maybe—

Excuse me, Barney. The stuff is wearing off, the shots they gave me. I didn't feel anything. I mean, I knew somebody's daughter went to see her father and he killed her. And cut his throat. But it didn't mean anything.

Alan's note, they gave me that but then they took it away. Why did they have to do that? His last handwriting, the last words he wrote before his hand picked up the, before he—

I remember it. *"Sudden and light as that, the bonds gave And we learned of finalities besides the grave. The bonds of our humanity have broken, we are finished. I love—"*

I'm all right, Barney, really. Who wrote that, Robert Frost? *The bonds gave* . . . Oh, he said, tell Barney: *The terrible rightness*. What does that mean?

You can't answer that, Barney dear. I'm just writing this to stay sane, I'll put it in your hidey-hole. Thank you, thank you, Barney dear. Even as blurry as I was, I knew it was you. All the time you were cutting off my hair and rubbing dirt on my face, I knew it was right because it was you. Barney, I never thought of you as those horrible words you said. You were always Dear Barney.

By the time the stuff wore off I had done everything you said, the gas, the groceries. Now I'm here in your cabin. With those clothes you made me put on I guess I do look like a boy, the gas man called me "Mister."

I still can't really realize, I have to stop myself from rushing back. But you saved my life, I know that. The first trip in I got a paper, I saw where they bombed the Apostle Islands refuge. And it had about those three women stealing the Air Force plane and bombing Dallas, too. Of course they shot them down over the Gulf. Isn't it strange how we do nothing? Just get killed by ones and twos. Or more, now they've started on the refuges . . . Like hypnotized rabbits. We're a toothless race.

Do you know I never said "we" meaning women before? "We" was always me and Alan, and Amy of course. Being killed selectively encourages group identification . . . You see how sane-headed I am.

But I still can't really realize.

My first trip in was for salt and kerosene. I went to that little Red Deer store and got my stuff from the old man in the back, as you told me—you see, I remembered! He called me "Boy," but I think maybe he suspects. He knows I'm staying at your cabin.

Anyway, some men and boys came in the front. They were all so *normal*, laughing and kidding. I just couldn't believe, Barney. In fact I started to go out past them when I heard one of them say "Heinz saw an angel." An *angel*. So I stopped and listened. They said it was big and sparkly. Coming to see if man is carrying out God's will, one of them said. And he said, Moosenee is now a liberated zone, and all up by Hudson Bay. I turned and got out the back, fast. The old man had heard them too. He said to me quietly, "I'll miss the kids."

Hudson Bay, Barney, that means it's coming from the north too, doesn't it? That must be about 60°.

But I have to go back once again, to get some fishhooks. I can't live on bread. Last week I found a deer some poacher had killed, just the head and legs. I made a stew. It was a doe. Her eyes; I wonder if mine look like that now.

* * *

. . . I went to get the fishhooks today. It was bad, I can't ever go back. There were some men in front again, but they were different. Mean and tense. No boys. And there was a new sign out in front, I couldn't see it; maybe it says Liberated Zone too.

The old man gave me the hooks quick and whispered to me, "Boy, them woods'll be full of hunters next week." I almost ran out.

About a mile down the road a blue pickup started to chase me. I guess he wasn't from around there, I ran the VW into a logging draw and he roared on by. After a long while I drove out and came on back, but I left the car about a mile from here and hiked in. It's surprising how hard it is to pile enough brush to hide a yellow VW.

Barney, I can't stay here. I'm eating perch raw so nobody will see my smoke, but those hunters will be coming through. I'm going to move my sleeping bag out to the swamp by that big rock, I don't think many people go there.

. . . Since the last lines I moved out. It feels safer. Oh, Barney, how did this *happen?*

Fast, that's how. Six months ago I was Dr. Anne Alstein. Now I'm a widow and bereaved mother, dirty and hungry, squatting in a swamp in mortal fear. Funny if I'm the last woman left alive on Earth. I guess the last one around here, anyway. Maybe some holed out in the Himalayas, or sneaking through the wreck of New York City. How can we last?

We can't.

And I can't survive the winter here, Barney. It gets to 40° below. I'd have to have a fire, they'd see the smoke. Even if I worked my way south, the woods end in a couple hundred miles. I'd be potted like a duck. No. No use. Maybe somebody is trying something somewhere, but it won't reach here in time . . . and what do I have to live for?

No. I'll just make a good end, say up on that rock where I can see the stars. After I go back and leave this for you. I'll wait to see the beautiful color in the trees one last time.

I know what I'll scratch for an epitaph.

HERE LIES THE SECOND MEANEST
PRIMATE ON EARTH

Good-bye, dearest dearest Barney.

* * *

I guess nobody will ever read this, unless I get the nerve and energy to take it back to Barney's. Probably I won't. Leave it in a Baggie, I have one here; maybe Barney will come and look. I'm up on the big rock now.

The moon is going to rise soon, I'll do it then. Mosquitoes, be patient. You'll have all you want.

The thing I have to write down is that I saw an angel too. This morning. It was big and sparkly, like the man said; like a Christmas tree without the tree. But I knew it was real because the frogs stopped croaking and two bluejays gave alarm calls. That's important; it was *really there.*

I watched it, sitting under my rock. It didn't move much. It sort of bent over and picked up something, leaves or twigs, I couldn't see. Then it did something with them around its middle, like putting them into an invisible sample-pocket.

Let me repeat—it was *there.* Barney, if you're reading this, THERE ARE THINGS HERE. And I think they've done whatever it is to us. Made us kill ourselves off.

Why! Well, it's a nice place, if it wasn't for people. How do you get rid of people? Bombs, death-rays—all very primitive. Leave a big mess. Destroy everything, craters, radioactivity, ruin the place.

This way there's no muss, no fuss. Just like what we did to the screwfly. Pinpoint the weak link, wait a bit while we do it for them. Only a few bones around; make good fertilizer.

Barney dear, good-bye. I saw it. It was there.

But it wasn't an angel.

*I think I saw a real-estate agent.*

# Aztecs

Vonda N. McIntyre

Outside the field of science fiction, "romantic" stories characteristically tell of the joys and problems of human love, whereas in sf the great romantic dream has traditionally been to experience the wonders of new planets, new worlds. Here Vonda McIntyre, who was trained as a geneticist, employs her knowledge of science as well as of people to tell of a woman caught between those two dreams . . . but, though "Aztecs" could be called a romantic story and is certainly moving, it's basically a thoughtful exploration of the psychology of human wants and/or needs.

Vonda N. McIntyre won a Nebula Award in 1973 for her novelette "Of Mist, and Grass, and Sand," and has since published two novels, the second of which, *Dreamsnake*, is an extension of that earlier story.

---

She gave up her heart quite willingly.

After the operation, Laenea Trevelyan lived through what seemed an immense time of semiconsciousness, drugged so she would not feel the pain, kept almost insensible while her healing began. Those who watched her did not know she would have preferred consciousness and an end to her uncertainty. So she slept, shallowly, drifting toward awareness, driven back, existing in a world of nightmare. Her dulled mind suspected danger but could do nothing to protect her. She had been forced too often to sleep through danger. She would have preferred the pain.

Once Laenea almost woke: She glimpsed the sterile white walls and ceiling, blurrily, slowly recognizing what she saw. The green glow of monitoring screens flowed across her shoulder, over the scratchy sheets. Taped down, needles scraped nerves in her arm. She became aware of sounds, and heard the rhythmic thud of a beating heart.

She tried to cry out in anger and despair. Her left hand was heavy, lethargic, insensitive to her commands, but she moved it. It crawled like a spider to her right wrist and fumbled at the needles and tubes.

Air shushed from the room as the door opened. A gentle voice and a gentle touch reproved her, increased the flow of sedative, and cruelly returned her to sleep.

A tear slid back from the corner of her eye and trickled into her hair as she reentered her nightmares, accompanied by the counterpoint of a basic human rhythm, the beating of a heart, that she had hoped never to hear again.

Pastel light was Laenea's first assurance that she would live. It gave her no comfort. Intensive Care was stark white, astringent in odor, but yellows and greens brightened this private room. The sedative wore off and she knew she would finally be allowed to wake. She did not fight the continuing drowsiness, but depression prevented anticipation of the return of her senses. She wanted only to live within her own mind, ignoring her body, ignoring failure. She did not even know what she would do in the future; perhaps she had none anymore.

Yet the world impinged on her as she grew bored with lying still and sweaty and self-pitying. She had never been able to do simply *nothing*. Stubbornly she kept her eyes closed, but she could not avoid the sounds, the vibrations, for they went through her body in waves, like shudders of cold and fear.

*This was my chance,* she thought. *But I knew I might fail. It could have been worse, or better: I might have died.*

She slid her hand up her body, from her stomach to her ribs, across the adhesive tape and bandages and the tip of the new scar between her breasts, to her throat. Her fingers rested at the corner of her jaw, just above the carotid artery.

She could not feel a pulse.

Pushing herself up abruptly, Laenea ignored a sharp twinge of pain. The vibration of a heartbeat continued beneath her palms, but now she could tell that it did not come from her own body.

The amplifier sat on the bedside table, sending out low-frequency thuddings in a steady pattern. Laenea felt laughter bubbling up; she knew it would hurt and she did not care. She lifted the speaker: such a small thing, to cause her so much worry. Its cord ripped from the wall as she flung it across the room, and it smashed in the corner with a satisfying clatter.

She threw aside the stiff starched sheets; she rose, staggered, caught herself. Her breathing was coarse from fluid in her lungs. She coughed, caught her breath, coughed again. Time was a mystery, measured only by weakness: She thought the doctors fools, to force sleep into her, risk her to pneumonia, and play recorded hearts, instead of letting her wake and move and adjust to her new condition.

The tile pressed cool against her bare feet. Laenea walked slowly to a warm patch of sunshine, yellow on the butter-cream floor, and gazed out the window. The day was variegated, gray and golden. Clouds moved from the west across the mountains and the Sound while sunlight still spilled over the city. The shadows moved along the water, turning it from shattered silver to slate.

White from the heavy winter snowfall, the Olympic mountains lay between Laenea and the port. The approaching rain hid even the trails of spacecraft escaping Earth, and the bright glints of shuttles returning to their target in the sea. But she would see them soon. She laughed aloud, stretching against the soreness in her chest and the ache of her ribs, throwing back her tangled wavy hair. It tickled the back of her neck, her spine, in the gap between the hospital gown's ties.

Air moved past her as the door opened, as though the room were breathing. Laenea turned and faced the surgeon, a tiny, frail-looking woman with strength like steel wires. The doctor glanced at the shattered amplifier and shook her head.

"Was that necessary?"

"Yes," Laenea said. "For my peace of mind."

"It was here for your peace of mind."

"It has the opposite effect."

"I'll mention that in my report," the surgeon said. "They did it for the first pilots."

"The administrators are known for continuing bad advice."

The doctor laughed. "Well, Pilot, soon you can design your own environment."

"When?"

"Soon. I don't mean to be obscure—I only decide if you can leave the hospital, not if you may. The scar tissue needs time to strengthen. Do you want to go already? I cracked your ribs rather thoroughly."

Laenea grinned. "I know." She was strapped up tight and straight, but she could feel each juncture of rib end and cartilage.

"It will be a few days at least."

"How long has it been?"

"We kept you asleep almost three days."

"It seemed like weeks."

"Well . . . adjusting to all the changes at once could put you in shock."

"I'm an experiment," Laenea said. "All of us are. With experiments, you should experiment."

"Perhaps. But we would prefer to keep you with us." Her hair was short and iron-gray, but when she smiled her face was that of a child. She had long, strong fingers, muscles and tendons sharply defined, nails pared short, good hands for doing any job. Laenea reached out, and they touched each other's wrists, quite gently.

"When I heard the heartbeat," Laenea said, "I thought you'd had to put me back to normal."

"It's meant to be a comforting sound."

"No one else ever complained?"

"Not quite so . . . strongly."

They would have been friends, if they had had time. But Laenea was impatient to progress, as she had been since her first transit, in which life passed without her awareness. "When can I leave?" The hospital was one more place of stasis that she was anxious to escape.

"For now go back to bed. The morning's soon enough to talk about the future."

Laenea turned away without answering. The windows, the walls, the filtered air cut her off from the gray clouds and the city. Rain slipped down the glass. She did not want to sleep anymore.

"Pilot—"

Laenea did not answer.

The doctor sighed. "Do something for me, Pilot."

Laenea shrugged.

"I want you to test your control."

Laenea acquiesced with sullen silence.

"Speed your heart up slowly, and pay attention to the results."

Laenea intensified the firing of the nerve.

"What do you feel?"

"Nothing," Laenea said, though the blood rushed through what had been her pulse points: temples, throat, wrists.

Beside her the surgeon frowned. "Increase a little more, but very slowly."

Laenea obeyed, responding to the abundant supply of oxygen to her brain. Bright lights flashed just behind her vision. Her head hurt in a streak above her right eye to the back of her skull. She felt high and excited. She turned away from the window. "Can't I leave now?"

The surgeon touched her arm at the wrist; Laenea almost laughed aloud at the idea of feeling for *her* pulse. The doctor led her to a chair by the window. "Sit down, Pilot." But Laenea felt she could climb the helix of her dizziness: She felt no need for rest.

"Sit down." The voice was whispery, soft sand slipping across stone. Laenea obeyed.

"Remember the rest of your training, Pilot. Sit back. Relax. Slow the pump. Expand the capillaries. Relax."

Laenea called back her biocontrol. For the first time she was conscious of a presence rather than an absence. Her pulse was gone, but in its place she felt the constant quiet hum of a perfectly balanced rotary machine. It pushed her blood through her body so efficiently that the pressure would destroy her, if she let it. She relaxed and slowed the pump, expanded and contracted the tiny arterial muscles, once, twice, again. The headache, the light flashes, the ringing in her ears faded and ceased. She took a deep breath and let it out slowly.

"That's better," the surgeon said. "Don't forget how that feels. You can't go at high speed very long, you'll turn your brain to cheese. You can feel fine for quite a while, you can feel intoxicated. But the hangover is more than I'd care to reckon with." She patted Laenea's hand. "We want to keep you here till we're sure you can regulate the machine. I don't like doing kidney transplants."

Laenea smiled. "I can control it." She began to induce a slow, arrhythmic change in the speed of the new pump, in her blood pressure. She found she could do it without thinking, as was necessary to balance the flow. "Can I have the ashes of my heart?"

"Not just yet. Let's be sure, first."

"I'm sure." Somewhere in the winding concrete labyrinth of the hospital, her heart still beat, bathed in warm saline and nutrient solution. As long as it existed, as long as it lived, Laenea would feel threatened in her ambitions. She could not be a pilot and remain a normal human being, with normal human rhythms. Her body still could reject the artificial heart; then she would be made normal again. If she could work at all she would have to remain a crew member, anesthetized and unaware from one end of every journey to the other. She did not think she could stand that any longer. "I'm sure. I won't be back."

Tests and questions and examinations devoured several days in chunks and nibbles. Though she felt strong enough to walk, Laenea was pushed through the halls in a wheelchair. The boredom grew more and more wearing. The pains had faded, and Laenea saw only doctors and attendants and machines: Her friends would not come. This was a rite of passage she must survive alone and without guidance.

A day passed in which she did not even see the rain that passed, nor the sunset that was obscured by fog. She asked again when she could leave the hospital, but no one would answer. She allowed herself to become angry, but no one would respond.

Evening, back in her room: Laenea was wide awake. She lay in bed and slid her fingers across her collarbone to the sternum, along the shiny-red line of the tremendous scar. It was still tender, covered with translucent synthetic skin, crossed over just below her breasts with a wide band of adhesive tape to ease her cracked ribs.

The efficient new heart intrigued her. She forced herself consciously to slow its pace, then went through the exercise of constricting and dilating arteries and capillaries. Her biocontrol was excellent. It had to be, or she would not have been passed for surgery.

Slowing the pump should have produced a pleasant lethargy and eventual sleep, but adrenalin from her anger lingered and she did not want to rest. Nor did she want a sleeping pill: She would take no more drugs. Dreamless drug-sleep was the worst kind of all. Fear built up, undischarged by fantasy, producing a great and formless tension.

The twilight was the texture of gray watered silk, opaque and irregular. The hospital's pastels turned cold and mysterious. Laenea threw off the sheet. She was strong again; she was healed. She had undergone months of training, major surgery, and these final capping days of boredom to free herself completely from biological rhythms. There was no reason in the world why she should sleep, like others, when darkness fell.

A civilized hospital: Her clothes were in the closet, not squirrelled away in some locked room. She put on black pants, soft leather boots, and a shiny leather vest that laced up the front, leaving her arms and neck bare. The sharp tip of the scar was revealed at her throat and between the laces.

To avoid arguments, she waited until the corridor was deserted. Green paint, meant to be soothing, had gone flat and ugly with age. Her boots were silent on the resilient tile, but in the hollow shaft of the fire stairs the heels clattered against concrete, echoing past her and back. Her legs were tired when she reached bottom. She speeded the flow of blood.

Outside, mist obscured the stars. The moon, just risen, was full and haloed. In the hospital's traffic eddy, streetlights spread Laenea's shadow out around her like the spokes of a wheel.

A rank of electric cars waited at the corner, tethered like horses in an old movie. She slid her credit key into a lock to release one painted like a turtle, an apt analogy. She got in and drove it toward the waterfront. The little beast rolled slowly along, its motor humming quietly on the flat, straining slightly in low gear on the steep downgrades. Laenea relaxed in the bucket seat and wished she were in a starship, but her imagination would not stretch quite that far. The control stick of a turtle could not become an information-and-control wall; and the city, while pleasant, was of unrelieved ordinariness compared to the places she had seen. She could not, of course, imagine transit, for it was beyond imagination. Language or mind was insufficient. Transit had never been described.

The waterfront was shabby, dirty, magnetic. Laenea knew she could find acquaintances nearby, but she did not want to stay in the city. She returned the turtle to a stanchion and retrieved her credit key to halt the tally against her account.

The night had grown cold; she noticed the change peripherally in the form of fog and condensation-slick cobblestones. The public market, ramshackle and shored up, littered here and there with wilted vegetables, was deserted. People passed as shadows.

A man moved up behind her while she was in the dim region between two streetlamps. "Hey," he said, "how about—" His tone was belligerent with inexperience or insecurity or fear. Looking down at him, surprised, Laenea laughed. "Poor fool—" He scuttled away like a crab. After a moment of vague pity and amusement, Laenea forgot him. She shivered. Her ears were ringing, and her chest ached from the cold.

Small shops nestled between bars and cheap restaurants. Laenea entered one for the warmth. It was very dim, darker than the street, high-ceilinged and deep, so narrow she could have touched both side walls by stretching out her arms. She did not. She hunched her shoulders, and the ache receded slightly.

"May I help you?"

Like one of the indistinct masses in the back of the shop brought to life, a small ancient man appeared. He was dressed in shabby ill-matched clothes, part of his own wares: Laenea was in a pawnshop or secondhand-clothing store. Hung up like trophies, feathers and wide hats and beads covered the walls. Laenea moved farther inside.

"Ah, Pilot," the old man said, "you honor me."

Laenea's delight was childish in its intensity. Only the surgeon has called her "Pilot"; to the others in the hospital she had been merely another patient, more troublesome than most.

"It's cold by the water," she said. Some graciousness or apology was due, for she had no intention of buying anything.

"A coat? No, a cloak!" he exclaimed. "A cloak would be set off well by a person of your stature." He turned; his dark form disappeared among the piles and racks of clothes. Laenea saw bright beads and spangles, a quick flash of gold lamé, and wondered uncharitably what dreadful theater costume he would choose. But the garment the small man drew out was dark. He held it up: a long swath of black, lined with scarlet. Laenea had planned to thank him and demur; despite herself she reached out. Velvet-silk outside and smooth satin-silk within caressed her fingers. The cloak had one shoulder cape and a clasp of carved jet. Though heavy, it draped easily and gracefully. She slung it over her shoulders, and it flowed around her almost to her ankles.

"Exquisite," the shopkeeper said. He beckoned, and she approached: A dim and pitted full-length mirror stood against the wall beyond him. Bronze patches marred its irregular silver face where the backing had peeled away. Laenea liked the way the cape looked. She folded its edges so the scarlet lining showed, so her throat and the upper curve of her breasts and the tip of the scar were exposed. She shook back her hair.

"Not quite exquisite," she said, smiling. She was too tall and big-boned for that kind of delicacy. She had a widow's peak and high cheekbones, but her jaw was strong and square. Her face laughed well but would not do for coyness.

"It does not please you." He sounded downcast. Laenea could not quite place his faint accent.

"It does," she said. "I'll take it."

He bowed her toward the front of the shop, and she took out her credit key.

"No, no, Pilot," he said. "Not that."

Laenea raised one eyebrow. A few shops on the waterfront accepted only cash, retaining an illicit flavor in a time when almost any activity was legal. But few even of those select establishments would refuse the credit of a crew member or a pilot. "I have no cash," Laenea said. She had not carried any for years, since once finding in various pockets three coins of metal, one of plastic, one of wood, a pleasingly atavistic animal claw (or excellent duplicate), and a boxed bit of organic matter that would have been forbidden on Earth fifty years before. Laenea never expected to revisit at least three of the worlds the currency represented.

"Not cash," he said. "It is yours, Pilot. Only—" He glanced up; he looked her in the eyes for the first time. His eyes were very dark and deep, hopeful, expectant. "Only tell me, what is it like? What do you see?"

She pulled back, surprised. She knew people asked the question often. She had asked it herself, wordlessly after the first few times of silence and patient head-shakings. Pilots never answered. Machines could not answer, pilots could not answer. Or would not. The question was answerable only individually. Laenea felt sorry for the shopkeeper and started to say she had not yet been in transit awake, that she was new, that she had only traveled in the crew, drugged near death to stay alive. But, finally, she could not even say that. It was too easy; it would very nearly be a betrayal. It was an untrue truth. It implied she would tell him if she knew, while she did not know if she could or would. She shook her head, she smiled as gently as she could. "I'm sorry."

He nodded sadly. "I should not have asked . . ."

"That's all right."

"I'm too old, you see. Too old for adventure. I came here so long ago . . . but the time, the time disappeared. I never knew what happened. I've dreamed about it. Bad dreams . . ."

"I understand. I was crew for ten years. We never knew what happened either."

"That would be worse, yes. Over and over again, no time between. But now you know."

"Pilots know," Laenea agreed. She handed him the credit key. Though he still tried to refuse it, she insisted on paying.

Hugging the cloak around her, Laenea stepped out into the fog. She fantasized that the shop would now disappear, like all legendary shops dispensing magic and cloaks of invisibility. But she did not look back, for everything a few paces away dissolved into grayness. In a small space around each low streetlamp, heat swirled the fog in wisps toward the sky.

The midnight ferry chuttered across the water, riding the waves on its loud cushion of air. Wrapped in her cloak, Laenea was anonymous. After the island stops, she was the only foot passenger left. With the food counters closed, the drivers on the vehicle deck remained in their trucks, napping or drinking coffee from thermoses. Laenea put her feet on the opposite bench, stretched, and gazed out the window into the darkness. Light from the ferry wavered across the tops of long low swells. Laenea could see both the water and her own reflection, very pale. After a while, she dozed.

The spaceport was a huge, floating, artificial island, anchored far from shore. It gleamed in its own lights. The parabolic solar mirrors looked like the multiple compound eyes of a gigantic water insect. Except for the mirrors and the launching towers, the port's surface was nearly flat, few of its components rising more than a story or two. Tall structures would present saillike faces to the northwest storms.

Beneath the platform, under a vibration-deadening lower layer, under the sea, lay the tripartite city. The roar of shuttles taking off and the scream of their return would drive mad anyone who remained on the surface. Thus the northwest spaceport was far out to sea, away from cities, yet a city in itself, self-protected within the underwater stabilizing shafts.

The ferry climbed a low ramp out of the water and settled onto the loading platform. The hum of electric trucks replaced the growl of huge fans. Laenea moved stiffly down the stairs. She was too tall to sleep comfortably on two-seat benches. Stopping for a moment by the gangway, watching the trucks roll past, she concentrated for a moment and felt the increase in her blood pressure. She could well understand how dangerous it might be, and how easily addictive the higher speed could become, driving her high until like a machine her body w[illegible] for now her energy began returning and th[illegible] in her legs and back slowly seeped away.

Except for the trucks, which purred off quickly around the island's perimeters and disappeared, the port was silent so late at night. The passenger shuttle waited empty on its central rail. When Laenea entered, it sensed her, slid its doors shut, and accelerated. A push-button command halted it above Stabilizer Three, which held quarantine, administration, and crew quarters. Laenea was feeling good, warm, and her vision was sparkling bright and clear. She let the velvet cloak flow back across her shoulders, no longer needing its protection. She was alight with the expectation of seeing her friends, in her new avatar.

The elevator led through the center of the stabilizer into the underwater city. Laenea rode it all the way to the bottom of the shaft, one of three that projected into the ocean far below the surface turbulence to hold the platform steady even through the most violent storms. The shafts maintained the island's flotation level as well, pumping sea water in or out of the ballast tanks when a shuttle took off or landed or a ferry crept on board.

The elevator doors opened into the foyer where a spiral staircase reached the lowest level, a bubble at the tip of the main shaft. The lounge was a comfortable cylindrical room, its walls all transparent, gazing out like a continuous eye into the deep sea. Floodlights cast a glow through the cold clear water, picking out the bright speedy forms of fish, large dark predators, scythe-mouthed sharks, the occasional graceful bow of a porpoise, the elegant black-and-white presence of a killer whale. As the radius of visibility increased, the light filtered through bluer and bluer, until finally, in violet, vague shapes eased back and forth with shy curiosity between dim illumination and complete darkness. The lounge, sculpted with plastic foam and carpeted, gave the illusion of being underwater, on the ocean floor itself, a part of the sea. It had not been built originally as a lounge for crew alone, but was taken over by unconscious agreement among the starship people. Outsiders were not rejected, but gently ignored. Feeling unwelcome, they soon departed. Journalists came infrequently, reacting to sensation or disaster. Human pilots had been a sensation, but Laenea was in the second pilot group; the novelty had worn away. She did not mind a bit.

Laenea took off her boots and left them by the stairwell. She recognized one of the other pair: She would have been hard put not to recognize those boots after seeing them once. The scarlet leather was stupendously shined, embroidered with jewels, and inlaid with tiny liquid-crystal-filled discs that changed color with the temperature. Laenea smiled. Crew members made up for the dead time of transit in many different ways; one was to overdo all other aspects of their lives, and the most flamboyant of that group was Minoru.

Walking barefoot in the deep carpet, between the hillocks and hollows of conversation pits, was like walking on the sea floor idealized. Laenea thought that the attraction of the lounge was its relation to the mystery of the sea, for the sea still held mysteries perhaps as deep as any she would encounter in space or in transit. No one but the pilots could even guess at the truth of her assumption, but Laenea had often sat gazing through the shadowed water, dreaming. Soon she too would know; she would not have to imagine any longer.

She moved between small groups of people half hidden in the recesses of the conversation pits. Near the transparent sea wall she saw Minoru, his black hair braided with scarlet and silver to his waist; tall Alannai hunched down to be closer to the others, the light on her skin like dark opal, glinting in her close-cropped hair like diamond dust; and pale, quiet Ruth, whose sparkling was rare but nova bright. Holding goblets or mugs, they sat sleepily conversing, and Laenea felt the comfort of a familiar scene.

Minoru, facing her, glanced up. She smiled, expecting

him to cry out her name and fling out his arms, as he always did, with his ebullient greeting, showing to advantage the fringe and beadwork on his jacket. But he looked at her, straight on, silent, with an expression so blank that only the unlined long-lived youthfulness of his face could have held it. He whispered her name. Ruth looked over her shoulder and smiled tentatively, as though she were afraid. Alannai unbent and, head and shoulders above the others, raised her glass solemnly to Laenea. "Pilot," she said, and drank, and hunched back down with her elbows on her sharp knees. Laenea stood above them, outside their circle, looking down on three people whom she had kissed good-bye. Crew always said good-bye, for they slept through their voyages without any certainty that they would wake again. They lived in the cruel childhood prayer: "If I should die before I wake . . ."

Laenea climbed down to them. The circle opened, but she did not enter it. She was as overwhelmed by uncertainty as her friends.

"Sit with us," Ruth said finally. Alannai and Minoru looked uneasy but did not object. Laenea sat down. The triangle between Ruth and Alannai and Minoru did not alter. Each of them was next to the other; Laenea was beside none of them.

Ruth reached out, but her hand trembled. They all waited, and Laenea tried to think of words to reassure them, to affirm that she had not changed.

But she had changed. She realized the surgeon had cut more than skin and muscle and bone.

"I came . . ." But nothing she felt seemed right to tell them. She would not taunt them with her freedom. She took Ruth's outstretched hand. "I came to say good-bye." She embraced them and kissed them and climbed back to the main level. They had all been friends, but they could accept each other no longer.

The first pilots and crew did not mingle, for the responsibility was great, the tensions greater. But Laenea already cared for Ruth and Minoru and Alannai. Her concern would remain when she watched them sleeping and ferried them from one island of light to the next. She understood why she was perpetuating the separation even less than she understood her friends' reserve.

Conversations ebbed and flowed around her like the tides as she moved through the lounge. Seeing people she knew, she avoided them, and she did not try to join an unfamiliar group. Her pride far exceeded her loneliness.

She put aside the pain of her rejection. She felt self-contained and self-assured. When she recognized two pilots, sitting together, isolated, she approached them straightforwardly. She had flown with both of them, but never talked at length with either. They would accept her, or they would not; for the moment, she did not care. She flung back the cloak so they would know her, and realized quite suddenly—with a shock of amused surprise at what she had never noticed consciously before—that all pilots dressed as she had dressed. Laced vest or deeply cut gowns, transparent shirts, halters, all in one way or another revealed the long scar that marked their changes.

Miikala and Ramona-Teresa sat facing each other, elbows on knees, talking together quietly, privately. Even the rhythms of their conversation seemed alien to Laenea, though she could not hear their words. Like other people, they communicated as much with their bodies and hands as with speech, but the nods and gestures clashed.

Laenea wondered what pilots talked about. Certainly it could not be the ordinary concerns of ordinary people, the laundry, the shopping, a place to stay, a person, perhaps, to stay with. They would talk about . . . the experiences they alone had; they would talk about what they saw when all others must sleep near death or die.

Human pilots withstood transit better than machine intelligence, but human pilots too were sometimes lost. Miikala and Ramona-Teresa were ten percent of all the pilots who survived from the first generation, ten percent of their own unique, evolving, almost self-contained society. As Laenea stopped on the edge of the pit above them, they fell silent and gazed solemnly up at her.

Ramona-Teresa, a small, heavy-set woman with raven-black hair graying to roan, smiled and lifted her glass. "Pilot!" Miikala, whose eyes were shadowed by heavy brow ridges and an unruly shock of dark brown hair, matched the salute and drank with her.

This toast was a tribute and a welcome, not a farewell. Laenea was a part of the second wave of pilots, one who would follow the original experiment and make it work practically, now that Miikala and Ramona-Teresa and the others had proven time-independence successful by example. Laenea smiled and lowered herself into the pit. Miikala touched her left wrist, Ramona-Teresa her right. Laenea felt, welling up inside her, a bubbling, childish giggle. She could not stop it; it broke free as if filled with helium like a balloon. "Hello," she said, and even her voice was high. She might have been in an Environment on the seafloor, breathing oxy-helium and speaking donaldduck. She felt the blood rushing through the veins in her temples and her throat. Miikala was smiling, saying something in a language with as many liquid vowels as his name; she did not understand a word, yet she knew everything he was saying. Ramona-Teresa hugged her. "Welcome, child."

Laenea could not believe that these lofty, eerie people could accept her with such joy. She realized she had hoped, at best, for a cool and condescending greeting not too destructive of her pride. The embarrassing giggle slipped up and out again, but this time she did not try to stifle it. All three pilots laughed together. Laenea felt high, light, dizzy: excitement pumped adrenalin through her body. She was hot and she could feel tiny beads of perspiration gather on her forehead, just at the hairline.

Quite suddenly the constant dull ache in her chest became a wrenching pain, as though her new heart were being ripped from her, like the old. She could not breathe. She hunched forward, struggling for air, oblivious to the pilots and all the beautiful surroundings. Each time she tried to draw in a breath, the pain drove it out again.

Slowly Miikala's easy voice slipped beyond her panic, and Ramona-Teresa's hands steadied her.

"Relax, relax, remember your training . . ."

Yes: Decrease the blood-flow, open up the arteries, dilate all the tiny capillaries, feel the involuntary muscles responding to voluntary control. Slow the pump. Someone bathed her forehead with a cocktail napkin dipped in gin. Laenea welcomed the coolness and even the odor's bitter tang. The pain dissolved gradually until Ramona-Teresa could ease her back on the sitting shelf, onto the cushioned carpet, out of a protective near-fetal position. The jet fastening of the cloak fell away from her throat and the older pilot loosened the laces of her vest.

"It's all right," Ramona-Teresa said. "The adrenalin works as well as ever. We all have to learn more control of that than they think they need to teach us."

Sitting on his heels beside Laenea, Miikala glanced at the exposed bright scar. "You're out early," he said. "Have they changed the procedure?"

Laenea paled: She had forgotten that her leavetaking of hospitals was something less than official and approved.

"Don't tease her, Miikala," Ramona-Teresa said gruffly. "Or don't you remember how it was when you woke up?"

His heavy eyebrows drew together in a scowl. "I remember."

"Will they make me go back?" Laenea asked. "I'm all right. I just need to get used to it."

"They might try to," Ramona-Teresa said. "They worry so about the money they spend on us. Perhaps they aren't quite so worried any more. We do as well on our own as shut up in their ugly hospitals listening to recorded hearts—do they still do that?"

Laenea shuddered. "It worked for you, they told me—but I broke the speaker."

Miikala laughed with delight. "Causing all other machines to make frantic noises like frightened little mice."

I thought they hadn't done the operation. I wanted to be one of you so long—" Feeling stronger, Laenea pushed herself up. She left her vest open, glad of the cool air against her skin. "We watched," Miikala said. "We watch you all, but a few are special. We knew you'd come to us. Do you remember this one, Ramona?"

"Yes." She picked up one of the extra glasses, filled it from a shaker, and handed it to Laenea. "You always fought the sleep, my dear. Sometimes I thought you might wake."

"Ahh, Ramona, don't frighten the child."

"Frighten her, this tigress?"

Strangely enough, Laenea was not disturbed by the knowledge that she had been close to waking in transit. She had not, or she would be dead; she would have died quickly of old age, her body bound to normal time and normal space, to the relation between time-dilation and velocity and distance by a billion years of evolution, rhythms planetary, lunar, solar, biological: subatomic, for all Laenea or anyone else knew. She was freed of all that now.

She downed half her drink in a single swallow. The air now felt cold against her bare arms and her breasts, so she wrapped her cloak around her shoulders and waited for the satin to warm against her body.

"When do you get your ship?"

"Not for a month." The time seemed a vast expanse of emptiness. She had finished the study and the training; now only her mortal body kept her Earthbound.

"They want you completely healed."

"It's too long—how can they expect me to wait until then?"

"For the need."

"I want to know what happens, I have to find out. When's your next flight?"

"Soon," Ramona-Teresa said.

"Take me with you!"

"No, my dear. It would not be proper."

"Proper! We have to make our own rules, not follow theirs. They don't know what's right for us."

Miikala and Ramona-Teresa looked at each other for a long time. Perhaps they spoke to each other with eyes and expressions, but Laenea could not understand.

"No." Ramona's tone invited no argument.

"At least you can tell me—" She saw at once that she had said the wrong thing. The pilots' expressions closed down in silence. But Laenea did not feel guilt or contrition, only anger.

"It isn't because you can't! You talk about it to each other, I know that now at least. You can't tell me you don't."

"No," Miikala said. "We will not say we never speak of it."

"You're selfish and you're cruel." She stood up, momentarily afraid she might stagger again and have to accept their help. But as Ramona and Miikala nodded at each other, with faint, infuriating smiles, Laenea felt the lightness and the silent bells overtaking her.

"She had the need," one of them said, Laenea did not even know which one. She turned her back on them, climbed out of the conversation pit, and stalked away.

The sitting-place she chose nestled her into a steep slope very close to the sea wall. She could feel the coolness of the glass, as though it, not heat, radiated. Grotesque creatures floated past in the spotlights. Laenea relaxed, letting her smooth pulse wax and wane. She wondered whether, if she sat in this pleasant place long enough, she would be able to detect the real tides, whether the same drifting plant-creatures passed again and again, swept back and forth before the window of the stabilizer by the forces of sun and moon.

Her privacy was marred only slightly, by one man sleeping or lying unconscious nearby. She did not recognize him, but he must be crew. His dark, close-fitting clothes were unremarkably different enough, in design and fabric, that he might be from another world. He must be new. Earth was the hub of commerce; no ship flew long without orbiting it. New crew members always visited at least once. New crew usually visited every world their ships reached at first, if they had the time for quarantine. Laenea had done the same herself. But the quarantines were so severe and so necessary that she, like most other veterans, eventually remained acclimated to one world, stayed on the ship during other planetfalls, and arranged her pattern to intersect her home as frequently as possible.

The sleeping man was a few years younger than Laenea. She thought he must be as tall as she, but that estimation was difficult. He was one of those uncommon people so beautifully proportioned that from any distance at all their height can be determined only by comparison. Nothing about him was exaggerated or attenuated; he gave the impression of strength, but it was the strength of litheness and agility, not violence. Laenea decided he was neither drunk nor drugged but asleep. His face, though relaxed, showed no dissipation. His hair was dark blond and shaggy, a shade lighter than his heavy mustache. He was far from handsome: His features were regular, distinctive, but without beauty. Below the cheekbones his tanned skin was scarred and pitted, as though from some virulent childhood disease. Some of the outer worlds had not yet conquered their epidemics.

Laenea looked away from the new young man. She stared at the dark water-wall at light's-end, letting her vision double and unfocus. She touched her collarbone and slid her fingers to the tip of the smooth scar. Sensation seemed refined across the tissue, as though a wound there would hurt more sharply. Though Laenea was tired and getting hungry, she did not force herself to outrun the distractions. For a while her energy should return slowly and naturally. She had pushed herself far enough for one night.

A month would be an eternity; the wait would seem equivalent to all the years she had spent crewing. She was still angry at the other pilots. She felt she had acted like a little puppy, bounding up to them to be welcomed and patted, then, when they grew bored, they had kicked her away as though she had piddled on the floor. And she was angry at herself: She felt a fool and she felt the need to prove herself.

For the first time she appreciated the destruction of time during transit. To sleep for a month: convenient, impossible. She first must deal with her new existence, her new body; then she would deal with a new environment.

Perhaps she dozed. The deep sea admitted no time: The lights pierced the same indigo darkness day or night. Time was the least real of all dimensions to Laenea's people, and she was free of its dictates, isolated from its stabilities.

When she opened her eyes again she had no idea how long they had been closed, a second or an hour.

The time must have been a few minutes, at least, for the young man who had been sleeping was now sitting up, watching her. His eyes were dark blue, black-flecked, a color like the sea. For a moment he did not notice she was awake; then their gazes met, and he glanced quickly away, blushing, embarrassed to be caught staring.

"I stared, too," Laenea said.

Startled, he turned slowly back, not quite sure Laenea was speaking to him. "What?"

"When I was a grounder, I stared at crew, and when I was crew I stared at pilots."

"I *am* crew," he said defensively.

"From—?"

"Twilight."

Laenea knew she had been there, a long while before; images of Twilight drifted to her. It was a new world, a dark and mysterious place of high mountains and black, brooding forests, a young world, its peaks just formed. It was heavily wreathed in clouds that filtered out much of the visible light but admitted the ultraviolet. Twilight: dusk, on that world. Never dawn. No one who had ever visited Twilight would think its dimness heralded anything but night. The people who lived there were strong and solemn, even confronting disaster. On Twilight she had seen grief, death, loss, but never panic or despair.

Laenea introduced herself and offered the young man a place nearer her own. He moved closer, reticent. "I am Radu Dracul," he said.

The name touched a faint note in her memory. She followed it until it grew loud enough to identify. She glanced over Radu Dracul's shoulder, as though looking for someone. "Then—where's Vlad?"

Radu laughed, changing his somber expression for the first time. He had good teeth, and deep smile lines that paralleled the drooping sides of his mustache. "Wherever he is, I hope he stays there."

They smiled together.

"This is your first tour?"

"Is it so obvious I'm a novice?"

"You're alone," she said. "And you were sleeping."

"I don't know anyone here. I was tired," he said, quite reasonably.

"After a while . . ." Laenea nodded toward a nearby group of people, hyper and shrill on sleep repressers, energizers. "You don't sleep when you're on the ground when there are people to talk to, when there are other things to do. You get sick of sleep, you're scared of it."

Radu stared toward the ribald group that stumbled its way toward the elevator. "Do all of us become like them?" He held his low voice emotionless.

"Most."

"The sleeping drugs are bad enough. They're necessary, everyone says. But that—" He shook his head slowly. His forehead was smooth except for two parallel vertical lines that appeared between his eyebrows when he frowned; it was below his cheekbones, to the square-angled corner of his jaw, that his skin was scarred.

"No one will force you," Laenea said. She was tempted to reach out and touch him; she would have liked to stroke his face from temple to chin, and smooth a lock of hair rumpled by sleep. But he was unlike other people she had met, whom she could touch and hug and go to bed with on short acquaintance and mutual whim. Radu had about him something withdrawn and protected, almost mysterious, an invisible wall that would only be strengthened by an attempt to broach it, however gentle. He carried himself, he spoke, defensively.

"But you think I'll choose it myself."

"It doesn't always happen," Laenea said, for she felt he needed reassurance; yet she also felt the need to defend herself and her former colleagues. "We sleep so much in transit, and it's such a dark time, it's so empty . . ."

"Empty? What about the dreams?"

"I never dreamed."

"I always do," he said. "Always."

"I wouldn't have minded transit time so much if I'd ever dreamed."

Understanding drew Radu from his reserve. "I can see how it might be."

Laenea thought of all the conversations she had had with all the other crew she had known. The silent emptiness of their sleep was the single constant of all their experiences. "I don't know anyone else like you. You're very lucky."

A tiny luminous fish nosed up against the sea wall. Laenea reached out and tapped the glass, leading the fish in a simple pattern drawn with her fingertip.

"I'm hungry," she said abruptly. "There's a good restaurant in the Point Stabilizer. Will you come?"

"A restaurant—where people . . . buy food?"

"Yes."

"I am not hungry."

He was a poor liar; he hesitated before the denial, and he did not meet Laenea's glance.

"What's the matter?"

"Nothing." He looked at her again, smiling slightly: That at least was true, that he was not worried.

"Are you going to stay here all night?"

"It isn't night, it's nearly morning."

"A room's more comfortable—you were asleep."

He shrugged; she could see she was making him uneasy. She realized he must not have any money. "Didn't your credit come through? That happens all the time. I think chimpanzees write the bookkeeping programs." She had gone through the red tape and annoyance of emergency credit several times when her transfers were misplaced or miscoded. "All you have to do—"

"The administration made no error in my case."

Laenea waited for him to explain or not, as he wished. Suddenly he grinned, amused at himself but not self-deprecating. He looked even younger than he must be, when he smiled like that. "I'm not used to using money for anything but . . . unnecessaries."

"Luxuries?"

"Yes, things we don't often use on Twilight, things I do not need. But food, a place to sleep—" He shrugged again. "They are always freely given on colonial worlds. When I got to Earth, I forgot to arrange a credit transfer." He was blushing faintly. "I won't forget again. I miss a meal and one night's sleep—I've missed more on Twilight, when I was doing real work. In a few hours I correct my error."

"There's no need to go hungry now," Laenea said. "You can—"

"I respect your customs," Radu said. "But my people never borrow and we never take what is unwillingly given."

Laenea stood up and held out her hand. "I never offer unwillingly. Come along."

His hand was warm and hard, like polished wood.

At the top of the elevator shaft, Laenea and Radu stepped out into the end of the night. It was foggy and luminous, sky and sea blending into uniform gray. No wind revealed the surface of the sea or the limits of the fog, but the air was cold. Laenea swung the cloak around them both. A light rain, almost invisible, drifted down, beading mistily in tiny brilliant drops on the black velvet and on Radu's hair. He was silver and gold in the artificial light.

"It's like Twilight now," he said. "It rains like this in the winter." He stretched out his arm, with the black velvet draping down like quiescent wings, opened his palm to the rain, and watched the minuscule droplets touch his fingertips. Laenea could tell from the yearning in his voice, the wistfulness, that he was painfully and desperately homesick. She said nothing, for she knew from experience that nothing could be said to help. The pain faded only with time and fondness for other places. Earth as yet had given Radu no cause for fondness. But now he stood gazing into the fog, as though he could see continents, or stars. She slipped her arm around his shoulders in a gesture of comfort.

"We'll walk to the Point." Laenea had been enclosed in testing and training rooms and hospitals as he had been confined in ships and quarantine; she, too, felt the need for fresh air and rain and the ocean's silent words.

The sidewalk edged the port's shore; only a rail separated it from a drop of ten meters to the sea. Incipient waves caressed the metal cliff obliquely, sliding into darkness. Laenea and Radu walked slowly along, matching strides. Every few paces their hips brushed together. Laenea glanced at Radu occasionally and wondered how she could have thought him anything but beautiful. Her heart circled slowly in her breast, low-pitched, relaxing, and her perceptions faded from fever clarity to misty dark and soothing. A veil seemed to surround and protect her. She became aware that Radu was gazing at her, more than she watched him. The cold touched them through the cloak, and they moved closer together; it seemed only sensible for Radu to put his arm around her too, and so they walked, clasped together.

"Real work," Laenea said, musing.

"Yes . . . hard work with hands or minds." He picked up the second possible branch of their previous conversation as though it had never gone in any other direction. "We do the work ourselves. Twilight is too new for machines—they evolved here, and they aren't as adaptable as people."

Laenea, who had endured unpleasant situations in which machines did not perform as intended, understood what he meant. Older methods than automation were more economical on new worlds where the machines had to be designed from the beginning but people only had to learn. Evolution was as good an analogy as any.

"Crewing's work. Maybe it doesn't strain your muscles, but it is work."

"One never gets tired. Physically or mentally. The job has no challenges."

"Aren't the risks enough for you?"

"Not random risks," he said. "It's like gambling."

His background made him a harsh judge, harshest with himself. Laenea felt a tinge of self-contempt in his words, a gray shadow across his independence.

"It isn't slave labor, you know. You could quit and go home."

"I wanted to come—" He cut off the protest. "I thought it would be different."

"I know," Laenea said. "You think it will be exciting, but after a while all that's left is a dull kind of danger."

"I did want to visit other places. To be like— In that I was selfish."

"Ahh, stop. Selfish? No one would do it otherwise."

"Perhaps not. But I had a different vision. I remembered—" Again, he stopped himself in mid-sentence.

"What?"

He shook his head. "Nothing." Laenea had thought his reserve was dissolving, but all his edges hardened again. "We spend most of our time carrying trivial cargoes for trivial reasons to trivial people."

"The trivial cargoes pay for the emergencies."

Radu shook his head. "That isn't right."

"That's the way it's always been."

"On Twilight . . ." He went no further; the guarded tone had disappeared.

"You're drawn back," Laenea said. "More than anyone I've known before. It must be a comfort to love a place so much."

At first he tensed, as if he were afraid she would mock or chide him for weakness, or laugh at him. The tense muscles relaxed slowly. "I feel better after flights when I dream about home."

The fortunate dreamer; if Laenea had still been crew, she would have envied him. "Is it your family you miss?"

"I have no family—I still miss them sometimes, but they're gone."

"I'm sorry."

"You couldn't know," he said quickly, almost too quickly, as though he might have hurt her rather than the other way around. "They were good people, my clan. The epidemic killed them."

Laenea gently tightened her arm around his shoulder in silent comfort.

"I don't know what it is about Twilight that binds us all," Radu said. "I suppose it must be the combination—the challenge and the result. Everything is new. We try to touch the world gently. So many things could go wrong."

He glanced at her, his eyes deep as a mountain lake, his face solemn in its strength, asking without words a question Laenea did not understand.

The air was cold. It entered her lungs and spread through her chest, her belly, arms, legs . . . she imagined that the machine was cold metal, sucking the heat from her as it circled in its silent patterns. Laenea was tired.

"What's that?"

She glanced up. They were near the midpoint of the port's edge, nearing lights shining vaguely through the fog. The amorphous pink glow resolved itself into separate globes and torches. Laenea noticed a high metallic hum. Within two paces the air cleared.

The tall frames of fog-catchers reared up, leading inward to the lights in concentric circles. The long wires, touched by the wind, vibrated musically. The fog, touched by the wires, condensed. Water dripped from wires' tips to the platform. The intermittent sound of heavy drops on metal, like rain, provided irregular rhythm for the faint music.

"Just a party," Laenea said. The singing, glistening wires formed a multilayered curtain, each layer transparent but in combination translucent and shimmering. Laenea moved between them, but Radu, hanging back, slowed her.

"What's the matter?"

"I don't wish to go where I haven't been invited."

"You are invited. We're all invited. Would you stay away from a party at your own house?"

Radu frowned, not understanding. Laenea remembered her own days as a novice of the crew; becoming used to one's new status took time.

"They come here for us," Laenea said. "They come hoping we'll stop and talk to them and eat their food and drink their liquor. Why else come here?" She gestured—it was meant to be a sweeping movement, but she stopped her hand before the apex of its arc, flinching at the strain on her cracked ribs—toward the party, lights and tables, a tasselled pavilion, the fog-catchers, the people in evening costume, servants and machines. "Why else bring all this here? They could be on a tropical island or under the Redwoods. They could be on a mountaintop or on a desert at dawn. But they're here, and I assure you they'll welcome us."

"You know the customs," Radu said, if a little doubtfully.

When they passed the last ring of fog-catchers the temperature began to rise. The warmth was a great relief. Laenea let the damp velvet cape fall away from her shoulders and Radu did the same. A very young man, almost still a boy, smooth-cheeked and wide-eyed, appeared to take the cloak for them. He stared at them both, curious, speechless; he saw the tip of the scar between Laenea's breasts and looked at her in astonishment and admiration. "Pilot . . ." he said. "Welcome, Pilot."

"Thank you. Whose gathering is this?"

The boy, now speechless, glanced over his shoulder and gestured.

Kathell Stafford glided toward them, holding out her hands to Laenea. The white tiger followed.

Gray streaked Kathell's hair, like the silver thread woven into her blue silk gown, but her eyes were as dark and young as ever. Laenea had not seen her in several years, many voyages. They clasped hands, Laenea amazed as always by the delicacy of Kathell's bones. Veins glowed blue beneath her light-brown skin. Laenea had no idea how old she was. Except for the streaks of gray, she was just the same. They embraced.

"My dear, I heard you were in training. You must be very pleased."

"Relieved," Laenea said. "They never know for sure if it will work till afterward."

"Come join us, you and your friend."

"This is Radu Dracul of Twilight."

Kathell greeted him, and Laenea saw Radu relax and grow comfortable in the presence of the tiny self-possessed woman. Even a party on the sidewalk of the world's largest port could be her home, where she made guests welcome.

The others, quick to sense novelty, began to drift nearer, most seeming to have no particular direction in mind. Laenea had seen all the ways of approaching crew or pilots: the shyness or bravado or undisguised awe of children; the unctuous familiarity of some adults; the sophisticated nonchalance of the rich. Then there were the people Laenea seldom met, who looked at her, saw her, across a street or across a room, whose expressions said aloud: *She has walked on other worlds, she has traveled through a place I shall never even approach.* Those people looked, and looked reluctantly away, and returned to their business, allowing Laenea and her kind to proceed unmolested. Some crew members never knew they existed. The most interesting people, the sensitive and intelligent and nonintrusive ones, were those one seldom met.

Kathell was one of the people Laenea would never have met, except that she had young cousins in the crew. Otherwise she was unclassifiable. She was rich, and used her wealth lavishly to entertain her friends, as now, and for her own comfort. But she had more purpose than that. The money she used for play was nothing compared to the totality of her resources. She was a student as well as a patron, and the energy she could give to work provided her with endurance and concentration beyond that of anyone else Laenea had ever met. There was no sycophancy in either direction about their fondness for each other.

Laenea recognized few of the people clustering behind Kathell. She stood looking out at them, down a bit on most, and she almost wished she had led Radu around the fog-catchers instead of between them. She did not feel ready for the effusive greetings due a pilot; she did not feel she had earned them. The guests outshone her in every way, in beauty, in dress, in knowledge, yet they wanted her, they needed her, to touch what was denied them.

She could see the passage of time, one second after another, that quickly, in their faces. Quite suddenly she was overcome by pity.

Kathell introduced people to her. Laenea knew she would not remember one name in ten, but she nodded and smiled. Nearby Radu made polite and appropriate responses. Someone handed Laenea a glass of champagne. People clustered around her, waiting for her to talk. She found that she had no more to say to them than to those she left behind in the crew.

A man came closer, smiling, and shook her hand. "I've always wanted to meet an Aztec . . ."

His voice trailed off at Laenea's frown. She did not want to be churlish to a friend's guests, so she put aside her annoyance. "Just 'pilot,' please."

"But Aztecs—"

"The Aztecs sacrificed their captives' hearts," Laenea said. "We don't feel we've made a sacrifice."

She smiled and turned away, ending the conversation before he could press forward with a witty comment. The crowd was dense behind her, pressing in, all rich, free, trapped human beings. Laenea shivered and wished them away. She wanted quiet and solitude.

Suddenly Kathell was near, stretching out her hand. Laenea grasped it. For Kathell, Kathell and her tiger, the guests parted like water. But Kathell was in front. Laenea grinned and followed in her friend's wake. She saw Radu and called to him. He nodded; in a moment he was beside her, and they moved through regions of fragrances: mint, carnation, pine, musk, orange blossom. The boundaries were sharp between the odors.

Inside the pavilion, the three of them were alone. Laenea immediately felt warmer, though she knew the temperature was probably the same outside in the open party. But the tent walls, though busily patterned and self-luminous, made her feel enclosed and protected from the cold vast currents of the sea.

She sat gratefully in a soft chair. The white tiger laid his chin on Laenea's knee, and she stroked his huge head.

"You look exhausted, my dear," Kathell said. She put a glass in her hand. Laenea sipped from it: warm milk punch. A hint that she should be in bed.

"I just got out of the hospital," she said. "I guess I overdid it a little. I'm not used to—" She gestured with her free hand, meaning: everything. My new body, being outside and free again . . . this man beside me. She closed her eyes against blurring vision.

"Stay awhile," Kathell said, as always understanding much more than was spoken. Laenea did not try to answer; she was too comfortable, too sleepy.

"Have you eaten?" Kathell's voice sounded far away. The words, directed elsewhere, existed alone and separate, meaningless. Laenea slowed her heart and relaxed the arterial constricting muscles. Blood flowing through the dilated capillaries made her blush, and she felt warmer.

"She was going to take me to . . . a restaurant," Radu said.

"Have you ever been to one?" Kathell's amusement was never hurtful. It emerged too obviously from good humor and the ability to accept rather than fear differences.

"There is no such thing on Twilight."

Laenea thought they said more, but the words drowned in the murmur of guests' voices and wind and sea. She felt only the softness of the cushions beneath her, the warm fragrant air, and the fur of the white tiger.

Time passed, how much or at what rate Laenea had no idea. She slept gratefully and unafraid, deeply, dreaming, and hardly roused when she was moved. She muttered something and was reassured, but never remembered the words, only the tone. Wind and cold touched her and were shut out; she felt a slight acceleration. Then she slept again.

Laenea half woke, warm, warm to her center. A recent dream swam into her consciousness and out again, leaving no trace but the memory of its passing. She closed her eyes and relaxed, to remember it if it would come, but she could recall only that it was a dream of piloting a ship in transit. The details she could not perceive. Not yet. She was left with a comfortless excitement that upset her drowsiness. The machine in her chest purred fast and seemed to give off heat, though that was as impossible as that it might chill her blood.

The room around her was dim; she did not know where she was except that it was not the hospital. The smells were wrong; her first perceptions were neither astringent antiseptics nor cloying drugs but faint perfume. The sensation against her skin was not coarse synthetic but silky cotton. Between her eyelashes reflections glinted from the ceiling. She realized she was in Kathell's apartment in the Point Stabilizer.

She pushed herself up on her elbows. Her ribs creaked like old parquet floors, and deep muscle aches spread from the center of her body to her shoulders, her arms, her legs. She made a sharp sound, more of surprise than of pain. She had driven herself too hard: She needed rest, not activity. She let herself sink slowly back into the big red bed, closing her eyes and drifting back toward sleep. She heard the rustling and sliding of two different fabrics rubbed one against the other, but did not react to the sound.

"Are you all right?"

The voice would have startled her if she had not been so nearly asleep again. She opened her eyes and found Radu standing near, his jacket unbuttoned, a faint sheen of sweat on his bare chest and forehead. The concern on his face matched the worry in his voice.

Laenea smiled. "You're still here." She had assumed without thinking that he had gone on his way, to see and do all the interesting things that attracted visitors on their first trip to Earth.

"Yes," he said. "Of course."

"You didn't need to stay . . ." But she did not want him to leave.

His hand on her forehead felt cool and soothing. "I think you have a fever. Is there someone I should call?"

Laenea thought for a moment, or rather felt, lying still and making herself receptive to her body's signals. Her heart was spinning much too fast; she calmed and slowed it, wondering again what adventure had occurred in her dream. Nothing else was amiss; her lungs were clear, her hearing sharp. She slid her hand between her breasts to touch the scar: smooth and body-temperature, no infection.

"I overtired myself," she said. "That's all . . ." Sleep was overtaking her again, but curiosity disturbed her ease. "Why did you stay?"

"Because," he said slowly, sounding very far away, "I wanted to stay with you. I remember you . . ."

She wished she knew what he was talking about, but at last the warmth and drowsiness were stronger lures than her curiosity.

When Laenea woke again, she woke completely. The aches and pains had faded in the night—or in the day, for she had no idea how long she had slept, or even how late at night or early in the morning she had visited Kathell's party.

She was in her favorite room in Kathell's apartment, one gaudier than the others. Though Laenea did not indulge in much personal adornment, she liked the scarlet and gold of the room, its intrusive energy, its Dionysian flavor. Even the aquaria set in the walls were inhabited by fish gilt with scales and jeweled with luminescence. Laenea felt the honest glee of compelling shapes and colors. She sat up and threw off the blankets, stretching and yawning in pure animal pleasure. Then, seeing Radu asleep, sprawled in the red velvet pillow chair, she fell silent, surprised, not wishing to wake him. She slipped quietly out of bed, pulled a robe from the closet, and padded into the bathroom.

Comfortable, bathed, and able to breathe properly for the first time since her operation, Laenea returned to the bedroom. She had removed the strapping in order to shower; as her cracked ribs hurt no more free than bandaged, she did not bother to replace the tape.

Radu was awake.

"Good morning."

"It's not quite midnight," he said, smiling.

"Of what day?"

"You slept what was left of last night and all today. The others left on the mainland zeppelin, but Kathell Stafford wished you well and said you were to use this place as long as you wanted."

Though Kathell was as fascinated with rare people as with rare animals, her curiosity was untainted by possessiveness. She had no need of pilots, or indeed of anyone, to enhance her status. She gave her patronage with affection and friendship, not as tacit purchase. Laenea reflected that she knew people who would have done almost anything for Kathell, yet she knew no one of whom Kathell had ever asked a favor.

"How in the world did you get me here? Did I walk?"

"We didn't want to wake you. One of the large serving carts was empty so we lifted you onto it and pushed you here."

Laenea laughed. "You should have folded a flower in my hands and pretended you were at a wake."

"Someone did make that suggestion."

"I wish I hadn't been asleep—I would have liked to see the expressions of the grounders when we passed."

"Your being awake would have spoiled the illusion," Radu said.

Laenea laughed again, and this time he joined her.

As usual, clothes of all styles and sizes hung in the large closets. Laenea ran her hand across a row of garments, stopping when she touched a pleasurable texture. The first shirt she found near her size was deep green velvet with bloused sleeves. She slipped it on and buttoned it up to her breastbone, no farther.

"I still owe you a restaurant meal," she said to Radu.

"You owe me nothing at all," he said, much too seriously.

She buckled her belt with a jerk and shoved her feet into her boots, annoyed. "You don't even know me, but you stayed with me and took care of me for the whole first day of your first trip to Earth. Don't you think I should—don't you think it would be friendly for me to give you a meal?" She glared at him. "Willingly?"

He hesitated, startled by her anger. "I would find great pleasure," he said slowly, "in accepting that gift." He met Laenea's gaze, and when it softened he smiled again, tentatively. Laenea's exasperation melted and flowed away.

"Come along, then," she said to him for the second time. He rose from the pillow chair, quickly and awkwardly. None of Kathell's furniture was designed for a person his height or Laenea's. She reached to help him; they joined hands.

The Point Stabilizer was itself a complete city in two parts, one a blatant tourist world, the second a discrete and interesting permanent supporting society. Laenea often experimented with restaurants here, but this time she went to one she knew well. Experiments in the Point were not always successful. Quality spanned as wide a spectrum as culture.

Marc's had been fashionable a few years before, and now was not, but its proprietor seemed unperturbed by cycles of fashion. Pilots or princes, crew members or diplomats could come and go; Marc did not care. Laenea led Radu into the dim foyer of the restaurant and touched the signal button. In a few moments a screen before them brightened into a pattern like oil paint on water. "Hello, Marc," Laenea said. "I didn't have a chance to make a reservation, I'm afraid."

The responding voice was mechanical and harsh, initially unpleasant, difficult to understand without experience. Laenea no longer found it ugly or indecipherable. The screen brightened into yellow with the pleasure Marc could not express vocally. "I can't think of any punishment terrible enough for such a sin, so I'll have to pretend you called."

"Thank you, Marc."

"It's good to see you back after so long. And a pilot, now."

"It's good to be back." She drew Radu forward a step, farther into the range of the small camera. "This is Radu Dracul, of Twilight, on his first Earth landing."

"Hello, Radu Dracul. I hope you find us neither too depraved nor too dull."

"Neither one at all," Radu said.

The headwaiter appeared to take them to their table.

"Welcome," Marc said, instead of good-bye, and from drifting blues and greens the screen faded to darkness.

Their table was lit by the blue reflected glow of light diffusing into the sea, and the fish watched them like curious urchins.

"Who is Marc?"

"I don't know," Laenea said. "He never comes out, no one ever goes in. Some say he was disfigured, some that he has an incurable disease and can never be with anyone again. There are always new rumors. But he never talks about himself and no one would invade his privacy by asking."

"People must have a higher regard for privacy on Earth than elsewhere," Radu said drily, as though he had had considerable experience with prying questions.

Laenea knew boorish people too, but had never thought about their possible effect on Marc. She realized that the least considerate of her acquaintances seldom came here, and that she had never met Marc until the third or fourth time she had come. "It's nothing about the people. He protects himself," she said, knowing it was true.

She handed him a menu and opened her own. "What would you like to eat?"

"I'm to choose from this list?"

"Yes."

"And then?"

"And then someone cooks it, then someone else brings it to you."

Radu glanced down at the menu, shaking his head slightly, but he made no comment.

"Do you wish to order, Pilot?" At Laenea's elbow, Andrew bowed slightly.

Laenea ordered for them both, for Radu was unfamiliar with the dishes offered.

Laenea tasted the wine. It was excellent; she put down her glass and allowed Andrew to fill it. Radu watched scarlet liquid rise in crystal, staring deep.

"I should have asked if you drink wine," Laenea said. "But do at least try it."

He looked up quickly, his eyes focusing; he had not, perhaps, been staring at the wine, but at nothing, absently. He picked up the glass, held it, sniffed it, sipped from it.

"I see now why we use wine so infrequently at home."

Laenea drank again, and again could find no fault. "Never mind, if you don't like it—"

But he was smiling. "It's what we have on Twilight that I never cared to drink. It's sea water compared to this."

Laenea was so hungry that half a glass of wine made her feel lightheaded; she was grateful when Andrew brought bowls of thick, spicy soup. Radu, too, was very hungry, or sensitive to alcohol, for his defenses began to ease. He relaxed; no longer did he seem ready to leap up, take Andrew by the arm, and ask the quiet old man why he stayed here, performing trivial services for trivial reasons and trivial people. And though he still glanced frequently at Laenea—watched her, almost—he no longer looked away when their gazes met.

She did not find his attention annoying; only inexplicable. She had been attracted to men and men to her many times, and often the attractions coincided. Radu was extremely attractive. But what he felt toward her was obviously something much stronger; whatever he wanted went far beyond sex. Laenea ate in silence for some time, finding nothing, no answers, in the depths of her own wine. The tension rose until she noticed it, peripherally at first, then clearly, sharply, almost as a discrete point separating her from Radu. He sat feigning ease, one arm resting on the table, but his soup was untouched and his hand was clenched into a fist.

"You—" she said finally.

"I—" he began simultaneously.

They both stopped. Radu looked relieved. After a moment Laenea continued.

"You came to see Earth. But you haven't even left the port. Surely you had more interesting plans than to watch someone sleep."

He glanced away, glanced back, slowly opened his fist, touched the edge of the glass with a fingertip.

"It's a prying question but I think I have the right to ask it of you."

"I wanted to stay with you," he said slowly, and Laenea remembered those words, in his voice, from her half-dream awakening.

" 'I remember you,' you said."

He blushed, spots of high color on his cheekbones. "I hoped you wouldn't remember that."

"Tell me what you meant."

"It all sounds foolish and childish and romantic."

She raised one eyebrow, questioning.

"For the last day I've felt I've been living in some kind of unbelievable dream . . ."

"Dream rather than nightmare, I hope."

"You gave me a gift I wished for for years."

"A gift? What?"

"Your hand. Your smile. Your time . . ." His voice had grown very soft and hesitant again. He took a deep breath. "When the plagues came, on Twilight, all my clan died, eight adults and the four other children. I almost died, too . . ." His fingers brushed his scarred cheek. Laenea thought he was unaware of the habit. "But the serum came, and the vaccines. I recovered. The crew of the mercy mission—"

"We stayed several weeks," Laenea said. More details of her single visit to Twilight returned: the settlement in near collapse, the desperately ill trying to attend the dying.

"You were the first crew member I ever saw, the first offworlder. You saved my people, my life—"

"Radu, it wasn't only me."

"I know. I even knew then. It didn't matter. I was sick for so long, and when I came to and knew I would live it hardly mattered. I was frightened and full of grief and lost and alone. I needed . . . someone . . . to admire. And you were there. You were the only stability in our chaos, a hero . . ." His voice trailed off in uncertainty at Laenea's smile, though she was not laughing at him. "This isn't easy for me to say."

Reaching across the table, Laenea grasped his wrist.

The beat of his pulse was as alien as flame. She could think of nothing to tell him that would not sound patronizing or parental, and she did not care to speak to him in either guise. He raised his head and looked at her, searching her face.

"When I joined the crew I don't think I ever believed I would meet you. I joined because it was what I always wanted to do, after . . . I never considered that I might really meet you. But I saw you, and I realized I wanted . . . to be something in your life. A friend, at best, I hoped. A shipmate, if nothing else. But—you'd become a pilot, and everyone knows pilots and crew stay apart."

"The first ones take pride in their solitude," Laenea said, for Ramona-Teresa's rejection still stung. Then she relented, for she might never have met Radu Dracul if they had accepted her completely. "Maybe they needed it."

"I saw a few pilots, before I met you. You're the only one who ever spoke to me or even glanced at me. I think . . ." He looked at her hand on his, and touched his scarred cheek again, as if he could brush the marks away. "I think I've loved you since the day you came to Twilight." He stood abruptly, but withdrew his hand gently. "I should never—"

She rose too. "Why not?"

"I have no right to . . ."

"To what?"

"To ask anything of you. To expect—" Flinching, he cut off the word. "To burden you with my hopes."

"What about my hopes?"

He was silent with incomprehension. Laenea stroked his rough cheek, once when he winced like a nervous colt, and again: The lines of strain across his forehead eased almost imperceptibly. She brushed back the errant lock of dark blond hair. "I've had less time to think of you than you of me," she said, "but I think you're beautiful, and an admirable man."

Radu smiled with little humor. "I'm not thought beautiful on Twilight."

"Then Twilight has as many fools as any other human world."

"You . . . want me to stay?"

"Yes."

He sat down again like a man in a dream. Neither spoke. Andrew appeared, to remove the soup plates and serve the main course. He was diplomatically unruffled, but not quite oblivious to Laenea and Radu's near departure. "Is everything satisfactory?"

"Very much so, Andrew. Thank you."

He bowed and smiled and pushed away the serving cart.

"Have you contracted for transit again?"

"Not yet," Radu said.

"I have a month before my proving flights." She thought of places she could take him, sights she could show him. "I thought I'd just have to endure the time—" She fell silent, for Ramona-Teresa was standing in the entrance of the restaurant, scanning the room. She saw Laenea and came toward her. Laenea waited, frowning; Radu turned, froze, struck by Ramona's compelling presence: serenity, power, determination. Laenea wondered if the older pilot had relented, but she was no longer so eager to be presented with mysteries, rather than to discover them herself.

Ramona-Teresa stopped at their table, ignoring Radu, or, rather, glancing at him, dismissing him in the same instant, and speaking to Laenea. "They want you to go back."

Laenea had almost forgotten the doctors and administrators, who could hardly take her departure as calmly as did the other pilots. "Did you tell them where I was?" She knew immediately that she had asked an unworthy question. "I'm sorry."

"They always want to teach us that they're in control. Sometimes it's easiest to let them believe they are."

"Thanks," Laenea said, "but I've had enough tests and plastic tubes." She felt very free, for whatever she did she would not be grounded: She was worth too much. No one would even censure her for irresponsibility, for everyone knew pilots were quite perfectly mad.

"Don't use your credit key."

"All right . . ." She saw how easily she could be traced, and wished she had not got out of the habit of carrying cash. "Ramona, lend me some money."

Now Ramona did look at Radu, critically. "It would be better if you came with the rest of us." Radu flushed. She was, all too obviously, not speaking to him.

"No, it wouldn't." Laenea's tone was chill. The dim blue light glinted silver from the gray in Ramona's hair as she turned back to Laenea and reached into an inner pocket. She handed her a folded sheaf of bills. "You young ones never plan." Laenea could not be sure what she meant, and she had no chance to ask. Ramona-Teresa turned away and left.

Laenea shoved the money into her pants pocket, annoyed not so much because she had had to ask for it as because Ramona-Teresa had been so sure she would need it.

"She may be right," Radu said slowly. "Pilots, and crew . . ."

She touched his hand again, rubbing its back, following the ridges of strong fine bones to his wrist. "She shouldn't have been so snobbish. We're none of her business."

"She was . . . I never met anyone like her before. I felt like I was in the presence of someone so different from me—so far beyond—that we couldn't speak together." He grinned, quick flash of strong white teeth behind his shaggy mustache, deep smile lines in his cheeks. "If she'd cared to." With his free hand he stroked her green velvet sleeve. She could feel the beat of his pulse, rapid and upset. As if he had closed an electrical circuit, a pleasurable chill spread up Laenea's arm.

"Radu, did you ever meet a pilot or a crew member who wasn't different from anyone you had ever met before? I haven't. We all start out that way. Transit didn't change Ramona."

He acquiesced with silence only, no more certain of the validity of her assurance than she was.

"For now it doesn't make any difference anyway," Laenea said.

The unhappiness slipped from Radu's expression, the joy came back, but uncertainty remained.

They finished their dinner quietly, in expectation, anticipation, paying insufficient attention to the excellent food. Though annoyed that she had to worry about the subject at all, Laenea considered available ways of preserving her freedom. She wished Kathell Stafford were still on the island, for she of all people could have helped. She had already helped, as usual, without even meaning to.

But the situation was hardly serious; evading the administrators as long as possible was a matter of pride and personal pleasure. "Fools . . ." she muttered.

"They may have a special reason for wanting you to go back," Radu said. Anticipation of the next month flowed through both their minds. "Some problem—some danger."

"They'd've said so."

"Then what do they want?"

"Ramona said it—they want to prove they control us." She drank the last few drops of her brandy; Radu followed suit. They rose and walked together toward the foyer. "They want to keep me packed in styrofoam padding like an expensive machine until I can take my ship."

Andrew awaited them, but as Laenea reached for Ramona-Teresa's money Marc's screen glowed into brilliance. "Your dinner's my gift," he said. "In celebration."

She wondered if Ramona had told him of her problem. He could as easily know from his own sources; or the free meal might be an example of his frequent generosity. "I wonder how you ever make a profit, my friend," she said. "But thank you."

"I overcharge tourists," he said, the mechanical voice

so flat that it was impossible to know if he spoke cynically or sardonically or if he were simply joking.

"I don't know where I'm going next," Laenea told him, "but are you looking for anything?"

"Nothing in particular," he said. "Pretty things—" Silver swirled across the screen.

"I know."

The corridors were dazzling after the dim restaurant; Laenea wished for gentle evenings and moonlight. Between cold metal walls, she and Radu walked close together, warm, arms around each other. "Marc collects," Laenea said. "We all bring him things."

"Pretty things."

"Yes . . . I think he tries to bring the nicest bits of all the worlds inside with him. I think he creates his own reality."

"One that has nothing to do with ours."

"Exactly."

"That's what they'd do at the hospital," Radu said. "Isolate you from what you'll have to deal with, and you disagree that that would be valuable."

"Not for me. For Marc, perhaps."

He nodded. "And . . . now?"

"Back to Kathell's for a while at least." She reached up and rubbed the back of his neck. His hair tickled her hand. "The rule I disagreed with most while I was in training was the one that forbade me any sex at all."

The smile lines appeared again, bracketing his mouth parallel to his drooping mustache, crinkling the skin around his eyes. "I understand entirely," he said, "why you aren't anxious to go back."

Entering her room in Kathell's suite, Laenea turned on the lights. Mirrors reflected the glow, bright niches among red plush and gold trim. She and Radu stood together on the silver surfaces, hands clasped, for a moment as hesitant as children. Then Laenea turned to Radu, and he to her; they ignored the actions of the mirrored figures. Laenea's hands on the sides of Radu's face touched his scarred cheeks; she kissed him lightly, again, harder. His mustache was soft and bristly against her lips, against her tongue. His hands tightened over her shoulder blades, moved down. He held her gently. She slipped one hand between their bodies, beneath his jacket, stroking his bare skin, tracing the taut muscles of his back, his waist, his hip. His breathing quickened.

At the beginning nothing was different—but nothing was the same. The change was more important than motions, positions, endearments; Laenea had experienced those in all their combinations, content with involvement for a few moments' pleasure. That had always been satisfying and sufficient; she had never suspected the potential for evolution that depended on the partners. Leaning over Radu, with her hair curling down around their faces, looking into his smiling blue eyes, she felt close enough to him to absorb his thoughts and sense his soul. They caressed each other leisurely, concentrating on the sensations between them. Laenea's nipples hardened, but instead of throbbing they tingled. Radu moved against her and her excitement heightened suddenly, irrationally, grasping her, shaking her. She gasped but could not force the breath back out. Radu kissed her shoulder, the base of her throat, stroked her stomach, drew his hand up her side, cupped her breast.

"Radu—"

Her climax was sudden and violent, a clasping wave contracting all through her as her single thrust pushed Radu's hips down against the mattress. He was startled into a climax of his own as Laenea shuddered involuntarily, straining against him, clasping him to her, unable to catch his rhythm. But neither of them cared.

They lay together, panting and sweaty.

"Is that part of it?" His voice was unsteady.

"I guess so." Her voice, too, showed the effects of surprise. "No wonder they're so quiet about it."

"Does it—is your pleasure decreased?" He was ready to be angry for her.

"No, that's not it, it's—" She started to say that the pleasure was tenfold greater, but remembered the start of their loveplay, before she had been made aware of just how many of her rhythms were rearranged. The beginning had nothing to do with the fact that she was a pilot. "It was fine." A lame adjective. "Just unexpected. And you?"

He smiled. "As you say—unexpected. Surprising. A little . . . frightening."

"Frightening?"

"All new experiences are a little frightening. Even the very enjoyable ones. Or maybe those most of all."

Laenea laughed softly.

They lay wrapped in each other's arms. Laenea's hair curled around to touch the corner of Radu's jaw, and her heel was hooked over his calf. She was content for the moment with silence, stillness, touch. The plague had not scarred his body.

In the aquaria, the fish flitted back and forth before dim lights, spreading blue shadows across the bed. Laenea breathed deeply, counting to make the breaths even. Breathing is a response, not a rhythm, a reaction to levels of carbon dioxide in blood and brain; Laenea's breathing had to be altered only during transit itself. For now she used it as an artificial rhythm of concentration. Her heart raced with excitement and adrenalin, so she began to slow it, to relax. But something disturbed her control: The rate and blood pressure slid down slightly, then slowly slid back up. She could hear nothing but a dull ringing in her inner ear. Perspiration formed on her forehead, her armpits, along her spine. Her heart had never before failed to respond to conscious control.

Angry, startled, she pushed herself up, flinging her hair back from her face. Radu raised his head, tightening his hand around the point of her shoulder. "What—?"

He might as well have been speaking underwater. Laenea lifted her hand to silence him.

One deep inhalation, hold; exhale, hold. She repeated the sequence, calming herself, relaxing voluntary muscles. Her hand fell to the bed. She lay back. Repeat the sequence, again. Again. In the hospital and since, her control over involuntary muscles had been quick and sure. She began to be afraid, and had to imagine the fear evaporating, dissipating. Finally the arterial muscles began to respond. They lengthened, loosened, expanded. Last the pump answered her commands as she recaptured and reproduced the indefinable states of self-control.

When she knew her blood pressure was no longer likely to crush her kidneys or mash her brain, she opened her eyes. Above, Radu watched, deep lines of worry across his forehead. "Are you—?" He was whispering.

She lifted her heavy hand and stroked his face, his eyebrows, his hair. "I don't know what happened, I couldn't get control for a minute. But I have it back now." She drew his hand across her body, pulling him down beside her, and they relaxed again and dozed.

Later, Laenea took time to consider her situation. Returning to the hospital would be easiest; it was also the least attractive alternative. Remaining free, adjusting without interference to the changes, meeting the other pilots, showing Radu what was to be seen: Outwitting the administrators would be more fun. Kathell had done them a great favor, for without her apartment Laenea would have rented a hotel suite. The records would have been available, a polite messenger would have appeared to ask her respectfully to come along. Should she overpower an innocent hireling and disappear laughing? More likely she would have shrugged and gone. Fights had never given her either excitement or pleasure. She knew what things she would not do, ever, though she did not know what she would do now. She pondered.

"Damn them," she said.

His hair as damp as hers, after their shower, Radu sat down facing her. The couches, of course, were both too low. Radu and Laenea looked at each other across two sets of knees draped in caftans that clashed violently. Radu lay back on the cushions, chuckling. "You look much too undignified for anger."

She leaned toward him and tickled a sensitive place she had discovered. "I'll show you undignified—" He twisted away and batted at her hand but missed, laughing helplessly. When Laenea relented, she was lying on top of him on the wide, soft couch. Radu unwound from a defensive curl, watching her warily, laugh lines deep around his eyes and mouth.

"Peace," she said, and held up her hands. He relaxed. Laenea picked up a fold of the material of her caftan with one of his. "Is anything more undignified than the two of us in colors no hallucination would have—and giggling as well?"

"Nothing at all." He touched her hair, her face. "But what made you so angry?"

"The administrators—their red tape. Their infernal tests." She laughed again, this time bitterly. " 'Undignified'—some of those tests would win on that."

"Are they necessary? For your health?"

She told him about the hypnotics, the sedatives, the sleep, the time she had spent being obedient. "Their redundancies have redundancies. If I weren't healthy I'd be back out on the street wearing my old heart. I'd be . . . nothing."

"Never that."

But she knew of people who had failed as pilots, who were reimplanted with their own saved hearts, and none of them had ever flown again, as pilots, as crew, as passengers. *"Nothing."*

He was shaken by her vehemence. "But you're all right. You're who you want to be and what you want to be."

"I'm angry at inconvenience," she admitted. "I want to be the one who shows you Earth. They want me to spend the next month shuttling between cinderblock cubicles. And I'll have to if they find me. My freedom's limited." She felt very strongly that she needed to spend the next month in the real world, neither hampered by experts who knew, truly, nothing, nor misdirected by controlled environments. She did not know how to explain the feeling; she thought it must be one of the things pilots tried to talk about during their hesitant, unsyncopated conversations with their insufficient vocabularies. "Yours isn't, though, you know."

"What do you mean?"

"Sometimes I come back to Earth and never leave the port. It's like my home. It has everything I want or need. I can easily stay a month and never see an administrator or have to admit receiving a message I don't want." Her fingertips moved back and forth across the ridge of new tissue over her breastbone. Somehow it was a comfort, though the scar was the symbol of what had cut her off from her old friends. She needed new friends now, but she felt it would be stupid and unfair to ask Radu to spend his first trip to Earth on an artificial island. "I'm going to stay here. But you don't have to. Earth has a lot of sights worth seeing."

He did not answer. Laenea raised her head to look at him. He was intent and disturbed. "Would you be offended," he said, "if I told you I am not very interested in historical sights?"

"Is this what you really want? To stay with me?"

"Yes. Very much."

Laenea led Radu through the vast apartment to the swimming pool. Flagstones surrounded a pool with sides and bottom of intricate mosaic that shimmered in the dim light. This was a grotto more than a place for athletic events or children's noisy beachball games.

Radu sighed; Laenea brushed her hand across the top of his shoulder, questioning.

"Someone spent a great deal of time and care here," he said.

"That's true." Laenea had never thought of it as the work of someone's hands, individual and painstaking, though of course it was exactly that. But the economic structure of her world was based on service, not production, and she had always taken the results for granted.

They took off their caftans and waded down the steps

into body-warm water. It rose smooth and soothing around the persistent soreness of Laenea's ribs.

"I'm going to soak for a while." She lay back and floated, her hair drifting out, a strand occasionally drifting back to brush her shoulder, the top of her spine. Radu's voice rumbled through the water, incomprehensible, but she glanced over and saw him waving toward the dim far end of the pool. He flopped down in the water and thrashed energetically away, retreating to a constant background noise. All sounds faded, gaining the same faraway quality, like audio slow motion. Something was strange, wrong . . . Laenea began to tense up again. She turned her attention to the warmth and comfort of the water, to urging the tension out of her body through her shoulders, down her outstretched arms, out the tips of spread fingers. But when she paid attention again, something still was wrong. Tracing unease, slowly and deliberately, going back so far in memory that she was no longer a pilot (it seemed a long time), she realized that though she had become well and easily accustomed to the silence of her new heart, to the lack of a pulse, she had been listening unconsciously for the echo of the beat, the double or triple reverberation from throat and wrists, from femoral artery, all related by the same heartbeat, each perceived at a slightly different time during moments of silence.

She thought she might miss that, just a little, for a little while.

Radu finished his circumnavigation of the pool; he swam under her and the faint turbulence stroked her back. Laenea let her feet sink to the pool's bottom and stood up as Radu burst out of the water, a very amateur dolphin, hair dripping in his eyes, laughing. They waded toward each other through the retarding chest-deep water and embraced. Radu kissed Laenea's throat just at the corner of her jaw; she threw her head back like a cat stretching to prolong the pleasure, moving her hands up and down his sides.

"We're lucky to be here so early," he said softly, "alone before anyone else comes."

"I don't think anyone else is staying at Kathell's right now," Laenea said. "We have the pool to ourselves all the time."

"This is . . . this belongs to her?"

"The whole apartment does."

He said nothing, embarrassed by his error.

"Never mind," Laenea said. "It's a natural mistake to make." But it was not, of course, on Earth.

Laenea had visited enough new worlds to understand how Radu could be uncomfortable in the midst of the private possessions and personal services available on Earth. What impressed him was expenditure of time, for time was the valuable commodity in his frame of reference. On Twilight everyone would have two or three necessary jobs, and none would consist of piecing together intricate mosaics. Everything was different on Earth.

They paddled in the shallow end of the pool, reclined on the steps, flicked shining spray at each other. Laenea wanted Radu again. She was completely free of pain for the first time since the operation. That fact began to overcome a certain reluctance she felt, an ambivalence toward her new reactions. The violent change in her sexual responses disturbed her more than she wanted to admit.

And she wondered if Radu felt the same way; she discovered she was afraid he might.

In the shallow water beside him, she moved closer and kissed him. As he put his arm around her she slipped her hand across his stomach and down to his genitals, somehow less afraid of a physical indication of reluctance than a verbal one. But he responded to her, hardening, drawing circles on her breast with his finger-tips, caressing her lips with his tongue. Laenea stroked him from the back of his knee to his shoulder. His body had a thousand textures, muted and blended by the warm water and the steamy air. She pulled him closer, across the mosaic step, grasping him with her legs. They slid together easily. Radu entered her with little friction between them. This time Laenea anticipated a long, slow increase of excitement.

"What do you like?" Radu whispered.

"I—I like—I" Her words changed abruptly to a gasp. Imagination exaggerated nothing: The climax again came all at once in a powerful solitary wave. Radu's fingers dug into her shoulders, and though Laenea knew her short nails were cutting his back, she could not ease the wire-taut muscles of her hands. Radu must have expected the intensity and force of Laenea's orgasm, but the body is slower to learn than the mind. He followed her to climax almost instantly, in solitary rhythm that continued, slowed, finally ceased. Trembling against him, Laenea exhaled in a long shudder. She could feel Radu's stomach muscles quiver. The water around them, which had seemed warmer than their bodies, now seemed cool.

Laenea liked to take more time with sex, and she suspected that Radu did as well. Yet she felt exhilarated. Her thoughts about Radu were bright in her mind, but she could put no words to them. Instead of speaking she laid her hand on the side of his face, fingertips at the temple, the palm of her hand against deep scars. He no longer flinched when she touched him there, but covered her hand with his.

He had about him a quality of constancy, of dependability and calm, that Laenea had never before encountered. His admiration for her was of a different sort entirely than what she was used to: grounders' lusting after status and vicarious excitement. Radu had seen her and stayed with her when she was as helpless and ordinary and undignified as a human being can be; that had not changed his feelings. Laenea did not understand him yet.

They toweled each other dry. Radu's hip was scraped from the pool steps, and he had long scratches down his back.

"I wouldn't have thought I could do that," Laenea said. She glanced at her hands, nails shorter than fingertips, cut just above the quick. "I'm sorry."

Radu reached around to dry her back. "I did the same to you."

"Really?" She looked over her shoulder. The angle was wrong to see anything, but she could feel places stinging. "We're even, then." She grinned. "I never drew blood before."

"Nor I."

They dressed in clean clothes from Kathell's wardrobes and went walking through the multileveled city. It was, as Radu had said, very early. Above on the sea it would be nearing dawn. Below only street cleaners and the drivers of delivery carts moved here and there across a mall. Laenea was more accustomed to the twenty-four-hour crew city in the second stabilizer.

She was getting hungry enough to suggest a shuttle trip across to #2, where everything would be open, when ahead they saw waiters arranging the chairs of a sidewalk café, preparing for business.

"Seven o'clock," Radu said. "That's early to open around here, it seems."

"How do you know what time it is?"

He shrugged. "I don't know how, but I always know."

"Twilight's day isn't even standard."

"I had to convert for a while, but now I have both times."

A waiter bowed and ushered them to a table. They breakfasted and talked, telling each other about their home worlds and about places they had visited. Radu had been to three other planets before Earth. Laenea knew two of them, from several years before. They were colonial worlds, which had grown and changed since her visits.

Laenea and Radu compared impressions of crewing, she still fascinated by the fact that he dreamed.

She found herself reaching out to touch his hand, to emphasize a point or for the sheer simple pleasure of contact. And he did the same, but they were both right-handed and a floral centerpiece occupied the center of their table. Finally Laenea picked up the vase and moved it to one side, and she and Radu held left hands across the table.

"Where do you want to go next?"

"I don't know. I haven't thought about it. I still have to go where they tell me to, when there's a need."

"I just . . ." Laenea's voice trailed off. Radu glanced at her quizzically, and she shook her head. "It sounds ridiculous to talk about tomorrow or next week or next month . . . but it feels so right."

"I feel . . . the same."

They sat in silence, drinking coffee. Radu's hand tightened on hers. "What are we going to do?" For a moment he looked young and lost. "I haven't earned the right to make my own schedules."

"I have," Laenea said. "Except for the emergencies. That will help."

He was no more satisfied than she.

"We have a month," Laenea said. "A month not to worry."

Laenea yawned as they entered the front room of Kathell's apartment. "I don't know why I'm so sleepy." She yawned again, trying to stifle it, failing. "I slept the clock around, and now I want to sleep again—after what? Half a day?" She kicked off her boots.

"Eight and a half hours," Radu said. "Somewhat busy hours, though."

She smiled. "True." She yawned a third time, jaw hinges cracking. "I've got to take a nap."

Radu followed as she padded through the hallways, down the stairs to her room. The bed was made, turned down on both sides. The clothes Laenea and Radu had arrived in were clean and pressed. They hung in the dressing room along with the cloak, which no longer smelled musty. Laenea brushed her fingers across the velvet. Radu looked around. "Who did this?"

"What? The room? The people Kathell hires. They look after whoever stays here."

"Do they hide?"

Laenea laughed. "No—they'll come if we call. Do you need something?"

"No," he said sharply. "No," more gently. "Nothing."

Still yawning, Laenea undressed. "What about you, are you wide awake?"

He was staring into a mirror; he started when she spoke, and looked not at her but at her reflection. "I can't usually sleep during the day," he said. "But I am rather tired."

His reflection turned its back; he, smiling, turned toward her.

They were both too sleepy to make love a third time. The amount of energy Laenea had expended astonished her; she thought perhaps she still needed time to recover from the hospital. She and Radu curled together in darkness and scarlet sheets.

"I do feel very depraved now," Radu said.

"Depraved? Why?"

"Sleeping at nine o'clock in the morning? That's unheard of on Twilight." He shook his head; his mustache brushed her shoulder. Laenea drew his arm closer around her, holding his hand in both of hers.

"I'll have to think of some other awful depraved Earth customs to tempt you with," she said sleepily, chuckling, but thought of none just then.

Later (with no way of knowing how much later) something startled her awake. She was a sound sleeper and could not think what noise or movement would awaken her when she still felt so tired. Lying very still, she listened, reaching out for stimuli with all her senses. The lights in the aquaria were out, the room was dark except for the heating coils' bright orange spirals. Bubbles from the aerator, highlighted by the amber glow, rose like tiny half-moons through the water.

The beat of a heart pounded through her.

In sleep, Radu still lay with his arm around her. His hand, fingers half curled in relaxation, brushed her left breast. She stroked the back of his hand but moved quietly away from him, away from the sound of his pulse, for it formed the links of a chain she had worked hard and wished long to break.

The second time she woke she was frightened out of sleep, confused, displaced. For a moment she thought she was escaping a nightmare. Her head ached violently from the ringing in her ears, but through the clash and clang she heard Radu gasp for breath, struggling as if to free himself from restraints. Laenea reached for him, ignoring her racing heart. Her fingers slipped on his sweat. Thrashing, he flung her back. Each breath was agony just to hear. Laenea grabbed his arm when he twisted again, held one wrist down, seized his flailing hand, partially immobilized him, straddled his hips, held him.

"Radu!"

He did not respond. Laenea called his name again. She could feel his pulse through both wrists, feel his heart as it pounded, too fast, too hard, irregular and violent.

"Radu!"

He cried out, a piercing and wordless scream.

She whispered his name, no longer even hoping for a response, in helplessness, hopelessness. He shuddered beneath her hands.

He opened his eyes.

"What . . . ?"

Laenea remained where she was, leaning over him. He tried to lift his hand, and she realized she was still forcing his arms to the bed. She released him and sat back on her heels beside him. She, too, was short of breath, and hypertensive to a dangerous degree.

Someone knocked softly on the bedroom door.

"Come in!"

One of the aides entered hesitantly. "Pilot? I thought— Pardon me." She bowed and backed out.

"Wait—you did right. Call a doctor immediately."

Radu pushed himself up on his elbows. "No, don't, there's nothing wrong."

The young aide glanced from Laenea to Radu and back to the pilot.

"Are you sure?" Laenea asked.

"Yes." He sat up. Sweat ran in heavy drops down his temples to the edge of his jaw. Laenea shivered from the coolness of her own evaporating sweat.

"Never mind, then," Laenea said. "But thank you."

The aide departed.

"Gods, I thought you were having a heart attack." Her own heart was beginning to slow in rhythmically varying rotation. She could feel the blood slow and quicken at her temples, in her throat. She clenched her fists reflexively and felt her nails against her palms.

Radu shook his head. "It was a nightmare." His somber expression suddenly changed to a quick but shaky grin. "Not illness. As you said—we're never allowed this job if we're not healthy." He lay back, hands behind his head, eyes closed. "I was climbing, I don't remember, a cliff or a tree. It collapsed or broke and I fell—a long way. I knew I was dreaming and I thought I'd wake up before I hit, but I fell into a river." She heard him and remembered what he said, but knew she would have to make sense of the words later. She remained kneeling and slowly unclenched her hands. Blood rushed through her like a funneled tide, high, then low, and back again.

"It had a very strong current that swept me along and pulled me under. I couldn't see banks on either side—not even where I fell from. Logs and trash rushed along beside me and past me, but every time I tried to hold on to something I'd almost be crushed. I got tireder and tireder and the water pulled me under—I needed a breath but I couldn't take one . . . have you felt the way the body tries to breathe when you can't let it?"

She did not answer but her lungs burned, her muscles contracted convulsively, trying to clear a way for the air to push its way in.

"Laenea—" She felt him grasp her shoulders; she

wanted to pull him closer, she wanted to push him away. Then the change broke the compulsion of his words and she drew deep, searing breath.

"What—?"

"A . . . moment . . ." She managed, finally, to damp the sine-curve velocity of the pump within her. She was shivering. Radu pulled a blanket around her. Laenea's control returned slowly, more slowly than any other time she had lost it. She pulled the blanket closer, seeking stability more than warmth. She should not slip like that: Her biocontrol, to now, had always been as close to perfect as anything associated with a biological system could be. But now she felt dizzy and high, hyperventilated, from the needless rush of blood through her brain. She wondered how many millions of nerve cells had been destroyed.

She and Radu looked at each other in silence.

"Laenea . . ." He still spoke her name as if he were not sure he had the right to use it. "What's happening to us?"

"Excitement—" she said, and stopped. "An ordinary nightmare—" She had never tried to deceive herself before, and found she could not start now.

"It wasn't an ordinary nightmare. You always know you're going to be all right, no matter how frightened you are. This time—until I heard you calling me and felt you pulling me to the surface, I knew I was going to die."

Tension grew: He was as afraid to reach toward her as she was to him. She threw off the blanket and grasped his hand. He was startled, but he returned the pressure. They sat cross-legged, facing each other, hands entwined.

"It's possible . . ." Laenea said, searching for a way to say this that was gentle for them both, "it's possible . . . that there is a reason, a real reason, pilots and crew don't mix."

By Radu's expression Laenea knew he had thought of that explanation too, and only hoped she could think of a different one.

"It could be temporary—we may only need acclimatization."

"Do you really think so?"

She rubbed the ball of her thumb across his knuckles. His pulse throbbed through her fingers. "No," she said, almost whispering. Her system and that of any normal human being would no longer mesh. The change in her was too disturbing, on psychological and subliminal levels, while normal biorhythms were so compelling that they interfered with and would eventually destroy her new biological integrity. She would not have believed those facts before now. "I don't. Dammit, I don't."

Exhausted, they could no longer sleep. They rose in miserable silence and dressed, navigating around each other like sailboats in a high wind. Laenea wanted to touch Radu, to hug him, slide her hand up his arm, kiss him and be tickled by his mustache. Denied any of those, not quite by fear but by reluctance, unwilling either to risk her own stability or to put Radu through another nightmare, she understood for the first time the importance of simple, incidental touch, directed at nothing more important than momentary contact, momentary reassurance.

"Are you hungry?" Isolation, with silence as well, was too much to bear.

"Yes . . . I guess so."

But over breakfast (it was, Radu said, midafternoon), the silence fell again. Laenea could not make small talk; if small talk existed for this situation she could not imagine what it might consist of. Radu pushed his food around on his plate and did not look at her: His gaze jerked from the sea wall to the table, to some detail of carving on the furniture, and back again.

Laenea ate fruit sections with her fingers. All the previous worries, how to arrange schedules for time together, how to defuse the disapproval of their acquaintances, seemed trivial and frivolous. The only solution now was a drastic one, which she did not feel she could suggest herself. Radu must have thought of it; that he had said nothing might mean that volunteering to become a pilot was as much an impossibility for him as returning to normal was for Laenea. Piloting was a lifetime decision, not a job one took for a few years' travel and adventure. The way Radu talked about his home world, Laenea believed he wanted to return to a permanent home, not a rest stop.

Radu stood up. His chair scraped against the floor and fell over. Laenea looked up, startled. Flushing, Radu turned, picked up the chair, and set it quietly on its legs again. "I can't think down here," he said. "It never changes." He glanced at the sea wall, perpetual blue fading to blackness. "I'm going on deck. I need to be outside." He turned toward her. "Would you—?"

"I think . . ." Wind, salt spray on her face: tempting. "I think we'd each better be alone for a while."

"Yes," he said, with gratitude. "I suppose . . ." His voice grew heavy with disappointment. "You're right." His footsteps were soundless on the thick carpet.

"Radu—"

He turned again, without speaking, as though his barriers were forming around him again, still so fragile that a word would shatter them.

"Never mind . . . just . . . oh—take my cape if you want, it's cold on deck in the afternoons."

He nodded once, still silent, and went away.

In the pool Laenea swam hard, even when her ribs began to hurt. She felt trapped and angry, with nowhere to run, knowing no one deserved her anger. Certainly not Radu; not the other pilots, who had warned her. Not even the administrators, who in their own misguided way had tried to make her transition as protected as possible. The anger could go toward herself, toward her strong-willed stubborn character. But that, too, was pointless. All her life she had made her own mistakes and her own successes, both usually by trying what others said she could not do.

She climbed out of the pool without having tired herself in the least. The warmth had soothed away whatever aches and pains were left, and her energy was returning, leaving her restless and snappish. She put on her clothes and left the apartment to walk off her tension until she could consider the problem calmly. But she could not see even an approach to a solution; at least, not to a solution that would be a happy one.

Hours later, when the grounder city had quieted to night again, Laenea let herself into Kathell's apartment. Inside, too, was dark and silent. She could hardly wonder where Radu was; she remembered little enough of what she herself had done since afternoon. She remembered being vaguely civil to people who stopped her, greeted her, invited her to parties, asked for her autograph. She remembered being less than civil to someone who asked how it felt to be an Aztec. But she did not remember which incident preceded the other or when either had occurred or what she had actually said. She was no closer to an answer than before. Hands jammed in her pockets, she went into the main room, just to sit and stare into the ocean and try to think. She was halfway to the sea wall before she saw Radu, standing silhouetted against the window, dark and mysterious in her cloak, the blue light glinting ghostly off his hair.

"Radu—"

He did not turn. Her eyes more accustomed to the dimness, Laenea saw his breath clouding the glass.

"I applied to pilot training," he said softly, his tone utterly neutral.

Laenea felt a quick flash of joy, then uncertainty, then fear for him. She had been ecstatic when the administrators accepted her for training. Radu did not even smile. Making a mistake in this choice would hurt him more, much more, than even parting forever could hurt both of them. "What about Twilight?"

"It doesn't matter," he said, his voice unsteady. "They refused—" He choked on the words and forced them out. "They refused me."

Laenea went to him, put her arms around him, turned him toward her. The fine lines around his blue eyes were deeper, etched by distress and failure. She touched his cheek. Embracing her, he rested his forehead on her shoulder. "They said . . . I'm bound to our own four dimensions. I'm too dependent . . . on night, day, time . . . my circadian rhythms are too strong. They said . . ." His muffled words became more and more unsure, balanced on a shaky edge. Laenea stroked his hair, the back of his neck, over and over. That was the only thing left to do. There was nothing at all left to say. "If I survived the operation . . . I'd die in transit."

Laenea's vision blurred, and the warm tears slipped down her face. She could not remember the last time she had cried. A convulsive sob shook Radu, and his tears fell cool on her shoulder, soaking through her shirt. "I love you," Radu whispered. "Laenea, I love you."

"Dear Radu, I love you too." She could not, would not, say what she thought: *That won't be enough for us. Even that won't help us.*

She guided him to a wide low cushion that faced the ocean; she drew him down beside her, neither of them really paying attention to what they were doing, to the cushions too low for them, to anything but each other. Laenea held Radu close. He said something she could not hear.

"What?"

He pulled back and looked at her, his gaze passing rapidly back and forth over her face. "How can you love me? We could only stay together one way, but I failed—" He broke the last word off, unwilling and almost unable to say it.

Laenea slid her hands from his shoulders down his arms and grasped his hands. "You can't fail at this, Radu. The word doesn't mean anything. You can tolerate what they do to you, or you can't. But there's no dishonor."

He shook his head and looked away: He had never, Laenea thought, failed at anything important in his life, at anything real that he desperately wanted. He was so young . . . too young to have learned not to blame himself for what was out of his control. Laenea drew him toward her again and kissed the outer curve of his eyebrow, his high cheekbone. Salt stung her lips.

"We can't—" He pulled back, but she held him.

"I'll risk it if you will." She slipped her hand inside the collar of his shirt, rubbing the tension-knotted muscles at the back of his neck, her thumb on the pulse point in his throat, feeling it beat through her. He spoke her name so softly it was hardly a sound.

Knowing what to expect, and what to fear, they made love a third, final, desperate time, exhausting themselves against each other beside the cold blue sea.

Radu was nearly asleep when Laenea kissed him and left him, forcibly feigning calm. In her scarlet-and-gold room she lay on the bed and pushed away every concern but fighting her spinning heart, slowing her breathing. She had not wanted to frighten Radu again, and he could not help her. Her struggle required peace and concentration. What little of either remained in her kept escaping before she could grasp and fix them. They flowed away on the channels of pain, shallow and quick in her head, deep and slow in the small of her back, above the kidneys, spreading all through her lungs. Near panic, she pressed the heels of her hands against her eyes until blood-red lights flashed; she stimulated adrenalin until excitement pushed her beyond pain, above it.

Instantly she forced an artificial, fragile calmness that glimmered through her like sparks.

Her heart slowed, sped up, slowed, sped (not quite so much this time), slowed, slowed, slowed.

Afraid to sleep, unable to stay awake, she let her hands fall from her eyes, and drifted away from the world.

In the morning she staggered out of bed, aching as if she had been in a brawl against a better fighter. In the bathroom she splashed ice water on her face; it did not help. Her urine was tinged but not thick with blood; she ignored it.

Radu was gone. He had told the aide he could not sleep, but he had left no message for Laenea. Nor had he left anything behind, as if wiping out the traces of himself could wipe out the loss and pain of their parting. Laenea knew nothing could do that. She wanted to talk to him, touch him—just one more time—and try to show him, insist he understand, that he could not label himself with the title failure. He could not demand of himself what he could break himself—break his heart—attempting.

She called the crew lounge, but he did not answer the page. He had left no message. The operator cross-checked, and told Laenea that Radu Dracul was in the crew hold of A-28493, already prepared for transit.

An automated ship, on a dull run, the first assignment Radu could get: Nothing he could have said or done would have told Laenea more clearly that he did not want to see or touch or talk to her again.

She could not stay in Kathell's apartment any longer. She threw on the clothes she had come in; she left the vest open, defiantly, to well below her breastbone, not caring if she were recognized, returned to the hospital, anything.

At the top of the elevator shaft the wind whipped through her hair and snapped the cape behind her. Laenea pulled the black velvet close and waited. When the shuttle came she boarded it, to return to her own city and her own people, the pilots, to live apart with them and never tell their secrets.

# *Tropic of Eden*

## Lee Killough

Karen Lee Killough has published few stories so far, but she's established herself as a writer worth watching (and reading). In "Tropic of Eden" she tells a richly imaginative story of a new art-form and the attempt of the narrator to create a portrait of the most beautiful woman in the world. But the "tropic" sculpture fails to capture her essence—because she's hiding a dreadful secret.

Ms. Killough lives with her husband in Kansas, where, in addition to writing, she works in the Radiology Department of the local veterinary hospital.

---

Eden Lyle still lives in Aventine. I see her occasionally at a distance, slim and graceful as ever in the Neohellan dresses that were her trademark, but her face is always veiled. I sometimes wonder what she thinks, living there above the Lunamere, looking out over a world she no longer allows to see her, and what she has to say to Hebe—and how much she hates me.

The news she had taken Mad Simon's villa shook Aventine like an earthquake, a rare event. Normally the rich and famous are considered commonplace. With the international airport and the stargate on Diana Mountain just an hour away by cableferry, we are virtually next door to the universe, yet remote enough to make a good retreat. Jessica Vanier wrote her poetry in a cabin on Birch Cove; Xhosar Kain cast his sonic masterpiece *I, the Living* in the studio next to mine; and Thomas Bradley Jerome lived on the cliffs above the Heliomere long before Congress investigated him in its hearings on black-market transplants. But Eden Lyle was another matter. She was not merely an actress, not merely one of the most beautiful women alive; she was a legend, Eve and Lillith, Penelope and Circe. She had been the guest of every world leader in the past decade and slept, so gossip claimed, with half of them.

"And she arrived here last night," Clive Harrison announced dramatically, bringing the news to me at my studio. He opened his arms to the sculpture I was working on. " 'Hail, Moonflower, who pales the sun; My poor heart sickens for love of you; And lives its days as night eternal; All while—' "

"For god's sake, Clive," I interrupted, "you should know better than to talk at a sculpture with a sonatropism. Look what the sounds are doing to it."

The sculpture was twisting like a corkscrew and leaning toward him.

Clive grinned sheepishly. "Maybe you could let me finish and then title it *The Lovesick Poet.*" But he patted the trope and backed away.

I started humming at it, coaxing it out of its spiral. Sound would always affect it to some degree, of course; the dynamic nature of the medium is the beauty of tropic sculpture. Once I had my basic concept imprinted, the piece would be permeated with a stabilizing gas, and its subsequent alterations would be only variations on the theme, but now every sound affected it profoundly.

And just as I almost had the piece back to its original form, I heard the door behind me open. I grimaced. What I did not need now was another interruption. Throwing a muffling cloth over the trope, I turned frowning.

With the light of the summer sun behind her, I could not really see the woman in the doorway, only her silhouette sheathed from head to wrists and ankles in a cowled Neo-hellan dress. It was a very nice silhouette, too, and something in the poised assurance of her carriage stopped the unfriendly greeting in my throat long enough for her to speak first.

"Drummond Caspar?" she asked.

The voice was low and rich, husky almost to the point of masculinity—and instantly identifiable. I think I swallowed audibly before speaking.

"Miss . . . Lyle."

Eden Lyle came forward, pushing back the cowl. Around me the world blurred, and all I could see in the universe was flawless skin, regal cheekbones, eyes as deeply purple and velvet as pansy petals, and silver-blond hair hanging straight and silky to her waist. It had to be one of the few remaining naturally beautiful faces in the world, just perceptibly asymmetrical, free of the monotonous perfection of cosmesculpturing. Seeing her in person, I could well believe the story that following a hovercraft accident some time ago she had chosen to spend a year in traction waiting for the shattered bones of her leg to heal rather than risk a transplant that might not match perfectly.

Behind me I heard Clive sigh. He began softly, " 'Hail, Moonflower.' "

It occurred to me I should say something, not just stand staring. "May I help you?" I asked.

She smiled. It sent a hot flash clear to my toes. "I hope so," she said. "I need something to fill the sterile spots in the villa I've just taken. I'm told you have the best tropic sculpture in both Aventine and Gateside."

Margo Chen, my agent, would have loved to be able to record that. "I have what I consider some very nice pieces," I said.

"Do you have photo- and sonatropes?"

I did. I worked with most of the available tropisms: photo, sona, thermo, and kinetitropes, even a few psychotropes. With Clive following, I took her over to the corner I used for a gallery, and while she studied the sculptures, we studied her. Once, crossing glances with Clive, we exchanged blissful smiles.

"It's very difficult to decide; they're all so magnificent." Eden backed off until she stood in the middle of the area and turned slowly, tapping her lower lip with a thoughtful finger. "I think I'll take the one called *Sunspots,* and *Mercury's Child* over there," she said, then sighed. "But none of the sonatropes are quite what I had in mind to fill—"

"I like that one over there."

Neither she nor Clive had spoken, and I certainly had not. Our heads snapped in the direction of the timid voice. It was something of a shock to realize there was a fourth person in the studio, and a double shock a moment later when, on thinking back, I realized I had actually been aware of the girl all the time but had somehow avoided seeing her.

I looked at her now. She appeared about sixteen or seventeen and closely resembled Eden, which was, perhaps, what made the difference all the more striking. There was the same body, same bones, same coloring—but the silver hair was crudely hacked short and without make-up her pale face looked virtually featureless. She wore her dress, a copy of Eden's, like a shapeless rag.

With all of us staring at her, her face did take on color, an unattractive bright pink. She stepped back, stumbling over a low kinetitrope which had reacted to her movement near it by stretching out sideways. The girl recovered her balance by turning the fall into a smooth backward somersault but straightened pinker than ever. She pointed to a small pyramid of interlocking loops. Almost inaudibly, she repeated, "That one?"

It was an early piece, *Möbius Mountain,* a very minor work. I kept it more out of sentiment than any hope of selling it. It was one of the first tropes I had attempted, and I was still amused at the way it rattled its rings in response to being whistled or talked at.

Eden looked it over from a distance and shook her head. "I'm afraid it isn't suitable." She looked around once more. "I'm sorry; I don't see anything else that attracts me at the moment. I'll just take the phototropes." She paused. "Can I arrange to have them delivered?"

"I'll be happy to bring them round," I said.

She smiled. "Thank you. Do you know where I am?"

I nodded.

A credit card appeared out of her purse. "Add a ten percent bonus to cover your trouble."

I began, "That isn't—"

Her hand on my arm interrupted me. "Please." Both her voice and velvet eyes insisted.

I made out the ticket.

The girl spoke, and though soft, the sound of her voice startled me again. Somehow I had forgotten her. "Could I have the little piece—for my room?"

"No," Eden said. She held out a hand to me. "Thank you so very much for your time."

The hand was soft and cool. I found myself kissing it. I was tempted to say something like "My time is ever slave to yours," but controlled the impulse. Clive was the poet. Instead, I said, "I'll bring the pieces out this afternoon."

Clive and I followed her to the door and watched them climb into a chauffeured limousine. As it hummed away, I heard Clive whistle. He pointed at the license.

"That's Bradley Jerome's number. What do you suppose she has to do with him?"

"I'm more curious about the girl," I said.

"Her?" Clive shrugged. "That's just Hebe, a cousin, I think. Eden is her guardian."

Which explained the likeness. I dismissed the girl. "What do you think of Eden Lyle in person?" I asked Clive.

He sighed ecstatically. "I'm going to finish my moonflower poem and nail it to her door."

The world was coming back into focus. I shook the last heady clouds of enchantment out of my brain and pushed him toward the door. "Fine. Finish it. Meanwhile. I'd better get back to work on that sonatrope before the traffic through here ruins it."

I uncovered the trope but just sat staring at it. Imposing precise, brisk lines on it was impossible when all I could think about was velvet purple eyes and long silver hair. Finally I gave up, rewrapped it, and called Margo in Gateside to tell her about the sale.

Her reaction was one hundred percent commercial. "Get her to pose for you."

My reaction was to laugh. "Right. Offer her five dollars an hour and please don't play compsynth tapes while I'm working."

"I mean it, Cas," Margo insisted. "Her portraits are worth thousands. Or think of its drawing value at exhibitions."

"I don't see how I can impose on her by asking her to give up her time for my profit, much as I'm attracted by the idea of being able to see her every day."

"Ah, another conquest." Margo's voice came back drily over the line. "What is there about the woman that makes weak men slaves and strong men swoon?"

"She's very beautiful."

"And beautiful women like to be admired, my lad, so get on out and sweet-talk her into sitting for you."

Margo knows her business and I usually follow her suggestions, but Eden Lyle—Eden was different. I thought about it, though. I was still thinking about it when I loaded the phototropes in the van and headed out Cliffside Road toward Mad Simon's.

There were several theories regarding Simon Broussard's architectural preferences: He was a claustrophobic; he was paranoid and wanted to be able to see his enemies coming; or he needed to feel surrounded by the elements in order to write his music. Whatever the reason, he had had the cantilevered cliff-villa built completely of polarized plastics, even to the roof and floor. Outside, it was a coppery mirror, but inside a transparent shell awash in dusky sunlight and splashed with rainbows reflected from the water of the Lunamere some forty feet below.

I tried not to look down as I dollied the sculptures to the sites Eden had chosen for them. The sites were perfect. The phototropes would catch every change of light from dawn until sunset, and the size and form of each complemented its surrroundings. Eden's choices could not have been better and I told her so.

She blew me a kiss. "Only because I had quality work to choose from. Brad was right." Her gaze slid past me. She looked thoughtful. "I still need one more space filled. Perhaps you'll have a suggestion."

She led the way to an atrium in the middle of the house. At one end water splashed down the sides of a flat-topped pyramid of stones into an oval pool—though that was not the first feature to attract my attention. The girl Hebe was there, too, working out nude on a board exercise mat. I saw now how she had managed the morning's somersault over the kinetitrope. Her every movement was smooth and controlled. She flowed from stretch to bend to twist with the fluid grace of a cat.

She stopped as we came in and looked questioningly at Eden.

Eden circled the mat to the pool. "Don't let us interrupt you."

Wordlessly, Hebe resumed her exercises, though they now had a self-conscious stiffness.

Eden pointed to the waterfall. "That's where I wanted to put the sonatrope. I thought the water would provide an interesting stimulus for it." She looked up at me. "Could you do a piece especially to put there?"

It was too good a chance to miss. "Yes," I said, "but I'd like to use a psychotrope instead, and . . . I'd like to represent you."

Her brows rose. "A psychotropic portrait." She studied the waterfall. "What an intriguing idea." When she looked back up at me the velvet of her eyes was so thick the color looked near black. "I'd like that. When would you like to begin?"

My answer was a bit hoarse. "Whenever it's convenient for you."

"Tomorrow morning is convenient, but I have one condition. I dislike going out except when necessary. Would you mind bringing your materials and working here?"

Work here, alone with her, every day? I could hardly say yes fast enough.

She looked back at the waterfall, smiling, absently pushing her hair back from her forehead. I noticed a thin, nearly invisible surgical scar just under the hairline. I looked more closely. It was the type made by face-lifting. Her age was impossible to guess, but I realized that she was not the mere girl she first appeared to be.

Noticing my scrutiny, Eden abruptly backed away from me into the comparative shadow of the salon entrance. "I think there's nothing more to discuss, then," she said. "I'll see you at ten o'clock tomorrow. Hebe, finish inside, out of the sun."

It was clearly dismissal. Leaving, I cursed myself for staring. I was lucky that Eden had not been so offended that she canceled the sittings.

The next morning, though, I wondered whether I had imagined her offense. She greeted me with a smile that would have melted the polar caps. "Do come in. May I call you Drummond?"

"Everyone calls me Cas."

"Cas, then. I have a space cleared for you in the salon."

Aside from the uncomfortable feeling the transparent floor gave me of walking on air, I approved of her choice. The entire room was bright, but the light was best over the small table she had set up for me. I suggested an area rug be laid where I would be working. That solved the problem of vertigo, and I was ready to go to work.

The dress Eden wore today was based on Minoan styles. It bared her breasts and was slit to the hip, revealing a long expanse of smooth leg with each step. She curled up on a couch in front of me.

"I've never sat for tropic sculpture before. Do I do anything in particular?" she asked.

"Just relax and be yourself. With this tropism, both of us are needed to imprint the concept. I do the basic shaping; then your personality determines the final form. Don't be disturbed, but I'm going to just look at you for a while," I warned her.

She laughed. "I've been looked at by a good many people. I thrive on it."

She certainly appeared to. While I leaned on the wrapped block, forearms folded, and studied her through half-closed eyes, building an image in my mind, she stared back with velvet eyes and a slight smile curving her mouth. Then I unwrapped the block and began roughing out my mental image. It was to be slim and softly curved, all lightness, delicacy, and grace, yet sensual, too.

Eden watched with fascination. "It's extraordinary how they change shape. I know they're mutated from sensitive plants like the mimosa group, but I've always wondered how they come to artists like you in those nice big blocks."

"They're cultured from the breeder's parent stock from slips or, more commonly, by cloning."

Her eyes regarded me steadily. "I didn't know cloning was done commercially."

"Of course. It's the best way to reproduce the qualities in a particular individual. There was even a fad for cloning people a while back."

"I remember." She glanced at a table chronometer and stood up. "I'm afraid that's all the time I have today." She softened the dismissal with a smile and a blown kiss. "Tomorrow at the same time?"

Of course tomorrow at the same time. My only concern was what to do the rest of the day that would not seem anticlimactic.

On the way out I passed Hebe standing still and silent in the doorway, but not until I was in the van did it occur to me that I had not so much as nodded a greeting to her. What was it about the girl that made her so easy to ignore? It must be difficult growing up as a ward of someone as overwhelming as Eden Lyle. I resolved to make a point of acknowledging her presence the next time I saw her.

As it turned out, I need not have worried about the rest of my day. It was spent entertaining half the population of Aventine, it seemed, a constant parade of my friends and fellow artists along Callisto Avenue who wanted to ask what Eden Lyle was like. The traffic was so bad I finally locked the door and pretended to be out in order to get any work done on my other commissions.

Eden was very amused by it when I told her several days later. She laughed aloud. "I should have warned you what you were letting yourself in for. I'm sorry." The warm velvet of her eyes belied the words, though. "Do you want to stop?"

I did not. However much trouble it might cause the rest of the day, I would not have given away one of those mornings with Eden Lyle at any price.

I heard a soft slither on the floor behind me and looked around to see Hebe slipping barefooted into the room. I remembered my resolve.

"Hello," I said.

She stopped short, eyes startled, and looked quickly past me toward Eden. "Hello," she whispered and, turning, fled.

I cocked a brow at Eden. "Did I do something wrong?"

"She's just shy." Eden came over to stroke the emerging shape of the sculpture. "It's progressing beautifully."

I wished it had been. I would not tell her, but the trope was resisting me. The form was only partially what I intended. The rest was its own idea. I lay awake some nights wondering what was wrong with it.

However, there was a bright side to the problem, too. Every difficulty meant another day I could spend with Eden, and they were hours I would remember the rest of my life. While I worked, she—"performed" would be the best word, I suppose, adding the force of her personality to the shaping of the sculpture. She recreated bits of past roles, told witty anecdotes about the famous and powerful men she knew, and danced or sang. The sinuously graceful dance steps reminded me of Hebe's exercises. The songs were mostly unfamiliar. One of them haunted me for days, though, until I finally identified it as one my mother used to sing when I was a boy.

I told Eden. It was the second faux pas of the day. The first had been bringing *Möbius Mountain* out to give to Hebe. I am not sure why I did it. Out of guilt, probably, compensation for having mostly ignored the girl day after day.

Once she was past initial disbelief, Hebe was radiant with delight. She hugged the little sculpture to her. "Thank you." She even managed a normal tone of voice. "No one ever—" She broke off, coloring, and bolted.

Eden said, "You didn't have to do that." Her voice was light, polite, correct for the situation, but her face was taut, and before her eyes went opaque, I caught a quick glimpse of disapproval and something that looked strangely like fear.

Tension stretched uncomfortably between us. To break it I said, "I know where one of your songs comes from," and told her about my mother.

The velvet in her eyes turned to gem-hard brilliance. Without a word she turned and walked out of the salon. I could only stare after her and wonder irritably what in the stars possessed the two of them. Was there something about Mad Simon's villa that drove its inhabitants as crazy as the old man? Maybe living suspended in midair did it.

On the way out I glimpsed Eden in the library, talking on the telephone. ". . . arrangements, Brad," she was saying. Her voice rose, sharpening. "It must be done as soon as possible."

I shut the door behind me rather harder than necessary.

A ringing phone greeted me at the studio. It was

Eden, contrite and apologetic. "I'm sorry for my rudeness, Cas. I hope you'll forgive me."

"Of course." I was only too happy to. "But would you tell me what happened?"

"It's silly. You suddenly reminded me of something I had to do, and I was out of the room before I realized I had just walked out and not explained to you."

I did not examine the plausibility of that too closely; I wanted to believe her.

"So don't think I'm angry with you," she went on, "but I can't sit tomorrow. I have an appointment I must keep."

"I could come in the afternoon," I offered hopefully.

"I'll probably have to be gone all day. I'm sorry."

I was, too. The day after tomorrow seemed like an eternity away. What could I do in the meantime? For one thing, I could go over to Gateside. I needed to pick up some supplies, and I really ought to stop by Margo's office and go over the details of an exhibition I had been invited to contribute to. I called Margo to warn her I was coming and early the next morning caught the cabletrain.

Margo greeted me with a sardonic smile. "Welcome back from paradise. How does it feel to be among mere mortals again?"

"Don't forget who it was that urged me to do this portrait," I replied.

She lifted a brow, then grinned. One finger drew a mark in midair.

Our ritual thrust and parry over with, she pulled out an envelope of information sent by the exhibition's promoters and we settled down to study it. Mostly it was a matter of deciding which pieces to send and how best to send them. That took most of the morning.

As we finished and stood to stretch, Margo said, "It's a bit early but why don't we catch lunch now—my treat—and then you can see about getting your supplies."

"If you're paying, it's a fine idea. Where shall we go?"

We went to the usual place, the Beta Cygnus. The food is excellent, it is enough out of the way that the tourists have not found it yet, and, perhaps most importantly, it is right across the street from Margo's office. We sat down at one of the sidewalk tables and ordered.

The waiter brought tea first. Margo settled back comfortably, sipping at hers.

"How is the Lyle portrait coming?"

I rubbed my nose, grimacing. "I don't know. I know what I *want* to do. Sometimes the piece flows right into the image, but other days it's like a wrestling match, and the best I can do is a draw. The trope is very stubborn about doing something else."

She leaned forward, setting her cup aside. "Like what?"

"That's what I don't know."

"It *is* a psychotrope," she pointed out. "Maybe the problem lies in your subject, or to be more exact," she hurried on when I opened my mouth to protest, "the difference between your subject and your concept of her. The trope may be responding exactly as it is supposed to."

I rejected that flatly. Eden was nothing like the form the psychotrope appeared to be trying to take. There was one other possibility, of course. Until it was stabilized, the trope could shape to any personality near it, and Eden did not live alone. I would not have thought, however, that Hebe's personality would be strong enough to override—

The thought broke off as I saw the subject herself sitting at a back table. Surprisingly, Hebe was alone. I called to her.

She hesitated, then smiled and waved shyly.

"Come on over and join us," I invited.

After a good deal of lip chewing, she did, holding her long skirt up to keep it from tangling with chair legs or her own feet. I introduced her to Margo, who looked the girl over with the same narrow-eyed speculation she used on the work of unknown artists.

"Gateside is an interesting place to poke around on your own, isn't it?" I asked.

Hebe's eyes widened with surprise. "I'm not alone. Eden is inside."

"She finished her appointment, then?"

"Appointment?" Hebe shrugged. "I don't know. This is where Mr. Jerome brought us. When Dr. Ascher came, Eden told me to wait out here."

It was the longest single speech I had ever heard her deliver.

Margo frowned. "Ascher. Dr. *Hugo* Ascher?"

Hebe bit her lip. "I don't know." Her eyes went past us toward the door of the Beta Cygnus. She brightened. "Ask him yourself. They're coming out."

Eden recognized me instantly. The brim of her hat hid her expression, but there was surprise in her posture as she halted in the doorway. She moved forward again almost immediately, and by the time she reached our table she was smiling in delight. I stood up to meet her.

She held out both hands to me. "Isn't this a marvelous coincidence. We get to see each other today after all, it seems. Oh, I'm forgetting my manners." She stepped aside and brought up the men behind her. "Drummond Caspar, Brad Jerome. You may have seen him around Aventine. This is Mr. Hans Feldman."

Jerome nodded. The other man made a stiff little forward jerk that looked like an aborted bow from the waist.

Eden sighed wistfully. "I wish we had time for a drink with you, but we have to go." She reached up and touched my cheek. "Tomorrow. Hebe."

She called the girl as someone might command a dog to heel. It was a disquieting thought.

Margo looked after them. "Feldman?" she murmured.

"Maybe Hebe heard wrong. She's a strange child."

"Strange, maybe, but not wrong. The man's name is Ascher, all right, and he used to be a doctor until someone sued him for malpractice a few years ago—I forget the circumstances just now—and his license was taken away."

I vaguely remembered the case, too.

Margo sipped her tea. "I wonder why she lied."

"Maybe Jerome told her to." After all, it was easy to see the possible connection between Mr. Thomas Bradley Jerome and an ex-doctor. Eden was probably along for the ride, and naturally Jerome would caution her against advertising his affairs. I put the matter out of mind.

To be more accurate, I made the decision to do so. In actual fact, it would not go away. It kept niggling at me, asking uncomfortable questions like: If Jerome wanted a confidential meeting, why not temporarily dismiss Eden as they had Hebe?

That may have been why the sittings went so poorly after that. Psychotropes are the most difficult to manipulate; they need full concentration and no external tension. Either I lacked the one or something was providing too much of the other, because I had no control over the sculpture any longer. It kept pulling away from my hands, slowly, in the way of tropes, but inexorably. The fluted edges defied being spread and insisted on curling like scrolls. I would coax one into opening, but when I turned my attention to another, the first started folding again.

"It seems to have gone psycho today," I quipped, giving up in disgust.

Eden tucked her arm through mine and rubbed her cheek against my shoulder. "Perhaps it's a faulty piece of wood. Or maybe"—she looked up at me—"it's something I'm doing wrong."

"I'm sure it isn't your fault," I assured her. "But I really don't care any longer. I'm tired of fighting it. Why don't we scrap it? I'll get a new block and start over."

Her finger smoothed the hair on my forearm. "There isn't time. Brad is going abroad soon and he's asked me to come with him."

The bottom went out of my stomach. "And you're going?"

"Oh, Cas." Raising herself on her toes, she kissed me lightly. "It isn't the end of the world, nor is it forever."

It would only seem so. I looked down at her. "So you want me to keep working on this piece as it is."

She stepped away from me and turned her attention on the sculpture. "I don't think it needs any more work."

I stared incredulously. "How can you say that when—"

She interrupted. "It may not be what you intended—sometimes a role I set out to play won't take the interpretation I would like, either—but it's still beautiful. I'd like to keep it as it is."

I eyed the trope with distaste. It was a piece of garbage. "I won't sign it."

"That's all right." She grinned mischievously. "I'll still know who did it."

I went on as though she had not spoken. "But I won't charge you for it, either. I don't approve, but if you want it, it's yours. I make you a gift of it."

The velvet of her eyes glowed richly. "Thank you very much, Cas. Would you set it up in the atrium, please?"

I carried it out and placed it on the flat surface above the waterfall. Then, leaving Eden admiring it, I gathered up my tools and glumly loaded them in the van. I left with only a perfunctory wave at Hebe, who was doing her exercises on the floor of the library. I could not understand how anyone with Eden's good eye for art could think the sculpture was beautiful. It was not at all what it was supposed to be, not at all Eden Lyle.

I did not see Eden again for almost a week. I picked up the phone a couple of times to call but could think of nothing to say and hung up again. I kept hoping she would call me. She did not, and, finally, afraid that if I did not act I would lose the chance to see her at all before she left, I drove out to her villa one evening.

It was just getting dark but the lights had not been

turned on in the villa yet. It loomed opaquely against the sky. A figure in a long pale dress moved gracefully through the garden.

"Eden," I called.

The figure paused. I vaulted the low boundary wall and ran up the slight slope toward her. Not until I was beside her did I realize it was Hebe. What I had taken for long hair was the cowl of her dress.

I could not keep the disappointment out of my voice. "I thought you were—"

"Eden," she finished matter-of-factly. "She's out tonight."

My disappointment sharpened. The drive had been in vain. I felt I could not just leave, though, and so I said, "It's uncanny how much you look like your cousin in this light. If you wore some make-up and let your hair grow, the two of you would look like twins."

Hebe's eyes lifted to mine, dark, unreadable pools. "We are."

I did not immediately understand. "Are what?"

"Twins. Not cousins."

I laughed. "There's just a few too many months' difference in your ages for you to be twins," I pointed out.

"I'm a clone," Hebe said.

I realized several moments later that my jaw was hanging and snapped it back into place. I tried to talk. I did not succeed very well. "A—I thought—cousins, I was told—why would Eden—"

"I asked once," Hebe said. She sighed. "She wouldn't tell me why she had me made."

She turned toward the villa. I found myself following. She pulled a leaf off a low-hanging branch and absently shredded it as we walked. I watched her covertly.

A genetic duplicate of Eden, maybe, but nothing alike in any other respect. Why did she exist? I knew the reasons usually attributed to certain groups: homosexuals, male and female, and "liberated" women, in order that they might have children without having to involve the other sex; individuals whose vanity forbade the dilution of their germ plasm; eugenics faddists intent on perpetuating their ideas of racial perfection. Surely Eden did not fall into any of those categories.

We reached the villa. Dropping the remains of the leaf, Hebe led the way inside through the terrace door. With darkness, the perception of depth was gone, and the floor looked more substantial, though the moon and stars visible beyond the ceiling and the splintered reflection of the moon on the water below still gave the illusion of being immersed in a sea of lights. Hebe touched a hidden light switch and the illusion disappeared. Instead, we were surrounded by mirrors. Our distorted images reflected back at us from walls, ceiling, and floor.

She shook back the cowl of her dress, watching her reflections do the same. "Hebe was a servant," she said quietly.

Her mythology was poorly researched. "Not exactly a servant," I corrected her. "Hebe was the cupbearer of the gods, yes; she was also the goddess of youth and spring. One of her gifts was supposed to be the ability to restore youth."

Hebe focused on me for a moment; then her eyes went remote. "Next to physical perfection, Eden worships youth."

She turned away toward the atrium. "Come look at your sculpture. It keeps changing."

I could well imagine, if I had not known how it was supposed to look, I might have been able to admire the piece. It was tall and graceful, its color faintly luminous in the single spotlight shining up from its base, but where it should have been spread wide, catching the light and embracing the horizon, it was narrow, shadowed, folded in upon itself. It stirred, reacting to our presence. Slowly, several of the fluted edges unrolled.

"Watch," Hebe said.

She moved around the pool. The sculpture quivered. It turned, following her progress.

The skin down my spine prickled. I have worked with tropes of every kind but none that ever reacted like that, not even kinetitropes. I moved around the pool in the opposite direction, but the sculpture did not react to me.

"Only me," Hebe said.

She moved closer. The sculpture leaned toward her, more of its edges opening, reaching, groping for her. With a shiver, Hebe backed away and walked quickly into the salon.

I followed. "When are you leaving?" I asked.

"Day after tomorrow." She did not turn on the lights but stood at the wall looking down over the Lunamere. "For Switzerland."

"Your cou—Eden seems partial to mountains."

Hebe looked around inquiringly.

"Both Aventine and Switzerland have mountains," I explained.

"We're going there because of some spa Eden wants to visit." By the light I could see her wrinkle her nose. "I even have to go."

"It won't hurt you. Most of those places provide plenty of rest, nutritious food, and exercise."

She just looked at me. After a bit she said, "I get that here."

I laughed. "Which spa is it?"

"Nebenwasser, near Schoneweis."

Nebenwasser. I had heard of it somewhere. I groped for the memory but it eluded me.

"Dr. Ascher recommended it," Hebe said.

I knew, then, where I had heard of Nebenwasser, and, more, I remembered the details of Dr. Hugo Ascher's malpractice conviction. That answered other questions, too. I hated all of them. I felt as though I were suffocating.

"Where's Eden?" I asked hoarsely.

"With Mr. Jerome."

I did not even thank her; I just headed for the van. I had to find Eden.

I did not have to go far. She was climbing out of Jerome's limousine as I left the villa. She watched it drive away before she turned and saw me.

"Why, Cas," she began, "what a lovely sur—"

I grabbed her by the shoulders. "Would you really go that far to stay physically perfect?" I demanded.

It was too dark to read her face but I heard her sharp intake of breath. "What do you mean? Cas," she protested, "you're hurting me."

"I know what Hebe is."

"So?" Her voice cooled. "There's nothing wrong with cloning."

"But she doesn't know why you did it. I do. Eden," I pleaded, "don't do it."

Her muscles went diamond-hard under my hands. With a sudden, surprisingly strong movement she twisted loose and backed away. "I don't have the slightest idea what you're babbling about," she said coldly.

Then I was sure I was right. My voice went harsh. "You've heard of Nebenwasser, surely. Your friend Jerome owns the property, according to Congress. He calls it a health spa, but it's a hospital."

"I will give you the benefit of the doubt and assume you're merely drunk, not mad. Go home and sleep it off, Mr. Caspar."

I caught her elbow and locked both hands around it. "Dr. Hugo Ascher, whom you call Feldman, is a transplant surgeon. He was one of the top men in the field until he ran into a little bad luck. That one chance in a hundred happened, and a patient died because his transplant rejected. There would be absolutely no chance of that if recipient and donor were genetic duplicates."

"In one second," Eden hissed, "I am going to start screaming."

"The transplant," I went on, "was a brain transplant."

The scream that shredded the night around us came from behind me. I dropped Eden's arm and whirled. A pale figure was fleeing away from us toward the villa. Hebe must have followed me out. If so—

"My God," Eden whispered. "She must have heard everything. Hebe!" She ran after the girl. "Hebe, wait!"

The front door slammed behind them. When I reached it, it was locked. I pounded on it. I could hear Hebe screaming hysterically inside.

I lunged at the door but it was massive and solid. All I did was bruise my shoulder. The screaming went on, and under it, the murmur of Eden's voice. I remembered the terrace door Hebe and I had used earlier. I started around the villa toward it.

I could just make out some of Eden's words, knife-edged: ". . . lovesick fool . . . jealousy . . . keep us here . . . he's being vindictive . . . Nebenwasser . . . good time . . ."

*"Liar,"* Hebe shouted. "LIAR!"

Suddenly, as I reached the terrace door, Eden shrieked, "Hebe, *no, don't!*" She screamed once, then subsided into a keening wail of despair.

From the sound of their voices they were in the atrium. I ran for it. And stood paralyzed in the doorway.

The plastic wall panels reflected the scene, and reflected also the images of opposite walls, so that stretching away to infinity on all sides, with increasingly greater distortion, were countless Edens wailing beside countless pools, their arms reaching toward the waterfall at the end, where the psychotrope huddled dark and withered and countless Hebes stood pressing their cheeks to the searing hot metal of the small spotlight they had ripped from the base of the sculpture.

I broke my paralysis and vaulted the pool to jerk the spotlight away from Hebe.

She let it go, smiling. The entire side of her face was purple and shriveled. "Too late," she said triumphantly. "No surgery can make me perfect again." She swayed. "No use to her now."

I caught her as she fainted.

And around me reflections reflected reflections, and an infinity of Edens looked at me with loathing and sank to the floor of an infinity of atriums, covering their faces.

# Victor

## Bruce McAllister

*If you're a fan of old science-fiction movies, you'll remember that when Hollywood last ventured en masse into producing science-fiction movies, in the 1950s, the results were usually simpleminded and rather banal melodramas of alien invasions foiled by intrepid teenagers. Ever wonder what happened to those crewcut/ponytailed heroes and heroines in later life? Bruce McAllister has come up with an answer that says a lot about Life in These United States . . . .*

McAllister, a professor of English at the University of Redland, California, served as a consultant for the Harry Harrison/Brian Aldiss *Best SF* series a few years ago; he's written several short stories and one remarkable sf novel, *Humanity Prime.*

---

I am standing on a hill now with Jane. I am wearing baggy khaki pants and a Hawaiian sports shirt with orange hibiscus and a big collar. I have a crewcut, but it's too long because I haven't had it cut in weeks. Jane is wearing a kelly-green pleated skirt, and her hair is in a ponytail (she looks five years younger with it), and the ponytail is drooping a little from the dust and dirt. A minute ago I caught myself whistling a jazzy version of Eddie Fisher's *Any Time* and stopped myself.

It's over now. We've won. We're standing on this hill looking down into the valley at the carcasses of the big alien worms ("nudibranches," the Professor calls them) which we've finally beaten. Our "weapon"—or rather, the professor's—worked. The invasion from another world has failed . . .

They came from the "intergalactic void," of course. Professor Stapledon, Jane's father, figured it out in the nick of time and saved us. What they looked like in outer space we don't know. But they were different out there. They'd been traveling through the cold void of space for thousands of years, and when they neared Earth, our planet's gravity field woke them. So they were ready when they hit Earth's atmosphere. They did not burn up from friction. They quickly began spinning "chitinous" cocoons, using the little bits of "atmospheric molecules" and their own alien bodies. The cocoons were hard, hard enough that the atmosphere didn't burn through and hard enough that the worms were "cushioned" when they hit Earth.

It was touch and go for quite a while, and at one point it appeared that they would win. They landed at night, left their cocoons, and began feeding on the "crude fiber" of our city dump. Because it was night, they grew slowly, but an accident showed us what would happen when the dawn came. Some idiot shined a searchlight from the Frontage Theater on one of the worms, and, feeding on the bright light and dump trash, it enlarged in what the Professor calls a "geometric growth," and then it broke apart into smaller worms that looked like ordinary earthworms. (The Professor called this "imitation." In other words, the alien worms hoped to survive on our planet by "imitating" one of our life forms.) The little worms could burrow like lightning, and according to the Professor's calculations, by eating rock and trash and sunlight they would be as large as the "parent" worms in two or three days. Fortunately we were able to capture all of those first little worms, but we knew we wouldn't be able to contain all of them when daylight arrived and our sun's rays fell on the dozens of giant worms that were browsing now on the city dump like cattle. There would be simply too many "infant" worms.

We saw no solution, and the clock ticked on. We didn't even know how to kill the little worms we'd just captured (we were keeping them in jars of "formaldehyde" in a dark closet for the time being). The Professor pointed out that we couldn't use bullets—because they would just eat the bullets. And if we tried to smash them, there would be "seminal fragments" (pieces of the little worms), and these "fragments" would grow, and we'd never find all of them anyway. The Professor also said (and this is what made the situation look completely hopeless) that we couldn't bomb the big ones with TNT or nitro or an A-bomb because they'd just "feed" on the energy and "multiply" even more quickly.

The National Guard was called, and the highway patrol. So was the Pentagon. Everyone wanted to use bombs, and the Professor had to fight hard to keep that from happening. He must have explained the situation to a hundred different people, all of them wanting to use bombs. Other countries—and, of course, our Supreme Commander—were notified too, and no one had an answer. Was this the end of the human species?

Mere hours were left before dawn. The worms were feeding quietly, waiting for the sun to rise.

It was then that the Professor produced his first invention. It was a special insecticide—like DDT, but different—and it combined an ingredient normally used against tapeworms and garden snails, and another ingredient often used to kill tomato worms (which are the "larvas" of the monarch butterfly, he explained).

The spray didn't work.

The Professor got to work on another invention, and Jane and I waited patiently at the newspaper office for a phone call from him. The minutes flew by. No call. And then finally:

The phone rang. It was the Professor, and he wanted us to rush over to his lab immediately.

When we reached the lab, an ugly surprise awaited us. In his excitement the Professor had tripped on a piece of equipment and had hit his head. In fact, he was falling into a coma as we arrived. But before he went unconscious, he looked up at Jane—who was holding him in her arms:

*"The whistle,"* he croaked.

Now it was up to me and Jane. "The whistle?" we asked ourselves. We had no idea what he meant. I certainly wasn't a scientist, and Jane had never really paid close attention to her father's experiments (even though she loved him dearly, and she was the only family he had left).

We looked and looked. The whistle? What whistle?

Finally, when there were only a few minutes left before dawn, we found it. The whistle. The Professor had wrapped it up in a sock in a drawer. It was a special hunting whistle he'd devised and tried to patent when he was only an Assistant Professor.

We set up loudspeakers and also a relay to a radio station that was connected with other loudspeakers.

Then we stood in the middle of the dump and blew on it as hard as we could. When I was out of breath, Jane took a turn—and vice versa.

And it began to happen, just as the Professor had calculated.

The birds began coming.

Hundreds of thousands of them, and a thousand different species. They settled down around us, and in the first hint of dawn they spotted the big worms.

Wild from the instinctual craving that birds have for worms, they ignored the size of the creatures and began their work. The invaders tried to fight back—by "growing" and "dividing"—but there were simply too many birds.

The Professor's whistle had worked. A simple little device like that—remembered at the last minute—and the entire human species had been saved. We should never underestimate science and technology (mankind's achievements, and his hope and salvation), nor the courage and resourcefulness of individual men and women, like Jane and myself.

The Professor has come out of his coma now, and all the newspapermen are interviewing him about the whistle.

Jane and I are being interviewed, too, since we're the ones who blew the whistle.

Jane and I have decided to get married. We've announced our engagement to the same newsmen and hope that they'll mention it in their articles.

The sun is beginning to set, and the sunset is beautiful. But it's actually a dawn, Jane says. Just like my little Jane to say that. She's always right.

The newsmen don't come anymore. Up until a few weeks ago people from *Life, Look,* and the *Post* were still coming, but they've stopped now. So many photos have been taken of the bony platelike remains of the alien worms that no one's interested anymore. Most of the remains have been stolen or taken away by museums. The city sold them to the museums and is planning to use the proceeds for a couple of long-overdue projects—one involving the dump.

Someone came a month ago and was talking about doing a book about me. They're the same people who did books on Stevenson and those four ransomed fliers that were shot down over Hungary a while back. A week later I got a call from the guy in New York, and he said the book would have to be about both of us, Jane and me. And then a week after that some other fellow called from the same publisher to say that the articles in *Life* had covered us too thoroughly and that interest in us nationally had started to die anyway.

Today Jane went shopping with Martha (Christmas is only a month away), and I went to the hill, to look down at the few remaining worm bones on the dump. It was strange standing on that hill. It was so quiet. I think I'm wearing the same khaki pants and the same saddle shoes I was wearing the day it all happened. I started to whistle, but it felt silly, and so I stopped.

When I woke up this morning, I did it without waking Jane. I looked over at her, and she didn't look the same. Her hair was in curlers, and she looked heavier. I know it didn't happen overnight. But this morning was the first time I'd noticed it.

We've put the Professor in a convalescent home outside of Pomona. The doctors don't think it had anything to do with his accident that day in the lab. That was too long ago to be affecting him this way now.

I drink a lot of Pabst Blue Ribbon these days, and I don't remember when I first switched brands. I also watch a lot of television. I like *Face the Nation* and *Omnibus,* I suppose (Jane tells me I should), but I also get a kick out of *Captain Video, Dragnet,* and *Mr. I-Magination.* And *77 Sunset Strip* (it's the "ginchiest"!). Jane hates them. I work at the big molds factory in Covina, and one of the things we make—the most famous anyhow—is cast molds for hula hoops. We make molds for other things, too—like teethers and the plastic objects you can hang from your rear-view mirrors.

Jane's pregnant, and she smokes a lot now. Before these Toni's she sets her hair with these days, she wore her hair so that it looked like a yellow poodle, and she wears very red lipstick—which looks like someone slugged her. I've told her a hundred times I don't like either the hair or the lips that way, but it doesn't faze her. I wish she'd start wearing a ponytail again.

Right after Peter woke us up this morning (his teeth were killing him, Jane tells me), she and I started arguing. She says our life bores the hell out of her. I told her that if it's boring, it's because she doesn't know what to do with herself during the day—a baby doesn't take *that* many hours. This made her mad. She threw some four-letter words at me and broke the vase in the hallway when she ran outside. But it's funny. I think I agree with her. She's right, in fact. I'm bored a lot these days, too. But she blames *me,* and she doesn't know how boring *she* can be. She just isn't interested in many things, which isn't her fault, I suppose. I have my hobbies, and she doesn't have any. And the hair styles and lipstick aren't exactly exciting either.

She'll probably join one of those PTA groups and spend all of her time with that when Petey's older, and I'll spend my time with the guys at the factory. The bowling's fine; the cards I don't really like all that much, but Jerry makes it worth it with all his jokes. Or maybe I'll spend my time with Petey and his Cub Scouts or something.

Sometimes Petey's crying depresses the hell out of me. It certainly never bores me.

Jane's dad died two months ago, and Jane is still saying how it was all our fault, how we should have taken him in with us, how he died because he didn't have anyone truly loving him. She always starts crying, and I always start shouting at her. Today I almost hit her.

Pete is having trouble in his fifth-grade class, after so much trouble in the fourth grade. We just never made him read enough at home, I think. He should like reading more than he does; then he wouldn't have so much trouble. Maybe Jane's PTA people are right. Maybe it's our fault. We don't read much either. There's so much yardwork on the weekends, and the barbecues every other weekend, and the games on TV, and the Scouts. If Pete was a girl, Jane would have to do it—be a den mother or whatever—and it wouldn't look so much like my fault.

I tried to get up to the top of the hill today, but they've been excavating it for a tract of Transamerican Medallion homes—$25,000 and up—the last one there's room for in the valley, they say. They've got a cyclone fence up around the hill now. I heard from Bob at the Bodega Bowl the other night that the valley floor is covered over with asphalt for a parking lot for that new Truesdale Center shopping area—the biggest in the state—and it's been like that for nine months. Obviously I haven't been out to look at the spot where the worms came down for quite a while. But every once in a while I do put on those saddle shoes—the same ones (Jesus, they're twelve years old now!)—and I go down the street, past all the juniper and birds-of-paradise, and I whistle—anything at all—and it reminds me of what happened back then. It helps. I have some things I'd rather not be thinking about, and so it helps.

Pete was busted for having marijuana on him at Poly High yesterday. The school won't turn him in, but they've suspended him for three weeks, and he's failing two classes anyway. We so much wanted him to try State next year. We've told him again and again what he'd have to do to get in, but it's never had an effect on him. He's got his friends, and the candy-apple GTO, and to hell with everything else!

Nancy is still cute in a little-girl way, though she's starting to get gangly. She's also starting to like boys, and I've argued with Jane a hundred times about the twelve-year-old bra thing. The real problem is, she likes this guy who's *fifteen*. She's always been Jane's favorite, but at least Jane's as upset as I am about the boyfriend situation.

We started seeing lawyers the same day that our dear Vice-President resigned.

The government of this country is so damned corrupt. I never could understand how we could let other countries make us fight their wars for them.

Pete dropped by two nights ago covered with grease from the shop, and Jane and I were arguing loud, and so he went away. I got mad and left too. I went to a motel and called Dorothy and she came over and stayed the night. We talked about taking a trip across the United States, and we both liked the idea.

When I got up the next morning, I caught myself

whistling. I thought about whistling and whistles, and it depressed the hell out of me, and I stopped.

Dorothy drops me off in the morning and meets me for lunch. Jane was never that way. Dorothy's got quite an ass on her, and I'd hate to see her put on any more weight, but she's certainly fun when it counts. And she does like most of the things I like, and vice versa.

One thing, though. I do wish she was more interested in reading those books I keep trying to get her to read. I've tried to explain to her—and more than once—how logical it is that throughout history our gods would actually be alien visitors (after all, if there are worms out there, why not?) and that our religions and civilization would be gifts from them. I did hit a guy in a bookstore once—he laughed a little too loud when I was explaining the idea to her—and I think that turned her off a little.

The alimony hasn't hurt us too much, which is good, because Dorothy likes campers and motor homes practically as much as I do. We looked at a Revcon 456 the other day, and that's the one I think we'll get. It's streamlined, like a spaceship, and that's what I've been looking for.

# *The Family Monkey*

## Lisa Tuttle

"The Family Monkey" (whose title comes from a poem by Russell Edson) is about the visitation of Earth by aliens—specifically, one alien—but it isn't a tale of marauding invaders pitted against teenagers in acne-lotion armor. Instead, its alien is crashlanded and confused, is taken in by a kind family in Texas, and within the space of about one acre and a couple of decades of time the creature has startling adventures and influences the lives of several humans in unforgettable ways.

Tuttle says she got the idea from a news story originally published about the turn of the century: "At that time, it said, a small town in north Texas witnessed a strange airship which crashed into a windmill. Inside was a pilot, dead on impact, dressed in a suit of strange, silvery metal—and not quite human." It later turned out that the "news" story was a hoax designed to build a Dallas paper's circulation, but Tuttle found it intriguing anyway, and "The Family Monkey" was the result of her speculations on the possibilities suggested by the story.

Lisa Tuttle tied with Spider Robinson in 1974 for the John W. Campbell Award for best new writers in science fiction; she was only 22 years old at the time. She holds a B.A. in

English from Syracuse University, and is currently the television editor and daily columnist for the Austin *American-Statesman.*

---

## William

I was sitting with Florrie on the porch of her daddy's house, watching the night get darker and wondering about making a move. I was at that time living in a boardinghouse in Nacogdoches, and Florrie's father had made me an offer to work for him that came complete with a house to live in. I didn't know if I wanted to be that much obligated to the man: I still thought I might want to go back to Tennessee, and maybe I'd be better with nothing to keep me here.

But then there was Florrie. I still can't figure why I was so interested in that scrawny little old girl, but I was. I guess there weren't too many women in Texas then, but still—most of the time Florrie didn't seem more than a child. But it was those other times that made me wonder, and made me wait, staying on in Texas, a place I didn't much like and didn't at all belong.

I was just deciding that moving a little closer to her there on the porch couldn't do no harm when there was a sudden flash in the sky, much brighter than any falling star ever was. It began to drop, leaving a streaky, glowing trail behind as it blazed brighter and then disappeared into the pines.

"What was that?" Florrie asked, already standing.

"Falling star?" I got up beside her.

"If it was, it must have fallen right over in the graveyard, it was so big and bright," Florrie said. Then: "Let's go see! I'd love to see a star up close!"

I thought I'd like to see a star up close myself, not that Florrie gave me any time to agree or disagree. She just took off into the woods and I followed after as best

I could. I ran into a lot of things in those dark woods. I tried to take hold of Florrie's hand, but she was impatient with me and pushed me off, saying there wasn't room for but one on this path, and that was true. It wasn't much of a path, and it must have been made by children, or elves, because below the shoulders I was fine, but I kept running head-on into hanging vines and protruding branches. I scratched my face up pretty good, and I guess I was lucky not to lose an eye. And Florrie really trotted through those woods, although I kept calling to her to slow up.

Halfway there it suddenly dawned on me. "Hey, Florrie, how're we gonna see anything? It'll be pitch-black in that old graveyard, and we didn't bring a lantern."

"If you'll hurry we can get there before the star burns itself out. We'll see by the light of that."

So I saved my breath for keeping up with her, not wanting to be lost in the woods without a light *or* a girl.

"There—is that it?"

I came up close behind her and looked where she was pointing. Whatever it was had sure enough landed right in the graveyard, but if it was a star or not we couldn't tell, for it had burned itself out. The night grew thicker around us and about all you could make out was a big, odd-angled, collapsed shape, like a barn some giant had pitched across a pasture. Whatever it was, it had no business being in that graveyard.

"What is it?" Florrie whispered, but I had no inclination to find out. Because suddenly, maybe foolishly, I was wondering if something might not come crawling out of the wreckage.

"Let's leave it be," I whispered back. "We can come out in the morning and see what it is. It's too dark now."

"If we wait till morning something might happen to it," she objected. "I'll just run back and fetch a lantern—you stay here and watch it."

"Why don't I go for the lantern?"

"You might get lost. I can go quicker'n you."

"Why don't we both go?"

"Are you afraid?" she asked, suddenly understanding.

"Of course not!" I said, real quick.

"Then wait till I get back." And she took off running, and what could I do but stay? I didn't want her to think me a coward, and, besides, she was right—I would have gotten lost in those woods.

Now, I am not the type who gets nervous about graveyards, after dark or otherwise. I don't believe in ghosts, and back in Tennessee there was a girl I used to take to a graveyard to court, so I have a kind of fondness for the places. The thing that was bothering me was that thing which didn't belong there, that chunk of star or whatever it was that had fallen out of the sky.

And as I sat there, staring at it (I couldn't see anything, but I didn't like the idea of turning my back on it) I started to hear something—a scratchy, grating sound that seemed to poke at the roots of my teeth and needle me just under my skin—and yet, though it didn't seem to make any sense at the time, I wasn't at all sure I was really hearing it. It seemed to be somehow inside me, a noise that my body sensed more than heard, a noise that was somehow a part of me, like the sound of my own blood pounding in my ears when everything else is silent.

I wanted to break and run, but there was something—and it was something more than fearing to look a fool in Florrie's eyes, it was a kind of compulsion—that wouldn't let me leave. So I stood there sweating, and argued with my feet, which seemed bent on dragging me over to that thing.

"Mr. Peacock?" Florrie, with a light, burst out of the brush. "Oh, there you are. You weren't going to explore it without me?"

I looked at where I was: It seemed my feet had done a pretty good job despite my arguing.

"Why, no, ma'am," I said, but she wasn't paying attention. She held the lantern up and away from herself, and we looked.

The thing which had fallen from the sky was of some dull metal. We could feel the heat from it, and the ground around was charred. I couldn't make out what it was, because I'd never seen anything like it, but I thought, It's a flying machine, and it's come from far away. And then forgot it.

"What's that?" Florrie said, whispering again.

There was a hole in the thing, deep blackness that the lantern light didn't touch against the silvery metal, and I couldn't tell if it was an accidental hole or some kind of door or window. Then I saw what Florrie had seen. Something was moving inside the darkness of the hole, something trying to get out.

You might have expected a woman to go crazy then, and Florrie did, but not at all in the way you'd expect. She didn't grab me, and she didn't scream, and she didn't faint or cry or run for home. She said, "We gotta help him, Billy." Her voice was urgent, and she immediately started toward the hole without any fear or hesitation.

Most of all I noticed that she called me Billy. Next I noticed she'd said "him"—"We gotta help him"—and with that noticing, I hardly paid any attention to the fact that I was agreeing with her, and going with her to the hole, reaching in (carefully, afraid the sides might burn us) and catching hold of something, someone, and pulling it out. I was scared, but I couldn't stop doing what was scaring me so. The flesh beneath my fingers didn't feel like the flesh of any man, but it was not an animal we were grappling with. He was stuck, and we knew we were hurting him, but we knew we had to get him out. It had to be done: The urgency was as much there as if this had been my mother, pinned beneath a rockslide.

And then we got him out and stretched on the grass. He looked enough like a man—in that he wasn't a dog or a horse—but even in the lantern light it was plain he wasn't human. He was some kind of freak or monster. His skin was too big on him. It hung like a sheet draped over his bones, the way the skin of a fat man, suddenly starved, might hang. It was rough and pebbly to the touch, and later, in daylight, we saw that he was a greenish-gray color all over. His eyes were too round, and there was something funny about the eyelids, and he didn't have a regular nose but only a couple of slits with flaps of flesh over them in the center of his face. It gave me a real creepy feeling all over when I saw what he was doing with his throat—blowing out a sort of translucent bubble of skin, the way a certain kind of lizard does.

I wished we hadn't come. I wished like anything we hadn't come.

"We'll have to get him to shelter so we can look after him," Florrie said. She stared down at the creature. I looked at her, not wanting to look at it. I wondered why she sounded so sure of herself, and why she wasn't scared, why she didn't want to run from there the way I did.

Her face was tight, like she was hurting and trying not to let it bother her. "I wish I knew rightly what to do," she said quietly. "I know what's wrong, and I know what would make him worse, but . . . maybe there isn't anything I can do to make it better, maybe there isn't anything anyone here can do for him now. But we can try—we can make him more comfortable, anyway. We'll have to fix up some kind of stretcher, anyway, to bring him up to the house. I'll go—"

"You'll go? Why don't I?"

She looked at me scornfully. "Because you can't just go and get things out of my house without a lot of questions, that's why."

"What does it matter? I could get someone else to help if we're going to take him up there anyway."

"We're not."

"You said—"

"Your house, not mine."

"My house! I don't have a house. If you mean the boardinghouse, do you intend to carry him into town?"

"The guest house. That's what I meant. You'll be

moving in after a few days, and we can keep him hidden there till he gets better."

"What makes you so sure I'm going to move in?"

"Now, Billy, don't be like that. We're just wasting time—somebody might come and see him."

"Well, so what if somebody does come?" I was getting pretty exasperated with her. "So what? Why can't we take him up to your house? We could get a real doctor, since you're so concerned with his health."

I stopped just short of saying what else I believed—that this thing would be better off dead, that it didn't belong and had no right to be here. Something like it would be easier explained away and forgotten, dead. Tuck him down in the graveyard—the other bodies would be too far gone to have any complaints about their company.

Florrie straightened slightly and said flatly, "My daddy shot a nigger once for comin' round on his property. He doesn't hardly think niggers are people, so you can guess what he'd have to say about this one. He'd kill him like an animal and feel less guilt. Now you just wait here, while I go get some things."

"Why should I? Why should I wait here with this old monster?"

"Billy, you just have to." She looked at me with her gray eyes shining in lantern light, and I saw she wasn't a child at all. So I put my arm around her and made to kiss her, and she punched me in the gut.

Then she went off into the woods again while I was still hunched over. I started swearing, but I didn't go after her, and I didn't go off on my own. I stayed there with that thing, just like she wanted me to. Just like it wanted me to.

And we took it up to the guest house, and she tended it and nursed it, and just as she'd said, I moved into the house and went to work for her father, and never made it back to Tennessee. And in time I married her, despite that gut-punch and the way she had of bossing me. Pete—as we called the monster after the only sound, the only real sound, we ever heard him make, a sort of *ppppp-ttttt* sound in his throat—became a part of the family and didn't seem such a monster any more. In time, he looked just as natural to us as any other person did, although he never stopped making me uneasy. It really unsettled me the way he and Florrie seemed to understand each other, whereas he and I were always strangers to each other. Our kids, when they came in time, loved Pete, and he was good with them.

I guess in all it's been good, it's worked out. I've made a home for myself here, and a name, friends and family. I think about the Tennessee hills sometimes—it's too flat here, and too dusty, even in the piney woods, for my taste—and I miss them, and the people I used to know. But they're all dead now probably, or gone away, and if I was to go back there wouldn't be anyone that knew me. This is my place now, even if I still don't much like it.

## Adaptation

At first it seemed only an oddity that they left him alone during the hours of darkness. At first he was too immersed in his pain to notice how life around him slowed and consciousness moved to another level.

There was much to learn, once he had mended (as much as he would ever mend) and could turn his attention to things outside his body. Sleep intrigued him—it was strange to him.

Life was very boring here for him, injured and out of touch with his own people. He searched hungrily for new interests, knowing that he must keep himself going, keep himself intrigued, or die. Something had happened to him in the crash which made it harder for him to think. His mind seemed wrapped in gauze now; he was limited. He could not communicate with these creatures, could not understand nor be understood except on the fuzziest, most imprecise and primitive levels. He was frustrated by the multitude of things he could no longer do, some of them simple things learned in childhood. There were ranges and heights now forever barred to him.

He continued his work with the limited mental equipment left to him. He tried to go on being a scholar, to give his life some meaning.

Sleep: It fascinated him. Here was something which might be important, a mental-spiritual state alien to his people. All of these creatures slept: What did it mean? What did they take from their journey through it every night?

To find out, he set about trying to fall asleep, to study the phenomenon at first hand. But he had no experience and no knowledge to draw upon. How to attain it? How to abandon oneself to it? It took him years to learn—but he had years. And when, finally, he had it:

He couldn't get back. It rushed upon him, swallowed him whole; he was wrapped, weighted, and sinking, and it was beyond all fighting. He had wanted this: Why then did he now want so desperataly to fight it? What instinct was this which prompted him to hold it off?

But it was too late. He was lost to sleep, swathed in it like the humans who had rescued him.

If sleep was frightening, the dreams were worse. He could not control them, and they were not his. He'd fallen into a pit, the abyss mankind kept hidden behind the curtain of sleep.

He wandered through the dreams of others, not even of his own kind, was caught in them and forced to play them out. Gave nightmares as well as received them as he shambled through the sleeping world.

Woke to the sun, terrified. Felt pity for the human race, a rush of gratitude for his own mental structure. He would never, he vowed, sleep again.

But the next night the battle began again. Sleep had him now. He'd made the mistake of learning it, and once learned it would not be unlearned. It gripped him already with the force of undeniable habit.

Every night he fought it as long as he could, but it

always overpowered him, submerged him, and every morning he dragged himself, shivering, out of the strange and terrifying sea of human sleep.

He was not, and could not be, human. The sharing of humanity's nightmares did not make him more human, yet it made him less than what he had once been. He forgot things; memories were lost, replaced by new learnings and by the useless memories, grafted on during sleep, of others. He changed and adapted, worn down by the numbing effects of day after day of living in this new, limited, and limiting world.

## Emily

I looked through the dust-streaked window at the sunlit pine forest and could almost smell the baked resinous scent of the country where I had grown up. New York was far away now. I was bone-weary and longing for the jouncing train ride to end. Just then I didn't care that it was Texas I was going to, not Paris; I simply wanted to be at rest.

My fingers brushed the cover of the book in my lap. The poems of Byron. Paul had given me that book. I heard his voice again, and wondered if anyone would ever again say my name the way he had said it.

I put the book inside the brown valise at my feet. In the bottom of that valise lay two hundred pages written out in my best hand: my unfinished novel. Unfinished because I felt the hypocrisy of writing about love when I knew nothing about it, yet I wanted to write about nothing else.

The train was crawling along now. The Nacogdoches station would not be far away. It was good that I had come to Texas; it would be better for me—more real, and less romantic—than Paris could have been.

In Texas I would learn to write about something other than love. I would relearn the important things, forgotten since childhood.

When Florrie embraced me, holding me close in her strong, capable arms, it seemed Mama was alive again, and I could become a little girl. Was this my little sister?

"Emma Kate! Oh, honey, how are you? It's so good to have you home again!"

I hugged back, and kissed her, a little awkwardly through being out of practice. "I'm just fine; I'm just fine, Florrie." I felt like crying, and saw there were tears shining in Florrie's eyes, too.

"It's just so good to have you back!" One more squeeze and she moved back reluctantly. "Now, where's the porter with your bags? Oh, Billy's got them. Come on, now—we'll get you home and out of those stiff clothes." It did me good to hear Florrie rattling on. "Now, we'll have a good long talk once you're settled in. I hope you're going to stay a good long while? No, no; we'll talk about all that later."

Billy hugged me, and it seemed strange to me that he was family now. I'd not set eyes on him since the day he and Florrie wed. And their children! It startled me a bit to see their four children. Florrie had been getting on with her life while I had been up in New York, teaching and playing at being an intellectual.

Billy loaded my things into the wagon with the children and helped me into the seat up front, between himself and Florrie. Then he clucked to the horses and we started off, slow and swaying. I looked out at the dusty road, the scrubby pines, the clapboard houses, the poorly dressed people, the animals. It seemed foreign to me after the man-made world of New York City.

The road wound through forest then, and the trees gave shelter from the sun and hid the straggling remains of the town. But the forest wasn't as deep as I remembered it. There were vast bare patches, ugly and denuded of trees: the harvest of the family lumber mill. The land was scarred, as by a forest fire, with tiny saplings pushing up bravely to stitch closed the wound. The old landmarks were gone, and I couldn't be certain how far we were from home.

Florrie continued to talk, and sometimes I listened. Finally she patted my knee. "Here. Almost home." The horses tugged us wearily around one last bend. Home. "Ain't it nice?"

I had imagined, somehow, that they would still be living in the old bride's house, although Florrie's letters had been rich with details of the building of their new home.

"It's lovely, Florrie," I said, and hugged her.

The house was large and sturdy, yet managed to have some style, a certain gentle elegance. It was painted white, and the windows, upstairs and down, were decorated with green shutters like many of the houses in New Orleans. The little bridal house, a log cabin, still stood, not far across the sloping lawn. It had been Billy and Florrie's first home, but once the children started coming it must have quickly become more cramped than cozy.

A colored woman came out of the side door as we rolled up the looping ribbon of driveway, hurrying toward us and beaming. This was Mattie, who hugged me while Florrie told me what a great help Mattie was with the children and the cleaning.

I looked suddenly from Mattie's dark face to my sister's smile. "Where's Daddy?"

Florrie's smile tightened. "We'll go see him as soon as you get cleaned up." She took my arm and walked me up toward the house, Billy following behind with my bags, the children scattering like a flock of birds uncaged.

"I thought he might have come up here to meet me," I said.

"Well, we asked him to supper, of course, But he won't come up here. He's as stubborn as he ever was. He don't like niggers around the place."

Of course. Why had I thought he would mellow with age?

"It's not so much Mattie and Tom," Florrie said.

"They're help—he might get used to ignoring them. But it's Pete he won't forgive us for."

"Who's Pete?" I didn't want to see my father. Every word Florrie said made me more certain.

"Pete," said Florrie. Her voice was odd. "Didn't I tell you about Pete? I suppose I never did. Well, you'll meet him by and by."

We entered by the back door, walking into a warm, good-smelling kitchen. But Florrie didn't give me time to gaze around, walking me quickly through a dark-wood hall and up uncarpeted stairs. "Right now you'd best get freshened up and go over to Daddy's. You know how cranky waiting makes him."

I did know, and I didn't like discovering that I still feared his anger.

My room was fresh and airy-feeling, from the white curtains sprigged with green to the patchwork quilt on the big brass bed. But I couldn't lie down on that bed for a nap; I couldn't even take a bath. Now that I knew Daddy was waiting for me I became rushed and clumsy, knocking over the china pitcher after I had poured water into the washbowl—almost breaking it, but it landed on the rag rug instead of the floor, spilling out the rest of the water but not cracking.

I washed my face, neck, hands—trembling and trying not to tremble as I exchanged my travel-stained dress for a clean one. I was a grown women. Say what he liked, he would not make me a girl again.

"Emily?" It was Florrie, peeking around the door. She hurried in and embraced me. "Oh, honey, don't be nervous!"

"Isn't it silly?" I said, trying to laugh. "I've faced down angry parents, and the headmaster at my school, but I'm afraid to see my own father. You were always the only one of us who could stand up to him, Florrie. I had to leave the state to be free of him."

We hugged again, and I clung to her a moment, trying to absorb some of her courage before I went to face our father.

He was waiting for me on the porch of the house I had grown up in. It was smaller in life than in memory, but he was not.

"It's about time you got here. Gossiping up there with your sister, I suppose."

"Hello, Daddy."

He got up to embrace me. We held each other awkwardly. I tried to kiss him, and his cheek rasped against mine.

"Come in and take dinner with me."

The kitchen too was smaller than I remembered it, and it was dirty, as it had never been when my mother was alive. Dinner was cornbread, beans, and ham, eaten sitting at the wooden table my father had built. It was much too large for just the two of us, but I suppose he didn't see any need to build himself a smaller one when this would do. He cooked and cleaned for himself now—Florrie might have done more for him, but I suspected it came down to a battle of wills between them.

We didn't speak much while we ate. That was my father's way. But the weight of the things we would say lay heavily on my tongue and I didn't eat much.

He commented on that, of course.

"Find a taste for fancy foods while you were up North?"

"I'm just not very hungry."

He wiped up the last few beans and sauce from his plate with a hunk of cornbread, washed that down with a gulp of iced tea, and settled back heavily in his chair, the wood complaining at his weight.

"Well," he said. "So you've come home. You given up on schoolteaching?"

I had known the question would come, but I had hoped for more time to think about it, time to talk with Florrie.

"I don't know if I've given up," I said. "I might just be here on a visit. Maybe I could see about getting a job near here—maybe do some tutoring." His eyes mocked me. He didn't believe me. He demanded some further explanation of myself and, unnerved, I made a mistake. I blurted out something I had meant to keep secret from him. "I thought I would do some writing while I'm here. I'm writing a novel."

His reaction was what I had known it would be: laughter; an outraged snort of laughter. "So now you want to be a writer. Why didn't you stay in New York with all those other writers, with all those intellectuals?"

"I may go back," I said. "I told you I hadn't really decided yet. I . . ."

But he wasn't listening; he never listened to me. "You thought that since the life you chose for yourself didn't work out that you'd come back here where your family would take care of you and you could play at writing without having to worry about being good or making a living at it. You could play at being an intellectual without having to prove yourself. You're like your mother, Emmie."

There were tears in my eyes, and I concentrated on not letting them fall.

He was silent, as I was—perhaps because he was sorry, or because he was thinking of my mother. Then he sighed and shook his head. "You shoulda got married, Emmie. You scared 'em all off with your learning and your books. Now you know you need a husband—but you might have done better to stay in New York, because there aren't any men in Texas who are gonna want a thirty-two-year-old spinster with too much book learning."

I wanted to refute him. I wanted to be cool and precise and witty—to laugh in his face as I told him how wrong he was, that I had never wanted to marry and that I had known far more of life than he ever had. That I had seen great actors on the New York stage, had been driven about in a motor car, had conversed once at a party with Dr. William James and his brother, the novelist, Mr. Henry James, had heard Samuel Clemens lecture, and had won the love of a fine man who would, I was certain, be known as a writer some day.

But actors, according to my father, were immoral; he wouldn't know who William James or Henry James or

Samuel Clemens were; motor cars were a silly fad; and this fine, undiscovered writer who loved me was a married man.

And I was a spinster, as he said, and I was getting old, and I had come back to Texas, where my book learning meant nothing, and my father was still my father and could preach to me as he chose. I was silent for a long while, on the verge of tears as I stared down at the cold lumps of food on my plate.

He began to feel more kindly toward me in my defeat. "Well, Emmie," he said. "There have been spinsters that lead worthwhile lives before you. Now that you're back home you can make yourself useful by looking after me and caring for this old house. It needs a woman's hand—I can't do woman's work, myself. And your sister and I, we just can't get along in the same house together. She's too strong-willed for a woman." He chuckled, rather pleased. "She's too much like me, I guess."

I no longer wanted to cry. I wanted to scream. Terror crept up into my throat, choking me. Take my mother's place? Be bullied and bossed by my father until that far-distant day when he allowed himself to die?

"What d'you say, Emmie? You can move right into your old room—have it to yourself now that Florrie has a house of her own. You can even work on that novel of yours in your spare time if you like." He was growing benevolent, almost jolly, with the prospect of capturing me once again.

I shook my head wildly, unable to speak, and raised my face to his. I suppose the wild animal look in my eyes, my terror, must have shocked him: The smile slid right off his face.

"Now see here, Emily Kate, you're not a child anymore. You've got some duties, and since you never married, your duties are still to me. You can't just flutter through your life like a butterfly—for one thing, you haven't got the looks or the spirit to get away with it. And your sister don't have room for you and she don't need you. She'll have another child one of these days and need your room for it. You don't know nothing about babies, so you won't be any help there." He spoke ponderously, leaning and bumping against me with his words, sure of wearing me down, just as a horse will hit against a door with a worn latch until the door falls open before the animal's dumb persistence.

I clung to the thought that this time I must not give in, I must not let him wear me down. I was not demanding anything from him, only trying to keep my freedom. I would not come back under his roof and be imprisoned; I did not owe him that much.

"Or maybe you plan on trying to teach in town? Well, you could try, but they like to have men—a woman can't handle some of these rough country boys. Also, I think they've got enough teachers in town—they don't need to hire someone who's practically a stranger. And people will talk, they'll sure wonder why this nice maiden lady is letting her old daddy live alone and uncared for. Maybe, they'll say, she ain't really such a nice—"

I suddenly recalled my last major confrontation with my father. How I had wanted to go to school, to go East and earn a degree, and how my father had cornered me and knocked down every one of my reasons for going, telling me what a fool I was to consider it, telling me there wasn't enough money, telling me I was needed at home, telling me it wasn't fair to my sister, telling me I would never be any good, telling me women didn't need to know much, telling me if I liked to read I could stay home and read, and I, numbed into silence simply by the power of his presence, had begun to nod along with him, seeing my dreams char and burn to ash. And then—

"Harold."

We had both turned at the unfamiliar sound of the name, and the unfamiliar steel in the familiar soft voice. My mother had been unsmiling. "Harold," she said again, she who always called him Darlin' or Husband or Hal-honey. "I want to talk to you. Emma honey, go help Florrie out in back."

I was slow in doing what I was told, lingering to hear what my gentle mother could do against my powerful father.

"Harold, the girl is going to school. That is already settled. She is going to have a chance. She's smart, and we can well afford to send her and we aren't going to deny her this one thing that she wants. It's her *life* and I won't let you ruin it."

I could hardly believe that was my soft, wheedle-tongued mother speaking. Perhaps my father was as startled as I, for instead of bullying her into tears as I had seen him do so many times before, he let her have her way. I did go to school; my mother had freed me.

But now my mother was dead; she couldn't fight my battles for me.

"And if you want to write a book—why, honey, you can go right ahead and write it. I won't stop you. All I ask is that you keep the house clean, do my mending, and cook meals for the two of us. That's certainly not much to ask." My father was sure this battle was already won.

"It is too much to ask," I said grimly. I moved, rather shakily, out of my chair and away from the table. I had to get out; I was terrified that he would raise his voice to me and I'd start crying. "I won't keep house for you, Daddy. I've got to live my own life—I'm grown up now." I didn't feel grown up at all. "You can get yourself a maid if you want someone to cook your meals. I didn't come back to Texas to be your slave."

"Now, Emma Kate, that's no way to talk to your father—" There was the barest trace of uncertainty beneath the bluster. My rebellion, small as it was, had shaken him.

"I've got to go now," I said. "I told Florrie I'd come right back. We have a lot to discuss." I backed toward the door, keeping out of his reach, afraid he might try to stop me physically.

But he had decided to let me go this time. Shaking his head like an old dog bothered by flies, he said, "We'll talk about this some more when you've settled down. You're still tired from your trip and you need a chance to rest and give some thought to your life. There's plenty of time to work things out—you can move in whenever you like. This is always your home, Emma Kate."

The trace of gentleness—which I knew to be a trap—almost undid me, but I managed to get out onto the porch before I tossed my quavering good-bye at him.

And then I ran back through the woods—ran like my father's little girl, and not at all like the aging spinster who had just defied him.

Florrie looked up from the game she played on the lawn with two of her children, concern on her features at the sight of me as I burst through the woods: red-faced, panting, hair straggling like a hoyden's. She got up at once, with a word to her children, and hurried to my side.

"Emmie honey," she said, gripping my arm.

"I'm all right. I—ran—through the woods—all the way—back." My panting slowed almost to normal as we walked up the lawn to the house.

"What happened?"

I shook my head. "It was terrible."

Upstairs in my room I washed my face and combed out my hair while Florrie began to unpack my bags, laying out fresh clothes for me.

"Florrie, he wants me to move in with him again. He wants everything to be just as if I had never escaped from him, as if I didn't have all my learning. He thinks I owe my life to him simply because I've never married." I began to pant again, this time with emotion.

Florrie took me in her arms and held me tightly. "Hush, now, honey."

"He—he said you don't have room for me here, and that no one wants me—"

"Emmie, stop it. You know we love you and you'll always be welcome here, just as long as you want. Don't let him scare you so. You're doing just fine with your life, and it's foolish for you to even worry about what he thinks."

I pulled away from her and busied myself unpacking. "I—I know that, Florrie. But he goes on at me so—I'm afraid that one day I'll agree with him—he'll bully me into moving into his house—and then I won't ever be free again. I can't take it, Florrie. I think I've got a life of my own, and a mind of my own, but then he yells at me and I go all over like a little child again."

"You're tired," Florrie said gently. "Just tell yourself that you have your own life to live and it doesn't matter what he says. You'll start believing in it after a while."

"It's hard to do," I said. "I'm not like you, Florrie. I never could stand up to him—I could only run away. I haven't got your backbone. I'm more like Mama—I let him wear me down."

"Emily." I looked at her. "Don't underestimate yourself *or* Mama. You are more like Mama than I am, but Mama was never weak. She was gentle, and she let Daddy have his way when it would keep peace, but for anything important—she wouldn't stop fighting until she had won. Remember how she stood up for you when you wanted to go to college? She faced Daddy down because—"

"Yes," I said. "I thought of that today. But she fought Daddy for *me*. She fought to protect us because she loved us. But she would never fight for something on her own behalf. She'd go without anything, put up with anything, unless it hurt us. And then she'd go to war. But for herself, she wouldn't raise a finger. And I'm afraid that I'm like that. Perhaps I might protect my child, if I had one, but I don't know how to fight to save myself."

Florrie looked at me with love and pain in her eyes, and I looked back. In a moment we might dissolve into tears, I thought, and to break the tension I said briskly, "Come now, Florrie. I need to get these things put away, and then I would love a nice hot bath."

"You could take your bath now," she suggested, "and I could put away the rest of your things."

I shook my head. "No. If we work together, it will give us a chance to talk. Oh, Florrie, I've missed talking with you so! There's so much that never gets said in a letter."

"You're right," Florrie said a little ruefully. "Why, I somehow never could tell you about Pete. Well, you'll meet him later."

"Florrie, don't tease me! Who is this Pete? When will I meet him?"

"In the morning. But now you tell me something. What made you decide to leave New York? You always seemed so happy there—at least, your letters made you sound very happy. Busy, working, meeting people. Did something happen, to change things? Why did you leave?"

As she spoke, by coincidence, I had in my hand the book of Byron's poems Paul had given me, and was casting about for a way of introducing him into the conversation. I turned to face her, and perhaps it was in my face.

"A man, Emily?" she asked softly.

"He was married."

"Oh, Emily . . ." Her arms went around me and again she held me tightly, comforting me. She drew back and looked at me tenderly. "Poor darling. Do you want to talk about it?"

We sat down side by side on the bed, holding hands, and I was reminded of confidences exchanged in childhood. Many years had passed since then and now, married and the mother of children, Florrie seemed the older sister.

"He was a teacher," I said. "We had similar interests. We met to talk about our work, about poetry and philosophy. We both wanted to be writers ourselves someday, and we showed each other work we didn't dare show anyone else. We criticized each other, both honestly and gently, and helped each other become better writers.

"I thought it was a platonic friendship. I met his wife and she didn't like me—she was jealous of what I shared with her husband. I thought she was foolish to be jealous—Paul and I had the sort of friendship two men would be fortunate to have."

"And then you realized you were in love with him?"

I looked at her without surprise—it was the natural assumption—and shook my head. "No—one evening he confessed his love for me. Of course, I told him I did not return his feelings."

Florrie squeezed my hand.

"I thought we could continue to be friends," I said. "I thought that if I discouraged him, and kept talk away from romance, we could still be friends. I couldn't—perhaps I should have refused to see him, but I didn't like the thought of losing his friendship, and since I didn't love him somehow I didn't really believe that he loved me, either." I didn't feel proud of myself, telling Florrie. My own excuses sounded feeble in my ears. Perhaps I had been leading him on, afraid he might be my last chance for a different kind of life and afraid to let him go.

"Finally he—he offered to leave his wife for me. He wanted to take me with him to Paris. Morality is different there, and it would be easier to live together. And of course, he knew how I wanted to live in Europe. So I left. I gave up my job and came down here because it would have been too easy to give in and go with him—let him ruin his life."

Florrie sighed. "Oh, Emily, how noble of you."

Noble. That was a word Paul had used, too—misunderstanding. I thought "coward" might be an apter choice.

"But I didn't love him," I said to Florrie. "I wasn't being noble. If I had really loved him"—loved, in the way of the heroine of a novel or play—"really, wholeheartedly loved him, then I wouldn't have hesitated. Then I would have given myself to him, Florrie; I would have run away with him at once."

That is what I believed. And, later, when I was alone, I thought more on my ideal of love, and wondered if I would ever experience anything I would think worthy of the name love. There would be—could be—no questions and no doubts, as there had been with Paul. Neither laws nor morals would keep me from the man I loved; I would stop at nothing, I would do anything he asked, give myself utterly.

I sat up in bed, brooding on the question of love. The house was quiet, everyone asleep. I had thought I would sleep, but although I was bone-weary, my body eager to slide into the healing lake of sleep, my mind was still active, jumping between thoughts of my father, thoughts of the career I had left behind, thoughts of Paul, thoughts of what love would mean to me.

I got up, then, and went to the bottom drawer of the dresser, where I had stored my unfinished novel. I lifted out the manuscript, remembering all the time that had gone into the writing and rewriting of the pages. I carried it to the bedside table and perched on the bed with it in my lap and began to read it by the light of the lamp.

It was the story of a perfect love between a man and a woman: the man an idealized Paul, the woman an idealized Me. I had been halted in my writing because, since I did not intend the novel to be a tragedy, I did not know where to go with this perfect love.

As I read over the pages of my novel, these pages that were the best I could write, my cheeks began to blaze. I felt feverish and unhappy, embarrassed by the prose. I imagined my father coming upon the manuscript and reading it, and laughing. I imagined Florrie being kind. I felt a sudden revulsion toward Paul, who had encouraged me in this sickly, silly fantasy about love.

I knew nothing about love, and probably never would. I was, as my father had said, a thirty-two-year-old spinster, and my ideas about love had come from books. How many of those books had been written by other people who knew as little about love as I?

I put the pages aside, my hands trembling, feeling sick at heart. I could not go on with it. I had thought to build a new life in these pages, and they would be better ash.

This thought firmly in mind, I rose and took the pile of paper to the washstand, and there I burned it, page by page. The sight of the flame licking at the first page, the curling of the paper, the way the writing changed color and disappeared, word by word, invigorated me. I would start fresh, write about something new, but not until I knew something to write about. I would forget this novel as if it had never existed. I would not write something my father could laugh at—until I could write something good and strong and true I would write nothing at all. I would give up my pretensions.

The second page went quickly. I burned my finger on the third. On the fortieth I felt a sudden sick surge of regret: What if I was wrong? But the fortieth burned, too, and the forty-first—which I paused to read—made me certain again.

Halfway through, a wave of exhaustion made me sway, and I feared I might swoon. But I was determined to see it through. I burned my fingers again, several times, but I saw every page of my novel become ash.

I woke in the morning feeling hollow inside, with the certainty that something that was important to me was gone forever. I opened my eyes, then, and remembered the novel. It was for the best, I thought. I did not regret it.

I had slept late, being so exhausted from the events of the preceding day, and breakfast had already been cleared away when I came downstairs.

"Mattie will fix you whatever you like for breakfast," Florrie said, kissing me on the cheek. "I thought you needed all the sleep you could get."

"I feel much better," I said, although I didn't. I felt drained and wished I were still asleep.

Florrie joined me in the kitchen for a cup of tea while I ate the scrambled eggs and sausage Mattie had fried up for me. I was just beginning to relax, to consider telling Florrie what I had done with my novel, when the door flew open and Florrie's eldest boy, Joe Bob, burst in.

"Young man, is that any way to come into a house?" Florrie said indignantly.

He grinned engagingly. Then he looked at me. "Grandaddy says whenever you feel like gettin' up he wants you to go over and have a talk with him."

I lost all appetite for breakfast. Florrie looked at me sharply. "Now, Emmie. You eat a good breakfast. You don't have to go hoppin' over there everytime he says 'frog.' You need a chance to relax and get your courage up. And I want you to meet Pete first, anyway."

"Very well," I said dully. I could not face my father so soon. First, I had to adjust to my life without the novel—my life without writing. I had to build a new life, and it would be fatal if my father began arguing at me again while I was without supports. I had nothing left with which to resist: I could only cling with determination to the idea of not giving in, of not going to live in my father's house, and hope that would be sufficient to carry me through his attacks upon me.

I pushed my eggs around on the plate, then looked up at Florrie. "I can't eat," I said. "Really. I'm too nervous."

She bit her lip, then nodded. "All right. I'll take you to meet Pete. He'll make you feel better."

I laughed, out of nervousness. "Really? I'm intrigued about this Pete person. Does he have another name?"

"No," she said, with a mysterious smile. "Come."

We went down the wide stretch of lawn dotted with pine trees and scrub oaks to the little cabin where Florrie and Billy had lived when they were first wed.

Florrie rapped sharply on the door once, then opened it, and we stepped into the dark cabin, where the sudden change from daylight dimmed my sight. I could make out somebody moving slowly, uncertainly forward from the far corner.

"Pete, it's Florrie. I've brought my sister Emily to meet you."

At that first meeting I thought him very old. He

moved with difficulty, shuffling and awkward as if plagued by pain and weakness. He was too small, the way an old man will seem shrunk down to his bones, although he was no shorter than I. I gave him my hand when Florrie pronounced our names, and felt the long, hard, thin fingers move lightly over my palm, as if reading it, the way a blind person might. But I didn't think he was blind, for the big round eyes shone, and looked directly into mine.

Except for those eyes—which were beautiful, but not normal in a human face—he was, I thought, very ugly. I thought at first he had no nose, and revulsion rose within me, only to be smothered at once by pity, or something like it, flowing smooth and heavy as molasses into my mind and drowning the revulsion before it was fully formed. I realized then that he did have a nose, but it wasn't like the noses I was used to: nothing more than a couple of slits with flaps of flesh over them.

The three of us went to the big table beside one window. Florrie and I sat and Pete disappeared into the kitchen. I looked at Florrie but I said nothing. I had questions, but for the moment they didn't matter.

Pete returned with a teapot and three cups and saucers, setting the tray down carefully on the table before Florrie, who poured out the tea and served us all.

I had a chance to examine Pete more closely now. His skin hung in folds and wrinkles from his slight frame, like an exaggeration of the shrinkage of age, but I no longer thought he was old, nor did I think he was ugly. He could not be compared with anyone else within my experience, so he was neither ugly nor beautiful, but only himself.

We sipped our tea and smiled at one another, and after a quarter of an hour Florrie rose and indicated that it was time for us to go. It was only then that I realized we had none of us spoken since the greeting, and Pete had never spoken at all. And yet never had I felt so comfortable, so instantly at ease with a stranger, as I had these past fifteen minutes.

Florrie and I said good-bye, and Pete nodded at us and blinked his bright eyes.

"You liked him," Florrie said, as we started back up to the big house.

"Yes. Florrie . . . who *is* he?"

"I don't know," she said, as if it did not matter. "I think Billy and I saved his life. And after that . . . he's just stayed with us." She was silent then, as we passed the two older children who were tumbling about on the grass. Then, just before we reached the house she spoke again. "I would hate to have him leave. He's closer than kin."

I took a nap before supper, and Florrie came upstairs to wake me, sitting beside me on the bed and gently touching my face.

I opened my eyes, feeling the dream fading past recall already. "I dreamed about Pete," I said, struggling to hold it.

Florrie nodded. "We all do. Good or bad?"

"Good." The dream was gone, not even an image remained, but I was left with a feeling of warmth toward him.

"My dreams about him are good ones, too. Sometimes I think—" She broke off.

"That he dreams about us, too?" I ventured.

Florrie nodded. "Mostly our dreams are good—sometimes the others have nightmares. I never do. But Sarah Jane"—that was her four-year-old—"has nightmares all the time about him. For some reason she is terrified of him. The other children love him and always want to play with him, but Sarah Jane cries whenever she sees him. I don't know why that is."

I couldn't understand it either. Pete might be frightening to a child only at first sight—he radiated such an air of harmlessness, of gentleness, that his looks soon become unimportant.

"I wonder if we give him nightmares," I said.

The next morning I did something I had not done since my college days: took out my sketchpad and went outside to try some sketches. Later, perhaps, I might return to my watercolors as well. Since I had abandoned my novel, I needed something to fill in the gap.

I took a canvas chair and set it beneath a large shade tree, not far from Florrie and the baby. I chose to sketch them: mother with child in sunlight.

I had not been long at work when I saw Pete traveling toward me in his slow, painful hobble—as if he fought against great weights with every step. He stood beside me and watched with interest as my fingers—now somewhat crippled by his regard—created penciled figures on the paper.

Mysteriously aware of his presence, the other two children (but not, of course, Sarah Jane) came running around the side of the house to play at being mountain goats upon poor Pete. I saw one of the dogs, a hunting hound who had been running with the children, turn tail at sight of Pete and slink off out of sight.

Wondering a little uneasily why dogs should fear Pete, I continued my sketch until it was done. It was crude, and I was annoyed by my clumsiness, but Pete seemed pleased with it. He indicated that he wanted the pad and pencil, and when I gave them to him he hunkered down in the grass and set to work.

He was not especially skilled, yet I knew the first face for mine; next Florrie's; then his own. They were not technically perfect, or even very good, yet there was a spark of life there, something which made it obvious what they represented.

Now, as I watched, he began to draw a story. Florrie—a very young Florrie—and a younger Billy; a starry night; a falling star; a crumpled, crashed vehicle—a flying machine—grounded in a graveyard.

I was so absorbed in what he was showing me that I scarcely noticed when Florrie and the baby went back up to the house. He drew me pictures of another land and, with a sudden shock, I recognized the landscape of my dreams the night before. I stopped his hand with mine and made him look at me—but his eyes were not human, and I could read nothing in them.

"Emily Katherine!" Like a whip cracked above my

head. I jerked my head up and saw my father standing some yards away. There it was again, that fear out of childhood. My stomach contracted and my mind, in old habit, nervously tried to remember what I had done that he might consider wrong.

"Come here, missy, I want to talk to you."

Whatever I had done, it was very bad indeed. My hands and feet felt like blocks of ice as I rose and walked to him. He grasped my arm, not gently, and walked me away.

"I know they preach nigger-loving up North," he said. "But you're a daughter of mine and I won't—I'd a damn sight sooner see you cuddlin' up to the biggest, blackest nigger in Texas than what I just saw." His voice was thick with fury, and his fingers were gouging my arm.

"Daddy, don't!" I tried to pull away. "I don't know what you're talking about!" I knew my voice was too shrill, and I couldn't stop shaking. How I hated him just then, for making me fear him so.

"What I'm talking about is that monster. It's bad enough that Florrie and Billy keep it—it's too much to see you nose to nose and making cow eyes at it. Can't you see that thing ain't human? It's an animal, and it doesn't belong here. It should be killed, just like you'd kill a snake, so it can't spread its poison around."

"Don't you call Pete a monster," I said, nearly in tears, "and don't you insinuate—"

"I ain't insinuating. I'm *telling*. That monster is trouble, and you'd better avoid it. If I ever see you cuddlin' up to that thing again—"

"Stop it!"

He let go of my arm. "Emily, you just do what your daddy tells you and keep away from that thing. Don't talk to it, don't touch it, and don't sit with it. Or you'll be sorry—I'll make you sorry."

Tears blinded me. He always reduced me to that, the child's refuge. I had never been able to defy my father except by running away to New York. And I was sure he saw it as running away—I would never be an adult in his eyes.

When I walked back toward the house I wasn't thinking of Florrie but of Pete. I wanted the peace his presence gave me, and I wanted to disobey my father at once. So I turned toward the little house where Pete lived, and saw him waiting for me on the porch. And when I saw him—the dear, already familiar, not-human ugliness of him—something like a bolt of pain went through me. And, although I have never fainted in my life, I thought that I would faint then, standing on the wooden porch staring at Pete.

He touched my arm and we went into the house together. I felt dazed and clumsy—I felt too large, as if all my skin had suddenly swollen, and my clothes were painfully constricting. Pete led me out of the main room and into the back room, his bedroom. It was a small room, and familiar. As children, Florrie and I had come here to play games with our dolls. It seemed very bare now, empty of the personal possessions one would expect to find in a bedroom. There was only the bed against one wall, and a chair beside the window, an old rag rug on the floor. I looked at the window which, although screened with vines, let in filtered sunlight. Sensing my concern, Pete crossed to the window and closed the shutters across it. I heard the small, wooden click as they closed together.

I wanted to speak to him. He seemed suddenly a stranger, standing across the room in the sudden darkness. He came close to me, and I could see his features again, and they were as well known as if I had seen them every day of my life. I no longer wanted to break the silence with words.

He placed his hand, palm down, against my bosom, on the stiff, smooth fabric of my dress, meaning: undress.

I could not look at him while I stripped off my clothes: I turned my back, and the rustling sounds as we both undressed filled the room with the sound of a flock of birds taking flight.

And my heart beat like a trapped bird's fluttering as I climbed naked into the bed. Pete laid his head against my breast, listening to it, and he kneeled beside the bed and stroked me slowly with the flat of one hand, soothing my shiverings as if they had been those of a horse.

When I was still and breathing only slightly faster than normal, he got into bed beside me, pressing close to me. His flesh was cool, so cool that it frightened me, and peppered roughly all over with what seemed to be goosebumps. I wondered if he was frightened too, and the possibility made me feel better.

He put his face closer to mine, and I closed my eyes, expecting to be kissed. I had been kissed before. But his lips never touched mine: Instead, I felt his breath warm against the skin of my face and a gentle fluttering touch which I later realized was his nose—rather, the flaps of skin over his nostrils, moving out and in as he sniffed.

I began to feel warm all over—much too warm—and his cool, pebbly flesh moving against mine was a friction I wanted and needed. I kept my eyes tightly shut: Since I had closed them I had not dared to open them again. I had glimpsed something—had glimpsed his male member—sprouting from the juncture of his legs, a frightening purplish vegetable. I felt it, warmer than the rest of his flesh, graze my leg now and again as he sniffed and stroked me.

I lay very still, hands clenched at my sides, clenched with wanting and with terror. I wanted to hold him and was afraid to touch him. I wished I would faint, that it would all suddenly be over with, that I would know what to do.

I made a soft sound in my throat. I thought I might cry. I was excited, desperate, and dreadfully confused. I had never before been in such a turmoil of conflicting desires. I moaned again, asking for his help, his pity.

I felt him move away from me suddenly, and my eyes flashed open. "Pete."

He looked at me and I couldn't read his eyes. What was he thinking? I noticed how green his skin was in the dim, filtered light, and saw how the hairless skin hung from his bones. I remembered what he was. Then I didn't faint or run away, but instead, most improbably, I felt a surging of love. It ran through my veins with the blood, heating me and making me brave enough to half sit up—trying desperately to forget my nakedness—and lean forward, reaching out for his hand, pulling him closer to me. I tried not to see the rising movement, the thing growing between his legs. He took me in his arms and I closed my eyes again, my mind rioting with senseless dream images, my thoughts a pathless jungle.

He parted my legs with his hands and I thought my heart would leap through my mouth. No—I didn't want it—I wanted to be safe and alone again—I did want it—I didn't—

I cried out at the first suggestion of pain—much more loudly than the discomfort warranted—and he stopped hurting me at once.

When he shifted position, my legs fell back together. Tears trickled from beneath my tightly shut lids—tears of fear and shame—and he licked them away.

He began stroking me again, and I realized that his fingertips had become warmer. They were raspily pleasant, like the tongue of a cat. They moved between my legs, caressing me more and more intimately until my legs fell apart and my body moved and I moaned and thought in strange, rapid, jagged images and my breath came as quickly as my thoughts, and I forgot about him and about my fear, it was as if I were alone with myself in my own bed, and so I clenched my teeth, my back arched, and I screamed silently, silently inside my head, bursting all the brilliant balloons of my thoughts.

Far away, yet very close, I felt him moving, and then the cool, rough length of his body was pressed along the length of mine and as I rocked toward sleep I was content. I seemed to feel Pete with my mind as well as with my body—we approached sleep together and his mind was joined to mine in a way our bodies had not been. His mind, I thought, was soothing mine as his hands had soothed my body. I was very sleepy and it was pleasant, even if utterly foreign to me, to be so close to another. So close, falling asleep together.

Then my father's face—a memory or a dream—shattered the moment, and I struggled to wake.

But I could not move, could not even open my eyes. As I fought it, I was drawn more deeply into the dream.

I saw my father sitting in his kitchen, cleaning out the gun he used for shooting squirrel and rabbit. But I knew, with the absolute certainty we have in dreams, that he did not intend to go hunting for his dinner this evening. His thoughts were open to me: I knew that he would go to some of the local men he knew, men ready to be frightened by the threat different-colored skin posed to their property and their women. My father thought of me: a spinster whose virginity had made her crazy, easy prey for the monster he now intended to kill or, at the least, to torture and disfigure and run out of the county.

I was humiliated by the vision my father had of me and, for a moment, I blazed with hatred.

His fingers tightened on the gun in his lap, and his face twitched. Had my hatred done that? He tried to set the gun aside, but could not. Rejoicing in my power, I made him stand.

My father got the bullets and loaded the gun—not at my direction, but of his own accord. I watched, seeing that he was thinking of Pete. His face was ugly with hate and anger, and his eyes whipped around the kitchen in restless search, as if he felt Pete's presence.

The gun moved—seemingly of its own accord—and my father, as his hands turned the gun to point at his own legs, struggled to turn it away.

The struggle was silent and fierce. I had Pete helping me, and his force magnified my own. I won't let you shoot him, I thought grimly at my father. You won't shoot Pete.

The gun barrel shifted, and for a moment I thought my father was winning. I made my father raise the gun. The position he held it in was unnatural and uncomfortable.

"Emily!" He said my name as if it were a curse. He was demanding again, not pleading. He would not acknowledge my power; even when I controlled his movements he still thought he could command me.

The gun was at his heart. I could have killed him if I chose.

"Emily!" The tone that could make me tremble, even in dreams. The barrel shifted slightly, caught in his will to move it, and mine to hold it still. Caught by my indecisiveness.

I shot him, and felt, for one impossible moment, the bullet tearing through his flesh.

I fainted then, or slept.

When I woke—feeling sick and miserable—Pete had already gotten up and dressed and was sitting beside the window. I dressed myself and left the house without speaking to him. He did not once turn to look at me.

I was the one who found my father lying in a pool of his own blood. It is likely that no one else would have stopped by to visit, and if I had not gone when I did, he would have died.

It was natural that I should be the one to stay with him, and look after him until he was completely well again. Everyone said how fortunate it was that I had come home. And after my father was healed, it seemed for the best that I continue to live in his house. After all, the house was too big for one man, and Florrie, with another baby on the way, could use the room I had been staying in.

My father said that he had accidentally shot himself while cleaning his gun—not knowing it was loaded. He never spoke—to me, or anyone else—of our struggle. Perhaps it was only a dream. I still get dreams from Pete, but that's the only time I am close to him. He makes me uncomfortable now, and I avoid him, except in my dreams. And no one would say that we can control what we do in our dreams.

## Living and Dying

The new woman, Florrie's sister, was a surprise to him. She was open and vulnerable, beaming her needs, her wants, her fears at him with more intensity than he thought a human could possess. He didn't have to search at all—she presented everything.

And, he was surprised to realize within moments of meeting her, he could fill her needs.

The understanding shook and intrigued him. Might it be possible that he need not remain a stranger forever? That he could have true communication with some one of these beings?

He both desired and feared the union which might be possible. Like sleep, which had so fascinated him as a key to understanding these aliens, might not this too be a trap? To grow closer to them, to any one of them, was to risk becoming too human, to risk losing all that made him what he was. He might become nothing more than a freakish, incomplete human.

But if he were to spend the rest of his life among humans, never to be among his own kind again, then he must try to build a new life here. He must become as involved with human society as possible. He could read them now with ease, and he could send feelings, but the idea of attaining something more, a more true and equal communication, tempted him strongly. The thought of what might be possible stirred up his loneliness again, and Emily's own open hunger struck a responsive chord within him. How lonely he was. How he missed his own kind. Were he home, he would be choosing his lifemate.

With that thought came an almost undeniable urge, and he resolutely made himself ignore all the things which made her physically strange—almost repugnant—to him, and to concentrate on the likenesses.

He began the task of knowing her by making himself known to her. First he sent a dream, then followed that up with pictures when she was waking, to let her know, most basically, that he came from another world.

But there was not time for the courtship to make its leisurely progress. She came to him one afternoon desperately in need and also projecting the idea that he was in danger from her father. There was no time for the courtship, no time to learn about each other, no time to grow naturally into a physical union.

Still, things were different on this world—events moved rapidly, these people lived their lives out so soon. He would adjust to this different pace—perhaps they might be mated in body and later in mind.

It might have worked; it might still have worked; but for Emily's fear. The fear rolled off her like a dreadful stench and it bewildered him, confused him, and made his genitals shrink. Fear had no place in lovemaking, and although with the room dim and his vision relaxed she might have been one of his own people, and although her desire for him aroused desire in him for her, her fear overwhelmed all desire and incapacitated him.

Yet she needed him—he could feel that—and when she reached out for him (bravely, against her own fear) he tried, his limbs trembling with confusion, to ignore her fear. But then he hurt her, and the pain and fear undid him completely.

What sort of creature was this to feel pain and fear and still desire? He suddenly saw her as if in a blaze of light, body and feelings all joined and hideously clear. She was an alien, a beast, a monster, unnatural and loathsome.

Yet he had hurt her, even if she was a monster, and he responded almost instinctively to stop her pain. He brought her to orgasm with his hand, meanwhile holding his emotions firmly in check. He wanted to run, to panic, to flee this revolting imprisoning planet.

He pushed her into deep sleep, knowing that he would have to follow, and cast about in search of her father, in search of the danger, wanting to think of anything but what he had just done with this alien creature. He wouldn't think of what he had almost shared with her, and he would never again consider mating with a human. He would deal with these creatures, his unsuspecting jailers, only as was necessary to sustain his life. He was a castaway, and had better get used to the life of a hermit and not think of coupling with beasts.

And so the years passed in solitude of his own choosing. He saw few humans and cared for none of them. Billy died, and Florrie after him, and he mourned neither of them. Others were born who continued to let him live in the little house and brought him food and occasional company, thinking of him as a strange old relative or family servant—an odd responsibility, but not very interesting. So he lived out his life like the days of a prison sentence and struggled against the involvement of dreams—knowing more about these people than he cared to, involved more than he wanted to be—and the tyranny of sleep every night.

And then one was born who, even in infancy, was different, who made herself felt. She had a potential he had seen in none of the humans he had encountered. She stirred something in him, an interest he had thought dead. And perhaps because he was of an age to be raising a child of his own, were he home, he cared for this child and began to teach it, to nurture its strange talent.

He wove dreams for her. He gave of himself to her, spending his nights in her dreams, becoming teacher and spiritual father to this strange child who became, under his care, something less or more than human.

**Jody**

As soon as I got off the bus I threw my thoughts on ahead to Pete, to see where he was and what he was feeling. And because it was a beautiful, blue-skyed day and I felt itchy and cramped and grouchy from sitting in school with a bunch of stupid kids and teachers—none of whom knew nearly as much as I did—I started to run just as soon as my feet hit the dusty side road which led off the highway and into the woods toward home.

But something was different. I found Pete's mind, like always, but he pushed me away. His thoughts were all agitated and rolling around. I couldn't understand it, and he wouldn't help me. I tried to get hold of something underneath all his thoughts. Was it fear? Anger? Suddenly I recognized it: joy. He was feeling joy, an almost unbearable excitement, and he didn't even want me around to share it.

I realized I had stopped stock-still in the road, my mouth probably hanging open. I started myself up again. My heart was lurching around like a dying fish. I didn't know what was going on, but it had to be something terrible. I couldn't even remember the last time Pete had pushed me out of his mind.

The walk down that interminable dusty road, striped with pine-shadows and blazing sunlight, was the most painful I ever took. I don't think I was reacting just to his pushing me away—I think I knew already, knew without understanding just why, that this was the end of Pete and me.

There were a whole bunch of strange cars pulled up on the circular gravel drive, and when I walked into the front hall the air was blue with smoke and ringing with voices.

They were all in the living room. They went on with their talking at first, not noticing me in the doorway. My folks were there, and my sister and her junior politician boyfriend had driven in from Austin, and there were reporters with cameras and tape recorders and some senior politicians and some very quiet men who couldn't be anything but plainclothes police. And Pete was there, the center of it all, sitting in the antique Italian chair that nobody but company ever got to sit in, with reporters buzzing like flies around a cow pattie.

I sent a cry out to Pete, but his wall was still up. My sister Mary Beth quit chatting to some woman, turned, and saw me.

"Jody!" She hurried toward me. "Thank goodness you're finally here—I was thinking of sending Duane in his car up to school to fetch you." Even while she was glad to have me here, I could feel her automatic assessment and disapproval of the way I looked. She couldn't understand how I could be so tacky as to wear baggy blue jeans, a shirt with a rip under one arm, and dusty boots to school. I made a face at her for her thoughts, and she looked a little shook up. She gripped my arm too tightly and whispered at me, "Jody, behave! There are some very important people here today and they're interested in Pete."

"So what?" Inside I felt like being sick. This was it. This was finally it. Somehow the government had found out about Pete and they had come to take him away. And Pete was just sitting there, stone ignoring me. He was going to let them take him away.

"Honey, are you all right?"

I must really have looked terrible for Mary Beth to ignore my rudeness.

"Yeah," I said. "What's going on?"

Instead of answering me, Mary Beth addressed the room at large. "Everybody," she said brightly, the sorority girl at a club meeting, "Jody's come home from school! She's always been able to communicate with Pete better than anyone else can—it's a special talent of hers."

They were all staring at me. A flashbulb flared.

"You can all go to hell," I said, but I said it so low, my chin down, blinking from the flash, that I don't think anyone but Mary Beth heard me. Her long nails pressed warningly into my skin.

I stared at the ground. I wasn't going to help them take Pete away. Mary Beth would have to do a lot more than pinch me to get me to talk, I thought.

"Jody," my mother said, her voice threatening in the most civilized manner. "No one is going to hurt Pete. We have just learned that Pete comes from another planet. And his friends—"

"You aren't his friends!" I cried. "None of you are! Pete doesn't have any friends except me!"

My mind was running around like a hamster on a wheel, trying to think of a way to get Pete and myself away from here. We had to get away. I knew how to drive, although I wasn't old enough for a license, and if I could get somebody's keys away from them—

Pete came into my mind then—maybe he'd been watching my thoughts all along and knew where I was headed—and ended it. He showed me himself surrounded by others who looked like him. They were his own people, his friends, and they had found him and come to take him home. And Pete was happy. Overwhelmingly, unbearably happy to be leaving the planet he'd been exiled to and to be going home again.

He was leaving *me*. Not simply a strange planet, but *me*. And he was happy.

Pete laid a comfort-touch on me, but I evaded it easily, his heart not being in it. He was so consumed by his own joy that he didn't have time for me. My sadness only irritated him.

My mother and Mary Beth's officious boyfriend were taking it in turns to tell me what I already knew. I was too numb to tell them to save their breath, that I didn't care about any of it. Pete had told me all I needed to know, and I didn't care about the details of the landing and the discovery. I didn't care what had been seen on TV or how the rest of the world was reacting.

"Mary Beth and I just happened to have the television on while we were having breakfast this morning—" Duane stopped suddenly, blushing. The biggest event in history had just happened and that fool thought people cared if he and Mary Beth had spent the night together.

"And there they were," Mary Beth said quickly, filling in for him. She would make a good little wife. "There they were on TV. We couldn't believe it at first—Duane thought it was a hoax, but I said, 'Why that looks like Pete! Our funny old Pete!'

"So Duane, after I'd told him about Pete, and after what the announcer said on the TV about these alien visitors looking for a lost comrade, well, Duane said that maybe he should call up his friend in the governor's office, and maybe also call up the newspaper, and . . ."

I turned around and started to leave. I wanted to be by myself.

"Jody, we haven't finished," Mary Beth said.

"I already know what you're saying," I said.

"But everyone's been waiting for you," Duane said. "Isn't there something Pete would like to say to all of us? Can't you tell us how he feels?"

I looked back at them all for a moment, at all of them and at Pete, who was bobbing gently in the good chair like a slightly dotty old man. The membrane at his neck was billowing gently and flaring orange. Since the photographer wasn't going crazy I guessed this was nothing new to him, although it was to me. It was a sign of extreme emotion, I knew, but I had never seen it before.

"He's very happy," I said finally. "He's very, very happy that his friends have come for him at last, and he can't wait to go home again. That's all. He doesn't have anything he needs to say, except to his friends." Then I went upstairs to my room and closed the door.

My mother came up a few hours later with some sandwiches and a piece of cake and glass of milk on a tray.

"I thought you'd like something to eat," she said, setting the tray down on my dresser.

"Thanks," I said, scooting across the bed to reach the food on the dresser. I was hungry and wished I wasn't. It didn't seem right that my whole life could be breaking up and I was still getting hungry at the usual times. I broke off a piece of the cake and tasted it.

My mother sat down on the bed beside me. "Jody," she said carefully. "You understand Pete awfully well. Do you—that is, I heard that his friends all speak, uh, with their minds. They don't make a sound that can actually be recorded, but to us it seems as if they are talking. At least, that's what I've heard. Can you—when you know what Pete wants, do you read his mind?"

"When he lets me," I said. My mother has been frightened of me since I was just a baby, although that's not something she will admit even to herself.

"Can you—" she stopped. She would never believe me if I answered her now, so I waited. "He speaks to you through, um, telepathic conversation?" She gave the word an odd emphasis, and I suspected she had heard it for the first time today.

"Yeah. I guess. Sort of," I said.

"Why can't he talk to the rest of us like that, then? These other aliens talk to everyone mind-to-mind. Why do you suppose Pete can't?"

I looked at her in surprise. I'd always taken it for granted that I was special in being able to understand Pete.

She steeled herself. "Jody, can you read our minds, too?"

"No," I said. "Look, I can only read Pete's mind when he lets me. He sort of gives it to me. I send my thoughts back to him. I don't know how I do it—I guess he taught me how when I was such a little baby that I just can't remember it. But when he doesn't want me to, I can't. And I can't read anyone else. It's like I can hear Pete, but nobody else is talking the way he is."

"I see." My mother bent her dark head to examine her well-kept nails. "I thought—well, you sometimes seem to know what I'm thinking or what I'm going to say, and I thought that maybe—"

"I can't read your mind," I said. "I guess I'm just real observant. I sort of put things together from how you move and what I know about you." This was true, but I wasn't going to tell her about the dreams. I wasn't going to tell her I could go into her dreams at night, or that it was her dreams which let me know so much about her.

"These aliens," I said, wondering about these creatures who could talk to everyone when Pete couldn't. "When are they getting here?"

"They'll arrive sometime tomorrow," she said. "They're all being flown in with a lot of government people, secret service, reporters—that whole lot. This is a big deal, you realize." She looked at me curiously. "Have you always known what Pete is?"

"Sure."

"And you never told anyone. Why?"

"Why should I?"

She looked at me in silence, looking like she might be feeling sorry for me.

"Poor Jody," she said, confirming my thought. "Pete's always been very special to you, hasn't he?"

That didn't even deserve an answer.

My mother looked at me like she wanted to put her arms around me, like she wanted to get into my mind. "Try not to take it so hard," she said. "Of course you'll miss him, but it's really for the best. You know he's never been entirely happy here—he wants to go home, where he belongs, to be among his own people. Think of how he feels."

I tried to block out her voice. I closed my eyes. I wished she would shut up and go away; she didn't know anything. There was no way she could understand how I felt. I was beginning to hate her.

I heard her sigh, and get off the bed. "Okay. Try to get some sleep, Jody. You'll feel better after some rest."

I twisted my head away when she bent down to kiss me, and she went out of the room without another word. I was already going away myself, reaching out for Pete. He was in his house and, I thought, by himself. His thoughts were strung taut and vibrating slightly. I couldn't get ahold of anything. He wasn't pushing me away, he just wasn't paying attention to me.

Then there was something—a little like static and a little like an electric shock—and I sat up in bed, trembling. I was nowhere near Pete. I was all alone in my room and I felt boxed in. And I knew what had just happened. I knew what it meant even though I had never encountered it before. Pete had been talking with someone else.

I didn't want anyone to see me and stop me, try to interfere or to help, so I was very careful as I crept down the back stairs and out the kitchen door. To get to Pete's little house I had to pass in front of the lighted living-room window. It was early twilight, and I might be seen, so I ran and cast the image of a dog about me so that anyone looking out the window would think that one of the dogs had run past.

I found Pete where I expected he would be: in his bedroom, sitting on the cane-bottom, straight-backed chair beside the useless window. The window was a mass of vines, and I could barely make out Pete's shape in the darkness.

"Pete?" I didn't try to touch his mind, knowing he'd probably still be locked in communication with some of his people. I hadn't liked the feeling when I'd bumped into it before. I hadn't liked it one little bit.

I waited in the dark for Pete to respond. I didn't mind the wait. I was starting to feel better, calmer. I was fooling myself, of course, since nothing had changed, but just being in the same room with Pete was a tremendous relief after the confusion and loneliness of the afternoon.

He touched my mind with a question. A familiar touch, but strange. He was different: He was happy. I felt uncomfortable, wondering if what I had always thought normal for him had been a constant state of unhappiness, or loneliness, or sickness. I felt guilty. I had never been able to make him happy.

But that wasn't my fault; I couldn't be expected to do that—he sent impressions rapidly into my mind. He had been lonely, physically sick as a reaction to our atmosphere and psychically sick with longing for home and friends. I could do nothing—I had made him as happy as it was possible for him to be on this strange planet. But all that I had done wasn't enough—now he was going home, to be among his own kind again.

"What about me?" I demanded, so upset that I spoke to him in words. "I'm like you—you *made* me be like you. I'm different from everybody else. I can't stay here if you're gone. You know what it's like to be lonely; think of how it will be for me! It isn't fair, it isn't right for you to go off and leave me after you've turned me into some kind of monster."

He tried to calm me—this was always his first defense against the destructive emotions of humans. But I wasn't just another human, and I didn't let it work on me.

"Don't leave me," I said. "I can't stand it if you go. I'll be all alone; I won't have anybody. I won't even be able to wait and hope that someday my people will come for me, because there's only you. There's only you and me, Pete. We belong together. Don't leave me here with strangers. Take me with you. Please, Pete. We need to be together."

He did love me; I know he did. And he must have seen what it would be like for me if he left me. He couldn't condemn me to a loneliness worse than the one he had been rescued from. I would be a stranger among his people, but I was a stranger among my own. If I stayed with him I would have only what I had always had.

He accepted me; he agreed. Pete would take me home with him.

By first light, the place was like a fairground or the site of a rock concert. Newspeople and security guards littered the grounds around the house, and there were plenty of gawkers who made their way down from the highway only to be run off again by police. I was up early after spending the night with Pete. He had shared vivid memories of his home planet with me, something he had done before, and this time they were even more real and special to me, because I would soon be going there myself. Finally, despite my excitement, I had drifted off to sleep. But I dreamed alone that night, for Pete only held me in his arms and lay wakeful on the bed all through the night.

I hung around with my mother in the kitchen while I waited for the motorcade bearing the aliens to arrive from the airfield. I helped her and Mary Beth make sandwiches and coffee to feed the visitors, and hoped they wouldn't guess that my mood had changed from sorrow to excitement. Because of course they would try to stop me. I knew I couldn't even say good-bye—I would have to slip away somehow—because if I did they would never let me go.

I saw the short strand of black cars from the window, and bolted out the door, taking a shortcut that zigzagged through the woods and running hard, suddenly afraid that I still might get left behind, despite Pete's promise.

The porch and grounds around Pete's little house were swarming with people, and just as I got there I heard them all exclaiming, and the motorcade pulled up in a fine mist of dirt and gravel.

I was craning as eagerly as everyone else to see the first alien step out of a car—but they weren't aliens, I chided myself. They were people, my people, and I would have to get used to them.

When the first one came out through the car door I reacted as if it were Pete, my mind leaping forward in greeting. But what I found was not Pete. My mind encountered something cold and unintelligible. I felt my mind touched in response, and then I was rebuffed.

There were two more of them, and they all looked the same to me. This might be expected from the rest of the humans, but I felt that I, at least, should be able to tell them apart. But I could see no individual differences among them, and they wore form-fitting skinlike suits which hid their sexual differences and protected their bodies from the poisons in the atmosphere which irritated Pete's skin.

Pete came out of the house, moving slowly as always, his neck membrane flaring brightly with his emotions at being reunited with his people after so long a time. He came down the porch steps, the onlookers moving away before him, as much to avoid his touch as to clear a path for him, and his alien brothers came forward and all four merged together in a large embrace which lasted long minutes. I felt very strange: uncomfortable, unhappy, left out, repelled.

Then one of the aliens spoke, and it was strange because I knew I was hearing it in my mind, the way I had heard Pete so many times, but this was not private or personal—I knew that everyone else was hearing it, too.

"We thank you people for your hospitality and kindness in caring for our injured brother. We will take him home with us now, and trouble you no further."

I felt a hand on my shoulder and twisted around to see my parents and Mary Beth and Duane. I shrugged off my father's hand.

Pete? I thought at him fiercely, but he wasn't looking at me or responding. Pete, tell them I am coming with you. I ran to him and threw my arms around him, hugging him tightly. Pete, you aren't going to leave me?

I felt the cold touch of one of the other aliens, and then he mind-spoke, not bothering to speak directly to me, letting everyone know: "You can't come with us. You must stay here with your own kind, child."

I was outraged and betrayed. Pete, tell them! "Pete," I said aloud, pleading.

And, reluctantly, he gave me his thoughts: He had asked, but the others were displeased by the very idea. They didn't want me; they refused to take me.

Pete was docile and bending before their wishes. He hadn't insisted, I realized. He was as weak and uncertain as a hospital patient. He seemed to have given up all his own wants and powers of decision in order to let them do all the deciding. He was as helpless before them as I was but, it seemed to me, of his own choice.

My mother touched my shoulder. "Darling. Let us all say good-bye to Pete; we'll miss him too, you know."

I resented her words, but I loosened my hold on Pete and stepped back. No one could miss Pete the way I would.

My mother hesitated a moment, a little timid now that Pete was an alien instead of an old member of the family. But he *had* been a member of the family, and so she conquered her fear and hugged him. My father shook Pete's hand and patted his shoulder as if he were one of the men who worked for him, about to leave on a long journey. My sister looked a little sick but made herself do the proper thing as she saw it, and hugged

Pete for the first and last time in her life. Pete put his hands out to them as if he wanted to talk to them, to express something important before he left. Then he looked at me, and I saw the wattles of skin at his neck darken and wave slightly, about to flare.

That terrified me, that sight of emotion, for I knew it meant Pete was saddened by having to leave me. And that meant that he *was* leaving me, and this was the end with no escape.

Suddenly I was crying, for the first time in years, and I threw myself at Pete. "Take me with you . . . Oh, please, take me with you." I was crying and begging with mind and voice, with all of me. I didn't want to be alone. All my life, I had never been alone, and I couldn't bear the thought.

My mother tried to pull me away, but she was too gentle, feeling sorry for me. Pete stood still, simply suffering my embrace. I stopped crying with an effort because I had thought of another chance. I wouldn't give in as Pete had; I would not be meek, I would keep trying. I released Pete and turned to my family.

"Look," I said, as calmly as I could. "Just let me go with him. Just in the car. Just up to the highway. I need to say good-bye to him, I need more time. Please. Let me. Please. Just to the highway—the driver can let me out there." If I could get in the car I might have half a chance to make the human driver forget to stop, forget I was there.

My mother looked very unwilling—she must have known I would desert her and all the earth for Pete.

"I'll come back, I will," I said. "I just want to drive with Pete up the road to the highway. Then—I need to be alone, to think for a while by myself. So I'll walk in the woods for a while. Okay?"

The need I projected got to her and she relented, nodding at the driver and the government security man who stood by the car. "It's up to them," she said. "If there's no room, or they don't have time . . ."

I looked at the man I figured to have the most power—it showed in the way he held himself—and gave it everything I had. I tried to fix in his mind the idea that it would be a good idea to take me, and stupid to leave me; that in fact they must take me, it was already decided, they would take me—

One of the aliens—I couldn't even tell which one—intercepted my projection, snapped it up, and nullified it just like a frog taking a fly from the air. They all three looked at me with their unreadable, alien expressions, and for just a moment they didn't look like Pete at all, and I was afraid of them.

"Ma'am," said the man I'd meant to aim my plea at, "I don't think it would be a good idea." He looked at my mother. "There's no point in dragging out these good-byes—it only makes the final parting more painful. And there'll be a lot of sightseers up by the highway—it might not be safe or wise to stop. I'm afraid I'm going to have to say no." He smiled.

I turned and ran back to the house, hating the tears that stung my eyes, hating the aliens, hating the man who smiled, hating my parents, hating Pete for doing nothing at all. I would have fought to keep him with me, I wouldn't have given in as he did. I would have fought all the armies of Earth for him, and he wouldn't even argue with his friends.

And that was the last of Pete for me. He was soon too far away for me to reach, although I'm sure that if he'd wanted to he could have reached *me* with his mind. But he didn't. And when they took him into space I knew it because I felt it, like a numbing shock. And then I knew about being alone. No more Pete. No more mind-talk. Ever.

I'm all alone among these humans I can communicate with no better than Pete ever could. At night I wander through their dreams, oppressed by their limited range, missing Pete beside me to show me things I cannot see alone.

And Pete is out there somewhere. If only I could reach him. I wonder if he's as lonely as me. Sometimes I believe he will come back for me. It's not something I should count on or believe in, but I do sometimes because it's all I have. I'm just afraid that if he does come back it may be too late. I may spend my life waiting for him, and die before he comes. But that is all I can do. He made me into his companion because he was lonely on this strange planet, but then his friends came and he left me here alone.

My parents are waiting for me to get over my misery. They think I miss Pete the way I would miss a friend or relative who died or went away. They think that I will get over it in time. They don't realize I am in mourning for my lost life.

They bought me a monkey, a bribe to cheer me up. What a joke. It almost makes me cry to look at it, sitting there on my bed and picking at things with its tiny hands, wearing a face no animal should wear, staring at me with those sorrowful, wise and stupid eyes, wishing I'd pretend to be its mother and teach it the ways of our tribe.

## Reunion

He was not accustomed to such excitement, not such excitement bursting from the inside to the outside, its source within himself. It had been so long, and he had become resigned to his way of life. Now—now he could barely control his thoughts and some of the more embarrassing body functions evaded control: Limbs twitched or spasmed at moments, the neck membrane bloomed and sank in meaningless indications. Worst of all, he still had the embarrassing habit of sleep, which he could not conquer. But his fellows assured him that all would be well, he could be cured and made whole again, once he was safely home.

And he was grateful to his fellows, for he knew he embarrassed them. Easier for them all if he'd had the grace to be dead. They had a defective on their hands now, a defective long presumed dead, to take home. But he thought of his friends waiting for him at home. They would be glad. They would welcome him in and cure his sick, weak body. His thoughts turned more and more toward home.

He had no time for the humans now. They could, at last, be shed. Jody embarrassed him—she clung so hard, making his leavetaking ambivalent at a time when he should be feeling only joy. Jody made his fellows feel scorn for him, he knew. There was a suggestion that such a close relationship with an alien creature was perverted and shameful. True, he must have been lonely. They expressed understanding and compassion, but he knew they did not understand at all, and for a moment he feared that Jody was right, that they both were monsters, alienated from their own races, at home only with each other.

He didn't like feeling uneasy; he wanted to return to the life he had known so long ago, the proper life for him. And so he submerged his will and let the others tell him what to do and what to think. He was, after all, an invalid; badly injured in the crash and seriously malformed by the years of living on this unhealthy planet.

The humans, seen now through the eyes of his fellows, began to look ugly again. They were unfamiliar, and their ugly plump-almost-to-skin-bursting bodies made him curl with distaste. He was seeing them for the first time. He saw only Jody still with his own eyes—she was still Jody, and he couldn't help regretting that he had to leave her. But she would be miserable on his planet—it would be harder for her to learn to survive there than it had been for him to adapt to her world. Her life span was too brief for such changes.

The others noticed Jody, too, for she was more noticeable than the other humans, made more like them than the others by her association with one of their kind. But their interest was only a passing spark—she made them uneasy, like an animal dressed in clothes to amuse or frighten.

He tried to make them see that she was different—but they responded that she was not different enough. She was a freak among her own people, but she was still only a human.

He was saddened by leaving Jody, but there was never any question but that he would leave her, never any question of his not going away with his own people. Although he quickly realized that he was almost as out of place among them as he was among the humans, still he had faith that soon everything would be as it had been. Soon he would be home among friends and family, he would be cured, and he would live out a proper life in comfort among his own kind. Jody, he thought to ease his mind, would find the same. She was young and would adjust. It was right and proper for a being to be among its own kind.

So he went away and never came back to Earth again.

## *A Rite of Spring*

**Fritz Leiber**

Fritz Leiber's stories are varied and unpredictable, which may account for the fact that he's won awards for everything from heroic fantasy to "hard-core" science fiction plus everything between (and alongside)—more sf/fantasy awards than any other writer, in fact. "A Rite of Spring" is a long and deliciously erudite novelette about sciences both modern and ancient, and combines scientific extrapolation with a love story that manages to be erotic without resorting to a single "dirty" word. It is, in fact, a *tour de force*—and Leiber's forces, as you'll see, are rather irresistible.

Fritz Leiber lives in San Francisco; he's a tall, knowledgeable man with the voice of a Shakespearean actor—which he's been. If ever anyone was designed to be a Superstar of Science Fiction, Fritz Leiber must be that person.

---

This is the story of the knight in shining armor and the princess imprisoned in a high tower, only with the roles reversed. True, young Matthew Fortree's cell was a fabulously luxurious, quaintly furnished suite in the vast cube of the most secret Coexistence Complex in the American Southwest, not terribly far from the U.S. Government's earlier most secret project, the nuclear one. And he was free to roam most of the rest of the cube whenever he wished. But there were weightier reasons which really did make him the knight in shining armor imprisoned in the high tower: His suite was on the top, or mathematicians', floor and the cube was very tall and he rarely wished to leave his private quarters except for needful meals and exercise, medical appointments, and his unonerous specified duties; his unspecified duties were more taxing. And while he did not have literal shining armor, he did have some very handsome red silk pajamas delicately embroidered with gold.

With the pajamas he wore soft red leather Turkish slippers, the toes of which actually turned up, and a red nightcap with a tassel, while over them and around his spare, short frame he belted tightly a fleece-lined long black dressing gown of heavier, ribbed silk also embroidered with gold, somewhat more floridly. If Matthew's social daring had equaled his flamboyant tastes, he would in public have worn small clothes and a powdered wig and swung a court sword at his side, for he was much enamored of the Age of Reason and yearned to quip wittily in a salon filled with appreciative young Frenchwomen in daringly low-cut gowns, or perhaps only one such girl. As it was, he regularly did wear gray kid gloves, but that was partly a notably unsuccessful effort to disguise his large powerful hands, which sorted oddly with his slight, almost girlish figure.

The crueler of Math's colleagues (he did not like to be called Matt) relished saying behind his back that he had constructed a most alluring love nest, but that the unknown love bird he hoped to trap never deigned to fly by. In this they hit the mark, as cruel people so often do, for young mathematicians need romantic sexual love, and pine away without it, every bit as much as young lyric poets, to whom they are closely related. In fact, on the night this story begins, Math had so wasted away emotionally and was gripped by such a suicidally extreme Byronic sense of futility and Gothic awareness of loneliness that he had to bite his teeth together harshly and desperately compress his lips to hold back sobs as he kneeled against his mockingly wide bed with his shoulders and face pressed into its thick, downy, white coverlet, as if to shut out the mellow light streaming on him caressingly from the tall bedside lamps with pyramidal jet bases and fantastic shades built up of pentagons of almost paper-thin, translucent ivory joined with silver leading. This light was strangely augmented at irregular intervals.

For it was a Gothic night too, you see. A dry thunderstorm was terrorizing the desert outside with blinding flashes followed almost instantly by deafening crashes which reverberated very faintly in the outer rooms of the Complex despite the mighty walls and partitions, which were very thick, both to permit as nearly perfect soundproofing as possible (so the valuable ideas of the solitary occupants might mature without disturbance, like mushrooms in a cave) and also to allow for very complicated, detectionproof bugging. In Math's bedroom, however, for a reason which will be made clear, the thunderclaps were almost as loud as outside, though he did not start at them or otherwise show he even heard them. They were, nevertheless, increasing his Gothic mood in a geometrical progression. While the lightning flashes soaked through the ceiling, a point also to be explained later. Between flashes, the ceiling and walls were very somber, almost black, yet glimmering with countless tiny random highlights like an indoor Milky Way or the restlessly shifting points of light our eyes see in absolute darkness. The thick-pile black carpet shimmered similarly.

Suddenly Matthew Fortree started up on his knees and bent his head abruptly back. His face was a grimacing mask of self-contempt as he realized the religious significance of his kneeling posture and the disgusting religiosity of what he was about to utter, for he was a devout atheist, but the forces working within him were stronger than shame.

"Great Mathematician, hear me!" he cried hoarsely aloud, secure in his privacy and clutching at Eddington's phrase to soften a little the impact on his conscience of his hateful heresy. "Return me to the realm of my early childhood, or otherwise moderate my torments and my loneliness, or else terminate this life I can no longer bear!"

As if in answer to his prayer there came a monstrous flash-and-crash dwarfing all of the storm that had gone before. The two lamps arced out, plunging the room into darkness through which swirled a weird jagged wildfire, as if all the electricity in the wall-buried circuits, augmented by that of the great flash, had escaped to lead a brief free life of its own, like ball lightning or St. Elmo's fire.

(This event was independently confirmed beyond question or doubt. As thousands in the big cube testified, all the lights in the Coexistence Complex went out for one minute and seventeen seconds. Many heard the crash, even in rooms three or four deep below the outermost layer. Several score saw the wildfire. Dozens felt tingling electric shocks. Thirteen were convinced at the time that they had been struck by lightning. Three persons died of heart failure at the instant of the big flash, as far as can be determined. There were several minor disasters in the areas of medical monitoring and continuous experiments. Although a searching investigation went on for months, and still continues on a smaller scale, no completely satisfactory explanation has ever been found, though an odd rumor continues to crop up that the final monster flash was induced by an ultrasecret electrical experiment which ran amok, or else succeeded too well, all of which resulted in a permanent increment in the perpetual nervousness of the masters of the cube.)

The monster stroke was the last one of the dry storm. Two dozen or so seconds passed. Then, against the jagged darkness and the ringing silence, Math heard his door's mechanical bell chime seven times. (He'd insisted on the bell's being installed in such a way as to replace the tiny fisheye lens customary on all the cube's cubicles. Surely the designer was from Manhattan!)

He struggled to his feet, half blinded, his vision still full of the wildfire (or afterimages) so like the stuff of ocular migraine. He partly groped, partly remembered his way out of the bedroom, shutting the door behind him, and across the living room to the outer door. He paused there to reassure himself that his red nightcap was set properly on his head, the tassel falling to the right, and his black robe securely belted. Then he took a deep breath and opened the door.

Like his suite, the corridor was steeped in darkness and aswirl with jaggedy, faint blues and yellows. Then, at the level of his eyes, he saw two brighter, twinkling points of green light about two and a half inches horizontally apart. A palm's length below them was another such floating emerald. At the height of his chest flashed another pair of the green points, horizontally separated by about nine inches. At waist level was a sixth, and a hand's length directly below that, a seventh. They moved a bit with the rest of the swirling, first a little to the left, then to the right, but maintained their positions relative to each other.

Without consciousness of having done any thinking, sought any answers, it occurred to him that they were what might be called the seven crucial points of a girl: eyes, chin, nipples, umbilicus, and the center of all wonder and mystery. He blinked his eyes hard, but the twinkling points were still there. The migraine spirals seemed to have faded a little, but the seven emeralds were bright as ever and still flashed the same message in their cryptic positional Morse. He even fancied he saw the shimmer of a clinging dress, the pale triangle of an elfin face in a flow of black hair, and pale serpents of slender arms.

Behind and before him the lights blazed on, and there, surely enough, stood a slim young woman in a long dark-green grandmother's skirt and a frilly salmon blouse, sleeveless but with ruffles going up her neck to her ears. Her left hand clutched a thick envelope purse sparkling with silver sequins, her right dragged a coat of silver fox. While between smooth black cascades and from under black bangs, an elfin face squinted worriedly into his own through silver-rimmed spectacles.

Her gaze stole swiftly and apologetically up and down him, without hint of a smile, let alone giggle, at either his nightcap and its tassel, or the turned-up toes of his Turkish slippers, and then returned to confront him anxiously.

He found himself bowing with bent left knee, right foot advanced, right arm curved across his waist, left arm trailing behind, eyes still on hers (which *were* green), and he heard himself say, "Matthew Fortree, at your service, mademoiselle."

Somehow, she seemed French. Perhaps because of the raciness of the emeralds' twinkling message, though only the top two of them had turned out to be real.

Her accent confirmed this when she answered, " 'Sank you. I am Severeign Saxon, sir, in search of my brother. And mooch scared. 'Scuse me."

Math felt a pang of delight. Here was a girl as girls should be, slim, soft-spoken, seeking protection, calling him "sir," not moved to laughter by his picturesque wardrobe, and favoring the fond, formal phrases he liked to use when he talked to himself. The sort of girl who, interestingly half undressed, danced through his head on lonely nights abed.

That was what he felt. What he did, quite characteristically, was frown at her severely and say, "I don't recall any Saxon among the mathematicians, madam, although it's barely possible there is a new one I haven't met."

"Oh, but my brother has not my name . . ." she began hurriedly; then her eyelashes fluttered, she swayed and caught herself. *"Pardonne,"* she went on faintly, gasping a little. "Oh, do not think me forward, sir, but might I not come in and catch my breath? I am frightened by ze storm. I have searched so long, and ze halls are so lonely . . ."

Inwardly cursing his gauche severity, Math instantly resumed his courtly persona and cried softly, *"Your* pardon, madam. Come in, come in by all means a rest as long as you desire." Shaping the beginning of another bow, he took her trailing coat and wafted her past him inside. His fingertips tingled at the incredibly smooth, cool, yet electric texture of her skin.

He hung up her coat, marveling that the silky fur was not so softly smooth as his fingertips' memory of her skin, and found her surveying his spacious sanctum with its myriad shelves and spindly little wallside tables.

"Oh, sir, this room is like fairyland," she said, turning to him with a smile of delight. "Tell me, are all zoze tiny elephants and ships and lacy spheres ivory?"

"They are, madam, such as are not jet," he replied quite curtly. He had been preparing a favorable, somewhat flowery, but altogether sincere comparison of her pale complexion to the hue of his ivories (and of her hair to his jets), but something, perhaps "fairyland," had upset him. "And now will you be seated, Miss Saxon, so you may rest?"

"Oh, yes, sir . . . Mr. Fortree," she replied flusteredly, and let herself be conducted to a long couch facing a TV screen set in the opposite wall. With a bob of her head she hurriedly seated herself. He had intended to sit beside her, or at least at the other end of the couch, but a sudden gust of timidity made him stride to the farthest chair, a straight-backed one, facing the couch, where he settled himself bolt upright.

"Refreshment? Some coffee perhaps?"

She gulped and nodded without lifting her eyes. He pushed a button on the remote control in the left-hand pocket of his dressing gown and felt more in command of the situation. He fixed his eyes on his guest and, to his horror, said harshly, "What is your number, madam . . . of years?" he finished in a voice less bold.

He had intended to comment on the storm and its abrupt end, or inquire about her brother's last name, or even belatedly compare her complexion to ivory and her skin to fox fur, anything but demand her age like some police interrogator. And even then not simply, "Say, would you mind telling me how old you are?" but to phrase it so stiltedly . . . Some months back, Math had gone through an acute attack of sesquipedalianism—of being unable to find the simple word for anything, or even a circumlocution, but only a long, usually Latin one. Attending his first formal reception in the Complex, he had coughed violently while eating a cookie. The hostess, a formidably poised older lady, had instantly made solicitous inquiry. He wanted to answer, "I got a crumb in my nose," but could think of nothing but "nasal cavity," and when he tried to say that, there was another and diabolic misfire in his speech centers, and what came out was "I got a crumb in my navel."

The memory of it could still reduce him to jelly.

"Seven—" he heard her begin. Instantly his feelings did another flip-flop and he found himself thinking of how nice it would be, since he himself was only a few years into puberty, if she were younger still.

"Seventeen?" he asked eagerly.

And now it was her mood that underwent a sudden change. No longer downcast, her eyes gleamed straight at him, mischievously, and she said, "No, sir, I was about to copy your 'number of years' and say 'seven and a score.' And now I am of a mind not to answer your rude question at all." But she relented and went on with a winning smile, "No, seven and a decade, only seventeen—that's my age. But to tell the truth, sir, I thought you were asking my ruling number. And I answered you. Seven."

"Do you mean to tell me you believe in numerology?" Math demanded, his concerns doing a third instant flip-flop. Acrobatic moods are a curse of adolescence.

She shrugged prettily. "Well, sir, among the sciences—"

"Sciences, madam?" he thundered like a small Doctor Johnson. "Mathematics itself is not a science, but only a game men have invented and continue to play. The supreme game, no doubt, but still only a game. And that you should denominate as a science that . . .

that farrago of puerile superstitions—! Sit still now, madam, and listen carefully while I set you straight."

She crouched a little, her eyes apprehensively on his.

"The first player of note of the game of mathematics," he launched out in lecture-hall tones, "was a Greek named Pythagoras. In fact, in a sense he probably invented the game. Yes, surely he did—twenty-five centuries ago, well before Archimedes, before Aristotle. But those were times when men's minds were still befuddled by the lies of the witch doctors and priests, and so Pythagoras (or his followers, more likely!) conceived the mystical notion"—his words dripped sarcastic contempt—"that numbers had a real existence of their own, as if—"

She interrupted rapidly. "But do they not? Like the little atoms we cannot see, but which—"

"Silence, Severeign!"

"But, Matthew—"

"Silence, I said! —as if numbers came from another realm or world, yet had power over this one—"

"That's what the little atoms have—power, especially when they explode." She spoke with breathless rapidity.

"—and as if numbers had all kinds of individual qualities, even personalities—some lucky, some unlucky, some good, some bad, et cetera—as if they were real beings, even gods! I ask you, have you ever heard of anything more ridiculous than numbers—mere pieces in a game—being alive? Yes, of course—the idea of gods being real. But with the Pythagoreans (they became a sort of secret society) such nonsense was the rule. For instance, Pythagoras was the first man to analyze the musical scale mathematically—brilliant!—but then he (his followers!) went on to decide that some scales (the major) are stimulating and healthy and others (the minor) unhealthy and sad—"

Severeign interjected swiftly yet spontaneously. "Yes, I've noticed that, sir. Major keys make me feel 'appy, minor keys sad—no, pleasantly melancholy . . ."

"Autosuggestion! The superstitions of the Pythagoreans became endless—the transmigration of souls, metempsychosis (a psychosis, all right!), reincarnation, immortality, you name it. They even refused to eat beans—"

"They were wrong there. Beans cassolette—"

"Exactly! In the end, Plato picked up their ideas and carried them to still sillier lengths. Wanted to outlaw music in minor scales—like repealing the law of gravity! He also asserted that not only numbers but all ideas were more real than things—"

"But excuse me, sir—I seem to recall hearing my brother talk about real numbers . . ."

"Sheer semantics, madam! Real numbers are merely the most primitive and obvious ones in the parlor game we call mathematics. Q.E.D."

And with that, he let out a deep breath and subsided, his arms folded across his chest.

She said, "You have quite overwhelmed me, sir. Henceforth I shall call seven only my favorite number . . . if I may do that?"

"Of course you may. God (excuse the word) forbid I ever try to dictate to you, madam."

With that, silence descended, but before it could become uncomfortable, Math's remote control purred discreetly in his pocket and prodded him in the thigh. He busied himself fetching the coffee on a silver tray in hemispheres of white eggshell china, whose purity of form Severeign duly admired.

They made a charming couple together, looking surprisingly alike, quite like brother and sister, the chief differences being his more prominent forehead, large strong hands, and forearms a little thick with the muscles that powered the deft fingers. All of which made him seem like a prototype of man among the animals, a slight and feeble being except for hands and brain—manipulation and thought.

He took his coffee to his distant chair. The silence returned and did become uncomfortable. But he remained tongue-tied, lost in bitter reflections. Here the girl of his dreams (why not admit it?) had turned up, and instead of charming her with courtesies and witticisms, he had merely become to a double degree his unpleasant, critical, didactic, quarrelsome, rejecting, lonely self, perversely shrinking from all chances of warm contact. Better find out her brother's last name and send her on her way. Still, he made a last effort.

"How may I entertain you, madam?" he asked lugubriously.

"Any way you wish, sir," she answered meekly.

Which made it worse, for his mind instantly became an unbearable blank. He concentrated hopelessly on the toes of his red slippers.

"There *is* something we could do," he heard her say tentatively. "We could play a game . . . if you'd care to. Not chess or go or any sort of mathematical game—there I couldn't possibly give you enough competition—but something more suited to my scatter brain, yet which would, I trust, have enough complications to amuse you. The Word Game . . ."

Once more Math was filled with wild delight, unconscious of the wear and tear inflicted on his system by these instantaneous swoops and soarings of mood. This incredibly perfect girl had just proposed that they do the thing he loved to do more than anything else, and at which he invariably showed at his dazzling best. Play a game, any game!

"Word Game?" he asked cautiously, almost suspiciously. "What's that?"

"It's terribly simple. You pick a category, say Musicians with names beginning with B, and then you—"

"Bach, Beethoven, Brahms, Berlioz, Bartok, C. P. E. Bach (J.S.'s son)," he rattled off.

"Exactly! Oh, I can see you'll be much too good for me. When we play, however, you can only give one answer at one time and then wait for me to give another—else you'd win before I ever got started."

"Not at all, madam. I'm mostly weak on words," he assured her, lying in his teeth.

She smiled and continued, "And when one player can't give another word or name in a reasonable time, the other wins. And now, since I suggested the Game, I insist that in honor of you, and my brother, but without making it at all mathematical really, we play a subvariety called the Numbers Game."

"Numbers Game?"

She explained, "We pick a small cardinal number, say between one and twelve, inclusive, and alternately name groups of persons or things traditionally associated with it. Suppose we picked four (we won't); then the right answers would be things like the Four Gospels, or the Four Horsemen of the Apocalypse—"

"Or of Notre Dame. How about units of time and vectors? Do they count as things?"

She nodded. "The four seasons, the four major points of the compass. Yes. And now, sir, what number shall we choose?"

He smiled fondly at her. She really was lovely—a jewel, a jewel green as her eyes. He said like a courtier, "What other, madam, than your favorite?"

"Seven. So be it. Lead off, sir."

"Very well." He had been going to insist politely that she take first turn, but already gamesmanship was vying with courtesy, and the first rule of gamesmanship is, Snatch Any Advantage You Can.

He started briskly, "The seven crucial—" and instantly stopped, clamping his lips.

"Go on, sir," she prompted. " 'Crucial' sounds interesting. You've got me guessing."

He pressed his lips still more tightly together, and blushed—at any rate, he felt his cheeks grow hot. Damn his treacherous, navel-fixated subconscious mind! Somehow it had at the last moment darted to the emerald gleams he'd fancied seeing in the hall, and he'd been within a hairsbreadth of uttering, "The seven crucial points of a girl."

"Yes . . . ?" she encouraged.

Very gingerly he parted his lips and said, his voice involuntarily going low, "The Seven Deadly Sins: Pride, Covetousness—"

"My, that's a stern beginning," she interjected. "I wonder what the crucial sins are?"

"—Envy, Sloth," he continued remorselessly.

"Those are the cold ones," she announced. "Now for the hot."

"Anger—" he began, and only then realized where he was going to end—and cursed the showoff impulse that had made him start to enumerate them. He forced himself to say, "Gluttony, and—" He shied then and was disastrously overtaken for the first time in months by his old stammer. "Lul-lul-lul-lul-lul—" he trilled like some idiot bird.

"Lust," she cooed, making the word into another sort of bird call, delicately throaty. Then she said, "The seven days of the week."

Math's mind again became a blank, through which he hurled himself like a mad rat against one featureless white wall after another, until at last he saw a single dingy star. He stammered out, "The Seven Sisters, meaning the seven antitrust laws enacted in 1913 by New Jersey while Woodrow Wilson was Governor."

"You begin, sir," she said with a delighted chuckle, "by scraping the bottom of your barrel, a remarkable feat. But I suppose that, being a mathematician, you get at the bottom of the barrel while it's still full by way of the fourth dimension."

"The fourth dimension is no hocus-pocus, madam, but only time," he reproved, irked by her wit and by her having helped him out when he first stuttered. "Your seven?"

"Oh. I could repeat yours, giving another meaning, but why not the Seven Seas?"

Instantly he saw a fantastic ship with a great eye at the bow sailing on them. "The seven voyages of Sinbad."

"The Seven Hills of Rome."

"The seven colors of the spectrum," he said at once, beginning to feel less fearful of going word-blind. "Though I can't imagine why Newton saw indigo and blue as different prismatic colors. Perhaps he wanted them to come out seven for some mystical reason—he had his Pythagorean weaknesses."

"The seven tones of the scale, as discovered by Pythagoras," she answered sweetly.

"Seven-card stud," he said, somewhat gruffly.

"Seven-up, very popular before poker."

"This one will give you one automatically," he said stingily. "However, a seventh son."

"And I'm to say the seventh son of a seventh son? But I cannot accept yours, sir. I said cardinal, not ordinal numbers. No sevenths, sir, if you please."

"I'll rephrase it then. Of seven sons, the last."

"Not allowed. I fear you quibble, sir." Her eyes widened, as if at her own temerity.

"Oh, very well. The Seven Against Thebes."

"The Epigoni, their sons."

"I didn't know there were seven of *them,*" he objected.

"But there should be seven, for the sake of symmetry," she said wistfully.

"Allowed," he said, proud of his superior generosity in the face of a feminine whim. "The Seven Bishops."

"Dear Sancroft, Ken, and Company," she murmured. "The Seven Dials. In London. Does that make you think of time travel?"

"No, big newspaper offices. *The Seven Keys to Baldpate,* a book."

*"The Seven Samurai,* a Kurosawa film."

*"The Seventh Seal,* a Bergman film!" He was really snapping them out now, but—

"Oh, oh. No sevenths—remember, sir?"

"A silly rule—I should have objected at the start. The seven liberal arts, being the quadrivium (arithmetic, music, geometry, and astronomy) added to the trivium (grammar, logic, and rhetoric)."

"Delightful," she said. "The seven planets—"

"No, madam! There are nine."

"I was about to say," she ventured in a small, defenseless voice, "—of the ancients. The ones out to Saturn and then the sun and moon."

"Back to Pythagoras again!" he said with a quite unreasonable nastiness, glaring over her head. "Besides, that would make eight planets."

"The ancients didn't count the Earth as one." Her voice was even tinier.

He burst out with "Earth not a planet, fourth dimension, time travel, indigo not blue, no ordinals allowed, the ancients—madam, your mind is a sink of superstitions!" When she did not deny it, he went on, "And now I'll give you the master answer: all groups of persons or things belong to the class of the largest successive prime among the odd numbers—your seven, madam!"

She did not speak. He heard a sound like a mouse with a bad cold, and looking at her, saw that she was dabbing a tiny handkerchief at her nose and cheeks. "I don't think I want to play the Game any more," she said indistinctly. "You're making it too mathematical."

How like a woman, he thought, banging his hand against his thigh. He felt the remote control and, on a savage impulse, jabbed another button. The TV came on. "Perhaps your mind needs a rest," he said unsympathetically. "See, we open the imbecile valve."

The TV channel was occupied by one of those murderous chases in a detective series (subvariety: military police procedural) where the automobiles became the real protagonists, dark passionate monsters with wills of their own to pursue and flee, or perhaps turn on their pursuer, while the drivers become grimacing puppets whose hands are dragged around by the steering wheels.

Math didn't know if his guest was watching the screen, and he told himself he didn't care—to suppress the bitter realization that instead of cultivating the lovely girl chance had tossed his way, he was browbeating her.

Then the chase entered a multistory garage, and he was lost in a topology problem on the order of: "Given three entrances, two exits, *n* two-way ramps, and so many stories, what is the longest journey a car can make without crossing its path?" When Math had been a small child—even before he had learned to speak—

his consciousness had for long periods been solely a limitless field, or even volume filled with points of light, which he could endlessly count and manipulate. Rather like the random patterns we see in darkness, only he could marshal them endlessly in all sorts of fascinating arrays, and wink them into or out of existence at will. Later he learned that at such times he had gone into a sort of baby-trance, so long and deep that his parents had become worried and consulted psychologists. But then words had begun to replace fields and sets of points in his mind, his baby-trances had become infrequent and finally vanished altogether, so that he was no longer able to enter the mental realm where he was in direct contact with the stuff of mathematics. Thinking about topological problems, such as that of the multilevel garage, was the closest he could get to it now. He had come from that realm "trailing clouds of glory," but with the years they had faded. Yet it was there, he sometimes believed, that he had done all his really creative work in mathematics, the work that had enabled him to invent a new algebra at the age of eleven. And it was there he had earlier tonight prayed the Great Mathematician to return him when he had been in a mood of black despair—which, he realized with mild surprise, he could no longer clearly recall, at least in its intensity.

He had solved his garage problem and was setting up another when "License plates, license plates!" he heard Severeign cry out in the tones of one who shouts, "Onionsauce, onionsauce!" at baffled rabbits.

Her elfin face, which Math had assumed to be still tearful, was radiant.

"What about license plates?" he asked gruffly.

She jabbed a finger at the TV, where in the solemn finale of the detective show, the camera had just cut to the hero's thoroughly wrecked vehicle while he looked on from under bandages, and while the soundtrack gave out with taps. "Cars have them!"

"Yes, I know, but where does that lead?"

"Almost all of them have seven digits!" she announced triumphantly. "So do phone numbers!"

"You mean, you want to go on with the Game?" Math asked with an eagerness that startled him.

Part of her radiance faded. "I don't know. The Game is really dreadful. Once started, you can't get your mind off it until you perish of exhaustion of ideas."

"But you want nevertheless to continue?"

"I'm afraid we must. Sorry I got the megrims back there. And now I've gone and wasted an answer by giving two together. The second counts for yours. Oh well, my fault."

"Not at all, madam. I will balance it out by giving two at once too. The seven fat years and the seven lean years."

"Anyone would have got the second of those once you gave the first," she observed, saucily rabbiting her nose at him. "The number of deacons chosen by the Apostles in Acts. Nicanor's my favorite. Dear Nicky," she sighed, fluttering her eyelashes.

"Empson's Seven Types of Ambiguity," Math proclaimed.

"You're not enumerating?"

He shook his head. "Might get too ambiguous."

She flashed him a smile. Then her face slowly grew blank—with thought, he thought at first, but then with eyes half closed she murmured, "Sleepy."

"You want to rest?" he asked. Then, daringly, "Why not stretch out?"

She did not seem to hear. Her head drooped down. "Dopey too," she said somewhat indistinctly.

"Should I step up the air conditioning?" he asked. A wild fear struck him. "I assure you, madam, I didn't put anything in your coffee."

"And Grumpy!" she said triumphantly, sitting up. "Snow White's seven dwarfs!"

He laughed and answered, "The Seven Hunters, which are the Flannan Islands in the Hebrides."

"The Seven Sisters, a hybrid climbing rose, related to the rambler," she said.

"The seven common spectral types of stars—B-A-F-G-K-M . . . and O," he added a touch guiltily because O wasn't really a common type, and he'd never heard of this particular Seven (or Six, for that matter). She gave him a calculating look. Must be something else she's thinking of, he assured himself. Women don't know much astronomy except maybe the ancient sort, rubbed off from astrology.

She said, "The seven rays of the spectrum: radio, high frequency, infrared, visible, ultraviolet, X, and gamma." And she looked at him so bright-eyed that he decided she'd begun to fake a little too.

"And cosmic?" he asked sweetly.

"I thought those were particles," she said innocently.

He grumphed, wishing he could take another whack at the Pythagoreans. An equally satisfying target occurred to him—and a perfectly legitimate one, so long as you realized that this was a game that could be played creatively. "The Seven Subjects of Sensational Journalism: crime, scandal, speculative science, insanity, superstitions such as numerology, monsters, and millionaires."

Fixing him with a penetrating gaze, she immediately intoned, "The Seven Sorrows of Shackleton: the crushing of the *Endurance* in the ice, the inhospitality of Elephant Island, the failure of the whaler *Southern Sky,* the failure of the Uruguayan trawler *Instituto de Pesca No. 1,* the failure on first use of the Chilean steamer *Yelcho,* the failure of the *Emma,* and the South Pole unattained!"

She continued to stare at him judicially. He realized he was starting to blush. He dropped his eyes and laughed uncomfortably. She chortled happily. He looked back at her and laughed with her. It was a very nice moment, really. He had cheated inventively and she had cheated right back at him the same way, pulling him up short without a word.

Feeling very, very good, very free, Math said, "The Seven Years' War."

"The Seven Weeks' War, between Prussia and Austria."

"The Seven Days' War, between Israel and the Arabs."

"Surely Six?"

He grinned. "Seven. For six days the Israelis labored, and on the seventh day they rested."

She laughed delightedly, whereupon Math guffawed too.

She said, "You're witty, sir—though I can't allow that answer. I must tell my brother that one of his colleagues—" She stopped, glanced at her wrist, shot up. "I didn't realize it was so late. He'll be worried. Thanks for everything, Matthew—I've got to split." She hurried toward the door.

He got up too. "I'll get dressed and take you to his room. You don't know where it is. I'll have to find out."

She was reaching down her coat. "No time for that. And now I remember where."

He caught up with her as she was slipping her coat on. "But, Severeign, visitors aren't allowed to move around the Complex unescorted—"

"Oh pish!"

It was like trying to detain a busy breeze. He said desperately, "I won't bother to change."

She paused, grinned at him with uplifted brows, as though surprised and pleased. Then, "No, Matthew," settling her coat around her and opening the door.

He conquered his inhibitions and grabbed her by her silky shoulders—gently at the last moment. He faced her to him. They were exactly the same height.

"Hey," he asked smiling, "what about the Game?"

"Oh, we'll *have* to finish that. Tomorrow night, same time? G'bye now."

He didn't release her. It made him tremble. He started to say, "But Miss Saxon, you really can't go by yourself. After midnight all sorts of invisible eyes pick up anyone in the corridors."

He got as far as the "can't" when, with a very swift movement, she planted her lips precisely on his.

He froze, as if they had been paralysis darts—and he did feel an electric tingling. Even his invariable impulse to flinch was overridden, perhaps by the audacity of the contact. A self he'd never met said from a corner of his mind in the voice of Rex Harrison, "They're Anglo body-contact taboos, but not Saxon."

And then, between his parted lips and hers still planted on them, he felt an impossible third swift touch. There was a blind time—he didn't know how long—in which the universe filled with unimagined shocking possibility: tiny ondines sent anywhere by matter transmission, a live velvet ribbon from the fourth dimension, pet miniwatersnakes, a little finger with a strange silver ring on it poking out of a young witch's mouth . . . and then another sort of shocked wonder, as he realized it could only have been her tongue.

His lips, still open, were pressing empty air. He looked both ways down the corridor. It was empty too. He quietly closed the door and turned to his ivory-lined room. He closed his lips and worked them together curiously. They still tingled, and so did a spot on his tongue. He felt very calm, not at all worried about Sevvereign being spotted, or who her brother was, or whether she would really come back tomorrow night. Although he almost didn't see the forest for the trees, it occurred to him that he was happy.

Next morning he felt the same, but very eager to tell someone all about it. This presented a problem, for Math had no friends among his colleagues. Yet a problem easily solved, after a fashion. Right after breakfast he hunted up Elmo Hooper.

Elmo was classed and quartered with the mathematicians, though he couldn't have told you the difference between a root and a power. He was an idiot savant, able to do lightning calculations and possessing a perfect eidetic memory. He was occasionally teamed with a computer to supplement its powers, and it was understood, as it is understood that some people will die of cancer, that he would eventually be permanently cyborged to one. In his spare time, of which he had a vast amount, he mooned around the Complex, ignored except when he came silently up behind gossipers and gave them fits because of his remarkable physical resemblance to Warren Dean, Coexistence's security chief. Both looked like young Vermont storekeepers and were equally laconic, though for different reasons.

Math, who, though no lightning calculator, had a nearly eidetic memory himself, found Elmo the perfect confidant. He could tell him all his most private thoughts and feelings, and retrieve any of his previous remarks, knowing that Elmo would never retrieve any of them on his own initiative and never, never make a critical comment.

This morning he found Elmo down one floor in Physics, and soon was pouring out in a happy daze every detail about last night's visit and lovely visitor and all his amazing reactions to her, with no more thought for Elmo than he would have had for a combined dictaphone and information-storage-and-retrieval unit.

He would have been considerably less at ease had he known that Warren Dean regularly drained Elmo of all conversations by "sensitive" persons he overheard in his moonings. Though Math wouldn't have had to feel that way, for the dour security man had long since written Math off as of absolutely no interest to security, being anything but "sensitive" and quite incapable of suspicious contacts, or any other sort. (How else could you class a man who talked of nothing but ivories, hurt vanities, and pure abstractions?) If Elmo began to parrot Math, Dean would simply turn off the human bug, while what the bugs in Math's walls heard was no longer even taped.

Math's happy session with Elmo lasted until lunchtime, and he approached the Mathematics, Astronomy and Theoretical Physics Commons with lively interest. Telling the human memory bank every last thing he knew about Severeign had naturally transferred his attention to the things he didn't know about her, including the identity of her brother. He was still completely trustful that she would return at evening and answer his questions, but it would be nice to know a few things in advance.

The Commons was as gorgeous as Math's apartment, though less eccentrically so. It still gave him a pleasant thrill to think of all the pure intellect gathered here, busily chomping and chatting, though the presence of astronomers and especially theoretical physicists from the floor below added a sour note. Ah well, they weren't quite as bad as their metallurgical, hardware-mongering brothers. (These in turn were disgusted at having to eat with the chemists from the second floor below. The Complex, dedicated to nourishing all pure science, since that provably paid off better peacewise or warwise than applied science, arranged all the sciences by floors according to degree of purity and treated them according to the same standards, with the inhabitants of the top floor positively coddled. Actually, the Complex was devoted to the corruption of pure science, and realized that mathematics was at least fully as apt as any other discipline to turn up useful ideas. Who knew when a new geometry would not lead to a pattern of nuclear bombardment with less underkill? Or a novel topological concept point the way to the most efficient placement of offshore oil wells?)

So as Math industriously nibbled his new potatoes, fresh green peas, and roast lamb (the last a particularly tender mutation from the genetics and biology floors, which incidentally was a superb carrier of a certain newly developed sheep-vectored disease of the human nervous system), he studied the faces around him for ones bearing a resemblance to Severeign's—a pleasantly titillating occupation merely for its own sake. Although Math's colleagues believed the opposite, he was a sensitive student of the behavior of crowds, as any uninvolved spectator is apt to be. He had already noted that there was more and livelier conversation than usual and had determined that the increase was due to talk about last night's storm and power failure, with the physicists contributing rather more than their share, both about the storm and power failure and also about some other, though related, topic which he hadn't yet identified.

While coffee was being served, Math decided on an

unprecedented move: to get up and drift casually about in order to take a closer look at his candidates for Severeign's brother (or half brother, which would account elegantly for their different last names). And as invariably happens when an uninvolved spectator abandons that role and mixes in, it was at once noticed. Thinking of himself as subtly invisible as he moved about dropping nods and words here and there, he actually became a small center of attention. Whatever was that social misfit up to? (A harsh term, especially coming from members of a group with a high percentage of social misfits.) And why had he taken off his gray kid gloves? (In his new freedom he had simply forgotten to put them on.)

He saved his prime suspect until last, a wisp of a young authority on synthetic projective geometry named Angelo Spirelli, the spiral angel, whose floating hair was very black and whose face could certainly be described as girlish, though his eyes (Math noted on closer approach) were yellowish-brown, not green.

Unlike the majority, Spirelli was a rather careless, outgoing soul of somewhat racier and more voluble speech than his dreamy appearance might have led one to expect. "Hi, Fortree. Take a pew. What strange and unusual circumstance must I thank for this unexpected though pleasant encounter? The little vaudeville act Zeus and Hephaestus put on last night? One of the downstairs boys suspects collusion by the Complex."

Emboldened, Math launched into a carefully rehearsed statement. "At the big do last week I met a female who said she was related to you. A Miss Severeign Saxon."

Spirelli scowled at him, then his eyes enlarged happily. "Saxon, you say? Was she a squirmy little sexpot?"

Math's eyebrows lifted. "I suppose someone might describe her in that fashion." He didn't look as if he'd care much for such a someone.

"And you say you met her in El 'Bouk?"

"No, here at the fortnightly reception."

"That," Spirelli pronounced, scowling again, "does not add up."

"Well," Math said after a hiatus, "does it add down?"

Spirelli eyed him speculatively, then shrugged his shoulders with a little laugh. Leaning closer, he said, "Couple weeks ago I was into Albuquerque on a pass. At the Spurs 'n' Chaps this restless little saucer makes up to me. Says call her Saxon, don't know if it was supposed to be last name, first, or nick."

"Did she suggest you play a game?"

Spirelli grinned. "Games. I think so, but I never got around to finding out for sure. You see, she began asking me too many questions, like she was pumping me, and I remembered what Grandmother Dean teaches us at Sunday school about strange women, and I cooled her fast, feeling like a stupid, miserably well-behaved little choirboy. But a minute later Warren himself wanders in and I'm glad I did." His eyes swung, his voice dropped. "Speak of the devil."

Math looked. Across the Commons, Elmo Hooper—no, Warren Dean—had come in. Conversation did not die, but it did become muted—in waves going out from that point.

Math asked, "Did this girl in 'Bouk have black hair?"

Grown suddenly constrained, Spirelli hesitated, then said, "No, blond as they come. Saxon was a Saxon type."

After reaching this odd dead end, Math spent the rest of the afternoon trying to cool his own feelings about Severeign, simply because they were getting too great. He was successful except that in the mathematics library *Webster's Unabridged*, second edition, tempted him to look up the "seven" entries (there were three columns), and he was halfway through them before he realized what he was doing. He finished them and resolutely shut the big book and his mind. He didn't think of Severeign again until he finished dressing for bed, something he regularly did on returning to his room from dinner. It was a practice begun as a child to insure he did nothing but study at night, but continued, with embellishments, when he began to think of himself as a gay young bachelor. He furiously debated changing back until he became irked at his agitation and decided to retain his "uniform of the night."

But he could no longer shut his mind on Severeign. Here he was having an assignation (a word which simultaneously delighted him and gave him cold shivers) with a young female who had conferred on him a singular favor (another word that worked both ways, while the spot on his tongue tingled reminiscently). How should he behave? How would she behave? What would she expect of him? How would she react to his costume? (He redebated changing back.) Would she even come? Did he really remember what she looked like?

In desperation he began to look up everything on seven he could, including Shakespeare and ending with the Bible. A cross-reference had led him to the Book of Revelations, which he found surprisingly rich in that digit. He was reading "And when he had opened the seventh seal, there was silence in heaven about the space of half an hour . . ." when, once again, there came the seven chimes at his door. He was there in a rush and had it open, and there was Severeign, looking exactly like he remembered her—the three points of merry green eyes and tapered chin of flustered, triangular elf-face, silver spectacles, salmon blouse and green grandmother's skirt (with line of coral buttons going down the one, and jade ones down the other), the sense of the other four crucial points of a girl under them, slender bare arms, one clutching silver-sequined purse, the other trailing coat of silver fox—and their faces as close together again as if the electric kiss had just this instant ended.

He leaned closer still, his lips parted, and he said, "The seven metals of the ancients: iron, lead, mercury, tin, copper, silver, and gold."

She looked as startled as he felt. Then a fiendish glint came into her eyes and she said, "The seven voices of the classical Greek actor: king, queen, tyrant, hero, old man, young man, maiden—that's me."

He said, "The Island of the Seven Cities. Antilia, west of Atlantis."

She said, "The seven Portuguese bishops who escaped to that island."

He said, "The Seven Caves of Aztec legend."

She said, "The Seven Walls of Ekbatana in old Persia: white, black, scarlet, blue, orange, silver, and (innermost) golden."

He said, " 'Seven Come Eleven,' a folk cry."

She said, "The Seven Cities of Cibola. All golden."

"But which turned out to be merely the pueblos of the Zuni," he jeered.

"Do you always have to deprecate?" she demanded. "Last night the ancients, the Pythagoreans. Now some poor aborigines."

He grinned. "Since we're on Amerinds, the Seven Council Fires, meaning the Sioux, Tetons, and so forth."

She scowled at him and said, "The Seven Tribes of the Tetons, such as the Hunkpapa."

Math said darkly, "I think you studied up on seven and then conned me into picking it. *Seven Came Through*, a book by Eddie Rickenbacker."

"The Seven Champions of Christendom. Up Saint Dennis of France! To the death! No, I didn't, but you know, I sometimes feel I know everything about sevens, past, present, or future. It's strange."

They had somehow got to the couch and were sitting a little apart but facing each other, totally engrossed in the Game.

"Hmph! Up Saint David of Wales!" he said. "The Seven Churches in Asia Minor addressed in Revelations. Thyatira, *undsoweiter*."

"Philadelphia too. The seven golden candlesticks, signifying the Seven Churches. Smyrna's really my favorite—I like figs." She clenched her fist with the tip of her thumb sticking out between index and middle fingers. Math wondered uncomfortably if she knew the

sexual symbolism of the gesture. She asked, "Why are you blushing?"
"I'm not. The Seven Stars, meaning the Seven Angels of the Seven Churches."
"You were! And it got you so flustered you've given me one. The Seven Angels!"
"I'm not anymore," he continued unperturbed, secure in his knowledge that he'd just read part of Revelations. "The seven trumpets blown by the Seven Angels."
"The beast with seven heads, also from Revelations. He also had the mouth of a lion and the feet of a bear *and* ten horns, but he looked like a leopard."
"The seven consulships of Gaius Marius," he said.
"The seven eyes of the Lamb," she countered.
"The Seven Spirits of God, another name for the Seven Angels, I think."
"All right. The seven sacraments."
"Does that include exorcism?" he wanted to know.
"No, but it does include order, which ought to please your mathematical mind."
"Thanks. The Seven Gifts of the Holy Ghost. Say, I know tongues, prophecy, vision, and dreams, but what are the other three?"
"Those are from Acts two—an interesting notion. But try Isaiah eleven—wisdom, understanding, counsel, might, knowledge, fear of the Lord, and righteousness."
Math said, "Whew, that's quite a load."
"Yes. On with the Game! To the death! The seven steps going up to Ezekiel's gate. Zeek forty twenty-six."
"Let's change religions," he said, beginning to feel snowed under by Christendom and the Bible. "The seven Japanese gods of luck."
"Or happiness. The seven major gods of Hinduism: Brahma, Vishnu, Siva, Varuna, Indra, Agni, and Surya. Rank male chauvinism! They didn't even include Lakshmi, the goddess of luck."
Math said sweetly, "The Seven Mothers, meaning the seven wives of the Hindu gods."
"Chauvinism, I said! Wives indeed! *Seven Daugh-*

*ters of the Theater*, a book by Edward Wagenknecht."

"The seven ages of man," Math announced, assuming a Shakespearean attitude. "At first the infant, mewling and puking—"

"And then the whining schoolboy—"

"And then the lover," he cut in, in turn, "sighing like furnace, with a woeful ballad made to his mistress' eye-brow."

"Have you ever sighed like furnace, Matthew?"

"No, but . . ." And raising a finger for silence, he scowled in thought.

"What are you staring at?" she asked.

"Your left eyebrow. Now listen . . .

> Slimmest crescent of delight,
> Why set so dark in sky so light?
> My mistress' brow is whitest far;
> Her eyebrow—the black evening star!"

"But it's not woeful," she objected. "Besides, how can the moon be a star?"

"As easily as it can be a planet—your ancients, madam. In any case, I invoke poetic license."

"But my eyebrow bends the wrong way for setting," she persisted. "Its ends point at the earth instead of sky-ward."

"Not if you were standing on your head, madam," he countered.

"But then my skirt would set too, showing my stock-ings. Shocking. Sir, I refuse! The Seven Sisters, mean-ing the Pleiades, those little stars."

Matthew's eyes lit up. He grinned excitedly. "Before I give you my next seven I want to show you yours," he told her, standing up.

"What do you mean?"

"I'll show you. Follow me," he said mysteriously and led her into his bedroom.

While she was ooh-ahing at the strangely glimmering black floor, walls, and ceiling, the huge white-fleeced bed, the scattered ivories which included the five regular solids of Pythagoras, the jet bedside lamps with their shades that were dodecahedrons of silver-joined pentagons of translucent ivory—and all the other outward signs of the U.S. Government's coddling of Matthew—he moved toward the lamps and switched them off, so the only light was that which had followed them into the bedroom.

Then he touched another switch and with the faintest whir and rustling the ceiling slowly parted like the Red Sea and moved aside, showing the desert night crusted with stars. The Coexistence Complex really catered to their mathematicians, and when Matthew had somewhat diffidently (for him) mentioned his fancy, they had seen no difficulty in removing the entire ceiling of his bedroom and the section of flat roof above and replacing them with a slightly domed plate-glass skylight, and masking it below with an opaque fabric matching the walls, which would move out of the way sidewise and gather in little folds at the urging of an electric motor.

Severeign caught her breath.

"Stars of the winter sky," Matthew said with a sweep of his arm and then began to point. "Orion. Taurus the bull with his red-eye Aldeberan. And, almost overhead, your Pleiades, madam. While there to the north is my reply. The Big Dipper, madam, also called the Seven Sisters."

Their faces were pale in the splendid starlight and the glow seeping from the room they'd left. They were standing close. Severeign did not speak at once. Instead she lifted her hand, forefinger and middle finger spread and extended, slowly toward his eyes. He involuntarily closed them. He heard her say, "The seven senses. Sight. And hearing." He felt the side of her hand lightly brush his neck. "Touch. No, keep your eyes closed." She laid the back of her hand against his lips. He inhaled with a little gasp. "Smell," came her voice. "That's myrrh, sir." His lips surprised him by opening and kissing her wrist. "And now you've added taste too, sir. Myrrh is bitter." It was true.

"But that's all the senses," he managed to say, "and you said seven. In common usage there are only five."

"Yes, that's what Aristotle said," she answered drily. She pressed her warm palm against the curve of his jaw. "But there's heat too." He grasped her wrist and brought it down. She pulled her hand to free it and he automatically gripped it more tightly for a moment before letting go.

"And kinesthesia," she said. "You felt it in your muscles then. That makes seven."

He opened his eyes. Her face was close to his. He said, "Seventh heaven. No, that's an ordinal—"

"It will do, sir," she said. She kneeled at his feet and looked up. In the desert starlight her face was solemn as a child's. "For my next seven I must remove your handsome Turkish slippers," she apologized.

He nodded, feeling lost in a dream, and lifted first one foot, then the other, as she did it.

As she rose, her hands went to his gold-worked black dressing gown. "And this too, sir," she said softly. "Close your eyes once more."

He obeyed, feeling still more dream-lost. He heard the slithering brush of his robe dropping to the floor, he felt the buttons of his handsome red silk pajama tops loosened one by one from the top down, as her little fingers worked busily, and then the drawstring of the bottoms loosened.

He felt his ears lightly touched in their centers. She breathed, "The seven natural orifices of the male body, sir." The fingers touched his nostrils, brushed his mouth. "That's five, sir." Next he was briefly touched where only he had ever touched himself before. There was an electric tingling, like last night's kiss. The universe seemed to poise around him. Finally he was touched just as briefly where he'd only been touched by his doctor. His universe grew.

He opened his eyes. Her face was still child-grave. The light shining past him from the front room was enough to show the green of her skirt, the salmon of her blouse, the ivory of her skin dancing with starlight. He felt electricity running all over his body. He swallowed with difficulty, then said harshly, "For my next seven, madam, you must undress."

There was a pause. Then, "Myself?" she asked. "*You* didn't have to." She closed her eyes and blushed, first delicately under her eyes, along her cheekbones, then richly over her whole face, down to the salmon ruffles around her neck. His hands shook badly as they moved out toward the coral buttons, but by the time he had undone the third, his strong fingers were working with their customary deftness. The jade buttons of her skirt yielded as readily. Matthew, who knew from his long studious perusals of magazine advertisements that all girls wore pantyhose, was amazed and then intrigued that she had separate stockings and a garter belt. He noted for future reference in the Game that that made seven separate articles of clothing, if you counted shoes. With some difficulty he recalled his main purpose in all this. His hands edged under her long black curving hair until his middle fingers touched her burning ears.

He softly said, "The seven natural orifices of the *female* body, madam."

"What?" Her eyes blinked open wide and searched his face. Then a comic light flashed in them, though Matthew did not recognize it as such. Saying, "Oh, very well, sir. Go on," she closed them and renewed her blush. Matthew delicately touched her neat nostrils and her lips, then his right hand moved down while his eyes paused, marveling in admiration, at the two coral-tipped crucial points of a girl embellished on Severeign's chest.

"Seven," he finished triumphantly, amazed at his courage while lost in wonder at the newness of it all.

Her hands lightly clasped his shoulders, she leaned her head against his and whispered in his ear, "No, eight. You missed one." Her hand went down and her fingers instructed his. It was true! Matthew felt himself flushing furiously from intellectual shame. He'd known *that* about girls, of course, and yet he'd had a blind spot. There was a strange difference, he had to admit, between things read about in books of human physiology and things that were concretely there, so you could touch them. Severeign reminded him he still owed the Game a seven, and in his fluster he gave her the seven crucial points of a girl, which she was inclined to allow, though only by making an exception, for as she pointed out, they seemed very much Matthew's private thing, though possibly others had hit on them independently.

Still deeply mortified by his fundamental oversight, though continuing to be intensely interested in everything (the loose electricity lingered on him), Matthew would not accept the favor. "The Seven Wise Men of Greece—Solon, Thales, and so on," he said loudly and somewhat angrily, betting himself that those old boys had made a lot of slips in their time.

She nodded absently, and looking somewhat smugly down herself, said (quite fatuously, Matthew thought), "The seven seals on the Book of the Lamb."

He said more loudly, his strange anger growing, "In the Civil War, the Battle of Seven Pines, also called the Battle of Fair Oaks."

She looked at him, raised an eyebrow, and said, "The Seven Maxims of the Seven Wise Men of Greece." She looked down herself again and then down and up him. Her eyes, merry, met his. "Such as Pittacus: *Know thy opportunity*."

Matthew said still more loudly, "The Seven Days' Battles, also Civil War, June twenty-fifth to July first inclusive, 1862—Mechanicsville, et cetera!"

She winced at the noise. "You've got to the fourth age now," she told him.

"What are you talking about?" he demanded.

"You know, Shakespeare. You gave it: the Seven Ages of Man. Fourth: 'Then a soldier, full of strange oaths and bearded like the pard, jealous in honor, sudden and quick in quarrel, seeking the bubble reputation even in the cannon's mouth.' You haven't got a beard, but you're roaring like a cannon."

"I don't care. You watch out. What's your seven?"

She continued to regard herself demurely, her eyes half closed. "Seven swans a-swimming," she said liltingly, and a dancing vibration seemed to move down her white body, like that which goes out from a swan across the still surface of a summer lake.

Matthew roared, "The Seven Sisters, meaning the Scotch cannon at the Battle of Flodden!"

She shrugged maddeningly and murmured, "Sweet Seventeen," again giving herself the once-over.

"That's Sixteen," he shouted. "And it's not a seven anyhow!"

She wrinkled her nose at him, turned her back, and said smiling over her shoulder, "Chilon: *Consider the end.*" And she jounced her little rump.

In his rage Matthew astonished himself by reaching her in a stride, picking her up like a feather, and dropping her in the middle of the bed, where she continued to smile self-infatuatedly as she bounced.

He stood glaring down at her and taking deep breaths preparatory to roaring, but then he realized his anger had disappeared.

"The Seven Hells," he said anticlimactically.

She noticed him, rolled over once, and lay facing him on her side, chin in hand. "The seven virtues," she said. "Prudence, justice, temperance, and fortitude—those are Classical—and faith, hope and charity—those are Christian."

He lay down facing her. "The seven sins—"

"We've had those," she cut him off. "You gave them last night."

He at once remembered everything about the incident except the embarrassment.

"*Seven Footprints to Satan,* a novel by Abraham Merritt," he said, eyeing her with interest and idly throwing out an arm.

"*The Seven-Year Itch,* a film with Marilyn Monroe," she countered, doing likewise. Their fingers touched.

He rolled over toward her, saying, "*Seven Conquests,* a book by Poul Anderson," and ended up with his face above hers. He kissed her. She kissed him. In the starlight her face seemed to him that of a young goddess. And in the even, tranquil, shameless voice such a supernatural being would use, she said, "The seven stages of loving intercourse. First kissing. Then foreplay." After a while, "Penetration," and with a wicked starlit smile, "Bias: *Most men are bad*. Say a seven."

"Why?" Matthew asked, almost utterly lost in what they were doing, because it was endlessly new and heretofore utterly unimaginable to him—which was a very strange concept for a mathematician.

"So I can say one, stupid."

"Oh, very well. The seven spots to kiss: ears, eyes, cheeks, mouth," he said, suiting actions to words.

"How very specialized a seven. Try eyebrow flutters too," she suggested, demonstrating. "But it will do for an answer in the Game. The seven gaits in running the course you're into. First the walk. Slowly, slowly. No, more slowly." After a while, she said, "Now the amble, not much faster. Shakespeare made it the slowest gait of Time, when he moves at all. Leisurely, stretchingly. Yes, that's right," and after a while, "Now the pace. In a horse, which is where all this comes from, that means first the hoofs on the one side, then those on the other. Right, left, right, see?—only doubled. There's a swing to it. Things are picking up." After a while she said, "Now the trot. I'll tell you who Time trots withal. Marry, he trots hard with a maid between the contract of her marriage and the day it is solemnized. A little harder. There, that's right." After a while she said, gasping slightly, "Now the canter. Just for each seventh instant we've all hoofs off the ground. Can you feel that? Yes, there it came again. Press on." After a while she said, gasping, "And now the rack. That's six gaits. Deep penetration too. Which makes five stages. Oh, press on." Matthew felt he was being tortured on a rack, but the pain was wonderful, each frightening moment an utterly new revelation. After a while she gasped, "Now, sir, the gallop!"

Matthew said, gasping too, "Is this wise, madam? Won't we come apart? Where are you taking me? Recall Cleobulus: *Avoid Excess!*"

But she cried ringingly, her face lobster-red, "No, it's

not sane, it's mad! But we must run the risk. To the heights and above! To the ends of the earth and beyond! Press on, press on, the Game is all! Epimenides: *Nothing is impossible to industry!*" After a while he redded out.

After another while he heard her say, remotely, tenderly, utterly without effort, "Last scene of all, that ends this strange, eventful history, is mere oblivion. Now Time stands still withal. After the climax—sixth stage—there is afterplay. What's your seven?"

He answered quite as dreamily, "The Seven Heavens, abodes of bliss to the Mohammedans and cabalists."

She said, "That's allowable, although you gave it once before by inference. The seven syllables of the basic hymn line, as 'Hark, the herald angels sing.' "

He echoed with "Join the triumph of the skies."

She said, "Look at the stars." He did. She said, "Look how the floor of heaven is thick inlaid with patens of bright gold." It was.

He said, "There's not the smallest orb which thou behold'st but in his motion like an angel sings. Hark." She did.

Math felt the stars were almost in his head. He felt they were the realm in which he'd lived in infancy and that with a tiny effort he could at this very moment push across the border and live there again. What was so wrong about Pythagoreanism? Weren't numbers real, if you could live among them? And wouldn't they be alive and have personalities, if they were everything there was? Something most strange was happening.

Severeign nodded, then pointed a finger straight up. "Look, the Pleiades. I always thought they were the Little Dipper. They'd hit us in our tummies if they fell."

He said, gazing at them, "You've already used that seven."

"Of course I have," she said, still dreamily. "I was just making conversation. It's your turn, anyway."

He said, "Of course. The Philosophical Pleiad, another name for the Seven Wise Men of Greece."

She said, "The Alexandrian Pleiad—Homer the younger and six other poets."

He said, "The French Pleiad—Ronsard and his six."

She said, "The Pleiades again, meaning the seven nymphs, attendant on Diana, for whom the stars were named—Alcyone, Celaeno, Electra, Maia (she's Illusion), Taygete (she got lost), Sterope (she wed war), and Merope (she married Sisyphus). My, that got gloomy."

Matthew looked down from the stars and fondly at her, counting over her personal and private sevens.

"What's the matter?" she asked.

"Nothing," he said. Actually, he'd winced at the sudden memory of his eight-orifices error. The recollection faded back as he continued to study her.

"The Seven Children of the Days of the Week, Fair-of-Face and Full-of-Grace, and so on," he said, drawing out the syllables. "Whose are you?"

"Saturday's—"

"Then you've got far to go," he said.

She nodded, somewhat solemnly.

"And that makes another seven that belongs to you," he added. "The seventh day of the week."

"No, sixth," she said. "Sunday's the seventh day of the week."

"No, it's the first," he told her with a smile. "Look at any calendar." He felt a lazy pleasure at having caught her out, though it didn't make up for a Game error like the terrible one he'd made.

She said, " 'The Seven Ravens,' a story by the Brothers Grimm. Another gloomy one."

He said, gazing at her and speaking as if they too belonged to her, "The Seven Wonders of the World. The temple of Diana at Ephesus, et cetera. Say, what's the matter?"

She said, "You said the World when we were in the Stars. It brought me down. The world's a nasty place."

"I'm sorry, Sev," he said. "You are a goddess, did you know? I saw it when the starlight freckled you. Diana coming up twice in the Game reminded me. Goddesses are supposed to be up in the stars, like in line drawings of the constellations with stars in their knees and heads."

"The world's a nasty place," she repeated. "Its number's nine."

"I thought six sixty-six," he said. "The number of the beast. Somewhere in Revelations."

"That too," she said, "but mostly nine."

"The smallest odd number that is not a prime," he said.

"The number of the Dragon. Very nasty. Here, I'll show you just how nasty."

She dipped over the edge of the bed for her purse and put in his hands something that felt small, hard, cold, and complicated. Then, kneeling upright on the bed, she reached out and switched on the lamps.

Matthew lunged past her and hit the switch for the ceiling drapes.

"Afraid someone might see us?" she asked as the drapes rustled toward each other.

He nodded mutely, catching his breath through his nose. Like her, he was now kneeling upright on the bed.

"The stars are far away," he said. "Could they see us with telescopes?"

"No, but the roof is close," he whispered back. "Though it's unlikely anyone would be up there."

Nevertheless he waited, watching the ceiling, until the drapes met and the faint whirring stopped. Then he looked at what she'd put in his hands.

He did not drop it, but he instantly shifted his fingers so that he was holding it with a minimum of contact between his skin and it, very much as a man would hold a large dark spider which for some occult reason he may not drop.

It was a figurine, in blackened bronze or else in some dense wood, of a fearfully skinny, wiry old person tautly bent over backward like a bow, knees somewhat bent, arms straining back overhead. The face was witchy, nose almost meeting pointed chin across toothlessly grinning gums pressed close together, eyes bulging with mad evil. What seemed at first some close-fitting, ragged garment was then seen to be only loathsomely diseased skin, here starting to peel, there showing pustules, open ulcers, and other tetters, all worked in the metal (or carved in even harder wood) in abominably realistic minuscule detail. Long empty dugs hanging back up the chest as far as the neck made it female, but the taut legs, somewhat spread, showed a long flaccid penis caught by the artificer in extreme swing to the left, and far back from it a long grainy scrotum holding shriveled testicles caught in similar swing to the right, and in the space between them long leprous vulva gaping.

"It's nasty, isn't it?" Severeign said drily of the hideous hermaphrodite. "My Aunt Helmintha bought it in Crotona, that one-time Greek colony in the instep of the Italian Boot where Pythagoras was born—bought it from a crafty old dealer in antiquities, who said it came from 'Earth's darkest center' by way of Mali and North Africa. He said it was a figure of the World, a nine-thing, *Draco homo*. He said it can't be broken, must not, in fact, for if you break it, the world will disappear or else you and those with you will forever vanish—no one knows where."

Staring at the figurine, Math muttered, "The seven days and nights the Ancient Mariner saw the curse in the dead man's eye."

She echoed, "The seven days and nights his friends sat with Job."

He said, his shoulders hunched, "The Seven Words, meaning the seven utterances of Christ on the cross."

She said, "The seven gates to the land of the dead through which Ishtar passed."

He said, his shoulders working, "The seven golden vials full of the wrath of God that the four beasts gave to the seven angels."

She said, shivering a little, "The birds known as the Seven Whistlers and considered to be a sign of some great calamity impending." Then, "Stop it, Math!"

Still staring at the figurine, he had shifted his grip on it, so that his thick forefingers hooked under its knees and elbows while his big thumbs pressed against its arched narrow belly harder and harder. But at her command his hands relaxed, and he returned the thing to her purse.

"Fie on you, sir!" she said, "to try to run out on the Game, and on me, and on yourself. The seven letters in Matthew, and in Fortree. Remember Solon: *Know thyself.*"

He answered, "The fourteen letters in Severeign Saxon, making two sevens too."

"The seven syllables in Master Matthias Fortree," she said, flicking off the lamps before taking a step toward him on her knees.

"The seven syllables in Mamsel Severeign Saxon," he responded, putting his arms around her.

And then he was murmuring, "Oh Severeign, my sovereign," and they were both wordlessly indicating sevens they'd named earlier, beginning with the seven crucial points of a girl ("Crucial green points," he said, and "Of a green girl," said she), and the whole crucial part of the evening was repeated, only this time it extended endlessly with infinite detail, although all he remembered of the Game from it was her saying "The dance of the seven veils," and him replying "The seven figures in the Dance of Death as depicted on a hilltop by Ingmar Bergman in his film," and her responding, "The Seven Sleepers of Ephesus," and him laboriously getting out, "In the like legend in the Koran, the seven sleepers guarded by the dog Al Rakim," and her murmuring, "Good doggie, good doggie," as he slowly, slowly, sank into bottomless slumber.

Next morning Math woke to blissful dreaminess instead of acutely stabbing misery for the first time in his life since he had lost his childhood power to live wholly in the world of numbers. Strong sunlight was seeping through the ceiling. Severeign was gone with all her things, including the purse with its disturbing figurine, but that did not bother him in the least (nor did his eight-error, the only other possible flyspeck on his paradise), for he knew with absolute certainty that he would see her again that evening. He dressed himself and went out into the corridor and wandered along it until he saw from the corner of his eye that he was strolling alongside Elmo Hooper, whereupon he poured out to that living memory bank all his joy, every detail of last night's revelations.

As he ended his long litany of love, he noticed bemusedly that Elmo had dropped back, doubtless because they were overtaking three theoretical physicists headed for the Commons. Their speech had a secretive tone, so he tuned his ears to it and was soon in possession of a brand-new top secret they did well to whisper about, and they none the wiser—a secret that just might allow him to retrieve his eight-error, he realized with a throb of superadded happiness. (In fact, he was so happy he even thought on the spur of the moment of a second string for that bow.)

So when Severeign came that night, as he'd known she would, he was ready for her. Craftily he did not show his cards at first, but when she began with "The Seven Sages, those male Scheherazades who night after night keep a king from putting his son wrongfully to death," he followed her lead with "The Seven Wise Masters, another name for the Seven Sages."

She said, "The Seven Questions of Timur the Lame—Tamurlane."

He said, "The Seven Eyes of Ningauble."

*"Pardon?"*

"Never mind. *Seven Men* (including 'Enoch Soames' and 'A. V. Laider'), a book of short stories by Max Beerbohm."

She said, *"The Seven Pillars of Wisdom,* a book by Lawrence of Arabia."

He said, *"The Seven Faces of Dr. Lao,* a fantasy film."

She said, "Just *The Seven Faces* by themselves, a film Paul Muni starred in."

He said, "The seven Gypsy jargons mentioned by Borrow in his *Bible in Spain."*

She said, "*Seven Brides for Seven Brothers,* another film."

He said, "The dance of the seven veils—how did we miss it?"

She said, "Or miss the seven stars in the hair of the blessed damosel?"

He said, "Or the Seven Hills of San Francisco when we got Rome's?"

She said, "*Seven Keys to Baldpate,* a play by George M. Cohan."

He said, "*Seven Famous Novels,* an omnibus by H. G. Wells."

She said, "*The Seven That Were Hanged,* a novella by Andreyev."

That's my grim cue, he thought, but I'll try my second string first. "The seven elements whose official names begin with N, and their symbols," he said, and then recited rapidly, poker-faced, "N for Nitrogen, Nb for Nobelium, Nd for Neodymium, Ne for Neon, Ni for Nickel, No for Niobrium, Np for Neptunium."

She grinned fiendishly, started to speak, then caught herself. Her eyes widened at him. Her grin changed, though not much.

"Matthew, you rat!" she said. "You wanted me to correct you, say there were eight and that you'd missed Na. But then I'd have been in the wrong, for Na is for Sodium—its old and unofficial name Natrium."

Math grinned back at her, still poker-faced, though his confidence had been shaken. Nevertheless he said, "Quit stalling. What's your seven?"

She said, "*The Seven Lamps of Architecture,* a book of essays by John Ruskin."

He said, baiting his trap, "The seven letters in the name of the radioactive element Pluton—I mean Uranium."

She said, "That's feeble, sir. All words with seven letters would last almost forever. But you've made me think of a very good one, entirely legitimate. The seven isotopes of Plutonium and Uranium, sum of their Pleiades."

"Huh! I got you, madam," he said, stabbing a finger at her.

Her face betrayed exasperation of a petty sort, but then an entirely different sort of consternation, almost panic fear.

"You're wrong, madam," he said triumphantly. "There are, as I learned only today—"

"Stop!" she cried. "Don't say it! You'll be sorry! Remember Thales: *Suretyship is the precursor of ruin.*"

He hesitated a moment. He thought, That means don't cosign checks. Could that be stretched to mean don't share dangerous secrets? No, too farfetched.

"You won't escape being shown up that easily," he said gleefully. "There are *eight* isotopes now, as I learned only this morning. Confess yourself at fault."

He stared at her eagerly, triumphantly, but only saw her face growing pale. Not ashamed, not exasperated, not contumacious even, but fearful. Dreadfully fearful.

There were three rapid, very loud knocks on the door.

They both started violently.

The knocks were repeated, followed by a bellow that penetrated all soundproofing. "Open up in there!" it boomed hollowly. "Come on out, Fortree! *And* the girl."

Matthew goggled. Severeign suddenly dug in her purse and tossed him something. It was the figurine.

"Break it!" she commanded. "It's our only chance of escape."

He stared at it stupidly.

There was a ponderous pounding on the door, which groaned and crackled.

"Break it!" she cried. "Night before last you prayed. I brought the answer to your prayer. You have it in your hands. It takes us to your lost world that you loved. Break it, I say!"

A kind of comprehension came to Math's face. He hooked his fingers round the figure's evil ends, pressed on the arching loathsome midst.

"Who is your brother, Severeign?" he asked.

"You are my brother, in the other realm," she said. "Press, press!—and break the thing!"

The door began visibly to give under the strokes, now thunderous. The cords in Math's neck stood out, and the veins in his forehead; his knuckles grew white.

"Break it for me," she cried. "For Severeign! *For Seven!*"

The sound of the door bursting open masked a lesser though sharper crack. Warren Dean and his party plunged into the room to find it empty, and no one in the bedroom or bathroom either.

It had been he, of course, whom Matthew, utterly bemused, had mistaken for Elmo Hooper that morning. Dean had immediately reactivated the bugs in Matthew's apartment. It is from their record that this account of Matthew and Severeign's last night is reconstructed. All the rest of the story derives from the material overheard by Dean (who quite obviously, from this narrative, has his own Achilles' heel) or retrieved from Elmo Hooper.

The case is still very open, of course. That fact alone has made the Coexistence Complex an even more uneasy place than before—something that most connoisseurs of its intrigues had deemed impossible. The theory of security is the dread one that Matthew Fortree was successfully spirited away to one of the hostiles by the diabolical spy Severeign Saxon. By what device remains unknown, although the walls of the Coexistence Complex have been systematically burrowed through in search of secret passageways more thoroughly than even termites could have achieved, without discovering anything except several lost bugging systems.

A group of daring thinkers believes that Matthew, on the basis of his satanic mathematical cunning and his knowledge of the eighth isotope of the uranium-plutonium pair, and probably with technological knowhow from behind some iron curtain supplied by Severeign, devised an innocent-looking mechanism, which was in fact a matter transmitter, by means of which they escaped to the country of Severeign's employers. All sorts of random setups were made of Matthew's ivories. Their investigation became a sort of hobby in itself for some and led to several games and quasi-religious cults, and to two suicides.

Others believe Severeign's employers were extraterrestrial. But a rare few quietly entertain the thought and perhaps the hope that hers was a farther country than that even, that she came from the Pythagorean universe where Matthew spent much of his infancy and early childhood, the universe where numbers are real and one can truly fall in love with Seven, briefly incarnate as a Miss S. S.

Whatever the case, Matthew Fortree and Severeign Saxon are indeed gone, vanished without a trace or clue except for a remarkably nasty figurine showing a fresh, poisonously green surface where it was snapped in two, which is the only even number that is a prime.

## Recommended Reading—1977

BRIAN ALDISS: "Where the Lines Converge," *Galileo*, April 1977.

GREGORY BENFORD: "Knowing Her," *New Dimensions 7*. "A Snark in the Night," *Fantasy and Science Fiction*, August 1977.

ROBERT CHILSON: "People Reviews," *Universe 7*.

ROBERT HOLDSTOCK: "A Small Event," *Andromeda 2*.

GEORGE R. R. MARTIN: "The Stone City," *New Voices in Science Fiction*.

CHARLES OTT: "The Astrological Engine," *Analog*, September 1977.

MARTA RANDALL: "The State of the Art on Alyssum," *New Dimensions 7*.

KIM STANLEY ROBINSON: "The Disguise," *Orbit 19*.

CARTER SCHOLZ: "The Ninth Symphony of Ludwig van Beethoven and Other Lost Songs," *Universe 7*.

CHARLES SHEFFIELD: "Legacy," *Galaxy*, June 1977.

CLIFFORD D. SIMAK: "Auk House," *Stellar #3*.

ROBERT THURSTON: "The Mars Ship," *Fantasy and Science Fiction*, June 1977.

JOHN VARLEY: "Air Raid," *Isaac Asimov's Science Fiction Magazine*, Spring 1977. (Under the penname "Herb Boehm.")
"In the Hall of the Martian Kings," *Fantasy and Science Fiction*, February 1977.

GENE WOLFE: "The Marvelous Brass Chessplaying Automaton," *Universe 7*.

# *The Science-Fiction Year*

## Charles N. Brown

Nineteen seventy-seven will go down in science-fiction history as the year of *Star Wars*. The movie opened in May to nearly universal praise and quickly became the largest-grossing film of all time. The question among sf fans was not "Have you seen *Star Wars*?" but "How many times have you seen *Star Wars*?" The entrepreneurs, remembering the *Star Trek* phenomenon of ten years ago, were ready in record time. Books, posters, blueprints, T-shirts, and tons of other paraphernalia appeared almost instantaneously. Ballantine/Del Rey Books, successful veterans of both the Tolkien and *Star Trek* crazes, got the lion's share of the proceeds. The novel version of *Star Wars* was on the paperback bestseller list for six months and sold 3.5 million copies. The calendars, blueprints, portfolios, etc., all published by Ballantine, are selling phenomenally well. 1978 should bring more of the same, and will strongly affect the literary-science-fiction field as well, as various publishers try to attract the huge *Star Wars* audience. Most of the imitations will probably be bad space opera, but many of the readers and new writers will adapt to the general science-fiction field and help rejuvenate and change it.

As I write this (early December 1977) a second science-fiction movie, *Close Encounters of the Third Kind,* has not yet opened, but advance reviews and previews indicate it will be second only to *Star Wars* in appeal and popularity. Nearly all of the film companies have announced science-fiction programs, and we will probably be inundated with a spate of good, bad, and indifferent flicks over the next few years. The only dismal note seems to be that *Star Trek* is still being announced and then canceled as a future movie or TV show, with monthly regularity—almost as if the producers were being affected by the phases of the moon.

The final figures on 1977 are not in yet, but the record of 954 titles (470 new, 484 reprint) published in 1976 will probably be beaten. The prices also went up again, and it is no longer unusual to pay $1.95 for a paperback or $8.95 for a hardcover book. Still, the percentage price differential between them has changed drastically. Twenty years ago a hardback cost twelve times as much as a paperback. Today it's less than five times as much. This has certainly affected sales. The average hardcover is selling around 6,000 copies—twice as many as it did five years ago. The average paperback is selling 50,000 copies—only slightly higher than five years ago. It's becoming increasingly rare for a major science-fiction novel to appear as an original paperback.

The paperback field is still dominated by the same four publishers: Ballantine/Del Rey, DAW, Ace, and Berkley; the hardcover field by Doubleday, the Science Fiction Book Club, Putnam/Berkley, and St. Martin's Press. These publishers were responsible for about 35 percent of the science-fiction books published in 1977. Ballantine/Del Rey has announced a major hardcover program for 1978. Ace, under new editor James Baen, a former editor of *Galaxy,* has announced an expansion program, as have DAW and Berkley.

Fawcett Books, recently purchased by CBS, paid the two largest advances of the year for paperback reprint rights: $236,500 for *Lucifer's Hammer,* a novel by Larry Niven and Jerry Pournelle; and $393,000 for reprint rights to a group of older André Norton books. Avon paid $85,000 for paperback rights to *All My Sins Remembered* by Joe Haldeman.

The third book in the "Riverworld" series, *The Dark*

*Design,* by Philip José Farmer (Putnam/Berkley), the most anticipated science-fiction novel of all time, finally appeared five years after its announcement. It's a triple-length novel—over 200,000 words—but, alas, it ends in the middle of a battle and we now have to wait for the *fourth* volume. The book sold 20,000 hardcover copies in 1977.

Frank Herbert's new book, *The Dosadi Experiment* (Putnam/Berkley), also sold well (37,000 copies). It's a nominal sequel to *Whipping Star* (1970), but you don't have to read the earlier book to appreciate this tightly plotted action-adventure novel.

*In the Ocean of Night* by Gregory Benford (Dial/James Wade) was the science-fiction novel that impressed me the most this year. It is not only a strongly realistic novel of the future with believable background, but succeeds in the difficult task of having both strong plotting and strong characters.

Other important science-fiction novels for the year were *Gateway* by Frederik Pohl (St. Martin's), a fine blend of hard science and psychology; *A Scanner Darkly* by Philip K. Dick (Doubleday), an effective anti-drug tract buried in a typical Dick novel; *Dragonsinger* by Anne McCaffrey (Atheneum), the latest volume in her "Dragon" series; *Time Storm* by Gordon R. Dickson, his best and longest novel to date; *Dying of the Light* by George R. R. Martin (Simon & Schuster), a somewhat overwritten but mostly successful first novel; *The Ophiuchi Hotline* by John Varley (Dial/James Wade), a flawed first novel with many fascinating ideas; and *Michaelmas* by Algis Budrys (Berkley/Putnam), a near-masterpiece by a major author who writes much too little.

In 1977, the fantasy publishing field, for decades the poor stepsister of the science-fiction field, became a major category of its own.

J. R. R. Tolkien's long-awaited book, *The Silmarillion* (Houghton-Mifflin), edited by his son Christopher, finally appeared in September to generally very favorable reviews. It turned out to be a sort of

Middle-Earth Bible and not much like *The Lord of the Rings,* but thanks to twenty years' anticipation and an excellent advance-publicity campaign, the book was an instant success. Houghton-Mifflin originally planned to publish 150,000 copies of the first printing, a huge number by any standards, but advance orders were so great they kept upping the print run and finally did a record 325,000 copies. Even this wasn't enough to fill advance orders, and within three months the publisher had a million copies in print—the largest number of any fiction hardcover book ever. The book zoomed to the top of all the hardcover bestseller lists and, after three months, is still there. *The Silmarillion,* together with the excellent animated TV version of *The Hobbit,* sparked a major Tolkien revival, which in turn helped rejuvenate a major interest in fantasy.

The Robert E. Howard boom reached its highest point so far with the republication of the "Conan" saga by Ace Books. The series had been tied up in litigation since Lancer Books ceased publishing in 1973. Berkley, Bantam, Zebra, and Baronet also got into the Robert E. Howard field, along with the limited-edition and semi-professional publishers. Everything Howard ever wrote, including half a ton of embarrassingly bad amateur work which the author would probably have burned if he had lived a little longer, has found its way into print. A "Conan" movie has also been announced.

*The Book of Merlyn,* T. H. White's "lost" sequel to *The Once and Future King,* appeared in 1977 from the University of Texas Press and made the bestseller list—a rare thing to happen to a University Press publication. White wrote it in 1941 and submitted it along with the revised text for *The Once and Future King*. The publisher used the paper shortage as an excuse not to publish it, and even in 1958, when the revised text of the first four books appeared, it was skipped, although White did incorporate two scenes from it into *The Sword in the Stone*. The reason it remained unpublished for so long is obvious: It's a strong anti-war tract which no British publisher would have touched in 1941 and is so full of preaching it weakens the rest of the series.

An excellent publicity campaign was at least partly responsible for the success of *The Sword of Shannara* by Terry Brooks, an imitation Tolkien fantasy published by Del Rey Books as an expensive ($6.95!) trade paperback. It sold 250,000 copies and also made the paperback bestseller lists.

My own personal favorite of all the fantasy novels published in 1977 was *The Chronicles of Thomas Covenant the Unbeliever* (Holt), a huge triple-decker by a new author, Stephen R. Donaldson. The novel was published in three volumes, *Lord Foul's Bane, The Illearth War,* and *The Power That Preserves,* and, despite its $30 price tag, sold out of its first edition of 10,000 copies by December. I read the entire 1100 pages practically at one sitting and wished it had been twice as long. The book owes a lot to Tolkien, of course, but, unlike *The Sword of Shannara,* it's not a carbon copy.

Other good fantasy novels of the year included *Our Lady of Darkness* by Fritz Leiber (Berkley/Putnam), a creepy-crawly set in modern San Francisco; *Sword of the Demon* by Richard Lupoff (Harper & Row), an exotic tale based on Japanese mythology; *Queens Walk in the Dusk* by Thomas Burnett Swann (Heritage), his final novel of classic mythology; *Heir of Sea and Fire* by Patricia A. McKillip (Atheneum), the sequel to her popular *The Riddle Master of Hed*; and *Silver on the Tree* by Susan Cooper (Atheneum), the fifth and final volume in her Arthurian fantasy series.

The magazine field improved again in 1977. All of the magazines except *Analog* showed increased circulation, with *Galaxy,* despite financial problems and some skipped issues, showing the greatest amount. J. J. Pierce took over as *Galaxy* editor when James Baen moved to Ace. *Isaac Asimov's Science Fiction Magazine,* a new magazine with George Scithers as editor, was extremely successful and outsold *Analog* on the newsstand. *Galileo,* which has no newsstand distribution at all, quadrupled its circulation in just four issues. *Cosmos,* a handsome large-size magazine, folded after four issues because of undercapitalization. The British magazine, *Vortex,* also ceased publication. A new magazine, *Destinies,* which will appear in paperback form, was announced for 1978.

Edmond Hamilton, seventy-two, died on February 1, 1977. His first story, "The Monster-God of Mamurth," appeared in *Weird Tales* in 1926. He was one of science fiction's most prolific authors of space opera, and at one time wrote a novel per issue for *Captain Future* magazine. Hamilton married Leigh Brackett in 1946. They commuted between homes in Ohio and California to accommodate her screenwriting career. Hamilton's most famous book, *The Star Kings,* appeared in hardcover in 1949. Although he kept writing until the late sixties, his later work was not well received. Because of *Star Wars,* we may see a revival of some of his space opera in 1978.

Ray Palmer, sixty-seven, died on August 15, 1977, after a series of strokes. Palmer was a former editor of *Amazing, Fantastic Adventures, Other Worlds,* and many other magazines as well as a pulp writer. He co-edited the first fanzine, *The Comet,* in 1930, and published one of the earliest and rarest limited-edition science-fiction books, *The Dawn of Flame and Other Stories* by Stanley G. Weinbaum. Palmer became editor of *Amazing* in 1938 and changed it into a juvenile action pulp. Its circulation skyrocketed. He started *Fantastic Adventures* in 1939 and edited both magazines until he founded his own publishing company in 1949. That era was famous (or infamous) for the Shaver Mystery, a blend of nut cult and sf which annoyed the sf fans but increased the circulation. Palmer started *Other Worlds* and other digest magazines in the fifties, but was caught in the general collapse of the pulp field in 1954. He turned to flying saucers and psychic phenomena, ending his involvement in science fiction.

Tom Reamy, forty-two, died on November 5, 1977, apparently of a heart attack. He was a longtime fan publisher, writer, and artist who turned to professional writing in 1973. His first story, "Twilla," was a Hugo and Nebula nominee; his second story, "San Diego Lightfoot Sue," won the Nebula. He won the John W. Campbell award for Best New Writer in 1976. His novel, *Blind Voices,* will be published in 1978.

Science-fiction authors H. H. Hollis, Henry Hasse, Walt Richmond, Paul Fairman, and David McDaniel also died in 1977.

The 1977 Nebula Awards were presented at the annual Nebula banquet in New York on April 30, 1977. Winners were: Best Novel: *Man Plus* by Frederik Pohl; Best Novella: "Houston, Houston, Do You Read?" by James Tiptree, Jr.; Best Novelette: "The Bicentennial Man" by Isaac Asimov; Best Short Story: "A Crowd of Shadows" by Charles L. Grant. The Grand Master Award went to Clifford Simak.

The 1977 Hugo Awards were announced at the World Science Fiction Convention in Miami on September 4, 1977. Winners were: Best Novel: *Where Late the Sweet Birds Sang* by Kate Wilhelm; Best Novella: "Houston, Houston, Do You Read?" by James Tiptree, Jr., tied with "By Any Other Name" by Spider Robinson; Best Novelette: "The Bicentennial Man" by Isaac Asimov; Best Short Story: "Tricentennial" by Joe Haldeman; Best Editor: Ben Bova; Best Professional Artist: Rick Sternbach; Best Fanzine: *SF Review*; Best Fan Artist: Phil Foglio; Best Fan Writer: Susan Wood and Richard Geis (tie). The John W. Campbell Award for Best New Writer was won by C. J. Cherryh, the Gandalf Award by André Norton, and a special award was given to George Lucas for *Star Wars.*

The 1977 *Locus* Awards, which receive more nominations than the Hugo and Nebula Awards combined, were announced in July 1977. Winners were: Best Novel: *Where Late the Sweet Birds Sang* by Kate Wilhelm; Best Novella: "The Samurai and the Willows" by Michael Bishop; Best Novelette: "The Bicentennial Man" by Isaac Asimov; Best Short Story: "Tricentennial" by Joe Haldeman; Best Collection: *A Song for Lya* by George R. R. Martin; Best Anthology: *The*

*Best Science Fiction of the Year # 5* edited by Terry Carr; Best Original Anthology: *Stellar 2* edited by Judy-Lynn del Rey; Best Publisher: Ballantine Books; Best Magazine: *Fantasy and Science Fiction*; Best Artist: Rick Sternbach; Best Critic: Spider Robinson; Best Fanzine: *Locus*; Best All Time Author: Robert A. Heinlein. Special awards were given to John Varley and Peter Weston.

The 1977 John W. Campbell Memorial Award was presented in Sweden on October 7, 1977. The winning novel was *The Alteration* by Kingsley Amis.

The 1977 World Fantasy Awards were presented October 30, 1977, in Los Angeles. Winners were: Life Achievement: Ray Bradbury; Best Novel: *Doctor Rat* by William Kotzwinkle; Best Short Fiction: "There's A Long, Long Trail A-Winding" by Russell Kirk; Best Collection: *Frights* edited by Kirby McCauley; Special Professional Award: Alternate World Recordings; Special Non-Professional Award: *Whispers* edited by Stuart Schiff; Best Artist: Roger Dean.

The 36th World Science Fiction Convention will be held in Phoenix, Arizona, August 31 to September 4, 1978. Guest of Honor is Harlan Ellison. For information on membership, write: Iguanacon, Box 1072, Phoenix AZ 85001.

The 37th World Science Fiction Convention will be held in Brighton, England, August 23–27, 1979. Guests of Honor include Fritz Leiber and Brian Aldiss. For information on membership, write: Seacon 79, 14 Henrietta Street, London WC2E 8QJ, United Kingdom.

*Charles N. Brown is the editor of* Locus, The Newspaper of the Science Fiction Field. *Copies are $1.00 each; subscriptions in North America are $9.00 per year, payable to Locus Publications, P.O. Box 3938, San Francisco CA 94119.*